All I Want for Christmas

A COLLECTION
OF HEARTWARMING
STORIES BY IRELAND'S
BEST-LOVED AUTHORS

Introduction by
Fergus Finlay and Lynda Wilson

For Dot,
I hope you enjoy it. Happy
Christmas!
    Lots of love,
        Caroline xxx

POOLBEG

Published 2012
by Poolbeg Press Ltd
123 Grange Hill, Baldoyle
Dublin 13, Ireland
E-mail: poolbeg@poolbeg.com
www.poolbeg.com

1

A catalogue record for this book is available from the British Library.

ISBN 978-1-84223-586-7

Typeset by Patricia Hope in Sabon 11.5/15.5

Printed and bound by CPI Group (UK) Ltd, Croydon, CR0 4YY

www.poolbeg.com

Introduction

First of all, all of us in Barnardos, in Northern Ireland and the Republic, are really grateful to Poolbeg for thinking of this collection, and to each of the authors who have given their time and talent to help put the project together.

The sale of the book in stores nationwide will bring smiles to many faces this Christmas – as well as raising much-needed funds to help us continue providing services for those who need us most.

These are challenging times for all of us, but particularly for the thousands of children and families we work with throughout the island. Many of these children face huge obstacles in their everyday lives, obstacles like poverty, educational disadvantage, neglect and even abuse.

At Barnardos, our goal is simple: to change children's lives for the better. We work as hard as we can to turn hardship and hopelessness into potential and achievement.

One of the biggest issues faced by a lot of children who live in disadvantage across the island of Ireland is literacy. Children who come from a background where reading isn't valued, or where educational disadvantage is passed from generation to generation, are often the children who start behind the others on their first day in school. Children who start behind often stay behind, and end up being the early school leavers. Early school leavers face the highest mountains in terms of jobs and careers. Their lives can often take a different turn – a drift into gangs, anti-social behaviour, even crime.

In short, the links between early literacy and success in later life are deep and profound.

A fundamental part of the solution, time and time again, is dead simple: stories. Stories like the ones in this book, that will make you smile, maybe bring a lump to your throat, and leave you in a hurry to turn the next page.

We all know children whose lives have been changed for the better because someone took the time and trouble to sit down with them and read them stories. In every one of our projects, story-time is usually the most treasured part of the day, when children will tell visitors to "shush!" because the reader is coming to the best bit of the story.

We hope you really enjoy reading this book and that it will serve to remind you of the joys and value of literacy and the need to promote it among children on our island. We'd like to say how grateful we are for your support. Remember – just like the people who wrote these stories, you're helping to change little lives for the better.

Fergus Finlay
Chief Executive
Barnardos (Republic of Ireland)

Lynda Wilson
Director
Barnardo's Northern Ireland

Contents

Last Christmas

Claire Allan

Pulling the shutters down, I rubbed my hands together to warm them from the cold and wrapped my coat and scarf tightly around me, pulling my hat down over my ears so I looked a little like Pootle from *The Flumps*. I kicked the snow off my Uggs and sighed, my breath frosting in front of me. In half an hour I would be in front of a fire, lying on the sofa, watching the flames lick higher and higher. I had closed up early – the shop had been quiet for the last hour, the bustle of last-minute Christmas shopping having faded away. Kate and Sam had looked at me expectantly each time I walked past them and, deciding not to come across all Ebenezer-Scrooge to their expectant little Bob-Cratchit-y faces, I had sent them on their way with an extra £50 each in their pockets to mark my gratitude for their help in the busy pre-Christmas season. We wouldn't open again until December 27th and I relished the thought of two days at home, blissfully lost in a world far removed from commercialism, retail and our temperamental cash register, which had bags of character and a personality all of its own.

"What I really want for Christmas," Kate had said, brushing her bright pink fringe off her face and exhaling loudly, "is a new cash register. One that you plug in. Which scans things and actually, you know, works."

"But Bessie has character," I'd said, sticking my tongue out and staring at the old metal till in front of me. "You wouldn't cast her out into the snow at Christmas?"

Kate had rolled her heavily kohled eyes at me. "I would, and I would take great joy in doing it," she said, pushing the drawer three times to try and get it to lock.

Yes, Bessie was probably on her last legs but I couldn't let her go. I had a certain affection for her – she'd been with me right from the very start of 'Grace and Favours' gift shop and I wasn't about to condemn her to the scrapheap.

"You're just grumpy because you were celebrating the festive season a little too much last night," I'd teased Kate and she smiled.

"It was a good night. You would have enjoyed it."

"I'm too old for that carry-on now," I said.

She tutted and went back to her work, rearranging the deliciously scented candles in the window display.

"Light a few," I'd told her, caught up in the Christmas glow. So, taking the lighter from her pocket she set some burning in their ornate glass holders, the faint glow lighting the shop window and glinting on the snow outside, while the soft aroma of cinnamon and spice permeated the air.

Kate and Sam had left, hand in hand, giggling and singing 'We Wish You a Merry Christmas' as they went. They had taken some mistletoe from the display beside Bessie and had tried to slap kisses on my cheeks. "On you go, you buck eejits," I'd teased them and off they went, no doubt headed for some bar or house party and not one bit of either of them dreaming of a long evening on the sofa in front of the fire.

I left one candle burning in the shop window as I pulled the door behind me and locked up – something in me felt it right to leave a light on for all those making their way home this Christmas Eve – but as I wandered through the town centre it seemed as if I was the only one in a rush to get back to the comfort of home. I tutted at the young women risking life and limb tottering by on high heels in the icy slush, their tanned legs only just hiding the blue from the cold. I definitely was getting old – stuck in my ways. Settled. That thought used to scare me. Now it made me smile. I hugged my coat closer to me and wandered on.

Passing the many bars between 'Grace and Favours' and the car park, I could hear the sound of Christmas Eve waft out on the thin, wintery air. The clinking of glasses, the calls of drunken 'Merry Christmas' greetings, the singing that came with the blessed relief that, for at least one day, everything would be still and everyone would have a day off work at last.

The last few weeks had been manic. It seemed as if everyone and his mother had left their Christmas shopping to the last minute – and everyone, it seemed, wanted "something a little different" this year. "It's been a tough year," they would say. "I want to treat her to something nice." And I had nodded and smiled softly before helping them choose an appropriate gift: a bracelet, a picture frame, a gilt-edged mirror or just a sign declaring that love was, indeed, all you need. I'd heard a thousand stories – sad stories – reasons why a special gift was important. "No gift vouchers this year," my customers told me. "I wanted to choose something myself. Something personal." I'd smiled and nodded and I completely understood: sometimes you wanted to say something in just the right way. Sometimes you wanted the gift to be something that truly took the recipient's breath away.

This is why I loved 'Grace and Favours' so much – there was so much love in every purchase. So much thought. And as I wrapped each present, in delicate red tissue paper with a thin gold bow tied around it, I would watch the smile spread across the face of the customers who made the shop as much a home as it was a place of work. And Kate would smile at me, her cheeky grin peeping out from under her pink fringe, and she would assure the customer they had made the perfect purchase. I know it sounds as cheesy as a packet of Wotsits, but for us it wasn't all about the sale. It wasn't about the profit margin – though I always was a fan of staying in business – it was about that anticipation of each gift being warmly received. It was knowing I

3

had helped someone choose the perfect gift. I had even helped Kate choose the perfect gift for Sam – the pair of us conspiring when he was in the stockroom or out on a run to buy some scones for morning tea. Kate had vowed to text me to tell me if he liked it as soon as he opened it on Christmas morning and I think I was maybe almost as giddy as she was about it. A smile danced across my face as I walked on, thinking of how he would react to the genuine *Stars Wars* artefact she sourced for him. I was only disturbed from my reverie when a tall, gangling man – nose as red as Rudolph's, beer-belly as wide as Santa's – stumbled out of the pub and grasped me in a bear-hug to steady himself. I should probably have been alarmed, but I knew he didn't pose a threat. He smiled, apologised profusely, spun me around and launched into his best Pogues impression, singing about the boys of the NYPD choir. He could have been someone, he sang loudly, with a joy that didn't quite match the sombreness of the piece but then again it was Christmas. No one really thinks about the words of that song – just the rousing chorus, the feeling that it's finally here, the "Sure isn't the *craic* great?" about it all. I smiled and wished him a happy Christmas, not taking up his offer to play Kirstie McColl to his Shane MacGowan, and walked on, almost at the car park – and almost on my way home.

I thought back to the previous Christmas Eve – how I had gone to the bar after work and met Jack there. He'd ordered me a half of Guinness – it was waiting for me on the table as I walked in, shaking the rain off my umbrella and smiling brightly because the shop had traded well and I had survived Christmas Eve without running out of scented candles, carrier bags and my sanity. "A half pint?" I had grumbled, raising my eyebrow to him. "A pint would have been a better shout."

He had smiled and pulled me in for a kiss and I had kissed him back.

"I'll get you another if you want, Grumpy-drawers," he teased.

"Indeed you will," I said. "Let the Christmas celebrations begin now!" I had reached up to him and kissed him again, brushing his dark hair from his face and feeling the delicious brush of his stubble against my cheek.

"Lila," he said, "that sounds like a plan!"

Kate and Sam had followed me into the bar and were sitting on two stools opposite, the last two empty seats in the place. "I can't believe how busy it is," Kate had said, fishing in her bag for her purse.

"I know," I had grinned. "What kind of eejit goes to a bar on Christmas Eve?"

As I walked on, reaching my car and brushing the snow off my windscreen, I smiled at the memory of the four of us eejits in the bar – sharing a few drinks, enjoying each other's company, singing along to the cheesy music. Of course as 'Fairytale' played Jack had swept me up onto the crowded dance-floor and serenaded me loudly and out of tune, looking me deep in the eyes as he promised the coming year would be for me and him.

I felt tears prick in my eyes and hastily brushed them away. I would not cry. There would be no tears shed. No – everything was good. Everything was okay. There was no need for excesses of emotion. Clearing the windscreen and climbing into the driver seat, I patted my hands together to warm them and switched on the ignition, revelling in the sound of the engine chugging into life. With the demisters on full pelt I switched on the radio and waited for the windscreens to clear. I was foolish to think the radio would be playing anything other than Christmas tunes and, as 'Have Yourself a Merry Little Christmas' washed over me I closed my eyes and drank in the soft, velvet tones of Judy Garland's voice. It was no good then – there was no fighting the tears. They were going to fall and I felt one slide down my cheek. This time I didn't brush it away. I just let it fall and land with a gentle thump on my coat. The last year had been momentous – life-changing. I wasn't one who coped with change well but for the last twelve months I had felt as if I were caught up in a whirlwind.

As Jack and I had walked home from the bar last Christmas Eve we had huddled against the softly falling rain – the soft fuzz that came with a few drinks and a few hours in good company only interrupted by the occasional glare of the headlights from passing cars. The roads were quieter by then. I imagined the only people out and about were tipsy revellers making their way home or parents doing the Santa run – collecting presents from grandparents' houses where they had been secreted for the previous few months. I had wrapped my arms around Jack and breathed in the warmth of his skin. It didn't matter that it was raining. It didn't matter one bit. We were blissfully happy – happier than I had ever been.

When we reached home, the glint of the Christmas-tree lights in the window caught my eye and I turned to scold Jack. "You shouldn't have left the lights on," I said as I fished for my key, our bubble of contentment broken. "The house could have burned down, for the love of God. You should have unplugged them." My voice sounded shrill and angry and I was annoyed with myself for shattering the calm of our evening. "We could have lost everything!" I exclaimed dramatically, running through to the living room and switching off the lights as if they posed a clear and present danger.

I was vaguely aware of Jack laughing. "We're fine," he said. "Calm down."

"I will not calm down!" I raged and felt my blood boil further as he reached behind me and switched the blasted lights back on.

Glaring at him, I turned to leave the room and felt his hand grab mine.

"Lila," he said softly, a hint of amusement still evident in his voice and I pulled against him, determined to walk on. "Lila," he said, more firmly this time, and I turned to face him and see him smiling like a Cheshire cat back at me.

"Don't try and win me over with that smile of yours," I answered, feeling my resolve melting away.

"I won't," he said, glancing towards the relit Christmas tree. "I promise I won't."

I followed his gaze to where a small gold package sat as the solitary present below the branches. "It's your Christmas present," he said. "Now I know how you feel about leaving Christmas presents under the tree, inviting burglars and all that carry-on – but sure it's grand and it's for you and if you look at the clock it has just turned twelve and now would be a perfect time to open it."

He let go of my hand and knelt down to reach under the tree, taking the box out and turning to face me, still on his knees. Well, more accurately on one knee.

"Lila, the most infuriating and safety-conscious woman in the world, I love you. I adore you. I want to be with you forever – for every Christmas as long as we both shall live."

He opened the box, and the diamond glinted at me as the tears rolled down my face and I nodded my response.

Sitting in the car, I wiped the tears away at the memory and thought of the candle glowing in the shop window. What would Jack say about that, I wondered? Lila Cassidy throwing caution to the wind, leaving a lit candle in an unsupervised shop. I smiled at the thought of his grin. He would no doubt find it hilarious.

Easing out of the car park onto the road to find the trail left by the gritters, I set off home – my body tired – more tired than it had ever been. I drove home, thinking of the wedding that followed just seven months later, the honeymoon spent on the Italian lakes, the days and evenings spent just being together. My heart soared just thinking of it all – how handsome he had looked on our wedding day – how he had taken my breath away time and time again over the last twelve months.

Perhaps tonight I would take his breath away. I thought of the small package in my handbag which I had carefully wrapped before leaving the shop that night. It was an original for sure – the perfect present. I was convinced he would love it. I knew he would and I was itching to give it to him. Pulling into the drive, the glint of the Christmas-tree lights made me smile. They were allowed on now – sure he was inside and making me soup and he assured me the fire was blazing.

"You don't want to go to the pub tonight?" he had asked that morning as I got dressed. "A little early Christmas celebration, perhaps?"

"Jack," I had smiled, "I am bone tired. Must be all the excitement we've had this year. If the truth be told when work is done I just want to come home, lie on the sofa with my gorgeous husband and spend some time together."

"I think you have broken me, Mrs Cassidy," he said. "Because that sounds infinitely more appealing than the pub."

"We're getting old, Jack," I teased. "Settled old marrieds now."

"Married, yes. Less of the old," he smiled and kissed me softly on the forehead.

God, I was lucky. Opening the door to our home, the smell of the cinnamon candle hit me as did the warmth of the blazing turf fire.

"You look frozen," Jack said, walking into the hall and hugging me before helping me out of coat and scarf. "Dinner will be ready soon," he smiled. "There's a bath run for you, if you want it. There are candles and everything."

I grinned. "I've trained you well," I teased.

"Don't get too excited," he smiled back. "I can't beat last year's Christmas present so a bubble bath and some candles are all part of the present package."

"Sounds perfect," I said, heading upstairs and sinking into the bubbles where I lay, smiling to myself about the package in my bag before drying off, putting on my pyjamas and dressing gown and padding down the stairs.

As I reached the bottom step, I reached into my bag and pulled out the small rectangular box and smiled. I could feel tears prick at my eyes again and I took a deep breath before walking through to the living room where my soup and freshly baked bread were waiting for me. Before sitting down I placed the box under the tree and I saw Jack look at me strangely.

"A present? Under the tree? Before the big day? The burglars will be breaking down our door," he teased.

"I know . . . well, it worked so well last year, I figured this year we would keep with tradition." I watched the curiosity in his eyes as I added softly, "It's for you."

As far as he was concerned, his Christmas present was a box set of *Game of Thrones* – and that definitely was not in keeping with the small box glinting from under the tree.

"You can open it now, if you want."

"You really are throwing caution to the wind all over the place tonight, Lila, aren't you?"

"That's nothing," I laughed, feeling slightly nervous. "I left a candle burning in the shop tonight – a wee light for all those coming home for Christmas."

"You rebel!" He smiled brightly. "I do love you."

"And I you, now open the present!"

"Bossy-boots," he teased as he reached down.

I could feel the emotion swell in me again. Damn it – I would not cry. Not again. But my emotions were all over the show. Please God he would like it – please God it would go some way to showing him how much he meant to me.

I watched as his fingers unwrapped the paper, my own hands trembling as I watched him. I watched as he took the lid from the box, opened the tissue paper and looked at what was inside. His face, it froze. His jaw dropped as he tried to process the contents. I was aware of the silence in the room, the slow hiss of the turf on the fire, the ticking of the clock, the blood rushing through my veins, the patter of the sleety snow on the windscreen.

"Does this mean what I think it means?" he asked, his eyes wide, and I nodded.

"Baby," he said, and I wasn't sure if it was a term of endearment or a statement of fact.

"Baby," I responded simply, looking to the pregnancy testing stick nestled in the box, tears pricking in my eyes again. Blasted hormones! They'd had me at every turn and here they were again.

It had been a remarkable year – this Christmas Eve so different to last. And the most exciting part was that next Christmas Eve would be different too – more magical again.

Jack reached over and kissed me and I melted into the kiss, tears running down my cheeks. "Happy Christmas, I love you, baby."

❦

Claire Allan is an author, columnist and journalist from Derry. She has published six novels with Poolbeg Press including *Rainy Days and Tuesdays*, *Feels Like Maybe* and, most recently, *What Becomes of the Broken Hearted?*. When not writing novels she holds down a full-time job on the staff of the *Derry Journal*. She is passionate about many things – her children, reading, singing in a choir – and she has a new-found love of baking. She is addicted to Twitter and Facebook. She is unashamedly romantic and believes in happy endings. Christmas makes her very emotional and her happiest Christmas memories include John Denver and the Muppets, her family and Sindy's Dream House.

Santa Baby

Shirley Benton

"Patrick, is that you? Christ, it is!"

"That's *Santa*," the eldest of four boys says to the open-mouthed woman.

"Sorry, pet. Of course it is." Patrick's ex-girlfriend Gemma stares at him incredulously.

He suddenly wants to die, unfair and all as that would be to the children of the world on Christmas Eve.

This *really* hadn't been part of Patrick's career path. How has he gone from being a wealthy architect to a shopping-centre Santa? The answer is a simple two-word one, of course – the recession – but at times like these, he really feels the impact of how far he's fallen. His career progression had been in full flow around the time he and Gemma had broken up. And although he knows he is lucky to have this job to tide him through the inevitable expense of Christmas, he can't stop himself from feeling embarrassed. Rightly or wrongly, he doesn't want Gemma to see him like this.

"Your accent hasn't changed anyway, Santa," Gemma says. She looks like she wants to laugh now.

A mongrel accent, that's what Gemma had always called it. It was ten years of Glasgow, eight years of his mother's hometown of Cork city after his parents had separated and his mother had moved home with him and his sister, and twenty-one of Dublin. He preferred to call it distinctive.

The eldest boy – around five, Patrick guesses – charges over to the elf photographer at the back of the grotto and bombards her with questions about her camera. His brother, who looks about four, follows him. The toddler and baby in the double buggy just stare at Patrick, like their mother.

"I suppose you're wondering how this came about," Patrick finds himself saying when the older boys are out of earshot.

Gemma shrugs.

"The previous guy did a Bad Santa and showed up trollied on the first day," Patrick continues. "My sister Ella is one of the centre's managers and told me they needed someone with immediate availability that didn't eat children for breakfast, or any other meal of the day. I'm not otherwise employed right now, so . . . here I am."

Up to that moment, he'd been happy to be there. Initially, he'd thought he'd hate the gig, that he'd be punching in hours and getting punched himself by wild kids. It was a pleasant surprise to find that it was actually rather good fun, bar the odd beard-yank elastic-prong injury from some of the younger children. Every morning when he arrived at the shopping centre, he'd try to see things from a child's perspective before stepping into Santa's boots. The elaborate Christmas decorations must have been spellbinding to a pair of young eyes. Animated displays were dotted all over the centre – Arctic scenes, dancing polar bears, winter wonderlands. They brought with them the promise of good things to come over the holiday season and, although Patrick couldn't anticipate anything good coming his way, he found himself slightly uplifted to think of the joy Christmas would bring to little children.

This would inevitably be followed by him asking himself what had got into him. He'd never been a children person. For all Ella knew when she offered him the Santa job, he could have been atrocious with kids – neither of them had any to test the waters with.

"As long as you stay sober you'll be doing better than the last fella," was all she said when Patrick asked her if she was sure about this. Her only condition was that he had to work on neutralising his accent so that the children would understand him. He practised the same few questions and phrases that needed to be asked over and over again, speaking as slowly as possible, and none of the children seemed to have had a problem with comprehending him – every child understood the word 'present' anyway. Maybe he's been slipping as it has come closer to Christmas Eve and the end of his gig, though. Gemma has rumbled him immediately.

He hadn't even recognised her when she'd walked in. Although they'd been together for nine years, ten more have passed since he's last seen her. Looking around at the four heads bobbing around the room in their knitted winter hats, she'd been busy – and although she is wrapped up in a huge coat and a thick woolly scarf, a baby bump is obvious. He shouldn't be surprised – her desire for children and his lack of it had been why they'd broken up, after all – but still! Almost *five* children! He can't imagine it.

"You don't need to explain yourself to me, Pa-Santa," Gemma says as the boys return. They don't look particularly like her, Patrick notices. She doesn't look like the person he'd once shared his life with either. She isn't blonde any more – her hair is now an auburn colour – at the ends, at least. She looks shorter, but then she'd always worn at least three-inch heels to augment her five-foot-four stature. Patrick can't imagine running around after this lot in three-inch heels – not that he can imagine wearing three-inch heels at all. If he had taken the notion to when they'd been together, though, Gemma would have been okay with it. She was good like that – open-minded, on for the *craic*. Nothing like her successor, Lucy.

"And weren't you boys very good to come out to see Santa in this snow?" Patrick says, aiming for his best Santa impression but suspecting that he sounds ridiculous.

When the kids ignore him, Gemma steps into the silence. "We

weren't going to come at all, but we figured it'd be quiet here today because of the snow."

Ireland had never seen snow like it. All month, the country had experienced widespread disruption to air, sea and road travel due to heavy snowfall coupled with overnight freezing and sub-zero temperatures. Severe weather advisories and promises of up to eight inches of overnight snow and black ice were becoming an everyday thing, and driving conditions were generally hazardous and sometimes treacherous. The centre had felt the impact of the weather on business over the Christmas period, and today has been the quietest Christmas Eve imaginable.

"I've been meaning to bring them over for weeks, but, well . . ."

"Santa can understand it's not easy to get around when there's a baby on the way and lots of snow to drive through," Patrick says. He realises he is only going downhill with this Santa thing.

"It did take us a good forty-five minutes to get here when it usually only takes five, but that's okay. But it wasn't so much the snow as the fact that I wanted to ignore Christmas this year."

Patrick notices that Gemma has started to well up.

"My husband Karl died in a car accident during the summer, you see," she whispers.

"Oh, feck, Gemma. I don't know what to say . . ."

"Mum, Santa cursed!" the eldest boy pipes up. "You always tell me not to curse or Santa won't come, but he does it himself!"

Gemma regains her composure somewhat. "He was just testing you to see if you knew what a curse was – and see, you did!"

"But –"

"Shhh! He might keep your presents if you continue talking about cursing!"

The boy adopts a sulky expression and wanders off towards the elf again.

"I realised at the last minute that it wasn't fair to the kids to have them miss out on their annual Santa trip just because I was feeling a bit off."

"A bit off? Gemma, this must be unbearably tough on you."

"Ah, there's always someone worse off, isn't there?"

Patrick doesn't say a word. He can't think of anyone he knows who is in a worse situation than Gemma, rearing four boys without a father and another child on the way. But that had always been Gemma's way – looking for the bright side even when there wasn't one. How life hasn't beaten that out of her, Patrick has no idea.

He suddenly feels ashamed. He's been going around for months – years – feeling sorry for himself, the former architect who had it all and lost it. Nobody had forced him to buy a detached five-bedroom house in an affluent part of town – and what need did a man who didn't see children as part of his future have with a five-bedroom house anyway? It was a house to impress, the type you'd bring your work colleagues to for weekend dinner parties – the type that screamed that you had money. Lucy had thought it was amazing. Nobody had been quite as impressed by it though when Patrick could no longer afford to pay his massive mortgage after the work dried up. The house had been repossessed, he'd gone on state benefits and he was now living in a tiny apartment, paid for by rent allowance.

The thought strikes him that he'd never have ended up in that mess if he'd stuck with Gemma. She hated ostentation, and would no doubt have talked him into some more modest dwelling place. Something on the outskirts of the city with a big garden that they could extend the house onto as they earned the money to do so. He thought he'd outgrown her, with her sensible civil-service job and her caution with finances. Now, he could see that *she'd* outgrown *him*. How cruel, though, that she'd got the large family she wanted only to have her husband snatched away.

Patrick is single now too – Lucy left him as soon as the money dried up – and lately he finds himself wondering if he's been wrong in thinking that having children isn't for him. It's probably too late now though. He has no way of meeting women any more, and it isn't as if he'd be an attractive prospect on a dating website. Sometimes he can't help feeling that he's a waste of space, a liability to the country with his dole payments. Sponging off the state even though he'd had his chance for a secure future. He'd earned plenty of money over the years, but had blown it on holidays and cars and other ridiculous things he'd brainwashed himself into thinking he needed. All of this torments him on a daily basis – that he'd had his chances in life and ruined them all. But he is alive and well, and he should be bloody grateful for that.

Gemma rubs her back.

"How's life been treating that friend of yours, Santa – Patrick? Is he well these days?"

"Patrick is doing okay," he lies. He can hardly complain in light of what he's just heard, can he?

"Did he ever marry?"

"No. There was a long-term relationship, but it didn't work out."

"No kids, I take it?"

"No kids."

"And is he happy? Forget that the question is coming from a woman who's lost her husband when answering."

She'd always been able to read him.

"Ah, he's fine. Probably not contributing much to the world though."

"Does that bother him?"

"Well, I suppose. He's a bit useless these days really."

"Useless? Aren't you being a bit harsh on him?"

"No."

"I think you should give Patrick a break." She frowns. "Santa, do you mind if I sit down there beside you for a minute? This baby is dancing a jig in there."

"You have to sit on his *lap*," the eldest says.

"Santa can't deliver the presents with broken femurs and chipped kneecaps," Gemma replies. She squeezes and heaves her way into the small space beside Patrick.

"Here, take the whole seat," he says, getting up. "I'm sorry, I should have already offered. There's nobody in the queue so you can rest for as long as you want. When's the baby due?"

"Two weeks."

Patrick tries to think of something fitting to say – 'not long now', or some other ludicrously obvious statement that might fit into the flow of a polite conversation – but all he can think about is the fact that Gemma's poor mite will be born without a father. He shakes his head, an act that he hadn't known he was about to commit until he does it.

"Stop feeling sorry for us, Patrick."

Blood rushes to his face. He still doesn't know what to say.

Gemma rescues him. "So what are you doing for Christmas Day?"

"Em . . ." How can he make the word 'nothing' sound good? Ella invited him over for dinner with her and her husband, but he declined. It will be their first Christmas as a married couple and he knows she only asked out of politeness.

"I'll probably . . . visit a few neighbours or something. I haven't decided yet."

"In other words, you'll spend the day sitting at home by yourself doing frig all."

There was blunt, and then there was Gemma. "You haven't changed," he says, trying to close the subject down with a laugh.

He is suddenly nostalgic for convivial Christmases spent with Gemma's family. The boozing would start with dinner, which was always served right after morning Mass to give everyone a clear run at the day. The annual reindeer tablecloth would be littered with cans of beer, fighting for space between the plates and knives and forks – Gemma's family weren't wine-with-dinner people. Many hours later, the table would be cleared (of plates and foodstuffs – the drink supplies would only increase) to accommodate Trivial Pursuit. Gemma's mother Judith would open a bottle of red wine and pour it in a bowl, then pour boiling water on top of the wine and throw in a few herbs from the spice rack. She'd plonk a soup ladle into it and lay it on the table with a stack of plastic cups and tell everyone to help themselves to her special mulled wine. They would all pour it down their gullets like folk who'd just come across water after finishing a marathon.

Trivial Pursuit and mulled-wine consumption would go on until the first of the evening guests arrived. For what? A Christmas session, of course – because what had gone on before that was only target practice. Gemma's siblings and cousins and aunts and uncles and grand-aunts and grand-uncles and every other imaginable relative would convene in the sitting room and drink the house dry until well into Stephen's Day. Their annual Christmas Day session was almost a public service of sorts, helping the bachelors and spinsters in the family to put down a somewhat unputdownable day. Patrick had loved the inclusivity of it. He missed it.

He'd missed Gemma too. For years afterwards, he'd craved her friendship. She wasn't able to handle a friendship scenario after breaking up, she'd said, and he'd respected that. But it had been hard.

Family Christmases with Lucy had always involved him being belittled. "You bought Lucy's Tiffany bracelet in *Brown Thomas*, Patrick?" Lucy's mother had said incredulously the first year they'd gone around for Christmas dinner. "Ah, that explains it." She took her present for Lucy out from under the tree – a present that turned out to be an exquisite hand-crafted necklace that made his bracelet look insignificant – before elaborating. "They wouldn't have the selection of New York, I suppose, only the most *basic* supplies. Still, you'll know better for next year!" When next year came, he gave Lucy a three-thousand euro watch that she'd been asking for all year. Later, when her mother was the worst for wear after a few sherries, the words "like something you'd get in a Lucky Bag" were mentioned about the watch in hushed tones that hadn't been hushed enough.

He'd never missed Lucy since she'd upped and left him. Not once.

Gemma stands up abruptly.

"Is everything okay?"

"Bit of a weird backache there. Just felt the need to stand u –" She lurches forward and puts her hands on her legs as her camel maternity trousers start to turn a darker colour. Within seconds, there is water on the floor.

The older children notice straight away, and go through an inevitable round of laughing at their mum weeing on herself.

18

"Oh my God . . . I thought the pains were Braxton Hicks. I've been getting them for weeks and wasn't taking any notice of them earlier!"

"Does this mean you're in . . . labour?" He mouths the last word for the children's benefit.

"Put it this way – Alfie was born forty-five minutes after my waters broke last time."

It takes Patrick a few seconds to react. Eventually, he manages to tell the elf to call an ambulance and to get security to put out a call for a doctor or midwife in the centre. The elf nods, looking relieved to be getting out of there.

"Take the boys with you!" Gemma shouts.

And that's when Patrick truly realises what is about to happen.

"Oh God, Patrick, this means I'm going to miss the session tomorrow. Mum'll kill me!"

Gemma sinks onto her knees and presses a hand against the wall. She closes her eyes as she starts to breathe in a raggedy-jaggedy fashion. Patrick thinks the protocol is deep breaths in, deep breaths out, but decides to keep quiet.

"Are you in pain? Is this a – contraction?"

She grimaces and reaches out, squeezing her eyes into oblivion and panting. Her hand connects with Patrick's beard, which she wrenches off as she starts to roar.

That answers his questions, then.

It all kicks in fast after that. Gemma repeats the process of leaning against a wall, bellowing, and reaching out for something of Patrick's to pull every few minutes. It isn't long before his moustache and Santa hat are gone too, along with the white furry trim around the neck of the Santa coat. In between, she orders Patrick to ring her mother to come and collect the boys – a surreal conversation in which Judith accepts that her daughter is in early labour, but can't quite fathom Patrick's involvement in the situation. He doesn't blame her.

Patrick throws frantic glances at the door every few seconds as he awaits the elf's return. Eventually, she pokes her head into the grotto and beckons frantically at him just as Gemma starts to wail again.

"Sorry, I had to find someone to mind the kids while I rang for an ambulance – no doctor or midwife has come forward, there's hardly anyone in the centre. The ambulance could be at least half an hour. They're only a few miles down the road, but you know what it's like out there . . ."

Gemma doesn't look like someone who has half an hour left in her.

"They're still on the line here and want to know how long there is between contractions."

"Okay." Patrick tries his best to stay calm. "I'll ask her."

He does. Gemma just howls. Not long, it seems.

Patrick takes the phone and moves to the door of the grotto. "She seems to be in bad pain every minute or so."

He has a feeling he knows what's coming, but it's still a shock to hear it articulated. "*You may have to deliver the baby.*" Suddenly, there is talk about getting Gemma comfortable and undressed from the waist down and fetching an endless list of things. He tells the elf to get the supplies needed and tentatively approaches Gemma, phone still in hand.

"The ambulance is on the way –"

"And so's this baby – any minute. Help me, Patrick!" Gemma says between gasping breaths. "It's in a hurr-*aaaaggggghhhhhhhh*!"

Patrick puts the phone on speaker. When the contraction passes, he immediately removes Gemma's lower clothing before another arrives. The pain is clearly gathering speed and amassing extra reserves, like a giant snowball thundering down a steep hill.

Gemma lies back on the ground and reaches out – for something to pull, Patrick assumes. As soon as she connects with Patrick's hand, she starts to push.

"Are you supposed to be pushing?" Patrick says frantically. Surely it is too soon? "*Is she supposed to be pushing?*" he yells into the phone.

He looks down and sees it. The tip of the baby's head. In the absence of blankets or other cushioning material, he whips off his Santa costume and places it between Gemma's legs where the baby will soon be. He knows it's a matter of seconds now, not minutes any more.

And then, Gemma is pushing again and Patrick sees a head coming at him. He reaches forward, ready to take the baby in his hands. He is terrified but determined not to fail this little life. With one more push, the baby rotates and its shoulders emerge. It slides right into Patrick's waiting hands.

"A girl," Gemma repeats over and over as soon as Patrick places the baby on her chest, the cord still attached – he has been told, to his relief, that there is no need to cut it.

Patrick just smiles. He can't quite believe what's just happened.

"I think you're lost on this Santa thing, Patrick," Gemma says without taking her eyes off the baby. "Maybe you've found your new career. Not so useless now, are you?"

Patrick can't believe Gemma's generosity of spirit, to even think of him and his troubles at this time.

"*You* did all the hard work. I think Karl must have been pulling a few strings for you up there though, to have all of that happen so easily."

"I had a dream last night in which he said I'd have a fast, uncomplicated labour as long as I called the baby Karoline – with a K. Egotistical fecker! But it did make me laugh – and it suits her, doesn't it?"

The elf returns with the supplies. Patrick and Gemma fuss and footer around the baby until the ambulance eventually arrives to take mother and child to hospital to be checked out, informing Gemma that her mother has arrived to collect the boys.

Patrick moves backwards as Gemma is wheeled out, suddenly ill at ease. She smiles shyly up at him. He knows he should say something, but what? He's just delivered her baby and somehow, against all rational assumptions, that hadn't been awkward – but *this* is.

He realises he doesn't want to have to say goodbye to them. How can you share something like this with someone and then never see them again? And yet, how else can things be? They are strangers now. If it had been any other pregnant woman whose baby he'd delivered, they'd go their separate ways and pray they'd never bump into each other in the shopping centre again. Why is this different?

"Thank you," she says before she and Karoline disappear through the door of the grotto. Patrick doesn't get a chance to reply. They are already gone.

By the time Patrick and the elf have cleaned up the grotto, it is six o'clock and he is officially unemployed again. He leaves the centre and fights his way through the fresh snow to his car, flitting between jubilation at the magic that he's just experienced and a huge sense of loss for something that was never his.

He arrives home several hours later after a tough battle with the roads and tries to stop wondering how Gemma and Karoline are doing. It feels disrespectful to Karl somehow, and yet how can he not wonder? Besides, he has a feeling Gemma could use a friend as much as he could right now. He finds himself thinking about ways he could help her out – maybe taking the four boys out to the playground or something. Could he handle minding four boys? He hasn't a clue, but he'd be willing to try . . .

He shakes his head. What is he *thinking*? He doesn't even have her phone number. He has to accept the night's events for what they were – a wonderful episode when, for the first time ever, he truly understood what life is all about. But that is all it can be.

He is contemplating going to bed at nine o'clock when his phone rings.

"Patrick, it's Judith. Gemma says you've no plans for tomorrow. We're down a Trivial Pursuit player if you and your liver are up for it . . ."

⁂

Shirley Benton is originally from the metropolis of Toomevara in Tipperary but now lives in Dublin with her husband and children. She studied English and French as part of her BA degree in Mary

Immaculate College of Education, Limerick, and completed a postgraduate Diploma in Systems Analysis in NUI Galway. After working full-time in IT for ten years, she left the industry in 2009 to pursue her dream of becoming a writer whilst working part-time as a freelance editor and proofreader. She has had two books published by Poolbeg, *Looking for Leon* and *Can We Start Again?*, and is currently working on her third. Shirley is also a book reviewer for the chicklit website www.chicklitclub.com. She is a lover of the Irish language and when she is not writing or reviewing, she can be found on her couch watching TG4 if you're looking for her.

A Christmas to Remember

Ann Carroll

Nine-year-old Jack Hennessey lived in the last cottage on Hollybank Lane with his mum and dad and his dog Bowsie. Banked by holly bushes, the lane wound along a stream which disappeared into the blackness of Warlock Woods just beyond Jack's home. This was a dense forest of ancient trees, so terrifying no local ever ventured there. People said demons lived in its depths and hunted for human blood. Stories travelled through the centuries of strangers seeking a short cut through the woods to the distant town – strangers who hadn't listened to warnings and were never seen again.

Sometimes from his attic bedroom, late at night, when he couldn't sleep, Jack heard shrieks and howls from the forest and shivered. And then he was glad to be inside the cosy cottage.

Next door lived Mrs Timson, a widow, who was very fond of Jack and often invited him to tea. The widow wasn't quite as fond of Bowsie because the dog was sometimes seized by fits of great energy and dug large holes in her garden. Then she would chase him into the lane, shouting abuse and waving the sweeping brush – not that she'd ever hit him.

At the top of the lane lived Jimmy Sullivan, one of a large

family and Jack's best friend. Jimmy's dad worked at Fergusons' Emporium in Hollybank village, half a mile from the lane.

The Emporium's banner, high across the village street, boasted:

Fergusons' Emporium
YOU NAME IT WE SELL IT

Someone must have named a snake and not collected it because one day that's what Mr Sullivan arrived home with, to the delight of all except his wife who promptly put on her coat and declared that either the snake went or she did. Her children must have hesitated, for she then expressed the hope that the snake was able to cook and look after a family. That clinched it and the snake left. Jack was a witness to the drama and only regretted that such things never happened in his own house. His dad managed a local farm and was unlikely to find snakes there or anything else exotic.

Jack was always around in Jimmy's and envied him his brothers and sisters. Sometimes he hated leaving the noise and laughter for the quiet of his own cottage. But he knew his parents were ace and couldn't do enough for him. They'd got Bowsie in case he was lonely and in Jack's world there was no one to match the black and white collie. Every weekday the dog sat in the porch waiting for his return from school. The minute Jack appeared in the lane, Bowsie shot out like an arrow and tried to bowl him over with affection. The collie was clever, able to open the pedal-bin in the kitchen and drop in wrappers, able to fetch shoes and press on the telly with a paw – though so far he'd made a right dog's dinner of using the remote control.

As winter came and the days grew short and cold, the boys began to look forward to Christmas. The Emporium set up a Christmas Fair with toys from all parts of the world. Santa's Den was a small wonderland of magical lights and gift-wrapped presents and each of the boys confided to Santa that the one thing they wanted this year was a mobile phone. They explained that everyone who was in any way grown-up had a mobile phone and, much to their delight, Santa agreed that their time had come.

Then, one mid-December night, disaster struck Fergusons'. While the village slept, a van moved quietly along the street and down the alleyway beside the shop. Silently five men got out and jemmied open the back entrance into the premises, found the safe and with great expertise blew it open and took a large metal box.

There was pandemonium next day when the robbery was discovered. A few people living nearby said they'd heard a loud bang in the middle of the night but thought they must be dreaming. Explosions didn't happen in Hollybank and there'd never been a robbery before. Everyone was stunned. A huge sum of money had been taken – some said tens of thousands, others put it higher. Many of the orders for Christmas had been paid for in advance and the money had been locked away safely, destined next morning for the bank in the distant town.

Police cars screeched down the street and the press arrived. The day was a hullabaloo of activity with detectives taking statements and reporters talking to anyone and everyone about the crime.

Then it emerged that Mr Ferguson's insurance was out of date by a few months. Things had been so busy he'd put off paying it – and so busy anyone could have posed as a customer and planned the robbery without the staff noticing. The only lead was a red van with a Dublin registration which a few people had spotted some weeks before. They remembered it because Hollybank village was rarely visited by Dubliners.

Once the police and press had gone, the excitement died down and Fergusons' was as busy as ever. People began to think that in time the shop would recover from the loss of all that money. The festive atmosphere returned and the village was decorated with fairy lights. Everywhere was decked with holly.

Soon the Christmas trees appeared in the cottages' windows and all the porch lanterns along the lane were switched on by early afternoon. Woodsmoke from the chimneys drifted into the icy air. Jack loved coming from school when it was dark, watching the night sky grow bright with stars. The warm lights welcomed him home and a cheerful fire beckoned, keeping at bay the immense darkness of Warlock Woods.

One evening Mrs Timson invited him to tea. Such meals were never boring since Mrs T didn't believe in the kind of healthy food Jack's mum prepared. Mrs T ditched the egg sandwiches and the beetroot salads in favour of cream cakes, apple tarts, ice cream and Belgian chocolates.

Now that Christmas was coming, Mrs T had felt she should make a proper effort with Bowsie and so she had invited him too. The collie was on his best behaviour and, putting his head to one side, he looked appealingly at the widow. She motioned him under the table in the kitchen where he tried to chew her slipper until she gave him a plate of ham and some superior doggy biscuits. Bowsie settled down.

Then she made two mugs of chocolate topped with cream, marshmallow and flakes and Jack tucked into a chocolate éclair.

"I wonder, Jack, do you remember my husband at all?" she asked.

Jack could see the answer was important, so he tried his best but shook his head.

Mrs T sighed, then brightened. "Maybe if I show you a picture . . ."

She took a small photo from her handbag and the boy studied it. The man was middle-aged. He was laughing, his eyes creased with merriment.

"Yes," Jack broke the silence. "I remember now. He used to swing me up in the air. And he put me on his shoulders at the circus so I could see the clowns. He was ace."

He stopped, struck by Mrs Timson's expression. She looked as if she might cry, or laugh, her face crumpled between sadness and pleasure.

"Oh my goodness," she said and then she was smiling. "You were only four when we took you to the circus, Jack. I'm glad you remember Henry, because he was very fond of you. We both were."

"I suppose you miss him," he said sturdily. "Just like I'd miss Bowsie if anything happened to him."

Mrs Timson's smile vanished.

"Not that anything will happen," he added quickly, to stop any worry on her part.

"That's a blessing, I'm sure," she said faintly. "But don't you think missing a dog is a bit different to missing a husband?"

"No." Jack was earnest. "I'd hate it if I didn't have Bowsie. He's the best. Is it all right if I take a chocolate?"

Mrs Timson handed him the plate and looked thoughtful.

"They're the nicest chocolates I've ever tasted," Jack said hopefully as he swallowed the last morsel.

"Have another," Mrs Timson said. "Have as many as you like."

Jack munched away.

"Henry was great company and he was wonderful and funny," she said.

"So's Bowsie. Wonderful and funny I mean, and great company," Jack said. "He can do all sorts. And I can talk to him 'cos he's a good listener. I'm lucky he's mine." He gave Bowsie an extra biscuit.

When he looked again Mrs Timson was staring at him as if she'd made a discovery.

"Do you know, you're right. You are lucky Bowsie is yours just as I was lucky Henry was mine." She leaned under the table and patted the dog. "Now whenever I see you," she told the collie, "I'll think of Henry – except that he didn't ever dig random holes in the garden."

Bowsie emerged, put his paws on her knees and tried to knock her off the chair. Jack explained that this was a sign of fondness and Mrs T laughed.

The collie had made his peace, at least for the moment.

The evening before the school holidays, when all seemed right with the world, there was a tremendous knocking at the door.

Mrs Hennessey opened it to Jimmy who had run so fast down the lane he had trouble breathing.

"What on earth's the matter?" She led the boy into the kitchen and made him sit down.

"It's Dad," Jimmy panted. "His job is gone!"

"That can't be," Jack's dad said. "Fergusons' is safe as houses."

The boy shook his head. "No. It's closing down after Christmas. Mr Ferguson said the robbery wiped him out. But that's not the worst. The worst is we'll have to leave Hollybank! Dad says he won't be able to pay the rent and we'll have to go."

"There must be other jobs," said Mrs Hennessey.

"Not around here. Dad says we'll have to move to the town."

He stopped, gazing at Jack as if his friend might have some solution. But Jack was overcome, trying to imagine life without Jimmy and without the Sullivans.

"Well, I won't go – I don't want to leave here." Jimmy wiped the back of his hand across his eyes and, afraid he might start crying in earnest, dashed up the hall and out the front door.

Mrs Hennessey patted Jack's shoulder. "Let him be for tonight," she told her son. "He won't want you to see him so upset."

"This is bad news indeed," Mr Hennessey said. "Fergusons' sell nearly all the farm produce. If it goes, the farm won't survive."

Things were very quiet in school next day. The news about Fergusons' had spread and the teachers were worried, knowing a lot of families might have to move. Things wouldn't be the same without the Emporium, they said. When it closed the life would go out of the village; it was only a matter of time before they all had to move and the village itself closed down. The end-of-term Christmas party was miserable and everyone was relieved when the principal decided to close the school early, glumly wishing them all a Happy Christmas.

The boys trudged into Hollybank Lane, each thinking how awful the future would be.

Jimmy stopped suddenly. "Where's Bowsie?"

They stared down the winding lane and walked faster, hoping the collie would suddenly appear and collide as usual with his master. But the only figure they saw was Jack's next-door neighbour, Mrs Timson, standing at her garden gate and waving frantically.

"Jack, Jack!" she called. "It's Bowsie!"

When the boys stopped, she shook her head sorrowfully. "Oh, Jack. I am so sorry. I was going to tell your mum but she's gone out."

"Tell her what?" Jack dreaded what she would say but had to know. "Tell her what, Mrs Timson?"

"Bowsie . . . he's . . . he's . . ."

"Dead?" Jimmy said, unable to stand the suspense.

She looked at him, amazed. "No, not dead. Why would he be dead, for heaven's sake?" She had found her tongue. "No, no, no. He was digging a hole in my garden, Jack, the way he does sometimes and I had to chase him out with the broom. I'm so sorry."

Hugely relieved, Jack said, "That's alright, Mrs T. But where is he?"

"That's what I'm trying to tell you. I chased him into the lane thinking he'd turn into your house but he ran past, so then I ran too, trying to stop him, only he disappeared into Warlock Woods."

Jack's sense of dread returned. No one ever came out of Warlock Woods.

No one spoke, trying to think.

Then Mrs Timson said, "You go home, Jack. Give Bowsie a bit of time and he'll come back. I'm sure of it." She didn't look at all sure, the way she was wringing her hands, but Jack nodded.

Silently he let himself into his home, Jimmy following.

"I'm going to look for Bowsie," Jack said.

"In Warlock Woods?"

"Yes, before Mum comes back. I'm going to pack some things and leave."

"Pack some things? How long will you be gone?"

"I don't know, do I? Until I find Bowsie. I'll need food and a torch and stuff."

Neither boy mentioned the fear that he could be gone for good.

"I'm going with you," Jimmy said. "Our place is a right misery-dump at the minute. Warlock Woods couldn't be worse." This was more bravado than bravery but Jack didn't discourage him.

They stuffed backpacks with orange juice, some left-over cake, cheese, biscuits and dog food. Jack found a torch and then they were ready.

They stood at the edge of the forest and looked back. Although it was early afternoon, daylight was fast fading and the first stars had appeared. A light snow began to fall and the lane looked magical, beckoning them to stay. Reluctantly they turned into the darkness.

The woods were deathly quiet as if silenced by their intrusion. Then the boys made their own noise pushing through brambles and undergrowth. Progress was impossible until the beam from Jack's torch caught the line of an ancient track. As they struggled onto it they might have jumped up and down in relief if the place hadn't been so eerie.

"You can't see any stars," Jimmy said.

"Or any snow," said Jack.

"And there's no noise."

"Not an animal or a bird."

"Nothing."

"Except breathing. Heavy, heavy breathing."

"That's us."

To stop frightening himself, Jack shouted, "Bowsie, Bowsie!" And the call came back twice as frightening, "*Bowwwwsie! Bowwwwsieee!*"

"It's only an echo," Jimmy said swiftly and shouted himself.

They made their way along the track calling non-stop for the collie. Any sound was better than none, even with a horrible echo.

After a while they did hear another sound, the gushing, tumbling noise of water.

"It must be our stream," Jack said.

The stream was part of the lane and the boys thought of it as an old familiar friend and rushed towards the sound, Jack's torch bobbing.

They were shocked at what they saw. Their brook had become a torrent, too wide to cross.

"If Bowsie went in there," Jack said, "he'd have been swept away."

"He wouldn't go in there." Jimmy was hopeful. "He might have followed it though."

Now they looked for some sign of the dog along the banks of the river and after almost half a mile, in a sudden patch of muddy, wet soil they came across paw-marks. This time they did jump up and down. Then the bank became dusty and hard again and the collie's tracks disappeared. But they kept going, calling his name by the rushing river until an age passed.

Sitting on a fallen tree they shared some food and tried to consider what they should do next.

"What's that?" Jimmy whispered.

Jack clutched his arm in fright. "What? What is it?"

"Look over there."

Jack followed his finger, pointing across the river. Lights!

"I think it's a house," Jimmy breathed.

They stood up and shouted till they were hoarse, hoping someone would hear and come out. But the river drowned their voices. Still, if there was a house maybe that's where Bowsie was.

"Let's find a way across."

They began to follow the river further but suddenly came upon a wide track.

"Look, look close!" Jack shone the torch downward onto the faint outlines of large tyre prints.

Intently now, they moved along the prints until they disappeared straight into some bushes which they saw must have been placed there to hide something. Swiftly they cleared some of the bushes away and discovered an old, wide stone bridge.

"Why would anyone want to hide a bridge?" Jack said.

"Maybe to hide the house too. You can't see it with the

bushes. You can only see it from that spot on the river where we were before and I bet nobody comes along there."

Whoever wanted to hide the house mightn't welcome visitors, they reasoned, and so they moved stealthily across the bridge. The building was neglected, the roof collapsing in places. To one side was an old shed, still sturdy though in disrepair. The house's lights cast a ghastly glow in the forest setting, creating eerie shadows.

Hearing voices, they approached the main window and hunkered down. Clutching the sill, they peered in. Five men were sitting round an old table, drinking from cans and eating bread and meat. Two of them were arguing loudly.

"We've got to shoot that dog!"

"No, we don't. No one's going to find him. I vote we let him go."

"He found us. His owner might do the same!"

"All the more reason for letting him go. His owner is tracking the dog, not us!"

"If we free him he could lead someone to us. Collies are clever."

The argument raged on and on. Jack raised his head to see if there was any sign of Bowsie in the room, then ducked down when one of the men swirled around.

"What was that? At the window. I thought I saw something."

"It's your nerves, Clancy."

Nevertheless the man who wanted shut of Bowsie pushed back his chair and strode to the door. The boys crept around the side of the house.

"Nothing! Like I thought. I'm going to check on that dog."

He made his way to the shed and opened the door with a key. At once Bowsie barked and snarled at him.

The man laughed. "Good thing you're tied up, matey. And soon you won't be alive to tell any tales." He locked the door and went back into the house where the row resumed.

The boys moved around the back of the house and made for the shed. Bowsie barked excitedly.

"Don't, Bowsie! You have to stay quiet."

Even with the noise of the river, the men might hear and then what would happen?

The dog gave a little groan but made no more noise.

"How are we going to rescue him?" Jack was desperate.

Jimmy pointed. "We can use a tree to climb up to that hole in the roof."

The shed was quite high, with no windows or ledges, but the rough bark of the tree gave them some footholds and they managed to get onto the roof without much noise. Then they swung down in turn from one of the beams inside onto the clay floor. Jack shone his torch around until he saw Bowsie tied to the bumper of a red van. The dog jumped up and down and made little noises but didn't bark and when Jack hugged him Bowsie tried to knock him down, always proof of fierce affection.

They stayed still, all three of them, listening for any sign from the house, but none came. Quickly, Bowsie was untied and gave himself a great shake to welcome freedom.

"How do we get out?" Jimmy said. "How do we get Bowsie out? The roof is too high for us to go back the same way. And anyway he certainly can't shimmy down that tree."

It was then Bowsie came into his own as a great excavator. He led them to the back of the shed where the wood was rotting at the base. Then he started digging like mad and the boys tore at the timber until there was enough room for each of them to push through.

Somehow the journey back was easier. For one thing, after snaffling some dog food, Bowsie kept his nose to the ground and led the way and the boys were happy to follow. For another their eyes were more accustomed to their surroundings so that the darkness became less black and they could see farther ahead than the torchlight. Now they recognised landmarks: the muddy soil by the river, a crooked tree, a small clearing. The woods were no longer so frightening.

"Maybe no one ever disappeared here," Jack said. "Maybe strangers were never seen again because they travelled on."

"And maybe there are no demons," Jimmy said, "only villains."

The forest was no longer silent. Apart from the sound of water they could hear rustles in the undergrowth, burrowing noises, and once an owl hooted and flew ahead of them.

"Maybe that's what I heard late at night," Jack said. "The owl and sometimes the wind."

"The woods are getting used to us," Jimmy said.

Now too they could see snow falling through the tree-tops and covering the branches.

They were still some distance from the edge of Warlock Woods when they saw the wavering lights spread out in a long line. The boys stopped dead, swallowing fear, thinking that somehow the men had got ahead of them and now were tracking them down.

But Bowsie raced ahead, barking madly. Galvanised, they yelled after him, "Come back! Come here, Bowsie!"

But the collie paid no heed. Instead voices they recognised hailed them, neighbours' voices, their dads' among them.

"Jack! Jack!"

"Jimmy, son!"

"Boys – over here!"

They drew closer and saw that all the men from the lane were there along with a dozen police.

There was great excitement and much hugging and pummelling. No one uttered a word of reproach. Everyone was overjoyed to see them and when they told the police their story they were hailed as heroes for their daring rescue of Bowsie.

A large sergeant told them solemnly, "You're brave boys and that's a clever dog. Now I wonder if you'd do us the favour of lending him to us for a while so he can lead us back to those villains? For I suspect they're the ones who robbed Fergusons'." When he saw Jack's hesitation, the sergeant added, "He'll come to no harm, I promise." And he bent down to pat Bowsie who immediately knocked him over.

"He likes you," Jack said and agreed they could take him.

Now the party split into two groups with the police heading deep into the woods and the others heading home. And this time when the boys looked back from the top of the lane, Warlock Woods held no fear.

No one from Hollybank ever forgot that Christmas. The money

from Fergusons' was found in the red van and the robbers were caught. Jobs were safe once more and the Sullivans could stay on in Hollybank Lane. Mrs Timson said she'd never give out to Bowsie again – he could make a crater out of her garden for all she cared. The dog bowled her over with gratitude.

Bowsie got a police medal for his part in the villains' capture and the boys received a citation for bravery.

In time folk ventured into Warlock Woods and none disappeared. Picnics and strolls along the river were common. Children played games of hide and seek and there were no more tales of demons.

In time too, Jack and Jimmy had other adventures.

But all that was still in the future.

Ann Carroll is a Dubliner, married with two grown-up children, who taught English at second level for many years. When she was four, her father used to read to her from *The Adventures of Mandrake the Magician*. Mandrake was American and always wore a tall hat and tux. His sidekick, Lothar, was a large, tough, bald man dressed in what looked like a woman's leopard-skin bathing suit. It was a considerable let-down when the author met real Americans to find their dress code was normal and this led to the discovery that often life was no match for fiction. Some years ago she attended a workshop on Writing Fiction for Children and this got her started on *Rosie's Quest*, the first of six Rosie novels for children. She has also written *Laura Delaney's Deadliest Day* and *Amazing Grace*. For her, reading and writing are great adventures. Ann is currently adapting Irish legends for Poolbeg's new imprint *In a Nutshell*.

A Card at Christmas

Claudia Carroll

You think you know someone. You might even think you know them well, then you get such a shock, it feels like a stab right to the solar plexus.

Initially, when the police interviewed me, I was in shock. Couldn't believe it. Still am reeling from it all, if I'm being perfectly honest. I mean, come on . . . this is Dublin, in the twenty-first century, for God's sake. People don't just disappear into thin air.

Do they?

My first interview/interrogation was with a Garda called Jake Evans: about my own age, tall, soft-spoken, intent, focused eyes and a warm crinkly smile. Shook my hand and said call me Jake and offered me tea from a plastic cup. Oh, and a terrific listener, but then I suppose they're trained to be in that line of work, aren't they?

He gently steered me away from the business of the main police station, and into a quiet 'interview' room down the end of a long corridor. Thank God for that small mercy; it was a mad busy Friday evening and frankly I was terrified standing in the main area outside, surrounded by drunks who'd been arrested for brawling on the streets not to mention a gang of what looked like drug addicts who'd just been brought in wearing handcuffs and threatening all around them. Not for the faint-hearted, believe me.

Jake offered me a seat which I gratefully accepted, then shuffled down opposite me with a notepad in front of him, ready to write down anything I said that might in some small way, help.

"Sorry to have to drag you in," he began, "but as you were the person who filed the missing-person report, I'm afraid we need a full statement from you."

I nodded nervously back at him, my limbs feeling like they were being operated by someone else's brain.

"So take your time and tell me in your own words exactly how you first met Kitty Allen. Remember, don't leave anything out. Even the most insignificant detail could prove to be vitally important to our investigation."

"Well," I began, my voice sounding tiny, like it was coming from another room, "we first met about two years ago, when she came to work at Eurosales."

"Which is . . . ?" he prompted helpfully.

"Oh sorry, a telesales company that we both work for. We're based in town and I've been there for about six months longer than Kitty."

"And you became pals?"

"Yes, almost immediately. She had the cubicle next to mine and, well, from day one we just clicked."

A vivid memory, but then Kitty was someone it wasn't easy to forget. She bounced in on that first day, wearing what looked like pyjamas under a bright red plastic mac with a pair of sandals, but it turned out to be a flowery leggings and T-shirt. She was the nuttiest dresser I ever saw. Like she just fell out of the bed first thing every morning and did a lucky wardrobe dip, grabbing whatever came to hand without, God forbid, doing anything as conventional as colour-coding.

"And you'd go out a lot together?"

"Yes, we started nipping out for lunch together, but then we always had such a great laugh that pretty soon we'd meet up at night too. She'd just arrived up in Dublin from Cork, she told me, and didn't really know too many people. So of course, I introduced her to my own gang and she hung out with us a lot." Then I tack on "Everyone really liked her," in case he thought we just felt sorry for an out-of-towner.

And everyone did adore her. It was hard not to. Kitty is mad and bad and dangerous to know and the best fun you can possibly imagine. The kind of girl you meet for a few drinks, then end up the following morning in Holyhead. And there wasn't a single guy working at Eurosales who didn't fancy her. With her slim figure, long skinny legs, jack-in-the-box springy curls and bright black eyes always full of fun, she was irresistible.

Always dragging me out places, egging me on to say and do things that for her were completely normal, but for me were totally out of character. I'm naturally cautious, you see, introverted. I'm a hand-wringer, a rule-follower, a designated driver-type. But in all the time I'd known Kitty, she did her level best to yank me out of my more conservative carry-on, to take risks, just for the hell of it. To throw sickies from work so the two of us could skive off and see a movie in the afternoon, something I'd never in all my born days even considered. To date guys I thought weren't for me, but who turned out to be brilliant fun. To let my hair down every now and then. To live a fuller, better life.

"Come on!" she'd yell at me from across a packed nightclub floor, me still in my work clothes as we'd gone for 'just the one' after work and somehow ended up still on the tiles past two in the morning. "You can't live your life in fear, you'll be a long time dead!" was her catchphrase and somehow, even now, I can still hear her voice saying that to me, clear as you like.

Which is why this is just all so completely surreal.

Like it's happening to someone else and not me.

"Did she ever talk about her family?" Call-me-Jake asks.

I have to rack my brains to answer that one. But the answer is no, I tell him. At least, not really. She would get vague if I asked about her parents, brothers, sisters, anything like that at all. I remember once asking her if she was going home for Christmas and she somehow evaded my question, just said she'd be staying up in Dublin and would be back to work early in the New Year. Funny, but it just all seemed so plausible back then. Nothing about what she said or didn't say ever struck me as remotely odd.

"So tell me in your own words then," Jake says softly, "exactly what happened the night of her disappearance."

It's like a slap across the face even hearing the word disappearance. Because Kitty isn't missing, I'm sure of it. Kitty just vanished off the face of the earth never to be seen again just doesn't sound like the kind of thing she'd do. Ever.

"Well," I begin tentatively, telling this story for what feels like the thousandth time, "one of the girls in the office was leaving, so a gang of us were giving her a bit of a send-off after work."

Kitty, I tell him, was the organiser and ringleader, as somehow she always was. She was so popular and cool, everyone just did what she said, followed wherever she led, knowing that would inevitably be where the party was at. "Ron Black's bar," she decreed. "Let's all start off there after work, down a few cocktails then head up to Krystal nightclub to dance the night away!"

"And did you notice anything strange or unusual about her behaviour that night?"

I've been asked this what feels like about a thousand times, and the answer is still the same. No, I genuinely didn't think anything was amiss. Kitty was, if anything, more bubbly and vivacious than ever that last night, though I do remember noticing that while the rest of us were knocking back mojitos to beat the band, she stayed on water for the night. Not a big deal, but it was just odd, given that Kitty never cared if she had a hangover the next day, as I would have done. She never worried or fussed like I did.

Jake is looking at me keenly.

"Anything else?"

I pause for a breath, feeling like I'm trying to snatch a dim memory from the deepest recesses of my mind, but it's a bit like trying to recall a dream: the more you try to catch it, the further it slips away from you, like mercury. But there's something . . . I'm sure there's some little thing . . . that if I could only grasp it, it might just make sense of this nightmare, like the final piece in a jigsaw puzzle.

"Just . . . just give me a minute," I half-whisper, willing my subconscious to do its job.

He nods, then produces a bulging brown file, stuffed full, and lays it out on the desk in front of me. A colour photo, taken at a guess about four or five years ago.

"I know this isn't easy for you," he says gently, "but I need to ask you to identify the person in the photo. Take your time."

I don't even need to study it, I'd know those dancing brown eyes a mile away. It's Kitty, but somehow looking an awful lot younger. Her hair's different, shorter, and she's got a fringe which is long grown out now. But there's a weird-looking shadow across her right eye, almost like a scar, which looks odd . . . makes her look so different.

I nod, suddenly getting an inconvenient lump in my throat.

"Yes, it's her. It's Kitty."

"In that case," says Jake, "what I have to tell you next may come as a bit of a shock. You know this woman as Kitty Allen, but in actual fact her name is Katherine Walker."

"I'm sorry?"

"Her married name, that is."

I look at Jake, speechless. Her married name? No, there must be some mistake, Kitty isn't married, she'd have told me . . .

"I know this is hard to hear, but I'm afraid we suspect your friend had a whole other identity which she'd run away from," says Jake, calmly producing photo after photo of Kitty from the file in front of him. "Her husband is called Tom Walker and recently . . . well, there's no easy way to tell you this, but only in the last week he's been released on parole from prison."

"*What?*"

"He'd been serving time, for assault and battery, you see. Domestic abuse."

Then he produces the most shocking and horrific photos I've ever seen. They're black-and-white police shots of Kitty, but this time she's barely recognisable. Her pretty face is covered in bruises and her eyes are so puffed-up and swollen, they won't even open.

The breath catches in the back of my throat.

"You see," Jake goes on the explain, "we believe that she was running from this man, that she was terrified that, when he'd be released, he'd track her down and harm her again. And that's why she changed her name and moved to Dublin. And now that he's just been released, we know from his social-security payments that he's moved up to Dublin as well. Very possibly to track her down. She may have heard about this or might even have seen him around and knew it was only a matter of time before he got to her again . . ."

"Then . . . that's why she had to leave," I say numbly, "without even saying goodbye."

And right then, when I least expect it, that last and final memory slots into place.

That last night. As Kitty and I were climbing into separate taxis to head home, her final words to me as she hugged me tight were "Remember, you can't live your life in fear. You'll be a long time dead!"

Did she know then? That she herself was in danger again and that she'd no choice but to up sticks, reinvent herself and move on?

A huge sadness comes over me. Not so much that I've lost my best friend, but that she feels has to spend the rest of her whole life running . . .

Already December. Almost Christmas.

Capetown is beautiful at this time of year, she thought, as she gazed from her sunbed right across the azure blue sea. On a clear day, from this beach you could sometimes see all the way to Table Mountain.

Course she didn't call herself Kitty any more. Too easy to

find. After all, he'd successfully tracked her down once and could so easily do it again. So these days she was Susan Lynch and she'd got a job as a waitress in a busy restaurant where the staff were warm and welcoming and, if you worked hard, the tips were good.

She yawned and stretched and checking her watch, realised she'd better get a move on or she'd be late for her shift.

But there was something she needed to do first. Something she'd wanted to do for the longest time, but only now felt safe enough to. At all costs, she had to keep herself safe. But there was one person she felt she could trust, one person she owed at least an explanation to.

She checked her beach bag to make sure the Christmas card was there, the mailing address carefully typewritten (she was taking absolutely no chances on her handwriting being recognised,) and reminded herself to give it to a pal at the restaurant who was going to London for the holidays and who'd promised to post it from there. For the last and final time, she read it back over again.

It's me. All well. Am so sorry for not saying goodbye. Please understand I had good reason for wanting to just slip away and to keep where I'm at now a secret. Though I could never keep a secret from you and absolutely know that you'll say nothing. Hope to see you to explain properly someday.

By the way, remember that trip you always talked about taking? Your dream holiday?

She smiled to herself. Only one person in the whole world would understand that she was referring to Capetown.

Anyway, you should definitely go there. And if you ever do, I hear the fish restaurants on the waterfront are well worth checking out.

Blue Fin, where she worked was in fact the only fish restaurant there. A coded message, but she was sure it would be enough to do the trick.

Much love and thank you for being a true friend when I needed one.

And remember, you can't live your life in fear. You'll be a long time dead!

⁘

Claudia Carroll is a full-time writer; the only job, she reckons, where you can turn up at your desk every morning in a slobby tracksuit, with manky three-day-old hair and no one's remotely bothered. She's published nine novels and the latest one, *A Very Accidental Love Story*, is out now. She's just finished a new book, *Me and You*, to be published by HarperCollins in 2013 and has spent the last few days celebrating by eating far too much Ben & Jerry's Karamel Sutra ice cream than is good for her.

The Sunny Side of Christmas

Fiona Cassidy

It was three weeks before Christmas and it could have been a scene from any picture postcard. The bustling town of Miller's Bay had been transformed into a winter wonderland of twinkling lights, soft snowflakes and hat-and-scarf-clad children all excitedly looking into decorative windows whilst their parents rushed from shop to shop making the necessary preparations.

It *could* have been a scene from a postcard but it wasn't and Izzy Grant wasn't in the mood for any more of her mother's sentimental musings about how lovely this particular time of year was. It was freezing cold, everyone had set themselves firmly on the road to bankruptcy and everywhere she went she had to encounter George Michael's warbling reminders of how she had catastrophically given someone her heart only to have it broken so badly she didn't think she'd found all the pieces yet.

As her mother pulled into practically the last available parking space in the middle of town, Izzy saw her reflection in the glass of the passenger window and tried to arrange her face into a neutral expression before being told that she was far too pretty to look so cross. Izzy disagreed. She had boring brown hair, a squat nose, far too many freckles and green eyes that made her look like a cat – but her mother insisted that she was a stunningly striking brunette and if she sent out the right signals she'd have men queuing up to take her out. But that was the real problem. There was only one man for her but unfortunately he wasn't interested and she could never picture herself with anyone else. So, basically, at the ripe old age of thirty-one she was declaring herself a spinster for the foreseeable future.

"Could you stop scowling for all of two minutes, please, darling? I swear one day I'm going to go into your bedroom and find that you've grown a crop of green fur overnight and answer to the name 'Grinch'."

"Perhaps I should change my name then, Mother, and that would dissuade everyone from being so annoyingly cheerful and happy. I should have been born a bear or something so that I could hibernate my way through this madness and wake up in time for spring when everyone is sensible again. God, but I hate Christmas!"

"A bear, you say," Amelia Grant answered thoughtfully. "That's a great idea. You and your temperament could sleep for six months and the rest of us could get to enjoy Christmas without your constant barrage of criticisms."

Izzy felt guilty for all of two seconds before reasoning that she was entitled to her opinion and, as everyone else felt the need to shove their joy of the season in her face, she felt just as inclined to show her displeasure. Christmas was just an excuse for people to get drunk, spend money they didn't have and proclaim love and peace to people they detested for the rest of the year. Of course, it was also a time when people like herself were 'singled' (pardon the pun) out and made to feel that their lack of partner made them into freaks of nature.

"Come now!" Amelia said, patting her daughter's arm brusquely. "We're going to have a lovely day. There's nothing nicer than going around town in the run-up to Christmas – the smells, the music, the atmosphere!"

The throbbing at Izzy's temples signalled the onslaught of another migraine and she longed for a darkened room away from her mother and the rest of the world. She regretted ever agreeing to come out at all. What on earth had possessed her? Didn't she know the torture that lay ahead? She would have to go into shops and be overcome to the point of near-unconsciousness with the overpowering scent of pine cones and cinnamon. She would have to listen to Bing Crosby droning on about what a wonderful time of the year it was and stand in queues listening while women tried to outdo each other as they talked about just how organised they were with reference to their Christmas shopping.

"I've mine nearly all done, Marjorie. I started back in September, you know."

"September's too late for me. I spent my summer holidays getting everything together."

"Gosh, you both left it very late, Jennifer! I started mine in the January sales last year. The minute I put the Christmas tree back in the attic I knew it was time to start planning for next year."

The women in Izzy's thoughts were all speaking like they had taken huge gulps of air from a helium balloon and were related to the chipmunks. They were wearing glow-in-the-dark reindeer antlers and long dangly Christmas-tree earrings and laughing manically. She shook her head and warned herself to stop thinking like a deranged person, as at the first opportunity her mother would willingly have her locked up in the nearest clinic, for a rest over the festive period (a rest for her mother, that is).

"Izzy! Presumably we're not going to sit here all day?" Amelia commented impatiently. "I have a million and one things to do and even if you refuse to get into the spirit of things I'd like to make this time special for everyone." She sighed before patting her daughter's arm again, this time in a comforting fashion. "I promise everything will get better, my darling. You won't always feel like this but you need to help yourself by being positive."

Izzy gave her mother a weak smile and got out of the car. She dug her hands into the pockets of her coat before following

Amelia up the street and having to endure her cheerfully greeting everyone, commenting on how cold it was and asking passing children what Santa was bringing this year.

As they entered the butcher's Izzy watched as the burgeoning queue of excitedly chattering women ebbed and swelled as they placed orders for their Christmas meat. You could almost feel their satisfaction and relief once they made the necessary arrangements for their December feast and Izzy swore that if the butcher had introduced a turkey ban there would have been fisticuffs and a row that would have made the London summer riots look like a street party.

"I'm going for a walk. I'll meet you back at the car in an hour," Izzy said, finding it hard to hide her disgust.

"Try not to scare off any small children or assault Santa Claus if you happen to be in the shopping centre."

Izzy had no intention of going anywhere near the heaving shopping centre and plonked herself on a bench in the centre of town.

This time last year Izzy had been positively glowing. She and Mark Devine had been together for almost four years and she couldn't have been more in love. He wasn't tall, dark and handsome in the traditional sense but there was something extremely alluring about him, with his lazy smile and penetrating blue eyes, and from the first moment Izzy met him she had been hypnotised. He had a reputation for being wild and untameable but had met his match in Izzy who was equally as headstrong and determined. She had never felt like that about anyone before.

Having met in the month of December, everyone, including her, had been hoping he might produce a present in a small box that sparkled and came with a lifetime guarantee of happiness and good times ahead. When Christmas morning came, however, there had been a designer scarf and tickets to see Michael Bublé live in concert which had been amazing but no box, small or otherwise. More worryingly there had also been a shift in their relationship and in hindsight Izzy realised that the signs had been there for months but she had either not noticed or was subconsciously ignoring them. Mark was distant and restless and his interest in her seemed to have diminished, so much so that when he asked her to come to dinner just after New Year's so they could 'talk' she had already predicted that the worst was to come and her fears were confirmed when he held her hands and told her that it wasn't working out. He said that it wasn't her, it was him. He said that their relationship no longer held a spark for him and announced that he wanted to go travelling with much emphasis on the word '*alone*'. Izzy had been totally devastated and even though almost a year had passed she still didn't feel any better. She had gone from planning a wedding in her head to the prospect of being alone forever and she thought that things couldn't get any worse. But that was where she was wrong.

Her father had been reading the paper one evening several weeks ago when he had suddenly jumped up in a state of panic and ushered her mother out of the room. Izzy hadn't paid much attention as Eddie Grant was quite highly strung and the headlines of the news normally sent his blood pressure soaring, especially if they indicated a further dip in the economy which threatened the future of the family-run furniture business. But her mother, instead of reappearing shaking her head and laughing softly at her husband's antics, had been ashen-faced when she came back. When she took her only daughter by the arm, told her to sit down and poured them both a large glass of wine, Izzy knew that whatever it was wasn't going to be good.

"I can't sugar-coat this for you, Izzy, and I hate being the bearer of bad news, my love, but I'd rather that you heard it from me than from someone else."

Izzy felt the blood drain from her face. The newspaper was rolled up so tightly in Amelia's hand that her knuckles were white.

"What the hell is wrong? Tell me now, Mum. You're starting to scare me."

"Mark Devine has come home from his travels."

"Is that it?" Izzy said, relieved, although her heart had started to beat so hard it sounded like a bongo drum in her head. "I thought you were going to tell me that someone had died."

Her mother looked like she might have preferred to be delivering the news of a death and slowly opened the paper to where Izzy could see the face of her former lover tanned and smiling and not alone. She grabbed the pages and leapt from her seat, scanning the words with her stomach in knots.

> When local man Mark Devine left Miller's Bay last spring to go travelling in South America I'm sure he expected to bring home a few souvenirs, but it seems that there was one very special thing that he couldn't leave behind. After a whirlwind romance he and his new wife, Emmanuelle, decided to get married in an intimate ceremony in state capital Lima before returning home to Ireland to have a reception for family and friends.

There had been a few more lines but Izzy had stopped reading and let the paper flop limply in her hands.

"He told me that he felt restless and needed to explore the world. He told me that he didn't want to settle down with anyone. He said that if Cheryl Cole had offered to walk him up the aisle he would have politely declined. I just don't understand how everything could change. Obviously when he said it was *him*, what he really meant to say was that it was *me*. I thought he'd go away and spread his wings but that maybe he would miss me and we could get back together. I've spent all this time pining after him and crying myself to sleep and all the time he was away falling in love with somebody else. How sad and stupid am I?"

Amelia had moved to put a comforting arm around her daughter but Izzy had walked away, declaring her need to be alone. Her pillow had been a sodden mass of tears the following morning and from then on sleep was a relatively alien concept to her as she constantly questioned what was so wrong with her that the man she loved felt the need to run away and marry the first girl he met in a foreign country. She continued to serve in her father's shop and deal with the orders and the accounts but seemed to be on autopilot. It was only when a worried and frazzled Eddie brought the Christmas tree down from its box in the store and started playing Bing Crosby's Christmas classics on a loop that Izzy started getting her spirit back . . . but there was nothing Christmassy about that spirit nor did it exude goodwill to anyone in particular.

The last few weeks had been incredibly difficult and the onslaught of Christmas and the legacy of the hopes and dreams she'd had last year were proving to be painful reminders of what could have been but would certainly never happen now and, as she made her way back to the car to meet her mother, she had never felt more miserable or alone.

The following day Izzy was at work and counting down the minutes to her lunch break when a man came in. He was of medium height with blonde hair and dressed casually in a pair of tracksuit bottoms and a T-shirt and wasn't typical of their usual clientele of this time of year. Most of their customers came bustling in full of talk of how they needed to redecorate before Christmas or buy presents for their newly married sons and daughters who were hosting Christmas dinner in their marital home for the first time. Izzy found these customers particularly soul-destroying and often thought that it was a good thing she was so fond of her father as, if the business had belonged to anyone else, she might well have been tempted to tell the whole lot of them where they could stick their fancy ideas and time-consuming demands.

She watched as her newest potential buyer looked around him with interest, paying particular attention to some of the sofas and chairs they had on display, before approaching the counter.

"Could I speak to the manager, please?" he asked in a friendly voice.

"My father's not here at the moment so I'll have to do," Izzy answered. "How can I help you?"

"I run a project for homeless people and we've just renovated our shelter in the middle of town and I was wondering if you had any shop-soiled furniture or seating that we could have a look at. We're totally reliant on contributions from the public and unfortunately our purse isn't as full as usual – and we're as busy as ever. I've been in all the charity and second-hand shops in the area today but nobody seems to have what we're looking for. I need sofas and chairs and that type of thing. I suppose, when you've been sleeping in a shop doorway or under a bridge, sitting on the floor doesn't matter but I'd just like to make things as comfortable for our clients as possible."

Izzy didn't know why she felt so surprised. After all, she knew that there were homeless people everywhere. Hadn't she walked past them enough times and ignored their requests for change, thinking in annoyance that they were a nuisance cluttering up the street?

"I don't know off-hand but I'll certainly ask my father if he can help."

"I also wondered if you'd put up a poster for me. We desperately need volunteers to help us over Christmas but offers really aren't plentiful and I suppose people can't be blamed for wanting to spend time with their loved ones."

The man looked crestfallen and sad for a moment and Izzy felt an unusual need to try and reassure him.

"Of course we'll put up some posters for you and I'll say to people that you're looking for help. Surely not everyone will be spending Christmas in a loved-up state with their partners?"

The man looked at Izzy in an amused fashion.

"Sorry, I didn't mean to sound quite so vehement," she said. "I just find this time of year tough."

"I know what you mean," he said, nodding in agreement. "I met my wife at Christmas and now that she's gone I tend to throw myself into work and can't understand why everyone else doesn't want to do the same. It's a self-preservation thing, I suppose. Keeps me from going mad."

"I know how you feel," Izzy commented ruefully. "My

boyfriend and I split up last year and I want to hurt Elvis Presley every time I hear him going on about how lonely it'll be this Christmas. It's like he's mocking me. If there's a spate of radios being hurled at the wall in this area you'll know who's responsible. When did you and your wife split up?"

"We didn't. She died two years ago from breast cancer."

If ever Izzy longed for a large hole to appear and swallow her up, she desperately yearned for one then. "I am so dreadfully sorry. Me and my big mouth. I didn't mean to be so flippant."

"You weren't to know, so don't worry about it. "I'm Jonathan, by the way. Jono for short. Workaholic and keen fan of comfy seats."

"Isabella, Izzy for short. Prone to sticking her foot in it, supplier of comfy seats and hater of all Christmas-inspired music."

Jono gave her a warm smile before giving her a card and walking out with a wave.

The Street Angel Project
Haven House
Sunnyside Street
Miller's Bay
Where second chances begin . . .

For the rest of the day Izzy did her work but was, as usual, preoccupied. Eddie watched as his daughter went through the moves of her job without apparently being in the room and sighed despairingly. If bloody Mark Devine (and there was nothing 'divine' about him) came anywhere near him he swore to God that he would kick him up and down the main street for turning his daughter into an emotional vegetable and leaving him with a walking zombie for an assistant manager. What he didn't realise was that for the first time in months, Mark Devine hadn't entered his daughter's head for hours.

Izzy hovered by the front door before she found the buzzer. A disembodied voice answered and she stated her name and the reason for her visit before a resounding click signalled that she was being allowed access.

"This is a surprise," Jono said, after one of his colleagues had called him.

"My father says he'd like to help you with your seating predicament. Besides, I thought I'd come and see the place for myself. I haven't been able to get you out of my head all day."

Izzy noticed Jonathan's counterparts grinning at each other and coloured as she realised what she had said.

"I didn't mean that like it sounded," she stammered. "What I meant was I couldn't stop thinking about the work you do. I wasn't actually thinking about you . . . although there's nothing wrong with you," she added, seeing Jono's amused expression and wondering why a total stranger was capable of making her lose all control of her tongue for the second time that day.

"Would you like me to show you around?" he asked. "A few of our volunteers are meeting in a short while so I have a bit of time on my hands if you're interested in learning a bit more about what we do?"

"I'd love to," Izzy said. "I'd actually like to know more about being a volunteer. I have plenty of time in the evenings and I'd be happy to help you. If nothing else it would stop my mother from dragging me to the shops."

"Well, if you're happy to help I promise to keep the playing of Christmas tunes to the bare minimum although we do have a carol service next week."

Izzy followed Jono as he introduced her to colleagues and allowed her to see the rooms and facilities that were available there for the short-term use of people who had the misfortune to find themselves on the streets. She listened as he told her how they patrolled the area and knew all the usual places to look for those that needed their help. As he spoke Izzy saw how animated he was.

Half an hour later Izzy found herself seated in a room in a circle with around four of the project's volunteers.

After introductions had been made, Jono said he wanted to do what he called a 'gratitude exercise' with everyone there.

"I want you all to think back to last year and what you were doing. The object of this is to look at your progression and how much you can achieve in a year."

Izzy groaned inwardly as she thought about what she had done in a year. She had moped. She had filled herself full of self-pity. She had driven her parents to distraction and she had been very determined: determined not to move on, that is. In short she had been a royal pain in the arse.

One by one, as the others spoke, Izzy's review of her last twelve months grew more and more shameful. One young girl by the name of Rainey had been a drug addict when she had been taken to the shelter but with the help of Jono and his team she had managed to turn her life around and was now clean. One man called Simon had been suicidal when the project had intervened and had him hospitalised. He said he still had tough days but that his life had improved dramatically since he had met Jono. The man sitting beside him had been an alcoholic and at that point Izzy switched off as she thought about how charmed her existence had been. She might have had her heart broken and been devastated but perhaps she should have come to the realisation a long time ago that if Mark had been able to replace her so quickly then obviously she'd had a lucky escape as he mustn't have loved her enough in the first place.

"What about you, Izzy? How far have you come in the last twelve months?"

"I think I've made more progress in the last five minutes than I have in the course of the past year. With all due respect to everyone here, sometimes you need to be given a reason to count your blessings and I think I've just found mine. You're all truly inspirational. This time last year I was sipping champagne in the warmth of my house and in the hub of my family but other things made me lose sight of how lucky I was."

After the meeting had ended and arrangements had been made for Izzy to work on Christmas Day, helping to serve dinner to their patrons, she and Jono walked out together.

"So apart from working here, have you any other plans for Christmas?" Jono asked.

"I'm going to spend time with my family and apologise profusely for being so difficult, take my mother out to the January sales with a smile on my face and try to convince my poor father that he doesn't need to get a new assistant because from now on I'm going to be there in both body and spirit."

"Sounds good," Jono commented. "I'm going to try to be more positive as well. Life is, after all, for living."

"Perhaps we can help each other," Izzy said.

"Perhaps we can."

As they walked out onto the street Izzy noticed the lights, the sounds and the atmosphere, and thought that it could have been a scene from any picture postcard. And for once the thought didn't make her flinch.

Fiona Cassidy (better known locally as Fionnuala McGoldrick) lives in Galbally, Co Tyrone, with her partner Philip and their six collective children (in a very noisy house that she wishes had an inbuilt self-cleaning mechanism!). Fiona is a full-time mother and creative-writing workshop-facilitator and tutor, teaching writing to adults, young people and children as a recreational activity, and to people who have suffered trauma as therapy. She has also worked as a mentor for aspiring writers. She is the author of two novels: *Anyone for Seconds?* and *Anyone for Me?*. To find out more about Fiona you can follow her blog and visit her at www.fionacassidy.net, become a fan on Facebook or follow her on Twitter: https://twitter.com/FionaCassidy

The Present

Carol Coffey

This fictional short story is dedicated to my late cousin,
Yellowknife writer, John Seagrave.

For the stories you didn't get to write.

Aiden Ruane pulled himself to the top of the hill and stood
panting against the solitary jack pine that overlooked the
snow-filled valley beneath him. As his breathing eased he
listened for the sound of his wife in labour but at this height he
could only hear her muffled cries coming from the tiny house
below. Slowly, he lowered himself down onto the deep snow,
oblivious to the sharp needles of the tree against his neck. He
leaned forward and unconsciously ran his bare hands over the
freezing flakes as the ice reddened his flesh and seeped up his
long bony fingers until he could no longer stand the pain.

He had been relieved when the local women from the
community shooed him out of the cramped cabin. He did not
think he could take another minute of seeing his wife in such
unbearable pain and could not meet her eyes as he skulked
around the wooden door and left the room, then ran up the
frozen hill as fast as his legs could carry him. The baby had not
been due for another four weeks and had taken them by surprise

as they prepared to go Christmas-shopping in the nearest town which was almost two hours away from the tiny hamlet they called home. Twenty-four hours had passed and his wife seemed no nearer to delivering the baby they had waited on for over fifteen years.

Aiden looked around at the snow-covered vista and tried to calm his racing heart by focusing on the serene landscape before him. He hoped he would never become impervious to the beauty of the Canadian winter. In the distance a cluster of black spruce and impressively tall tamaracks, naked from their winter shedding, swayed gently in the cold Arctic breeze. To his right, a group of white birch dotted the pristine landscape, their brilliant barks illuminated by the bright sun, sparkling in its slow climb in the winter sky. Beneath the small row of birch, the tiny footprints of a snow fox, left behind after the previous night's fall, meandered back and forth through the trees where the animal had searched for food. Aiden let out a long, lonely sigh and wondered how much longer his wife's labour would last.

As Aiden blew into his ice-cold hands, a cry shot out from below him, jolting him from his thoughts. He jumped to his feet and moved several slippery steps down the ravine. The scream subsided almost as soon as it had begun and he stopped in his tracks to peer down at the small house, hoping to see his wife's mother, a tiny Inuit woman by the name of Kesuk, beckoning for him, but instead his mother- in-law stood stone-faced at the open cabin door and signalled for him to stay where he was. He groaned and ran his hands through his thick fair hair. It was almost over, he reasoned to himself although he knew nothing of the sort. He sat down on the thick blanket of snow and buried his head in his hands.

As he settled onto the freshly fallen snow, he looked briefly at the watch his parents had bought him one Christmas and wondered why he wore it at all as time was of little importance in the North West territory of Canada he had come to call home. He realised that it was almost Christmas Day in Ireland. How different Christmases were here, he thought, than those of his childhood. He began to think about Christmas mornings in Ireland and of his parents whose untimely passing in a car accident almost seventeen years before had left him bereft and purposeless. He had not been there that morning when his father drove his mother out shopping in the heavy snow and often wondered how differently things might have turned out had he been there to drive them. After their funeral, he travelled from his tiny hometown in Ireland to Vancouver but within months of his arrival in the modern city he answered an advertisement for traders in the Northwest Territories, a place and a job he knew nothing about. Even now, he did not know what had drawn him to the frozen landscape all those years ago but somehow he had found himself here, living in the wilderness with only a few small Inuit communities and the odd traveller like himself for company.

He smiled weakly as he remembered his mother and how she would excitedly prepare for Christmas months in advance, writing Christmas cards to relatives in far-flung corners of the globe and buying up rolls of wrapping paper as though they were going out of fashion. And his father, his gentle kind father, would patiently drag himself through dozens of shops with her in search of the perfect present for their three beloved children and they would come home, drenched and spent, to sit by the fire and discuss their purchases and hope that their children would like them. How simple their life had been and how complete his parents were in each other's company. His sister had said it was a mercy that they had died together as she could not have imagined one of them living on without the other. But in his heart, the loss of them, the deficit that their passing created in his life, was still too raw to concede to his sister's conviction.

Aiden remembered each Christmas morning when they would huddle around the old kitchen table after Mass and dig into his mother's fried breakfast. His mouth watered as he remembered the smell of bacon and sausages, black and white pudding and his mother's soda bread, toasted and dripping with real butter. Then they would sit around the Christmas tree which would be weighed down heavily with familiar baubles and an odd arrangement of ornaments that his mother had collected over the years. His father would have an old LP of Christmas carols playing in the background. Together he and his brother and sister would join in with Dean Martin singing 'Silent Night' but only when he got to the part where the LP was scratched and their father's hero sang the same few words over and over. His father would stand up and feign annoyance with them before he deftly placed the needle beyond the scratch and returned to his seat to tap his foot off the linoleum floor. After steaming cups of strong tea and enormous slices of homemade Christmas pudding, they would open their presents and he and his siblings would, through raised eyebrows and rolling eyes, discreetly express their dissatisfaction about the homemade Aran sweaters they'd received from their grandmother or itchy woollen socks that would never see the light of day. His father would don one of those silly paper hats that made him look like a make-believe king and his mother would complain about the heat as she simultaneously looked around the room at her gathered brood, a smile of contentment and joy spreading across her round beaming face. He swallowed as he thought of them and wished for a moment that he could be there, that for just one moment he could travel back in time and stand in that scorching kitchen and laugh with them. His sister now lived next door to their abandoned house with her growing family. His brother was married with three boys in Darwin. He imagined Pat and Linda sitting on their porch in the searing Australian heat while he was surrounded by Arctic snow. How different all of their lives had turned out, how varied the paths they took. He briefly thought about that sad kitchen, normally alive with laughter and joy at this time of year, now darkened and lifeless, its one-time occupants separated by thousands of miles. After his mother's famous turkey and ham dinner, they would settle down to an evening by the fire, watching old movies that they had seen a hundred times before. His aunt and uncle and cousins who lived nearby would arrive and together they would play with whatever games Santa had brought, while his father snored happily in the background, the paper hat still placed firmly on his balding head. It was these happy, warm memories that he came back to time and time again and even now as a grown man he missed that sense of belonging to something larger than himself.

Aiden laughed as he thought of the conversations he had with his wife on all matters Irish and how she thought his notion of Christmas amusing. Most of the people in this tiny community had converted to Christianity due to the influence of early religious settlers and, while many of the families observed Christmas, it was not celebrated to the extent that it was in Ireland. Every Christmas since their marriage Shila would argue about the ridiculous notion of Christmas presents and would pretend not to buy him a gift. Each year he would play the game and would ceremoniously place her present under their makeshift tree, making as much noise as he could in the process in the hope that he would make her feel guilty. On Christmas morning he would wake to find a simply wrapped gift under the sparsely decorated tree marked *"From Santa"* and together they would laugh. There would be no early morning Mass and no Irish breakfast as no one in the small community had ever heard of black and white pudding. Instead they would have a simple breakfast of fried trout caught from the great lake only a few miles from their home which would be washed down with copious amounts of hot tea or coffee to protect them from the freezing climate. After breakfast they would take a walk through the majestic landscape and he would talk to his wife about some future Christmas where they might share their Santa joke with a child of their own. His wise wife would let him finish before pointing to the winter horizon and reminding him to listen and look at the beautiful day they were standing in and tell him not to wonder too much about the sun that would rise again tomorrow. It had always been that way with Shila. His wife seemed to know him better than he knew himself.

When he had first arrived at the trading outpost, the few white settlers that lived in the area warned him that Inuit men did not appreciate settlers taking an interest in their female relatives. Aiden had taken this advice to heart and had largely kept to himself in the first few months at the lonely outpost. It was Shila, who was employed at the store he worked in, who had taken an interest in the stranger who came from an island she had scarcely heard of and it was she who pursued him, inviting him to fish with her and her brother and attend local festivities with her large extended family. Years later, she told him that on the first night after they met she had heard the voice of a foreign woman in a dream, asking her to look after him and that she believed that the voice had belonged to his mother. Aiden had shrugged off the dream as nonsense. He did not believe in such things but, within months, Shila and he became inseparable and they had married within a year of his arrival.

Aiden breathed out and watched as his warm breath billowed out like steam into the crisp air. Despite his wife's warnings to live in the moment, the Christmas he dreamed of had finally come. Today he would be a father. Everything changes, he reasoned. Everything moves on. The old are replaced with the new, the past with the present, and the present with the future.

Aiden's happy thoughts were interrupted by the sounds of rustling coming from dense scrub behind him. Fear ran down his spine as he thought the noise might be caused by the brown bear that had been seen around for the last few nights. He gingerly turned his head around the old jack pine and peered into the white landscape. As the hind legs of an elk disappeared into the nearby trees, he breathed an audible sigh of relief. It would not do to get mauled by a bear on the same day that he was about to become a father.

He turned his gaze back to his cabin and waited for a sign of life. The silence that had descended on the house began to worry him. He had not thought that he would miss hearing his wife's cries but an overwhelming feeling that something was wrong began to trickle up his spine and bore into his consciousness. A small hum in the distance forced him to move his eyes from the cabin door to the almost invisible roadway. He squinted until a small snowmobile came into focus. He recognised the large red parka coat and the mangy dog bouncing around the back of the buggy. It was his wife's brother Nanuq's snowmobile. Aiden leapt to his feet as he noticed a second passenger holding onto Nanuq as the vehicle came to an abrupt stop outside the cabin. He raced down the hill, falling twice in his effort to make it down as fast as he could.

Aiden recognised the passenger immediately. It was Lisa Eldridge, a Toronto-born doctor whose love of the wild country had brought her to the remote community over ten years previously on a one-year tour of duty. Like him, she had never left and had embraced the people and the culture as though they were her own.

"What's wrong?" he shouted, aware that most of the local children were delivered by midwifes and local women.

When the doctor pushed by him and did not answer, he raced inside to find his wife writhing in agony on their bed, her light-brown face paler than he had ever seen it. Sweat dripped down her forehead and her thick black hair, soaked with perspiration, hung limply around her face.

"Shila!" he called but she did not open her eyes to look at him.

He grabbed her hand and began to pull roughly on her arm.

"Shila!" he shouted louder now, the urgency in his voice filling the tiny bedroom.

Aiden felt two small hands gently prise him off his wife and lead him away from the bed.

"She's okay," Dr Eldridge began. "She'll be okay . . . but I need you to go with Nanuq now. We'll call you as soon as there is news."

Aiden felt a larger pair of hands about his back and, as the door of the cabin opened, he was led down the laneway towards his brother- in-law's house.

In Nanuq's cabin, Oomailiq, Nanuq's wife, handed him a hot drink while simultaneously moving their children into another room out of his view. He could feel hot tears well in his eyes and he bit down on his lip.

"Come on, man!" Nanuq, who loved all things American including the accent, said.

On the tiny television, small children in a church choir sang Christmas carols. He grimaced as they began to sing 'Silent Night', his father's favourite. Oomailiq turned it off and looked closely at him.

"It's pretty singing," she said as she lowered her heavily pregnant body down onto the worn sofa beside him and pulled him to her where he cried openly in her arms.

Together the three adults sat in silence while they waited for news, Nanuq kicking his legs out rhythmically from the hard wooden stool where he sat, a Yankee's baseball cap pulled tightly down on his head, shading his eyes. Aiden stared at the brightly lit Christmas tree in the corner of Nanuq's living room. He tried to shake the image of his wife from his mind. Despite the fact that she was barely five foot tall, he had never seen her look so frail and helpless before. Of the two of them, Shila was the strong one. He breathed out a long slow breath and found himself yet again thinking of his parents, thinking of their home where he had felt safe and protected from all the danger and heartbreak in the world. He could not think of Shila and of what might happen. His wife would not like him to think of such things so he retreated once again to the Christmases of his childhood, to warm fires and familiar faces, to his past. He could see his mother folding her red holly-and-ivy Christmas tablecloth sadly and saying, "Well, that's it for another year!" before placing the bright cloth back in the same wrapping she bought it in when he was a small child. He remembered a red train set he had got one Christmas morning and how he had stored it in his sister's house before he left for Canada in the hope that some day his own child would play with it. He would send for it, he decided. As soon as this was over he would ask his sister to post the entire set over for his child to play with. That's what Shila would want him to do, focus on the positive, on the now. He willed other memories to come to mind and swallowed as he remembered his mother crying at the end of

Christmas when his brother left to return to work in Dublin and his sister to London. These were not the memories he had wanted to recall, memories of goodbyes and of change. He closed his eyes tightly and forced his family to sit at the dinner table, each one looking older and staring wide-eyed at him as though there was somewhere else they were supposed to be. He could see the table set with his mother's good dishes and the Christmas crackers, brightly lit in their red-and-gold tinsel, ceremoniously placed on each side plate by his father – but the cooker, his mother's old range, lay quiet and cold in the corner of the brightly lit kitchen.

"You can't have this, Aiden. Wake up," his father said sadly.

He jumped up from the sofa, startling Oomailiq who was seated quietly beside him, and noticed that his brother-in-law was gone.

"You were asleep," she said softly.

"I wasn't! I saw . . . I . . . never mind," he said as his heart sank further into despair.

"You were dreaming," she said simply.

Aiden shook his head and sat back down on the sofa as Oomailiq went about feeding her three children. He stared at the little Inuit children and wondered what his own child would look like. He was fair-haired with blue eyes but expected the baby to look like his wife with shiny black hair and large brown eyes.

"It will be soon," Oomailiq said as though reading his mind.

"I am tired of waiting, Oom," he said. He could hear the utter exhaustion in his voice and it saddened him.

"Everything happens at the right time," she replied softly.

Aiden thought about her words and how calmly she spoke them. He had noticed this about most of the Inuit he came into contact with and admired how they did not worry about the things they had no control over. He wished he could be like them and knew that Oomailiq was not just talking about the baby but that his uneasy ways were much talked about among the local tribe.

The door to the cabin opened suddenly and his brother-in-law stood panting on the other side.

"The lady doc is looking for you now!" he gasped.

Aiden felt his legs weaken as a shrill cry, which seemed to call to him, rang out through the tiny commune. He raced to the door, pulling it roughly behind him which caused a heavy drift of snow to fall from the roof as he passed. He threw open the door to his cabin and ran past the small group of local women who stood silently in the sitting room.

In the bedroom at the back of the cabin, Dr Eldridge looked up and smiled warmly at him. She moved away from the bed where his wife was propped up on pillows, revealing a tiny baby lying in her limp arms. Shila reached upwards, offering the child to him.

"Your daughter," she said weakly.

"Are you okay?" he whispered.

Shila nodded.

He bit down on his lip to avoid the show of emotion that he knew the women in the cabin would view as weakness. He took the child and peered down at her thick mop of coarse black hair, her button nose and tiny brown eyes that seemed to be already looking at him. A wave of love washed over him, stronger than the love he had for his siblings and his beloved parents, even stronger than the deep love he held for his wife. He had never seen anything so beautiful in his life. He pulled the baby tightly to his chest and his hands felt the warmth of her tiny body as her little heart beat in rhythm with his own.

"What will we name her?" he asked without taking his eyes from her.

"Ananak," his wife replied weakly. "It means 'grandmother' – in honour of your mother – so that your daughter will carry on her traditions in this land."

Aiden shook his head. It was time to move on, to look forward. His wife was right, he knew that now. He would never forget his parents or his homeland but this was his home now, this was his family.

"No – she needs a name of her own," he said lifting the tiny child up towards the brightly lit window.

"Buniq?" his mother-in-law, who had crept into the room behind him, offered.

"'Sweet daughter'," another woman who stood smiling in the doorway translated as, although his mother-in-law understood English, she spoke only Inuktitut.

"No."

"Adlartok?" his wife asked.

Aiden turned to look at Shila.

"'Clear sky'," she translated.

He smiled at the tiny face of the child in his arms.

"Adlartok Ruane it is," he replied.

"She is your present . . . from Santa," Shila teased.

Aiden laughed and moved to the bed where he gently placed the child in his wife's arms.

"Yes," he agreed. "She is my present . . . and my future."

⁂

Carol Coffey was born in Dublin and, after a ten-year stay in Australia, settled in County Wicklow. She has a degree in education and a Masters degree in behavioural disturbance. Carol is a teacher by profession and continues to work in the area of special education. Carol has used her extensive background in disabilities to bring the world of special needs to the wider population through her writing. Her first book, *The Butterfly State* centres on a young autistic girl. Her second book, *The Penance Room*, is set in outback Australia and provides an insight into the isolated world of a deaf child, while her third book, *Winter Flowers*, which is set in Dublin, examines the generational effects of dysfunctional upbringings on parents and their children. Her fourth book *The Incredible Life of Jonathan Doe* will be published Spring 2013.

Running on Empty

Martina Devlin

"I'm skint," Anne-Marie Morgan told the fridge, rummaging inside it for the milk carton. "Cleaned out, flat broke, running on empty." Lately, she had taken to discussing her finances with the household appliances in her tiny, shared apartment in Smithfield. It was more satisfying than talking them over with her flatmate, who became irritated when she ignored her advice. Household appliances might click or purr or rev their motors at her, but they would never scold her for being spendthrift.

"The thing is," she continued, "it's the day before Christmas Eve and Christmas is no time for cash-flow blockages. How am I supposed to buy presents? The money machine on the corner won't give me any more money and the credit card won't give me any more credit. And I never could get the hang of handmade gifts. Besides, they're cheap but they're not really free. You still have to shell out for ingredients and supplies."

The kettle reached boiling point and switched off, which Anne-Marie interpreted as a gesture of support. It was prepared to stop what it was doing and listen to her. She poured water onto coffee granules, untwisted the cap from the milk carton, and took a precautionary sniff. *Yeuw*! That's what came of having a flatmate who'd already gone home to Cork for Christmas. Anne-Marie never remembered to buy any milk. Black coffee it was.

"I know I have to shape up. It's my New Year's resolution. But what about presents? People always say they don't want anything but they never mean it."

She finished her coffee, cocooned herself in a cashmere scarf – the impulse buy that had pushed her bank account into the do-not-pass-go zone – and set off for the shops. Some retail therapy (sadly, just the theoretical variety) would set her up for the afternoon shift at work. Window-shopping was free, right?

Anne-Marie was a carer in a nursing home. It gave her job satisfaction, which was said to be worth its weight in gold, although she wouldn't have minded a little more recompense on the filthy-lucre front. She was fond of the residents, but it was demanding work, not just physically but mentally: lifting people in and out of bed with a hoist, washing and dressing them, listening to their stories of days gone by – in some cases, the same stories told over and over, because many of the residents were forgetful, poor souls. She didn't mind that, but it broke her heart trying to comfort them when their families didn't visit. Forgetfulness obviously ran in some families.

While Anne-Marie loved her work, it could be draining, and shopping was her way of keeping the shadows at bay. Shopping never provided a lasting rush, but it fizzed right at the moment when she needed an adrenalin surge. She always felt its power when she bought something, even if it was only a new brand of shampoo. It wasn't that she was extravagant, she told herself. The problem lay with her measly salary: there was always too much month left at the end of the money. A spark of antipathy towards her job ignited, but then she felt guilty. The residents were always so affectionate, so grateful for her time and attention. No matter how despondent she might be feeling, the glistening gum of their smiles never failed to bolster her.

If only she could be more like her friend Patrick, who actually managed to save some of his wages. Then again, he wasn't swayed by clutch-bags shaped like a pair of pouting lips, or necklaces fashioned from glass snowflakes. She considered touching Patrick for a loan to buy her Christmas presents, but reluctantly vetoed the idea. The last loan was never repaid. In the end, he let her off.

Anne-Marie had two hours to pass before her stint started at the Slievemore Nursing Home. No money for bus fare – she'd just have to walk. She detoured into the Jervis Centre, watching the spending frenzy. So much for austerity. She itched to join in. It was criminal having to be economical at the one time of year when the troika and the IMF programme were supposed to be with Scrooge in the naughty corner. She made her way into Debenham's, where an umbrella with a splash of sunflowers across its circumference caught her eye. It would be perfect for her sister. Anne-Marie opened her purse, checked all the compartments, and found nothing. But when she patted her pockets, a hole in the lining produced two coins, a two-euro and a one-euro. They wouldn't run to an umbrella but they would stretch to a fluffy coffee to keep her warm on the walk to work. She bought a takeaway, and headed up Henry Street.

A raindrop detonated on her forehead. No umbrella – especially not one with sunflowers on it – but she couldn't afford to get wet. Imagine if she caught a cold and spread her bugs among May and Seamus and Emily and Jim, and all the other senior citizens in her care! That would never do. But the umbrella was in the shop, and she was outside Dr Quirkeys Goodtime Emporium having spent her last euro, with a twenty-minute walk ahead. She pulled up her collar and hoped for the best.

All at once, it occurred to Anne-Marie that she might recycle some of the odds and ends lying round the flat as presents – the wooden lamp from Dunnes, for example: her mother would love that on her bedside table. Mind you, the shade had a stain on it shaped, oddly enough, like a penguin, thanks to a coffee spill. How about the tartan rug bought on her weekend break in Edinburgh? Would that do for Granny? Maybe the cigarette burn from their last party was a disadvantage. Anne-Marie racked her brains, but everything had suffered too much wear and tear. Re-gifting was a possibility, but she didn't have any unwanted gifts lying round. She found presents so exciting that she always pressed them into immediate use, even if they were a bit knobbly or bobbly.

Never mind, she'd think of something.

"Heard the good news?" Patrick paused, wheeling Emily away from the day room, where the hairdresser had set up shop to do her weekly wash-and-sets.

Emily, who had celebrated her eightieth birthday the previous month, preened in front of Anne-Marie, proud of her frothed-up curls.

"Look at those waves in your hair, Emily. One more wave and you'll be washed overboard." Anne-Marie hunkered down beside her, and the old lady smiled.

"I've always had good hair. Not like my friend May, she has thin hair – always did, even when she was a girl. 'May,' I said, 'you should get yourself a hair-piece, it would make all the difference.' But would she listen to me?" She shook her head. "Too proud."

"Sure everyone can't be as gorgeous as you," said Anne-Marie. "All the fellows here are mad about you. A little bird told me Jim keeps trying to get you under the mistletoe." She stood up and glanced at Patrick. "What good news?"

"The boss announced this morning we're being paid a fortnight early. The cash will be in our bank accounts tomorrow – Christmas Eve."

"Hallelujah!" Anne-Marie caught Emily's wheelchair and spun it full-circle. "'Christmas is coming and the geese are getting fat!'. My dad used to recite that to me when I was a kid. For a while there it looked as though I'd have no present to give him or Mum."

"I bought my mother an iPhone – it's been wrapped and ready since the first of December. I'm going to spend an hour on Stephen's Day showing her how to use it." Patrick radiated virtue.

Emily and Anne-Marie exchanged a look.

71

"I saw that. Where's the harm in being prepared?"

"I never could be doing with those boy scouts," said Emily.

"He even files his DVD collection alphabetically," said Anne-Marie.

"Feel free to talk about me as though I'm not here."

Patrick pushed Emily towards the bathroom, and Anne-Marie fell into step beside them.

"What have you picked out for your mother, Anne-Marie?" asked Emily.

Guilt rushed through her. She had considered a massage attachment that fitted onto an armchair, but it was out of her price range. "Still trying to decide." She changed the subject quickly. "Are you going to your son's house for Christmas dinner?"

"Not this year. He's taking the family to a hotel over the border for Christmas. Some class of a castle, with a golf course and leisure centre. Michael's been working so hard he hasn't had a proper break in ages. He says they all need a rest." She tilted her chin, absolving him. "They'll bring me for a run out on New Year's Day, Michael says, and somewhere smart for lunch. He's ever so generous, my boy."

Above the wheelchair, out of sight, Anne-Marie crossed her eyes at Patrick and he crossed his back.

"Here we are, Emily. Let's help you out of this chair. Can you manage on the Zimmer or would you like Anne-Marie to go in with you?"

"I can manage, thank you." Emily tottered, straightened and shuffled off into the bathroom.

"I'll wait here!" Patrick called after her. "Pull the emergency cord if you have any problems." He turned to Anne-Marie. "I'd love to throttle some of those relatives. Selfish pigs."

"It's a shame, Patrick. But out of sight is out of mind for some people. That's just how it is."

"I'd like to film the faces of Emily and May and all our residents when they hear their families can't be bothered to make time for them. I'd play it on continuous loop for their children. Then they'd have no excuse – they'd know exactly how hurtful their behaviour is."

"Lighten up, Patrick, it's Christmas."

"My point exactly."

It was Christmas Eve and Anne-Marie had chosen her family's presents. Mentally. That was the easy part. It just remained for the money to show up in her account today and she'd buy everything. She had plenty of time, after swapping days off with Patrick – his reluctance unable to withstand her persistence – the better to luxuriate in her trawl through the shops. She showered and dressed quickly, before making a beeline for the ATM machine in Centra. It was blank, without even a *not in service* sign on its screen. Never mind, she'd go to the hole-in-the-wall two streets away. It was blank too. "This is a conspiracy," Anne-Marie told the parking meter on the footpath beside her. Next, she tried the supermarket, which had a cash dispenser at the front of the store. Also blank.

Anne-Marie approached the manager, who looked as stressed as she felt.

"All the cash machines in town are out of commission, don't ask me why. Some kind of malfunction. Head office says a working ATM is as rare as hen's teeth. It's damaging my business – I've had customers asking me for tick. Tick! What do they think I'm running – a huckster's shop with a slate under the counter?"

Anne-Marie sucked her knuckle. She had been relying on this for her shopping spree. But if all the cash dispensers were out of order her plans were in jeopardy. Wait, she'd go to the bank and make a withdrawal at the counter. With funds in her account, they'd be obliged to hand over some of the readies. Nothing could be simpler.

Except the cashier declined to supply any cash. "You've exceeded your overdraft limit." He wouldn't meet her eye.

"But my salary was paid in this morning!"

"That's true, but it still leaves you overdrawn."

"Come on, give me a break – it's Christmas Eve."

He wriggled in his seat. "I'm sorry, I can't bend the rules. I don't have the authority."

"Fine, but I'm moving my account in the New Year."

The queue behind her grumbled at the delay, and she conceded defeat. "Bah humbug to you too!" Anne-Marie snapped at the cashier.

"It's not my fault," he said.

And he was right, she knew that. He wasn't the one who had ignored all those OD signs on the monthly statement, as though they'd miraculously reverse themselves.

But what now? How should she spend her day off? Window-shopping had lost its gloss, and she wasn't due at the family home thirty miles away until tonight, after her father collected her. She could text a friend to meet for lunch – provided the friend was willing to pay – but her mobile phone was out of credit. Nothing for it but to make tracks for the nursing home and wheedle a loan from Patrick. He'd scold and pull faces but he'd spring for the price of some cheap goodies. A scented candle for her mother, a hot-water bottle for her perma-frozen sister, whiskey for her dad and fancy shower gel for her brother. She'd add an IOU to each gift promising something lavish in the January sales. Well, maybe not lavish. But something else, definitely.

Patrick had been sent home an hour after turning up for work that morning.

"But he's never sick!" Anne-Marie was aghast.

"Don't worry, it's just a 24-hour bug," said the nursing-home manager. "Actually, now you're here you don't fancy working, do you? We're short-staffed. Patrick's not the only one down with this vomiting bug."

"Suppose I may as well."

Anne-Marie spent the day trying to be cheerful for the sake of the residents. Half of them were giddy with excitement because their families were taking them home for Christmas, the remainder were disappointed and defensive because their relatives wouldn't be making the day special for them. Anne-Marie pulled on Wellington boots and a plastic apron to give showers, and helped to feed residents who weren't able to manage by themselves. Finally, it was time to steep dentures and prepare everyone for bed.

Despite her chirpy manner, singing along to carols and wearing a piece of tinsel in her hair, Anne-Marie was feeling ashamed. She realised she had put her family last. Everyone would parrot that line about her presence mattering more than presents. But she had been careless with her money all year long, and that was a form of selfishness. If her dad hadn't volunteered to drive into the city and collect her, the only way she could get home to spend Christmas with the family would be by hitching.

"I'm a disgrace. I'm treating them as carelessly as some of our residents are treated," she told the hoist, wheeling it along the corridor to lift Emily into bed.

Emily's gummy smile raised her spirits. At least she could do something right.

"I won't forget that carrot for Rudolph you told me to leave out tonight, Emily."

"You're a good girl, Anne-Marie. I have something for you – over there on the bedside table."

Anne-Marie saw a box of chocolates the size of a Rockall.

"My son left them in. I'll never get through so many – I want you to have them, dear."

Anne-Marie was tempted: they weren't exactly the answer to her prayers, but they would save her from going home empty-handed. If only she was able to say yes. "I can't, Emily, I wish I could but I can't. The nursing home has strict rules about gifts."

"Even a box of chocolates? It's a Christmas present."

"Honestly, I can't, it's more than my job's worth. No presents allowed, for any reason. The rule protects you from staff who'd take advantage of you."

"I don't need protecting from you, Anne-Marie. Just slip them into your bag and nobody will be any the wiser."

"Tell you what, Emily, I'll settle for a great big Christmas hug instead."

Anne-Marie huddled at the meeting point agreed with her father, the forecourt of a garage and 24-hour shop. Her stomach was in knots at the prospect of arriving home without even a present for her mother. And her mum really wouldn't mind – that was the worst of it. She jumped up and down to keep warm, and as she did she spotted something glint on the ground. It was a coin. Finding money was lucky, but there wasn't much she could buy with a measly euro. Wait a minute: she could get some mints for the journey – her father was partial to them.

Anne-Marie walked through the automatic doors.

A fanfare jangled, coloured lights blinked on and off, and a grinning man with a Santa bow-tie materialised in front of her.

"Congratulations! You're our millionth customer!"

She was shepherded to a sign with the company name prominently displayed, where a photographer posed the pair for a series of shots and scribbled down her details. A deluxe hamper was thrust into her arms, along with a selection of gift vouchers, and the flash popped again.

"Shopping again, Anne-Marie?"

It was her father.

"Just collecting the Christmas presents, Dad."

❖

Martina Devlin is an author and journalist. Her books include the number one bestseller *Banksters*, a co-authored account of the Irish banking collapse; *Ship of Dreams*, a novel about the Titanic; and a memoir, *The Hollow Heart*. She won a Hennessy Literary Award for her first short story, and was shortlisted twice for the Irish Book of the Year awards. She writes a weekly current affairs column for the *Irish Independent* and in 2011 was named columnist of the year by the National Newspapers of Ireland. In 2009 she was writer-in-residence at the Princess Grace Irish Library in Monaco. Her website is www.martinadevlin.com and she tweets @DevlinMartina

What Really Matters

Caroline Finnerty

"I said I wanted it by close of business, so where is it?"

"I'm nearly finished." Redness crept up along the girl's face. She could feel the heat on her cheeks.

A few brave heads peeped over the tops of their partitions to see what was going on.

"Well, 'nearly' never won a race. Your CV – it said you had a first class honours degree?"

"I do –"

"Well, use it then!"

She turned on her heel and marched back down towards her office. The same heads ducked down again in case they came into her line of fire.

She slammed the door shut so that it reverberated against its timber frame. She sat back down at her desk overlooking the Dublin skyline and started to massage her temples in slow, circular movements. Looking out through the floor-to-ceiling glass, she watched the people filing out of offices on to the dark streets below her. They were all suited and booted in hats, scarves and gloves. Most had their hands stuffed deep down into their pockets as they hurried along, eager to get home out of the biting wind that was being channeled down the Liffey.

Just then the phone on her desk rang, disrupting her thoughts.

"I have your husband on the line for you, Anna," said Maria.

"You can put him through," she said curtly.

"Hiya, love!" Joe's cheery voice sang down the line.

"What's wrong?"

"Nothing – I was just wondering what time you'd be home?"

"I need to stay late – the imbeciles are at it again. Honestly, trained monkeys could do a better job than the people the HR team are giving me these days."

"*Again?* Your dinner is waiting for you."

"Well, just leave it in the oven then!" she snapped.

"Well, will I tell them you'll be back in time for their bedtime story?"

"No – I've too much to do here. Give them a kiss from me."

"You haven't seen them in three days, you know," he muttered.

"What?" she asked, distracted by an email that had just pinged into her inbox. "Look, I haven't got time for this," she said, irritated, and hung up the phone before picking it up again and dialling her PA's number.

"Maria, can you get Dan from Henson's on the line for me, please?"

"Sure – just hold the line, Anna."

Maria connected the call.

"Dan, how *are* you?"

"I'm good, thank you."

"So have you made up your mind yet?"

"I was just going to ring you, Anna. We've decided we'd like you to manage our funds – we were all very impressed with your forecasted returns for the coming year."

"That's fantastic! You won't regret it! Oh and Happy Christmas!"

This is why I do this job, she thought to herself as she hung up. She had been wondering about it a lot lately but the adrenalin rush when she achieved victory was like a drug. It made all the hard work and bad days fade away. She swung around a full 360 degrees in her chair before getting up and striding down to the MD's office. She knocked gently on his door before letting herself in.

"Guess who's going to be looking after Henson's funds for FY12?" she said triumphantly.

"Well done, Anna, you've managed to pull the rabbit out of the hat yet again! And I heard Morgan, Jones and Wiseman were all over them!"

He stepped out from behind the desk and pumped her hand. Henson's fund was worth a lot of money to the company.

"Myself and some of the others are just going to meet some clients for a few Christmas drinks –"

"Oh, that'd be great –" Finally, she was being included.

"It'll probably be a late one and I've a meeting at nine in the morning . . . you wouldn't mind doing it for me Anna, would you?"

"Oh, I see . . . okay, sure . . . no worries." She tried to mask her disappointment that her triumph was already forgotten. This was the third time this week that 'they' were going on a 'Christmas drinks' and the third time that she had not been invited.

She went back down to her office and started plugging numbers into a spreadsheet.

The kids were already in bed by the time she got home.

The next morning she rose early and crept quietly around the room in an attempt not to wake Joe.

"Tell me I'm seeing things," he said, sitting up in the bed and rubbing his eyes. "It's Christmas Eve, surely you're not going in to work today?"

"Stop it, Joe – I have to wrap things up before everything completely shuts down. Why the whole world needs to stop for a week and a half for some piddling religious holiday I'll never know!"

"But the office isn't even open today!"

"Exactly – it will be quiet and I'll have a chance to get stuck into things without every Tom, Dick and Harry running to me with their little problems."

"But we were supposed to be taking the kids to see Santa!"

"Oh God, I totally forgot! Look, you'll just have to go

without me. Bring them for a hot chocolate or something afterwards, yeah?"

And before he could argue any more she leant over to kiss him on the cheek. In her rush she kissed the air beside him instead but she didn't seem to notice. She ran out the door and down the stairs.

The kids came into the bedroom soon after. So much for a lie-in, he groaned inwardly but he knew they were excited. He pulled back the duvet and planted his two feet on the floor.

"So are you two all set?" he asked them.

"I couldn't sleep, Dad!" Peter, their six-year-old son, said giddily.

"Where's Mummy?" Alice asked, looking around the room.

"She's had to go to work, I'm afraid."

"But Mum said she would come!" Peter protested. "She always misses everything!"

"C'mon, we'll have great fun." Joe put his arm around his son's shoulder. "And if you're really good we'll go for a hot chocolate afterwards."

"Can I get marshmallows on mine?" He looked up wide-eyed at his dad.

"Absolutely."

They were at the stage where it was easy to appease them but it wouldn't be much longer until he wouldn't be able to distract them so easily when their mother had left them in the lurch yet again.

After he had made his specialty breakfast of Mickey-mouse-shaped pancakes doused in maple syrup, they all set off for Santa.

They waited in line for nearly an hour and when it was their turn to enter the grotto Peter sat up on Santa's knee but four-year-old Alice stood back, warily sizing up the man in the big red suit. Peter did the talking for both of them and then Santa gave them a small present each. The family went back outside into the cold biting wind again. They hurried along until they found a café. They had just ordered their hot chocolates and were clasping their cups in their hands, savouring the warmth against their frozen fingers when Joe's mobile rang.

"Joe – this is Fiona Loughlin calling from St Columba's."

"Oh yes?"

St Columba's was the nursing home where Anna's father resided.

"I'm afraid that Mr Ward – he's gone missing. He was sitting there having his lunch with the rest of the residents when his carer went to grab a cloth in the kitchen to clean up a spillage and when she came back he was gone!"

Joe struggled to hear what she was saying to him over the carol singers who were singing 'Santa Claus is Coming to Town' and shaking charity buckets full of coins outside the window. "We've searched everywhere – all the rooms of the house, the grounds, everywhere – but we've been unable to locate him. We've had to put an alert out with the Gardaí."

He sat up straighter. "But it's Baltic out there!"

"We know, we're really worried, Joe. I'm so sorry."

"Have you told Anna?"

"We've been trying to get hold of her but she isn't picking up."

Anna noticed her mobile had been ringing but she didn't bother to take it out of her bag – whoever it was, they could wait. She didn't need any more distractions. One of the benefits of the office being closed was that at least no one was able to reach her on the landline. After her mobile rang for the fifth time she sighed, resigned to the fact that she couldn't ignore it any longer. She opened up her bag and took out her phone. She looked at the display and saw it was Joe. He probably wanted to give her an update on how the visit to Santa went.

"What is it?" she asked impatiently.

"Anna – it's your Dad. The nursing home has been on to me."

"What's he done now?" She said it wearily. If this was another call about him refusing to take his tablets she wouldn't be held accountable for her actions. She didn't pay thousands of euro to the plush nursing home every month to get carers unable to handle a feeble old man. They were supposed to be nurses for God's sake!

"He's gone missing . . ."

"*What?*"

"He was at the dining table for lunch apparently and the carer turned her back for a minute and when she turned around again, he was gone."

"He's eighty-one years old – he can't have gone that far for heaven's sake! Have they checked the grounds?"

"Well, they said they've searched the place high and low and the grounds too but there's no sign of him. They're getting worried now because it's freezing out. They've put out an alert with the Gardaí."

This was enough to make her realise it was serious. She knew there was no way the nursing home would involve the Gardaí and risk their reputation unless they were really worried about his safety.

"Why did no-one tell me?" she shrieked down the phone.

"I've been trying to call you for the last hour and I even rang the office but I just kept getting a recorded message saying '*The office is now closed for Christmas*'!" He mimicked the automated voice.

She had assumed Joe was just calling for an uneventful chat, as he liked to do. He was a primary school teacher – he finished school at three o'clock every day and had endless holidays. Unlike her, he had time on his hands.

"Well, this is just bloody great – this is all I need now!"

Joe kept talking so she balanced the phone in the crook of her neck between her ear and shoulder while she took her camel mohair coat off the hanger and belted it around her waist. She packed up her belongings and slipped her hands into her leather gloves.

"Right, I'm leaving now," she told him.

"Come home," he said. "Then we can phone St Columba's and decide what to do. Hopefully by then he'll have turned up."

"I pay too much money for this kind of care!" she said angrily as she walked to the front door.

Outside the ominous grey clouds that had been looking treacherous all morning had broken and snow was starting to fall.

"Blast!" she muttered, almost falling over a homeless man

huddled on the ground outside the office door. "Why do you insist on sitting here?" she said brusquely. "Couldn't you find another doorstep to hang out on?"

"Sorry, Missus," he said, shifting himself and his grubby blanket to one side so as to get out of her way.

"Are you still there?" she said into her phone.

"Yes, I'm still here," Joe sighed.

"I'm on my way."

She rooted around in her oversized tote for her car keys. Eventually she found them and she quickly pressed the button to open the central locking. She sat into the cream leather upholstery of her Mercedes and pulled out onto the road. The roads were already starting to get slippery and every time she halted or moved forward again, her rear-wheel-drive car fishtailed slightly as it tried to get a grip. She loved her sleek red coupé but even she had to admit it was utterly useless in weather like this. The whole way home she tried to think of where her father could be. She looked at the bleak weather conditions and knew it didn't bode well. She cursed St Columba's staff for taking their eye off the ball.

Joe rushed to meet her as soon as she got in the door.

"Any word?"

"No." He shook his head. "I just rang St Columba's again but no news."

"Well, we'll have to try and look for him."

They all piled into the family car which was far more practical in weather like this. Joe drove and they set out in the direction of the nursing home, scanning the pavements as they went but there was no one matching her father to be seen. The people on the street were starting to blur together. She took off her glasses and rubbed her tired eyes.

"This is useless," she said eventually.

Her phone rang just then.

"Anna – the Gardaí just phoned – they think they might have located him." It was Fiona from St Columba's.

"Oh, thank God!" She felt the relief move down through her body. "Where did they find him?"

"In the zoo."

"The *zoo*? What in the name of God is he doing there?"

"We're not sure but they said that he's all right."

"I'm on my way."

Joe turned the car and drove to the zoo. They parked the car and ran towards the entrance.

The frozen cashier took in the family hurrying towards her. As they approached the desk, she wondered if they were actually insane – what family in their right mind would want to go to the zoo on a day like this at three o'clock on Christmas Eve? And they weren't alone, an old man had come in earlier muttering something about the lions. He had been a bit short on the admission fee but she had let him in anyway, it was Christmas after all.

Anna explained why they were there and the cashier brought them down to the staff tearoom. They all piled into the small room surrounded by ecru filing cabinets and wall-planners and photos of small animals with their keepers.

Her dad was sitting there on a chair in the centre of the room with a navy tartan rug over his shoulders. A woman was sitting chatting with him.

"Dad!" she cried out.

"Anna – thank God! Thank God you're here – the lions! They're not used to the snow, they're freezing out there. We need to feed them but I couldn't find them." He was wearing his shirt and pullover and corduroy trousers but no coat, hat or gloves. *Had he gone outside like that?*

She grabbed the small frame of her father, who used to be so big and strong, into her arms and held him there for a long time. He looked more frail and sorry than she had ever seen before. It was hard to accept that the man in front of her was the same big, strong dad who would lift her up on his shoulders so she thought she was on top of the world and then he would swing her around as she watched the world spin by. Tears were running down her cheeks. She didn't realise she was crying until one tear dropped onto her blouse and she felt the coolness of the wet silk against her skin. She thanked the staff who had found him and had sat with him until they had arrived.

As they made their way back to the car, snow had transformed the zoo into a magical place. The trees and black railings were now white-topped and the paths were pristine with virgin snow. It was so quiet and peaceful – the only sound to be heard was the snow crunching under their shoes as they walked.

In the car on the way home, the traffic stopped and started. It was heavy with people who had been making a last-minute dash to tick off the final items on their shopping lists and had been taken unawares by the snow. Christmas shoppers laden with cord-handled bags, with luxurious gift-wrapping peeping over the tops, zigzagged in and out between the stopped cars.

Her dad was sitting in the back with Peter and Alice, just like the third child that he had become.

"I hope we get home in time for Santa," Peter said from the backseat.

She could hear the worry in his voice.

"Of course we will, love."

"Santa is bringing me a car, you know," her father said confidently. "Last year it was a train-set but this year I just know it will be a car!"

She looked at his lined face in the rearview mirror. It was just like Peter's, full of nervous excitement and anticipation about Santa's visit. She felt her heart break a little bit more.

"Mum?" said Peter. "How will Santa know what Granddad wants – he never wrote a letter?" Panic was written all over the little boy's face.

"Don't worry, Santa is magic. He'll know what Granddad wants."

They sat in a queue held up by people filtering out of a car park and when she looked in the rearview again the three in the back were fast asleep. Her dad was slumped down, his head hopping off the window whenever the car moved on again.

The snow was coming down heavy now. It rushed at the windscreen, hypnotising her into a trance.

"Looks like we're going to have a white one this year," she said absently.

"Do you remember the last time we had a white Christmas?" Joe turned to her.

She did remember – how could she ever forget? They had just got engaged the week before and they were supposed to be travelling home to Cork on Christmas Eve to share the news with their friends and families but they had got snowed in. Christmas dinner had ended up being a frozen pizza with a side of garlic bread. It was all they had left in the freezer but it still ended up being one of their best Christmases ever.

After dinner and all the rituals of leaving out a carrot for Rudolph and some cake for Santa, the kids went to bed and Anna tucked her father up in the spare room. When she came back down the stairs Joe had uncorked a bottle of red wine.

"What a day, eh?"

"Boy, do I need this! Thanks." She took the glass from his hands.

She started to rub her left shoulder with her right hand, trying to massage out the usual knots which had wound even tighter after the day's events.

"Here, let me." He got up and stood behind her and used both hands to knead out the tension.

"That is so good – I had forgotten how good you are at that."

"I think we've both forgotten a lot of things."

"Thank you for today, Joe – if you weren't there – well, I don't even want to think what might have happened."

He stopped massaging for a moment and looked at her. It had been so long since she had thanked him for anything.

"You're welcome. I'm just glad he came to no harm."

"It's my own fault – he has been fixated on the zoo lately – he kept asking me to take him there every time I went to visit him. I kept putting him off, saying that we would go soon but really I never made the time for him."

"Don't beat yourself up about it – he's fine now – that's the main thing."

She started to sob then. "I'm such a horrible daughter. And wife and mother. I don't deserve any of you."

"Ah, love – no, you're not. Come here." He moved out from behind her and took her into his arms. They went and sat on the sofa.

"Well, that's it," she said. "Today was a wake-up call for me – things are going to change. From now on my family comes first. The kids are growing up right before my eyes and Dad won't be around for much longer either – I won't get this time back ever again. I've spent so many years chasing my tail trying to keep up with the younger and more energetic talent that comes into the office, always trying to prove myself. I thought when I was made a director that things might get a bit easier – you know, that I would have gained more respect? But the rest of the old boys' club still head off on their boozy lunches on a Friday afternoon or after-work drinks and never ask me along."

"But you've already proved yourself in there."

"It only lasts for so long and then there is something bigger to be fought for. You're only as good as your last investment. I'm always stressing myself at every so-called 'emergency' only to find then once it passes there is always another one waiting around the corner to replace it. Being the last person to leave every evening and eating my lunch at my desk. Going into the office at weekends when everyone else is off enjoying themselves and coming home from my holidays early – I'm tired of it all."

"You're good at your job, Anna, they know that."

"I know but it's not like it used to be – it's dog-eat-dog now, every man for himself. I just don't have the energy for it any more."

"It doesn't have to be like that – you know that. You put too much pressure on yourself."

"Well, I'm going to take the full Christmas off – I won't be going in at all. The place won't fall down and then I'm going to go back in January to hand in my notice."

"Now don't do anything hasty, love – you got a fright today, that's all. You love your job, you've worked hard to get where you are today."

"I love my family more. And, besides, I think I've been putting so much effort in for so long and at the end of the day the rewards aren't mine. I've been mulling it over for a while now about going out on my own, I know lots of my clients would come with me and at least I could work around the kids – be there to take them to school in the mornings and pick them up in the evenings. What do you think?"

"Wow!" He was taken aback. "That sounds like a great idea. Are you sure that's what you want?"

"I've been thinking about it for a while now and if I don't do it now, then I'll never do it."

"I know you'll make it a success."

They stayed talking in front of the log fire, the smell of smoked wood filling the air. They stayed up reminiscing until the logs had turned to embers in the grate. It had been a long time since they had been close.

Early the next morning she heard a soft knock on the bedroom door. She knew it was early because the bedroom was still heavy with darkness. She looked at her alarm clock; it was just after five. She knew that Peter and Alice were very excited. It was the same every year.

"Come on in!" she said, propping herself up on the pillows.

"Can we go down and see if Santa has come yet?" Alice said, her eyes wide.

Her soft blonde curls looked gorgeous against her red tartan pyjamas. Anna longed to snuggle her in close to her chest just like she had when she was a baby. Peter came running in behind her.

"Okay, well, put on your dressing gowns and I'll go and get Granddad."

She roused Joe by shaking his shoulder and went down the landing to where her father was sleeping. The door to the bedroom was open and when she went inside the room he wasn't there.

Oh no. Not again. She felt her blood run cold. She knew she should have locked the door to his bedroom last night as well as the front and back doors.

She hurried down the stairs and checked the front door. Thankfully it was still locked as she had left it the night before, with the key removed and the chain across it. She rushed into the kitchen to check the back door but it too was locked. She let out a heavy sigh of relief.

"Dad?" she called out. "Dad?" She could hear the mildly hysterical edge to her voice cutting through the quietness of the house.

"I'm in here," his voice answered back.

She pushed open the door into the living room to see him standing beside the tree in his dressing gown and slippers, staring in wonderment at the presents beneath.

"Santa Claus has come!" he said to her, full of excitement. "I didn't open them though – I'm waiting for Sheila."

Sheila was his younger sister who had died a few years back.

She swallowed back a lump in her throat. "That's good, Dad. Just hang on a minute for Peter and Alice too."

Peter and Alice came running through the door behind her, Joe in their wake.

"He came, he came!" they both shrieked happily.

They all sat down on the floor amongst the shiny wrapped presents. The kids dived in and started to check for the ones which bore their names.

Peter picked up a large rectangular box and shook it to see if he could work out what was inside. He picked up another red-and-green-wrapped parcel and read the name-tag.

"Granddad, this is for you!" he said excitedly, passing it over to him.

She watched her dad's eyes light up with glee as he instantly started untying the silver grosgrain ribbon and tearing open the wrapping paper. Inside the box was a vintage die-cast model racecar. She watched as her father ran his fingers over its glossy burgundy-red paintwork, his whole face lit up with joy.

"Santa knew! Santa knew!" Peter jumped up and ran around the living room in excited circles.

Joe looked at Anna in shock and a huge smile spread across his face. "How did you . . .?"

"See, didn't I tell you Santa was magic?"

Joe shuffled over beside her and put his arm around her shoulders and they sat watching the scene together. He leant into her and pulled her close so he could smell the lemony scent of her hair.

"This is what it's all about," she whispered to him as she nestled back into his arms. "This is what really matters – you, me. Our family."

Caroline Finnerty is originally from Celbridge, Co Kildare, but now lives nearby in the small village of Ardclough with her husband Simon, their three-year-old daughter Lila, baby twins Tom & Bea and their two dogs Harvey & Sam. Caroline completed an MSc in Bioinformatics in NUI Maynooth and a postgraduate diploma in business studies in the UCD Michael Smurfit Graduate School. When she is not singing 'The Wheels on the Bus', complete with actions, she loves to write. Her first novel *In a Moment* was published in 2012. Her second book *A Small Hand in Mine* will be released in 2013. You can find out more about Caroline on her website, www.carolinefinnerty.ie or on Facebook, www.facebook.com/carolinefinnertywriter.

One Snowy Christmas Eve

Caroline Grace-Cassidy

Susan Miley sat on her small suitcase and pushed down with all her weight. Damn these case weigh-ins for carry-on! Now she was beyond paranoid she wouldn't be able to fit everything in. "Yeah, well, if you have to sit on it, love . . ." she whispered to herself in her chilly London apartment.

The twinkling seasonal lights of Twickenham flicked in through her window as Christmas Eve broke over the city. It was a dark morning with snow forecast again and she prayed she'd get home to Dublin this afternoon. Well, *prayed* was a bit strong but she hoped.

Susan got off the case again and removed her favourite cream Avoca chunky jumper and a pair of Gap skinny jeans. "If I'm really honest with myself, the season that's in it, guys, I probably won't need you," she informed the dark denims as she threw them onto her bed, but she folded the jumper carefully. "In fact, I should start as I mean to go on," she said as she turned her back and was immediately in her kitchen. 'Roomy' was not a word that described her Twickenham apartment.

She reached for her strawberry-decorated biscuit tin and removed a Chunky Peanut Butter Kit Kat, her personal favourite

91

of the chunky range. Susan often thought about writing to Kit Kat to see if they might be interested in her designing some flavours for the chunky range. She knew she'd be incredible at that job. She was bursting with sweet ideas.

She had been living in London exactly a year to the day, she reminisced as she took a large bite. She let the peanut-butter filling melt in her mouth. She had left Dublin last Christmas Eve just as the first speckles of soft snow fell – on a last-minute flight. She had good reason to leave like that. Though Susan worked in sales on the north side of Dublin, her boss had surprised them and taken them into town for early Christmas Eve drinks on Grafton Street. She had opened the door of Neary's bar and stopped in her tracks. There in broad daylight was her fiancé tucked away in the corner kissing the face off a small blonde child. OK, so that was not exactly a fact but she was indeed around twenty and looked like a small elf, dressed as she was in skin-tight white jeans and a green cashmere sweater so tight Susan hoped it might cut off her circulation, She had those Christmas-tree earrings that light up that Susan so hated and her blonde hair tumbled around her like a pair of rich designer curtains you would see in a suite at the Four Seasons Hotel. In fact when the elf spoke the pitch of her voice proved Susan to be correct.

"You alright there, Rory? You seem a bit squashed," Susan had managed as he jumped like a scalded cat and the elf fell to the ground with a tiny thud. She had rubbed her head and a small squeak could be heard – obviously, she had disturbed the mouse in her brain. "Ror?" She looked up at him and held out her hand, her nails as long as a set of small sharp knives with blood on the tips. He wasn't that stupid. He knew he couldn't help her up. "Ror?" she squeaked again. "What's going on? I'm loike on the floor here and am loike totally beyond mortified, you know?" Elf didn't look at Susan.

Susan pulled her shoulders up and calmly re-tied her red silk scarf in a tidy knot. The pub was oblivious to them. A person on the floor of a bar on Christmas Eve was as common as Irish people telling you their Bono story. You were interested in the first one and after that you didn't care any more.

"Ror?" Susan managed and gave a small cough.

He jumped up now and stepped over the child. "It's not what you think, I mean in a minute I can explain – she's the new waitress and I was told by Malcolm to take her for a drink. I've had a few and it's all Christmassy in here and I – ah listen, I'm so, so sorry – please don't overreact now. I wouldn't be able."

Something about 'the season' being 'jolly' rang out on the stereo around them. Rory was fond of a few and he could be very scatty when he had a few. He was a chef in Tatero's on Leeson Street. He was supposed to be working until ten o' clock tonight. Then they were going to open a bottle when he got home. Susan never minded waiting up once there was a bottle to be opened. Tonight they were going to start on their wedding invites – on Christmas Eve – how romantic.

She was so shocked yet she was scarily calm. She couldn't understand her brain's reaction to this. Maybe in a way she was relieved she had caught him. She wouldn't be one of those women who forgave him, he should know her better that that. How many times had this happened, she wondered? If she hadn't walked in would he have taken her to Malcolm's knocking shop, as they so fondly had christened it, above the restaurant? A tall American man wearing thick-rimmed glasses pushed past her and ordered two pints of *Guinnessssssssssss* at the bar. She glanced at his hand and he was wearing his wedding ring. She knew he wasn't a Ror.

"Rooaaarrrr," she drew out the ridiculous shortening of his name by the elf, "go hump yourself!" Ring pulled off and flung at his face. Decorum out the window. Temper well and truly lost.

"Ah, come on now, Susan, you are way overreacting! It was only a kiss! Jesus, I could have done a lot worse!" Rory was pathetic.

Susan turned on her heel and headed for the door. The icy wind bit at her ears and she pulled her red scarf up around them now as her tears flowed onto her cheeks. Not hysterical tears by any means but tears she felt the situation she now found herself in deserved. Eight years she had been with Rory. The last two long years waiting for that proposal. She hailed a taxi at The Shelbourne Hotel and jumped in, just as she heard him call her from behind. "Clontarf, please." She composed herself and stared out the window. The Shelbourne was pure picture-postcard Christmas. Busy shoppers hurried down Baggot Street now as the taxi crawled by them, some nursing hot chocolates taking in the atmosphere, others frantically looking for those oversized slippers and CDs that deep down they knew loved ones already had. Red and green lights illuminated their faces. Children clutched the hands of their parents on this, the most exciting night of their lives.

Emergency shoppers. Susan had everything done; now Susan had nothing done.

She could already hear Amy's voice in her head – her best friend who had lived in London for the last nine years and who had no time for Rory whatsoever.

"Sure you have nothing in common with that man. He's not good enough for you. Why do you want to marry him?" had been her friend's reaction over the phone when she told her they had become engaged.

"I do. He's great and I love him!" Susan had protested, twirling her diamond ring around her finger. She had actually picked the ring and put the deposit on it herself some time ago, pushing Rory into the shop to pick it up on the afternoon of the engagement party.

"Susan, you are thirty-one years old, you have been with Rory since you were twenty-three. God knows I want you to be happy but I want it to be right for you. Tell him you want a year out and come and live with me in London for a while. If you still want to marry him then, you have my blessing."

Amy had been right and Susan should have listened to her friend.

Not long after that call Amy herself had fallen madly in love and quickly married Mark Pollit. They had moved to his townhouse on the other side of London. When Susan dashed away from Rory, she had called Amy. Her friend begged her to come and stay with them but Susan couldn't face sharing with the happy couple, so when Amy offered her vacant small apartment in Twickenham Susan had jumped at the offer. She moved in that fateful Christmas Eve and found a job days later in telesales and it suited her perfectly. Her mother had shipped over a box of her stuff and she hadn't heard from Rory from that night on.

Amy had been absolutely right. Susan hadn't missed him at all. Not one bit. She had settled into London wonderfully but now it was time to go home and face the music. Face the questions. The looks. What happened? Why had she run? Although the invites had never been written it was common knowledge that they were to get married on the following Christmas Eve.

Amy was already home in Dublin with Mark so Susan was looking forward to seeing her and her family too.

She finished her Kit Kat and looked at the small case again. Then she took a run and jumped on it, stomping up and down with all her might. Still no luck. She jumped again and again and shouted out in frustration now. *"Come on, will you! Do what you're told!"*

A soft knock came on her door.

"Hello?" She turned her head, still standing on the case.

"Is everything alright in there?" came a male voice.

"Yeah, why?" she answered.

"It's me, Graham, from downstairs. My ceiling seems about to cave in."

Susan shut her eyes tight. Her heart started to pound. Dishy Graham. He was outside her door. She couldn't open the door. Dishy Graham could not see her like this. The place was a bomb site, she wasn't dressed and had no make-up on.

"I'm doing Pilates!" She shut her eyes tight and hoped he'd buy that one.

"Is it nearly done?"

She knew he was smiling. "Yes, indeed, Graham, just finished!"

She was now actually doing some sort of yoga pose on the case. She pushed one leg out behind her and clasped her hands together prayer-like.

"Good, I have your post here – I met the postman on the stairs just now."

"Thank you." She tiptoed off the case and over to the door.

She peeked out the security hole. Dishy Graham was in jeans and a black T-shirt today. No suit. He was some sort of whizz financial banker and had a house in Notting Hill – however, he rented it and lived in this pokey complex. Amy had told her all this.

"Are you going to open the door?"

"Not today, no, I'm in a . . . I'm in a meditation place . . . in my head and it doesn't allow me to see another human being for another hour or so." She gritted her teeth to stop herself saying anything else.

"Fair enough, I will leave the post on the ground here and, Susan, there's a little card from me too, okay? Happy Christmas." He moved away.

"The very same to you, Dishy Graham!"

"Excuse me?" he said as the footsteps returned.

Jesus Christ! She banged her head against the door now. Hard. "Dishy, Graham? Do you need a dishy? It's just, I'll be away for a week and I've a load of dishes in here I won't be using, like? Pick a dishy if you will? Any dishy?"

"I'm good, thanks, Susan, I won't be using many dishes over Christmas myself but thanks anyway."

She bit her lip hard until it almost bled. "Stupid cow!" she muttered to herself and did a small but quiet dance on the spot.

She turned now and gave a small groan as the white drops of snow began to fall heavily. She hoped the flight wouldn't be delayed. She ran to her bathroom and jumped under the shower. She washed in a Christmas Body Shop Cranberry soap that her Kris Kindle had splashed out on and dried off quickly. She put on her light green combats with a white T-shirt, a white hoody and her green Puma runners. Susan stood in front of the mirror, her short black hair still wet as she slicked the blunt fringe to the side with a comb. She lined her bright blue eyes in dark kohl eyeliner and added dark mascara. A touch of foundation and blusher and that was it. She might just catch Graham before he left for the gym. Okay, so she knew his every move and had been known to get into a serious mood if he brought lady friends home. Which, to be fair to the man, was pretty much never. Susan thought about Graham 24/7.

"You are turning into a scary stalking hermit," Amy would say when she came down to visit. It was okay for her with her unreal Mark Pollit! He was simply the perfect man. Think the body of Brad Pitt in *Fight Club* (Mark was a rower), the face of a young Harrison Ford in *Indiana Jones* and the hair of Johnny Depp in *Chocolat* with the brains of Hilary Clinton. That was Mark.

"What else do you want me to do? I don't have friends here. I work in telesales and the people change every day. I have stopped talking to them as they are always gone the next day so it's a waste of time. I work. Make my money and think about Graham. I am perfectly happy."

"Why don't you talk *to* Graham?" Amy raised her hands in frustration at her friend.

"Don't be stupid, Amy, it's not that kind of relationship."

But today she had planned to talk to him. She had gone through the plan over and over again – it was military. But he hadn't been supposed to call to her before she did! She was going to wear exactly what she was wearing now, keeping it all very casual, and knock on his door with wet hair (the wet hair was very important as though she was just extra breezy and casual) and ask him to hold the spare key of her apartment while she was home for the week and water her geraniums. That way she could get a look into his place and see him too. Oh, they had exchanged pleasantries in the hall or at the front door lots and lots of times but nothing further. One night she had seen him in Piccadilly Square in the window of a fancy gastro pub with some lads. She had snuck around the corner and peered in until she saw him squint his eyes slightly and then slowly wave at her.

Horrors! She ran away so fast one of her cream Zara flats fell off and she didn't go back for it. She didn't even get one funny look on the tube. She had been red-faced for a week. Anyway, now was the time. She opened her door and picked up the post. The only one not stamped was from him obviously. She threw the letters on the side table. She made her way down the creaky blue-painted wooden stairs and knocked three times on his door, a little too loudly.

He opened it. Dishy Graham in his black tight T-shirt and jeans was in his bare feet. Susan couldn't look up. She was drawn to the feet like two majestically wonderfully rare creatures at a tropical zoo.

"Hi, Susan!" He was looking at his own feet now. They were perfect feet.

Look up! she screamed at herself and dragged her eyes from the evenly aligned toes. He was smirking. His short curly black hair was morning-messy and his dark-brown eyes mesmerising. "Good morning, Graham, I was hoping I could come in for a second to ask you a favour?" She knew the 'come in' bit was pushing it but he wasn't opening the door far enough so she could see inside. It was imperative for her Christmas dreaming that she could picture him in his own place.

"It's a bit of a tip, I'm afraid, but sure – come on." He pulled back the door and sure enough the place resembled Santa's Grotto.

"Wow, what are you? Santa's greedy little helper?" She took in every inch of the apartment and smelled a funny burning wine smell. It was clean though and there were his black socks tucked neatly into his white Converse runners. Susan imagined it was the first time in her life that she was envious of a pair of socks.

"Can I make you a cuppa? Eggnog?" He rubbed his hands together a little nervously.

"You actually have eggnog?" she asked and he nodded.

He had two small Christmas trees, one in the living room and one in the kitchen. Both twinkling simple white lights and smelling of pine.

"A massive pot!" He padded over to the pot.

The whole apartment was open plan and way bigger than Susan's. The view overlooking the old church was stunning. Susan watched people come and go from the church and wondered briefly what they were all asking God for – or were they just giving thanks on this very special day of the year?

"Holy Mickey! Where are ya going with a pot that size?" Susan startled him as she entered the kitchen and stood behind him.

Graham held his chest as though she'd frightened the daylights out of him and then grinned, showing the brightest straightest most perfect teeth she'd ever seen.

"Did you open my card then?" he mumbled as he poured the drinks, spilling a few drops over the side of the glass.

"Oh no – sorry, not yet. I was hoping you could water my geraniums while I'm back in Dublin for the holidays?" Susan had to say 'the holidays' – he could be a Muslim for all she knew. She pulled the small gold chubb from her combats. "That's if you're going to be here?"

"It would be my pleasure." He accepted the key and pushed it deep into his pocket. Note to self, Susan thought, never wash key.

"That snow's looking pretty grim for flying, I have to tell you," he said as he handed her the eggnog. They both looked out the window together in silence as Christmas Eve turned whiter and whiter. "Here, let me check in with my mate Dave, he works at Heathrow. It is Heathrow, isn't it?"

"Yes." Susan hadn't expected to be here this long and now her hair was drying and it was going to be frizzy as hell. She needed to get out. But she couldn't leave the side of this member of the species. She was as drawn to him as Usain Bolt was to a finishing line

As Graham hunted under his brown distressed leather sofa for his phone, she asked, "What's the craic with all the Christmas pheasants?" She gulped a bit now as the taste wasn't exactly Budweiser.

"The pheasants?" He stood up and looked out the window on his tippy-toes now.

Jesus, Susan! "Sorry, the presents?" She licked her fingers to try and pat down her hair.

"Oh yeah, well, welcome to Graham Wilson's Christmas. This is what I do." He looked a little sheepish now.

"What, have you a massive family or something?"

"I'm an orphan," he replied.

She hadn't meant to, she didn't know what happened but she spat the eggnog all over the lovely window. Susan coughed and spluttered and it ran down her chin, taking her newly applied make-up with it.

"Here, are you okay?" He handed her a soft tissue.

Graham had a box of tissues. She loved a man with a box of tissues. "Sorry. So sorry, it went down the wrong way, yes." She composed herself. "An orphan? Oh, Graham!"

He smiled at her and she felt like dissolving into the carpet. "Yep, ole orphan Graham that's me. It's quite alright – I'm pretty proud of it to be honest, it's nice to be a bit different." He raised his glass.

"So who are all these presents for then?" She stared at the tons and tons of toys and books on the floor. There was barely space to move. Rolls and rolls of colourful Christmas wrapping paper balanced on top of each other.

"Other orphans." He sipped his eggnog.

"Oh," Susan managed.

"Ah, there it is!" Graham pointed to the wrapping paper now and bent down to retrieve his iPhone.

Perfect bum.

"Let me call Dave."

Susan returned to the window, trying to wipe the eggnog on the glass with the tissue. She saw a mother and child, both dressed in red coats, leave the church. The mother bent down and pulled the child's collar up high and kissed the little girl on her cheek as she brushed the falling white snow from her shoulders. Then she scooped up the delighted child and they ran to their car.

"Yeah, Dave says all ok," she heard Graham say then. "What time's your flight?"

Susan turned back. "Two o'clock."

"Two? You better move it! You know what Heathrow's like this time of year." He twisted his wrist to show her his watch-face.

"Oh bugger, yes, sorry! I've to run back up and grab my stuff." She plonked the glass on his table. Bowl of fresh fruit. Nice. "Okay so Graham, bye bye then!"

He moved to follow her to the door. "Have a lovely Christmas, Susan. Amy called me last night and told me she was going home too. I'm sure the two of you will have a great time. Take a look at my Christmas card, won't you?"

He was still talking but all Susan could think of was that Amy had his number. She'd never told her that! She knew she couldn't listen in to his voice messages, the *News Of The World* had put an end to that particular service, but it would be nice to have it just the same. Maybe she could text him on Christmas Day? The excitement.

"Okay, bye, Graham!"

She turned on her heel and flew up the stairs to collect her bulging case.

CANCELLED. One simple word. So much hassle. Susan had been underground on the tube for an hour so hadn't been aware of the worsening snow. As she took the free shuttle towards Heathrow Arrivals the heavy snow fall hit her hard.

"Titties!" she whispered as a pair of loved-up lesbians draped in pink tinsel walked past her. "No, no, not you guys!" They gave her a strange look and spoke back in a foreign language. Now she stood under the electronic sign with hundreds of other disgruntled passengers. People with festive jumpers wearing Red-nosed Reindeers and Singing Santas clutched their beautifully wrapped festive gifts and swore mercilessly at the screen.

Susan headed for the bar. She ordered a pint of Bud and dragged out her phone. No answer. She left a message on the home phone: "Mam, the flight's cancelled." Christmas Eve started at one o' clock in the Miley house, down to the High

Chaparral, a Christmas Quiz, then a few drinks and then the carols started. Maureen Farrell always started off with 'Silent Night' and it was all anyone could do to stop the laughter. If Simon Cowell was judging he'd have shot her.

Susan sipped. She knew she wouldn't really be missed. She rummaged in her bag for inspiration. What could she do? Go home to her apartment? She could stay in the airport and wait. Then it hit her. Susan really didn't want to go home for Christmas. There was no underlying reason. It wasn't about Rory – in fact, she sometimes wished him well. Susan wanted to get back to her own life and her own apartment, small as it was. Her own life. Graham.

Oh, the card! She'd stuffed her post in the front of her case. She fished further and found the green envelope. Tearing it open, she removed it. *To the one I love at Christmas . . .* Oh great, he'd given her the wrong bloody card! Who the hell was this meant for? She roughly pulled it open.

Dearest Susan, my shyness won't allow me to say what I really want to say. So here it is – I think you are a very special girl. I hope you have a wonderful Christmas and I'd really like to take you out when you get back??? There, I've said it!

Love, Graham x

Susan belched. Loudly. She excused herself and a passing waitress acknowledged her manners. "Oh my God, he likes me!" she told the waitress. "Oh my God, he really likes me!" she told her again.

Then she ran, dragging her case behind her. Susan ran up the steps, ran for the first bus, then she ran down other steps, danced on the spot on the tube. Jumped off first. Ran up the steps for the second tube. Ran down the steps. Ran down Second Cross Road past the church and across to the apartment block. Breathe. Opened the new hall door. Up the blue steps, knocked on his door. Breathe. Fix fuzzy hair. He opened it.

"Hi," she panted, slicking her black hair back now with both hands.

"Susan! Hi!" His big brown eyes nearly popped out of his head.

"Cancelled!" she huffed.

"Good." He started to grin and opened the door and she stepped in. Every present was now beautifully wrapped and the eggnog was bubbling on the cooker.

"What happened?" she asked as she slowly sat on the couch and he knew immediately what she meant.

"A small aircraft over the desert in Vegas. They were at a wedding, I was with my only grandmother. It crashed. No survivors. My granny passed on 30th September that year and I turned four on 1st November. There was no one else. I was fostered a bit but then settled into a home in Coventry until I was eighteen. I worked in McDonalds and put myself through business school. I went into finance, I bought this place after three years and then I bought my dream home in Notting Hill."

"Why don't you live there?" she had to ask.

"It's an orphanage. I got it for the kids. It was always what I planned to do with my life. After I save enough money from finance to retire I will work with the kids full-time. I will be there soon enough, I hope." He stood tall now, over six feet she guessed, as he pulled on his socks and runners. "That's where I'm going now if you want to come?"

Did she? She stood. "My case?" she asked him as he zipped up his leather jacket. "Leave it here, if that's okay? The snow's fairly heavy so we'd better take my jeep. I'll make a start on these – can you grab a few?" She followed him out to the road into the snow and they made several trips back to fill the jeep with the presents.

On the drive he asked her, "Are you sad not to be with your family for Christmas?" She rubbed the cold window with her hand as they snailed along the soft white roads. It was picture perfect. Clean. Untouched.

"No. Not at all for some reason."

"Amy said, well, she thought, she . . ."

"Amy told you I fancied you, didn't she, Graham?"

"She mentioned something . . . about stalking?" He laughed now and so did she.

103

"I read your card, Graham."

"And?"

"This feels weird!" She shook her head.

"Why?"

He couldn't take his eyes from the road and that made it easier for Susan to say what she wanted to say.

"Well, I do think you are, well, seriously amazing. I was engaged and I caught him with . . . a girl . . . kissing . . . and I left . . . but I think I wanted to leave, you know? I was ready to leave. I've been doing the same thing the last eight years and I was well and truly bored trying to do the right thing. Trying to make my life what I thought it was supposed to be...as in married with kids... That's why this feels weird. You are only supposed to be my fantasy, I'm not supposed to actually get you."

"It is Christmas Eve," he said and she knew he was glad he didn't have to look at her either.

"It is," she answered and suddenly he turned up the music and the jeep was filled with Bing Crosby's voice and she got goosebumps.

"Here we go!" he announced after a while.

The house was stunning. A huge detatched redbrick with a long gravel driveway. Outside Christmas fairy-lights decorated a huge oak tree. The windows were stencilled with festive scenes and the most magnificent Christmas wreath with holly was hanging on the red hall door. A colossal tree stood tall in the main window.

"He's here!"

Susan could hear the shouts as Graham rang the bell. The door opened slowly and she couldn't help it, she felt a huge lump rise in the back of her throat. She swallowed hard. There in the hall stood a group of small boys. None of them older than six years old. All spotless in their Christmas pyjamas and matching slippers. Susan couldn't take her eyes off their little faces. Little Grahams. She head counted. Nine of them. She pulled the tissue from her combats and blew her nose.

"Graham! It's here! He's coming tonight!" The smallest boy ran and clung onto Graham's legs and a lady stepped in and gently tried to prise the child off.

Graham bent and scooped the small boy into his arms. "I know, Dick, can you believe it? I told you last week it would come, didn't I?" He turned his head and mouthed to the lady: "Gifts are in the jeep."

The lady disappeared to the back room and came back with two men.

"Thanks, guys," Graham said. "Susan, this is Tara and Paul and Cian – they all work here." Susan shook their hands warmly as they filed out to bring in the gifts.

They entered the living room and a row of little socks hung from the long mantelpiece over a roaring fire.

"Did you do what I said and leave out the carrots for Rudolf and the cake for Father Christmas?" Graham asked Dick.

"Yes, Graham, yes!" The little boy squealed with pure excitement as Graham tickled him and the other children crowded around them. "Early to bed, mind you! Santa Claus has a lot of work to do in this very special loving home."

Susan blew out a long hard breath to compose herself and Graham smiled.

"We have a big dinner to eat tomorrow so go easy on those selection boxes when you all wake up!" he said as the boys milled around excitedly.

This was Christmas.

Susan sat and Graham fussed around the children. She was having an out-of-the-body experience. Suddenly she knew she'd had a very lucky escape. It wouldn't have been the end of the world to have married Rory Moore and be sitting in the High Chaparral now listening to Maureen Farrell squawk but look where she was instead! Look what she was a part of. The deep feeling of contentment that came over her was electric. Graham looked at her and their eyes locked for moments. Thunderous eye contact.

"Who's this then, Graham?" A brown-haired boy with massive snowballs all over his pyjamas poked Susan in the face as he asked in his broad Liverpool accent.

"This is Susan, Keith She's special."

"Why?" Keith asked.

"Because she's going to be the first person I will ever wake up beside on Christmas morning and say 'I love you' to, since my parents passed. I hope."

"Oh." Keith wasn't overly impressed with Graham's answer.

Susan bloody was. She stood. Then she sat. Then she stood again.

"Come with me!"

He took her by the hand. Pins and needles. He led her out of the room, telling the boys to stay put, led her up the stairs and unlocked a door. All the presents Graham had wrapped and tagged were now placed on the floor of the bare room. They locked the door and sat on the small two-seater couch under the window.

"The very first Christmas Eve you moved in I was looking out the window," he said. "Wondering. You appeared out of nowhere. You were struggling with the key to the old hall door. I couldn't take my eyes off you. The small white snowflakes scattered on your dark hair. You looked so vulnerable and so alone. Just like me. I wanted to leave the apartment to help you but I was just too shy. Every day since, Susan, I've tried to talk to you but I don't know what to say. My palms sweat, my heart races. I knew this Christmas I had to try. Then when Amy called and gave me the nod . . . I'm sorry the card is so naff but I knew you were packing – I mean the whole building knew! I wanted to make my feelings known before you left. It was all I could think of." He laughed and ran his hand through his black curly hair, his brown eyes never leaving hers now. "What I'm trying to say is that the card was all I could think of to tell you how I feel about you."

Sweet day of justice, Susan Miley.

"That's . . . well, that's bloody great, Dishy Graham, it really is. I'm besotted with you and now, after seeing all this, I'm thinking you may well be the big man himself – Santa Claus that is!" She tried to catch her breath.

"Ho!" he moved closer on the couch. "Ho!" he leaned right

in and she could smell his crisp aftershave. "Ho!" he whispered and he kissed her softly on the lips.

She draped her arms around him and pulled him in tight.

Merry Christmas, Susan, she said in her head, and a Happy New Life.

Caroline Grace-Cassidy began her acting career on the BAFTA-winning *Custer's Last Stand Up*, playing Mary Mull. Since then she has gone on to appear in numerous productions for the BBC/ITV/RTE/TG4 & TV3. Her film career has seen her work with such respected directors as Jim Sheridan, Aisling Walsh, Dearbhla Walsh and David Gordon Green to date. She has written for the *Irish Student Press* and *Face-Up* magazine and has contributed to various publications. *When Love Takes Over*, her first novel, was published in 2012 and she is looking forward to the publication of her second, *Be Careful What You Wish For*, in 2013. Caroline has written three short films and is currently working on a screenplay. She will begin work on Graham Cantwell's feature film *Bere Island*, shooting in spring 2013.

Mummy's Christmas Star

Emma Hannigan

Veronique Miller had waited nine years two months and three days to have a baby.

Before they'd sought medical intervention she'd made her long-suffering husband Derek jump through hoops.

"Don't sit on that cold wall, Derek, it'll lower your sperm count."

"Don't eat spicy food, Derek, it might make you infertile."

Derek had nodded silently and gone along with most of it until the day Veronique had come home telling him he couldn't drink pints any more.

"Ah now," he'd said, looking affronted, "that's just crazy talk, Vee. I know you want a baby and all that but, taking inspiration from the words of Meatloaf, I'll do anything for you – but I won't do that."

"Derek, I'm reading a book about natural conception and how to boost our reproductive systems. The first thing it mentions is booze. It's the devil's own juice where conceiving is concerned."

"Then we'll have our own little Damien soon, won't we?" he said, patting her on the hand and striding over to sit on the sofa so he could crack open a can and watch the telly.

The leaky-eyes thing started once again. Veronique had never considered herself a whinger before all this baby lark. But as the months turned to years her desperation snowballed. Every time Derek did something she didn't like, she cried. Every time Derek did something she loved, she cried too.

"Why can't we get pregnant?" she asked him with desolation in her eyes. "We've tried everything over the last two years."

"Ah, come here, love," he said. "I think we should see the doctor. There's all sorts of pills and injections you can get now. Why don't we try those? I bet once we get the right drugs we'll be popping the babies out left, right and centre."

Veronique loved that about Derek. He never lost faith.

For his part Derek idolised his Veronique.

Their trip to the doctor led them swiftly to a specialist who prodded and poked her and sent her for tests she'd never imagined existed.

"I feel like a science experiment, Derek," she said unhappily.

"I'm sorry you're having such invasive tests, love," he answered guiltily. "It'll be my turn soon I'm sure." He was unable to hide the fear in his eyes.

The fertility specialist was quick to correct Derek however.

"The way we work here is that first we rule out any problems with yourself, Mrs Miller. If we can't find anything we'll move on to testing your husband."

Veronique had nodded and smiled, bravely agreeing to do whatever it took.

"I'm not into the idea of having my nether regions explored by the fellas in white coats," Derek whispered then.

"I know, love," she said, rubbing his arm. "It mightn't come to that."

As it turned out they discovered Veronique's fallopian tubes were the issue.

"You'll need IVF in order to conceive," the doctor explained. "I know it may come as a shock to you both. But at least we know where the problem lies and you have options."

"How much will that option cost us?" Derek asked, leaning closer to the consultant.

"Does it matter?" Veronique asked with wide eyes and a wobbly lip again. "There's no price on a baby's life, Derek."

"Yes, there bloody well is," he'd said as he winked at the doctor. "It's all written here on the leaflet."

So they scrimped and saved and found the money for their fertility treatment. The first failure was heartbreaking, but they consoled themselves with the knowledge that it only worked on approximately thirty-five per cent of couples aged between thirty-five and forty.

"We'll try again," Derek promised.

When the pregnancy didn't take the second time Veronique thought she'd die of a broken heart.

"I thought it would all happen so easily once we did what the clinic told us to do," she sobbed to Derek.

"I know, love. And we did it all right. I guess this just isn't our time."

The third attempt drained their life savings and nearly killed Veronique. Her body filled with fluid and she ended up in hospital on the critical list.

"We can't go again," Derek stated once he had Veronique home safely from the hospital. "None of it would be any use if you end up dead."

Reluctantly Veronique had to agree. They'd come to the end of the line financially. Or so they thought.

When her unmarried old-maid Auntie Marie died and left a sizeable amount of money to be split evenly between the cats' home and Veronique, Derek knew by the look on his wife's face where the money would go.

"This is the last time. I promise," she said.

Derek wanted to say no. He was worried sick something was going to happen to his precious wife. But the soulless look that had haunted her face for months had vanished at the spark of hope she was now feeling.

Reluctantly Derek agreed.

"You're pushing forty," the consultant said, pointing out the obvious. "The chances of success are slim. Are you sure you want to risk it?"

Veronique looked at Derek beseechingly.

"This is the very last time," he said firmly. "If you ask me to do this again the answer will be no. I can't take any more."

"I understand," she promised.

The angels, saints and holy fathers were obviously smiling down on them that time. Several weeks later the pregnancy was confirmed.

"Are you alright, love?" Derek asked his ashen-faced Veronique. "Did you hear what the doctor said? It worked! We're having a baby!"

Veronique sat perfectly still, staring at the wall in total silence for the longest time. Paralysed by emotion that her dream was finally becoming a reality, she felt utterly overcome. Derek had to lead her by the elbow from the surgery.

To say she tip-toed around for nine months was not an exaggeration. Nearly every book written about pregnancy and birth found its way through their front door. Veronique became an expert on antenatal care.

"Don't put that near me, Derek, it might harm the baby."

"It's a Snickers bar! What on earth is wrong with that?" he asked in shock.

"It has peanuts. They're potentially dangerous to unborn children. He or she could end up with a desperate peanut allergy, go into anaphylactic shock and die before his or her first birthday."

"It's not even born yet. Surely you'd have to consume it or feed it to the child after it's born? How could the baby have a reaction to a sealed bar of Snickers?" Her don't-mess-with-me-Derek-Miller expression told him it would be safer if he went out to the garden shed to sit on an upturned wheelbarrow and eat the bar. It was just easier.

The day the baby was born Veronique was a trooper. She

endured fifteen hours of labour and only took a few puffs of gas and air.

"I want the full experience," she managed to utter between contractions. As her face turned an alarming shade of violet and her eyes bulged, Derek wished it was still the 1950s where fathers waited with a cigar poised to be told the good news on the other end of the phone.

"Good girl, yourself," he said shakily as a scene akin to the worst horror movie he'd ever watched unfolded.

When they handed him his son swaddled in a blanket with soft peachy skin and a shock of dark hair just like his own, all the previous trials and tribulations melted away. None if it mattered any longer.

"He's perfect," he said as he sobbed. "Look at me, bawling like a little girl," he said grinning.

"Isn't he just beautiful, Derek?" Veronique asked proudly. "And he's all ours."

Bentley Derek Miller was christened a month later. Every family member, friend, neighbour and colleague they'd ever encountered came along to help them celebrate.

"This day has to be perfect," Veronique stated.

She'd spent the nine months of her pregnancy saving and organising the ceremony. The christening robe came from Italy. The catering was done by the chef from a five-star hotel. Everyone agreed Bentley was worth the long wait.

Books were still a massive influence on Veronique's mothering skills. When she wasn't tending to Bentley she was reading how best to do so.

"Cow's milk has larger molecules of fat which the body finds difficult to digest. So anything containing cow's milk is now barred from this house," she instructed Derek when weaning time came around.

Derek had taken up DIY as a hobby to replace long hours on the golf course away from his son. So he now owned a shed that was so impressively decked out most people would proudly live in it.

Unbeknownst to his wife, he installed a small fridge out there, filled with chocolate yoghurts and cream cakes. He figured they tasted even better because they were forbidden.

Veronique joined every mother and baby group in a five-mile radius. Herself and Bentley went to everything from baby yoga to music appreciation classes.

"There's no point in having a child if we're not going to spend time with him. I can't understand why people have children and leave them in crèches their entire lives," she scoffed.

"Well, some people have no choice, love," Derek reasoned. "Not everyone is as lucky as us. Circumstances can determine a lot. You shouldn't judge people harshly just because they don't do things the same way you do."

Veronique knew Derek was right but she couldn't help feeling a smug sense of superiority all the same.

By the time Bentley was ready to start Montessori, Veronique had researched and visited all the schools in the area. Satisfied she'd chosen the crème de la crème of establishments, she eagerly awaited his first day.

"I'll be feeling mixed emotions leaving him," she told Derek. "Heartbroken at the thought of being parted from him for even a few hours, but overwhelmingly proud that he's reached such a pivotal point in his young life."

"He'll be grand," Derek said, patting her hand. "And so will you. It'll do you good to have a couple of hours to yourself. You've yourself worked to the bone with that boy. Not that he doesn't deserve it. But I've never known a mother to be so dedicated."

Veronique knew it was outstanding that Bentley could read, almost fluently play pitch-perfect Suzuki-method violin, swim like a little fish and speak more French than his father. But she felt the time and effort she'd invested in their son would stand to him.

"He'll have so many doors open to him by the time he leaves school," Veronique insisted, with her eyes shut and a smug smile she couldn't hide. "I'm simply doing my job as a mother properly."

She knew some of the mothers at the school envied her. She'd caught a few of them glowering at her on more than one occasion. But she could deal with that. She justified it all by thinking they simply wished their children were as amazing as Bentley.

Play dates were a vital part of development according to all the books. So Veronique made certain to invite a good variety of children, both boys and girls, to the house regularly.

"Sharing is caring, Bentley," she'd say ad nauseam. "You must be kind and thoughtful so your friends know they are welcome here."

His birthday party was second to none. The gods were smiling down as the sun shone that late September day.

"Mothers and fathers are more than welcome to stay if little ones are nervous," Veronique announced.

Not only had she an amazing spread of home-baked cakes, biscuits and tiny finger sandwiches, but there was smoked salmon on bread, tasty tapas, wine and champagne on offer for the parents.

The face-painting distracted little people as the puppet show was set up. For those who didn't like the bouncy castle there was a young enthusiastic artist with a crafts table where the children could make masks, paint pictures and fashion animals from play dough.

"I know not all children enjoy rough and tumble," Veronique said wisely. "So I wanted to cater for all tastes. I'd hate to think of anyone leaving today saying they didn't have fun."

"Oh, I can't imagine that happening," Macy O'Rourke said.

Did Veronique detect a slight tone of sarcasm in the other woman's voice?

"Yes, God forbid," Anna Connolly said with an unmistakable sneer.

"So when are your children's birthdays and what plans have you made for their parties?" Veronique asked evenly with an unfaltering smile.

"Ah, Simon's birthday is during the Christmas holidays,

thank God," said Macy. "So I'll get away without doing a party. His brothers and two cousins can help him blow out candles. That'll do. When I have four children at home, believe me, the last thing I need is other people's landing in as well."

"I wish I could have the same complaint," Veronique clipped. "Derek and I would have loved more children. But I'm not going to spend my life being sour and dissatisfied with my lot."

Their cosy chat was interrupted by bloodcurdling screaming.

"Bentley, darling! What happened?" Veronique called out, rushing to her son's aid.

"Simon kicked me!" he sobbed.

"Simon!" Macy yelled. "Come here!"

"No, I won't!" Simon shouted rudely.

"Get over here, you little thug! I'll kill you!" Macy warned.

"Now, Macy," Veronique interjected, "there's no need to threaten the child that way. Please let's all sit calmly and take stock of the situation. If you can gather Simon to you, we'll talk it through. I'm sure once the boys realise that kicking isn't nice they'll think twice about doing it again."

"Whatever, Veronique," Macy said roughly. "Tell Bentley you're sorry," she instructed, holding a squirming Simon under his arms. "Say it!" she shouted.

"Sorry!" he yelled with a pout.

As she released him, he ran like a greyhound from a trap and flung himself back on the bouncy castle.

"I'm very unsure of your methods," Veronique said honestly. "I've read so many books which document the positive results of talking to your children and explaining other people's feelings. It helps them become mentally enriched."

"He's mental alright," Macy said, guffawing. "But I'm not sure how positive that'll be in years to come!"

The other women tittered so Veronique felt they mightn't be in the right frame of mind to listen openly to her theories.

Several week passed by and when Ms O'Neill, the Montessori teacher, sent a note home in Bentley's school bag that November asking for volunteers to help with the nativity play, Veronique felt a warm glow inside. This would be right up her alley.

"I've filled in the form and signed it in the correct place of course," Veronique told Ms O'Neill the following day. "But I wanted to make certain you understand I *did* intend ticking *all* the boxes. I can help with costumes, baking for the after-show party, make-up on the day *and* painting the backdrop."

"Well, that's above and beyond the call of duty!" said the teacher. "I'm very grateful and will be delighted to have someone so eh – organised – and efficient – to help out."

Veronique couldn't help but notice Macy and Anna sniggering like immature teenagers behind their hands.

"Everything okay there, ladies?" she asked curtly.

"Yup, just fine," Macy said, making a bad job of hiding her mirth.

The more Veronique encountered that woman the less she liked her.

"Am I missing out on a joke?" Veronique asked with one eyebrow raised and a frozen half-smile.

"Uh, nope. Not at all," the other woman said, snorting into her hand. "Anna and I were just talking about a funny incident with one of our kids last week." She elbowed Anna.

"Right," Veronique sighed. "Must've been hilarious if it's still making you both giggle a week on."

As it turned out, it was lucky for everybody Veronique stepped in when she did. Ms O'Neill might have been a fully qualified Montessori teacher, but that didn't mean she excelled when it came to organisational skills.

"According to your list here, there should be three sheep in the nativity play," Veronique said. "Unless you have another box of costumes you're two sheep short."

"What, the flock?" Anna said in mock outrage. "Ms O'Neill, how can you sleep at night?"

"Maybe she counts the sheep and nods off constantly, forgetting to fix the major disaster?" Macy suggested.

The teacher and two other mothers roared laughing.

Veronique smiled to show she was a good sport. Inwardly the silly behaviour was beginning to wear a bit thin with her.

"So who's playing Mary?" she asked, cutting to the chase.

"That'll be my Bethany," Anna said proudly.

"And before there's any sniff of a row," Macy cut in, "my Simon is being Joseph! Correct, Ms O'Neill?"

Veronique's head nearly revolved 360 degrees on her shoulders.

"Why?" she spat, forgetting her usual polite decorum.

"Yes, I promised Macy I'd let Simon be Joseph this year," said Ms O'Neill. "In fairness she's helped out at three previous nativity plays where all her boys have been cattle. So fair is fair, Simon gets the starring role!"

"That hardly seems fair at all," Veronique spat. "Surely it should be decided by the acting ability of the child?"

"Ah, they're only three, Veronique," Anna said condescendingly. "Unless we've a new Macaulay Culkin in our midst I reckon they're all pretty much the same!"

"Well, as it happens, Bentley has been at stage school on a Saturday since September. I know I might be a teensy-weensy bit biased, but I think he's exceptional. Even if I say so myself."

"I'm sure he's a marvel," Ms O'Neill said, "so we'll give him a little speaking part. How about he can be the first innkeeper Mary and Joseph come to? He can do the whole 'No room at the inn' thing. That part requires quite a bit of conviction."

"And he'd have to act like a horrible person," Anna said with a twinkle in her eye.

"Which won't come a bit naturally to him," Macy deadpanned.

"Right," Veronique said, looking furious. "If that's his part, so be it."

She went home that day via the haberdashery store and picked up some cream linen fabric with some stunning gold braiding. If her son was going to be an innkeeper, she was going to design the most wonderful costume for him.

It took a week and every bit of spare time Veronique could shoehorn in between violin, piano, swimming, drama, karate, athletics and horse riding. But she managed to fashion him a very striking tunic with matching headdress.

"Wow!" Ms O'Neill said in astonishment. "With all the gold braiding I think this would be more suited to one of the wise kings," she mused.

"Oh no," Veronique snapped. "This has been made to measure for Bentley."

"Right then," the teacher said uneasily. "Would you be so kind as to make the angel costume also? Macy has used an old rug to make the missing sheep. We've sourced a brown felt donkey from the year before last. Mary and Joseph are sorted too." She ticked off her list.

Veronique had taken it upon herself to write a list of suggested nibbles to be served with tea and coffee after the show.

"Eh, it's usually just a shop-bought mince pie in a napkin while people mill around," Ms O'Neill said.

"Well, let's start a new improved tradition!" Veronique suggested. "Please just leave it all to me. I don't mind, honestly."

As December dawned and the excitement of Christmas began to creep in, Ms O'Neill had a little announcement to make as the parents came for pick-up one Friday.

"Rehearsals will get under way from Monday. I have the costumes here and I hope this year's nativity play will be the best one ever!" She handed out slips of paper with the children's parts and lines neatly typed out.

Simon grinned from ear to ear and jumped up, punching the air as he was told he could be Joseph.

"I want to be Joseph!" Bentley yelled rudely.

"Bentley! Stop that!" Veronique said, flushing with embarrassment. "Wait until you hear who Ms O'Neill wants you to be," she said, praying he'd calm down.

"Yes, Bentley, you're going to be the first innkeeper!" Ms O'Neill announced.

"I won't!" he shouted, folding his arms and pouting. "I want to be Joseph. So I'm going to be Joseph and smelly Simon can be the stupid innkeeper!"

"Now, Bentley darling," Veronique said, bending down to take her son in her arms, "we must have a little chat about shouting and general behaviour." She spoke slowly and clearly. "Mummy wants you to listen while I explain things. Each year Ms O'Neill decides who will do what. This year she has thought it all through carefully and she has made her choices."

"I *hate* her choices," he said, wriggling free of his mother so he could roll on the floor and kick his legs. "I want to be Joseph!" And he burst into hot frustrated tears.

"Sorry about this, everyone," Veronique said, looking up at the disapproving gazes of the other mothers. "Once I explain this concept, Bentley will understand. Children only become unreasonable like this when they are threatened and confused. Darling, listen to Mummy . . ."

As Veronique reasoned and cajoled, Ms O'Neill handed out the rest of the parts.

"The only child in the universe is having another meltdown," Anna said, rolling her eyes as they departed.

"It's hardly his fault, God help him," Macy said. "Your woman is as mad as a brush. How could anyone expect the child to turn out any differently in fairness to him?"

Luckily Veronique was so intent on talking the tantrum through she didn't hear the hurtful remarks.

"So you see," she finished, "it's your duty to do your level best to be the most wonderful innkeeper you can. You inject your own style into your acting."

Ms O'Neill had cleared away all the painting stuff and put the last of the day's mess in the bin by the time Bentley had exhausted himself in the middle of the classroom floor.

Hiccupping and puffy-eyed, he waved limply while giving his teacher the daggers.

"Say good bye to Ms O'Neill properly and tell her you're sorry for getting so upset," Veronique encouraged.

"No," he pouted.

"Bentley, sweetie, the reason we must always do our best to be polite is this . . ."

"Okay. Sorry. Bye," he grumbled.

"Bye, Bentley," Ms O'Neill said wearily. "See you on Monday."

"Have a super weekend!" Veronique said cheerfully as she took her son's hand and led him out to the car. Chattering away happily acting as if the whole world was overrun by tweeting blue birds and blooming roses, she refused to allow the momentary lapse affect their day. Veronique knew *Supernanny*, along with many of the books she'd read, affirmed that moving on and not making small children feel bad about themselves was the way to go after an altercation. So she re-assumed her sunny outlook.

Things became fraught once again, however, when Veronique produced Bentley's lines to learn over the weekend.

"So when Mary and Joseph come to your inn," she explained, "Joseph will say 'Is there any room at the inn? My wife needs to have a baby and we've no place to stay.' You're meant to pretend to be rather mean and nasty. So put on a cross voice and say, 'No, I don't have any room! Now move away!' Do you get that?"

"I still want to be Joseph!" Bentley said, bursting into tears.

"That's enough of that now, son," Derek began. "You're the innkeeper – so get with the plot!"

"Derek!" Veronique chided crossly. "Talk the problem through, remember? Explain about others' feelings and how his negative actions may affect them," she warned in a hushed tone through gritted teeth.

"Are you sure about all this, Veronique?" Derek asked, looking doubtful. "In my day, if I talked to my parents like that I'd get a clip around the ear or a smack on the arse. That was the end of it."

"Times have moved on since that kind of brutal treatment of children was deemed acceptable," Veronique said, closing her eyes to block out such an image. "Young people today are nurtured and encouraged. It's so much more healthy and positive."

"Well, it did me no harm," Derek said doubtfully. "But I'll go along with whatever you say. I'll leave you to it. I'll be in the shed."

Veronique hadn't noticed the black cable running from the house to Derek's shed. She'd no idea he had a reclining leather chair and flat-screen television to keep the fridge company out there.

"Please just work with me for a few more minutes, Bentley," she begged.

"I don't want to do any more lines," Bentley sighed, his eyes glazed over and bored. "I want to watch *Ben 10*!"

"You can watch half an hour of television," Veronique promised. "But only once you've shown me you're going to comply with Ms O'Neill and be a good innkeeper."

"I don't want to be the stupid . . ."

Bentley stopped in his tracks. A sense of calm prevailed and his expression changed. "Okay, Mummy," he said sweetly. "I'll be the innkeeper."

"Good boy!" Veronique said, clapping, rewarding his good behaviour and putting aside the previous badness. "You're such a wonderful child. I'm so proud of you."

On the day of the show all the parents filled into the school hall. Veronique, Anna and Macy helped Ms O'Neill with the make-up and ensured all the children were dressed correctly in their costumes.

"The after-show teas and coffees are ready to rock and roll," Anna said. "The cakes you baked are really gorgeous, Veronique," she added grudgingly. "Fair play to you."

"Thank you! I'm thrilled you noticed. I spent hours on the icing." Veronique glowed.

The lights dimmed and the excitement was palpable as the tiny tots' nativity play got under way. All the parents and grandparents wiped little tears of pride and joy as each of their little dotes made his or her appearance.

Veronique and Derek felt like they'd burst such was the emotion that washed over them when Bentley's entrance approached. The cardboard door worked like a dream as Joseph knocked three times.

"What do you want? Why are you bothering me?" Bentley asked crossly as he answered the door.

Veronique looked over at Derek with glassy eyes brimming with pride.

"Isn't he brilliant?" she managed.

"Amazing," Derek agreed, shaking his head in awe.

In a monotone, little Simon, dressed in his Joseph costume, deadpanned. "Is there any room at the inn? My wife needs to have a baby and we've no place to stay."

As Mary and Joseph prepared to move to the next door, Bentley stood forward, opened his arms out widely and spoke cheerfully and clearly.

"Yes, I have a beautiful suite overlooking the mountains. You and Mary are very welcome. Come in!"

The last thing Veronique heard before she fainted from shock was the raucous laughter ringing out in the school hall.

❖❖

Emma Hannigan lives in Bray, Co Wicklow with her husband and two children.

She's the author of four bestselling novels *Designer Genes, Miss Conceived, The Pink Ladies Club* and *Keeping Mum* along with her memoir, *Talk to the Headscarf*.

Emma has made numerous television and radio appearances discussing both her writing and her candid approach to battling cancer. She is currently in remission for the eighth time and sincerely hopes her future continues to be bright and healthy.

For further information on Emma check out her website www.emmahannigan.com or follow her on Facebook AuthorEmmaHannigan or on Twitter @MsEmmaHannigan

Christmas Snow

Sarah Harte

"Is he coming?" a small voice says.

The hot breath of her daughter tickles her ear. She is a mass of hair and softness. Her butterball form rolls towards her mother.

"Yes," she says, unsure of whom her daughter means.

It is Christmas Eve, she realises. Her children have been crossing off the days on a calendar, marking each day with a red cross. Her eyes focus and come to rest on her son. He is standing by the door pivoting on one leg. He is wiry like his father.

"But will the snow make Dad not come?" he says.

His doubt clouds the room.

"I meant Santa," her daughter says, bouncing on the bed, her arms thrown above her head.

She swings her legs out of bed. The room is so cold she can see her breath. It must be early then. The heating comes on briefly every morning to coincide with their getting up. She looks out the window at the snow-blanketed road. The city is paralysed from the snow. She can feel her son's eyes hot on her back.

"Santa *and* Dad will come," she says.

They are making a snowman on the street. They do not have a garden. But no car can overcome the ice rink that is their road.

"Put the carrot on for his nose, Mammy," her daughter says.

She watches as her son carefully presses two stones onto the snowman's blank face.

He is eight. His sister is four. It has been harder on him. He understands more and does not have her easy way.

"They are his eyes," his sister says.

She blows onto her hands. The country is at a standstill. Cars crawl along only to be abandoned in the drifts of snow. People inch along the path, helping each other, calling out to each other. Ordinary things like benches and bins and roofs are topped with snow so that they become spotless and strangely elegant. There is a beauty to the scene, she knows, but she struggles to find it.

He left Ireland ten months ago with three hundred euro in his pocket, a qualification as a civil engineer and the promise of a job in Boston. They were going to lose their house. Or at least they had got behind in their mortgage payments. The sums didn't add up. It is a story that is by no means just theirs. There are many worse off, she knows. There are days when it seems like the whole country is in a bad mood.

At first, they thought they would be alright. Things would get better. He would find work. Then she lost her job as a sales assistant. Their debts mounted up quickly. That day in Dublin airport was awful. He walked through security quickly, not looking behind him. She knew why he did it like that. The sad, flat back of their son said it all though.

"I think our snowman is cool," she tells her children. "Does he have a name?"

Her daughter thinks for a second before saying "Snowy."

She wishes that her son might give a suggestion. But then she sees his back bending. He is picking up snow and balling it together in his red gloves. Her heart does a little jig. She pretends to run away.

"Don't you dare, Mister!"

Her daughter giggles.

"*Ow!*" she mock-cries as he pelts her.

They have a little snow fight. It is one of the good moments, she thinks afterwards.

"It's greedy to put up a stocking that is so big," her son says, standing by the mantelpiece.

She looks at him. He is eight years of age. Sometime she finds it hard to decipher what he is thinking. Does he know more than he should? They have tried to protect him. There are times now when she finds herself thinking that life is about learning to deal with loss but he is too young for that.

"It's *not*, sure it's not?" his sister says, looking towards her for reassurance.

"Santa will leave what he's going to leave," she says. "He doesn't mind what kind of a stocking you leave."

Her mobile begins to ring. She snatches it up and leaves the room.

"Dublin Airport is open again," her sister tells her.

"I know."

"Any news from him?"

"He's on the last flight tonight out of Boston. In theory at least."

He is camped out at the airport. She tries to imagine what it is like at Logan. Bedlam. she thinks. She has seen scenes from other airports on the telly. There is a snow blizzard there, he says, which makes her stomach churn.

"It's the last scheduled flight to arrive in Dublin," she says, trying to sound positive, "due to arrive at three forty in the morning." Then she adds, "He said the queue at the rebooking desk was miles long."

"Seán would manage it though if anyone could," her sister says, playing ball.

"Half the planes are in the wrong place, airports have run out of de-icer all over the place," she hears herself say with the authority of somebody who has been obsessively checking the news.

She could tell you all sorts of snow-related facts, like that it was the first time in a hundred and twenty-eight years that snow had fallen in Atlanta, Georgia.

"He'll make it – wait till you see."

"Yes," she says, the contours of his face swimming into her mind's eye.

She has seen him on Skype of course but is not the same. She longs to touch and be touched.

"Can you imagine how emigrants must have felt before?" he'd said in the too-bright voice she hates, "before Skype and before email?"

They are not good at this sort of communication. Their conversations are forced. Sometimes they are banal and she thinks that they have nothing to say.

"Can you imagine how isolated they must have felt?" he said.

She hopes that he is okay of course. But she wants him to be lonely too. She wants him to need her, to long for his little family.

She is amused at the thought of him cooking. In the long tradition of the son of an Irish Mammy he doesn't know how to boil an egg.

"I manage," he says.

Most likely he eats junk, she thinks. He washes his own clothes now apparently. He has had some disasters, he said. A red sock left in the drum by one of the other fellas. A guy from Portlaoise. Nice, he said, but a bit of an eejit. Fond of the jar.

That was a good conversation. She laughed when she imagined him wearing his pink T-shirt.

But there have been others that have not gone so well. One of the guys ended up in jail for a couple of days, he said, because of an argument with a woman. She wondered then about what sort of fellas he was shacked up with, about how they might influence him, about what kind of a hard-scrabble life they might be leading. He didn't like that.

"It was a misunderstanding," he said. "He's a good guy. It's not like I'll be influenced by anyone. I'm not a child."

She had hung up on him. That had been a bad couple of days.

She has always had a bit of a jealous streak and her mind played tricks on her. She is scared too that something is lost. In those months before he went they fought a lot. How can you not fight when you are crippled with worry? Love cannot remain untouched in those circumstances.

So she has imagined him in a house with five other Irish guys in a suburb of South Boston. They can't work all the time. They must get lonely. Seán is handsome. He is tall with nice smiling Irish eyes.

Seán is not that kind of a man. But still. Their son is not the only one with doubts.

She hasn't gone to Mass in years. Yet here she is in a pew clutching her children's hands.

"Will Santa come and think I'm not there or that I'm not in bed and not leave my presents?" her daughter says in the too-loud voice of a small child as they take their seats.

"No," she says, hushing her.

She focuses on the stained-glass window and blinks. The music is getting to her.

Her mother has sent a Christmas pudding and a Christmas cake. Her mother flings things into the oven without it costing her a thought. Baking is not her own strong suit though. At school she gave up home economics. She nearly drove her teacher, a nice but nervy woman, into the nuthouse with her burnt fairy cakes and grubby bits of fabric with stitches going the wrong way.

But this week she made buns for her kids so that the house would have the nice smell of baking she remembered from when she was small. The buns when she yanked them from the oven just in time were like mini Leaning Buns of Pisa but she had corrected the slant with icing and chocolate buttons. The kids were thrilled so she was pleased. Her son had licked the spoon and said he thought they were "gorgeous".

Her parents visit regularly but not now because of the snow. She thinks of them stuck outside in the white countryside near

Castlebar. After their visits there are always fifty-euro notes found in odd places. Now with the snow they have sent money in the post, for a turkey and ham and all the trimmings. The support should be flowing the other way, she thinks, her eyes welling.

The beautiful clear voice of the soprano rings out.

"*Oh Holy Night! The stars are brightly shining. It is the night of the dear Saviour's birth.*"

Her face is damp.

"Are you crying, Mammy?" her daughter asks.

"No," she says, dredging up a smile. She bends down and whispers, "I just think the singing is beautiful."

She reaches for her son's hand. She squeezes it. He does not take it away.

Afterwards they are invited next door for a drink. It will be late for her little girl to be up. They will not stay long. But they will go. Their neighbours have been good. Although he is older he has shovelled snow for her, clearing her path, checking on her. His wife has often bought things in the supermarket in duplicate "by mistake". People are kind, she thinks.

Later she stands in the neighbours' with a glass of something in her hand. She feels a little dazed. She had made an effort with her appearance but she feels shabby. Her roots need doing. She is too thin. Not sexy thin, the sort of thin that ages you. She doesn't really care. Not like she used to when she used to spend time and money on herself as if she was some sort of monument to be preserved.

The neighbours' house is comfortable. It's different, with lino and wallpaper and a pot plant in a brass pot on a stand inside the hall door. Their own 'two up two down' is all floorboards and white walls although now pockmarked with smudges and children's paw-prints. The loo seat is cracked. When he comes he can fix that. When he comes.

Here the fire is roaring up the chimney. There are sandwiches on the table and a box of biscuits from which her daughter is choosing, thrilled with herself. There are cards on the mantelpiece.

They do not have children. Her neighbour seems like the type who would have wanted them. She is so good to her two. She thinks she has seen a look in her eye. Everyone has their cross to bear, she tells herself. Other people have worries too.

She tries not to be bitter. If you were to let it, it could swallow you. That is the strange part, she thinks. She would never have thought of herself as that type of person but when she sees politicians mouthing on the telly, so-called experts sounding off about why Ireland has to pay back foreign debt she finds the bile rising in her throat. What do they know about ordinary people like them? She finds herself thinking nasty thoughts that scare her about big shots.

One day she saw a female politician on a walk-about outside the shopping centre. The kids had been at school. She looked at her in her fancy coat laughing with some supporters, click-lacking around in high heels with nice shiny blow-dried hair. She had seen a picture of her recently in the paper at some bun fight with a glass of champagne in her hand. She had stormed up to her like a madwoman, not knowing what she was going to say. She started giving out, using the F-word so that afterwards she thought of her mother at home in Mayo who would have been horrified. "You weren't brought up to talk like that," she imagined her mother saying. The anger had ripped through her. She had made garbled points about the banks and Seán. She had not given the woman a chance to respond, turning away instead and powering home on the heat of her anger. It was not strictly speaking the woman's fault. And yet she had wanted to punish her. It had frightened her how mad she had felt. She could see why people turned to crime.

Her neighbours' mother is talking to her, she realises. She is very old with white hair and a strong Dublin accent like her in-laws.

"God is good," she says to her, clutching her hand so that she is roused from her thoughts. "He'll bring your husband home to you."

She musters a smile. But the radio told her earlier that a plane destined for the States was left standing on the runway at Dublin Airport for seven hours. Then the passengers were asked to disembark. She imagines them trooping off tired and angry. For the first time then she thinks he will definitely not come.

"It's the tradition that the youngest gets to do it," she says, lighting the match.

"Is it so that Santa knows the way?" her daughter asks, standing on tiptoe to reach the sill.

She guides the small chubby hand.

"The lighted candle means that any weary traveller with no shelter knows that they are welcome in our home," she says.

"It's because Mary and Jesus couldn't find anywhere to stay," her son says. "They had to stay in a stable. It's to let them know that they could stay in our house."

"Yes," she says.

He is a clever little boy. His face upset her at the school Christmas concert. He was standing on the stage with the other boys, his recorder in his hand, about to murder some tune. She saw him looking out into the crowd. He was looking for her. But then she sensed him looking at the other daddies.

She does not like the vulnerability in his face, the way he goes silent. He needs his father there to witness his little triumphs and to help with the small failures and fears.

"Daddy will be proud," she said when he learnt how to tie his laces.

She thinks of what she heard on the radio.

"*Dublin Airport Authority has said it is working with airlines to provide accommodation for those passengers who remain stranded at Dublin Airport this evening. Thousands more remain stranded at other airports because of freezing conditions.*"

"Bedtime," she says. "Santa is making his way across the globe."

She, like many other parents, found herself in the run-up to Christmas saying things like "If you're not good Santa won't come." She wonders if that sort of talk is psychologically damaging.

It's much harder on your own. She has developed a new-found respect for single parents.

"And the cake and whiskey are on the table for Santa," her daughter says, checking this fact again.

"Yes."

"And the carrot for Rudolph?"

"Yes," she says, tucking her in.

Her daughter's conversation goes round and around. Will the other reindeers not be jealous that there are no carrots for them? Will Rudolph share his carrot with them? Will Santa get stuck in the chimney? She has endless energy for her cross-questioning.

Finally she says that she thinks she can hear sleigh-bells in the sky. Her daughter's eyes boggle and she shuts her eyes dramatically.

Then she makes her way over to her son's bed. He is facing the wall. She touches his hair. He does not move.

"Pet," she says, turning him gently.

"Dad's not coming," he says, his mouth twisted.

"He is so," she says, thinking that she might lose it.

There was one day when she did. She was trying to change a plug and she couldn't manage it. She was getting her period and everything got to her. She sat at the kitchen table and cried. She found an arm slung around her neck then.

"Are you okay, Mammy?" he had asked, his eyes round with concern so that she felt guilty.

That was bad parenting. But mainly she has coped, she thinks. There is a Christmas tree in the living room to prove it. She dragged it home herself. It is a little bit off kilter but she got it up and they decorated it. They listened to 'Fairytale of New York' which is a beautiful song but which caused her to turn her back on her children to steady herself. More Irish people leaving in search of a better life, she thought.

"You'll see," she says, wondering if she should be giving him false hope. "He'll come."

It is midnight and she throws another briquette on the fire. She will keep the fire going. The heating is on too so that the house is cosy. The last gas bill was huge. She cried when she opened the letter and her eye settled on the figure at the bottom. The Gas Board was good, they let you pay in increments, they worked with you – but Christmas was so expensive. She didn't want to think about January. It is Christmas night so she won't concern herself with that for now.

He had texted at seven. He said that cancelled flights were disappearing from the board but that his was still up. He was with a bunch of Irish guys. Another text came at eight. He thought they might be about to board the plane. Fingers crossed. She knew though that this did not necessarily mean that there was a bunch of Paddies winging their way home to their families. They have been through this palaver before. There had been two painful dress rehearsals. She has heard nothing since that last text.

There are young ones going up the road singing. Roaring, more like. She hears a great clatter of laughter.

"Ah Jaysus, hang onto me, you tool!"

She smiles. She remembers being like that herself. She looks at the picture of Seán's graduation on the wall. In the picture his parents look as if he has planted a flag on the moon. He is the first and only one in his family to go to college. His mother has his degree in her hall. His pose is jokey with his parchment balanced on his foot. She met him that night in Copper Face Jacks. They got plastered.

Life in those days seemed like one long party. You got up in the morning and unfurled yourself from sleep before eating brunch out and reading the papers. Money was not a real concern. They had a double income and no kids. They were the generation that thought they were worth it like the shampoo ad said.

She misses her job in the boutique. She liked advising women what to wear. She was good at it, she thought. People trusted her. She told the truth but in a nice way. She didn't let women walk out of the shop looking like holy frights like some might. They bought their house on the fringes of the city near the zoo, up from the Liffey. It was a daring thing to do so young. They bought it for too much, but not as much as some poor fools. He and his brothers did the bulk of the work on it. They had the kids. She felt blessed. He was doing well. The only way was up.

She has spoken to her parents.

"I wish I was there with you," her mother says.

"We'll be fine," she says, careful to conceal her worry.

"Ring, won't you, if you hear anything?" her mother says. "Please. No matter what time."

"I will," she said before setting down the phone.

She debates whether to uncork the wine that is sitting in her fridge. She decides against it. She might not stop at the glass or two. A bottle wouldn't satisfy her tonight. She settles for a cup of tea instead and sets the Santa presents under the tree: a bike for him, a doll and her house for her. She fills the Christmas stockings.

Eight inches of snow has fallen on Dublin airport the internet tells her.

She is tipsy. She allowed herself some wine. Too much. The bottle stands virtually empty, accusing her. It is five o'clock in the morning. She should go to bed. But she cannot bear to occupy that space in the centre of the bed again. She feels a little lightheaded. She can see the snowman's blue scarf through the window. She puts on her coat and goes outside. She will have a cigarette. Her sneaky pleasure. She forgets to close the door so that a pool of light follows her. The world glows. Fingers of light are streaking the sky. The flame of the match illuminates the snowman's face. He is not coming, she thinks. She has accepted that. She wonders what she will say to her son.

It is silent. She glimpses the lights of the city below. She thinks she hears a car. She cocks her head like an animal listening. Yes, she is right. Somebody is having a conversation at the end of their hill. She hears a car door dinging. She inches forward. The path is icy. She nearly slips. She makes her way a little further. Snowflakes melt in her hair.

She sees two figures coming up the hill. It's not him then. It's not fair, she thinks, trembling. She doesn't move.

Then she hears her name being roared. She stares. Her name rings out again. She doesn't move. He nearly falls but rights himself cursing.

"Seán," she says.

He is up close now. She feels shy. But then their bodies are flung together. They are kissing like in a movie. Her head is pressed against his breast then. When they part he says that his phone went dead. He couldn't ring when they landed. There was a scrum to get out of there anyway. He says something about giving a fellow a bed for the night. She thinks that he looks a little ragged. There is a man with reddish hair and bugsy teeth behind him. He is grinning too. They shared a taxi. Her husband gives her some rambling story about having to pay "through the nose" to persuade a taxi-man to bring them this far. They are a little drunk, she thinks. Of course they can give a stranger a bed, she says, it's Christmas Eve. There's a bloody candle lighting in the window. And she doesn't care about anything now. He's talking about the plane circling the airport. He thought that they might not be able to land. The words are washing over her. She can't stop crying. It's Christmas and he's back. It will be alright.

❧

Sarah Harte lives in Rathmines with her husband Jay and son Conn. She wanted to be a writer from when she was a little girl so signing to Penguin was a dream come true. She spent her childhood with her nose stuck in a book. Her favourite place to write is the corner of a café with a notebook and pot of tea. She likes to run, play tennis, cook, visit art galleries and most of all to read. Very often she is to be found loitering in bookshops. She has written for the *Irish Independent* and *Village Magazine*. She is the author of *The Better Half*. Her next book *Thick and Thin* will be published on 31 January 2013.

Lonely This Christmas

Emma Heatherington

"Oh, mistress, for definite!"

"You think?" asked Emily.

Tara watched the sharp-suited man almost break down the revolving door of Harvey's department store on his swift entrance.

"I don't think. I *know.*"

The man approached the perfume counter, his hands in pockets, his eyes darting around before he looked at the blur of fragrances that stood behind Tara and her colleague.

"Do you need some help, sir?" asked Tara.

She had seen it all before – the urgency, the nerves, the way he wanted to just choose it, have it wrapped and get out of that goddam department store before he bumped into someone who would recognise him.

"Just – just give me that one," he said.

"What one?" asked Tara.

"That one," he said, pointing to the most expensive fragrance on the shelf. "I'm in a hurry."

"Would you like it wrapped, sir?"

"Will it take long?"

"A few minutes."

"No, it will do like that," he said and swiped his card as quickly as he could, then tucked the fancy box inside his jacket pocket and scarpered towards the door of the department store.

"Happy Christmas," said Tara. "Have a nice day!"

"Men are tramps," said Emily.

"Agreed," said Tara. "A pack of dirty, rotten –"

"Yes, sir, what can I get you?" said Emily.

It was the same routine every day of the year and a game that kept Tara and Emily sane when the Christmas rush set in.

'I love you,' 'I'm sorry', 'Happy birthday,' 'Happy Christmas to my wife – my girlfriend – my lover – my mother –' The girls had seen it all. One man even bought the same perfume for his daughter, mistress and wife in one fell swoop and had the cheek to brag about it!

"No wonder I'm a cynical old bat," said Tara later, on lunch break as they sat in the tiny kitchen to the back of the perfume section of the department store "It will soon be a whole year since . . . since . . ."

"Ssh," said Emily. "Let's not go there. You have a box of Quality Street to get through after that soup and you can't possibly chew on a Toffee Penny and cry at the same time. Especially not over a man! He's gone, Tara. You have to just face it, babe."

Tara felt the rush of heated anxiety run through her veins, just as it did every time she thought of him. Everything at this time of year reminded her of him. The smells, the sounds, the songs, the mood . . . everything.

She played the moment he left her over and over again like a broken record – the things he said, how it stung so badly when he had to go – and now Christmas had come round again and like a raw, open wound the pain seeped deeper and deeper into her broken heart.

"You will get over it, you know," said Emily, licking a piece of chocolate from the side of her mouth. She had abandoned her turkey sandwich and gone for dessert. "I know you don't think so, but you will. The world is full of broken-hearted girls and 'tis the season to be jolly. Plus, you have the Christmas 'do' to look forward to tonight."

Tara reached for a Hazelnut Caramel, then another and another.

Her soup was getting cold and her head was banging from the eggnog she had unintentionally overdosed on the night before at her aunt's 60th birthday bash. The tights she had laid out to wear later under her brand new little black dress had a ladder that an overweight Santa could have easily climbed up and the hairdo she had saved for had been ruined in a flurry of snow when she'd popped out to get a last-minute Secret Santa present for the annual office bash.

She had built up more excuses not to go out than she used to do to get out of PE at school.

"I hate Christmas parties," she mumbled.

"You hate everything, Tara," her colleague replied. "You couldn't please you if David Beckham arrived at that counter out there and performed as a stripping carol singer."

Tara raised an eyebrow and tried not to laugh. "Probably not. But I do *not* hate everything. I like lots of things actually."

"Like what?"

"Em . . ."

"Exactly," said Emily. "Honestly, you need to shake him off! You're far too good a catch and far too good-*looking* to be sitting there as miserable as a wet weekend in Bundoran. Come on, I know it's hard but you *can* do this. I know you can!"

Emily had an answer for everything, always had, always would. She was the same age as Tara but a brighter, much bubblier version. She wore a Santa hat, bright-red lipstick, a skirt that was way too short for the bitter cold weather outside and her positive energy was draining Tara by the second.

"I'm smiling, see," said Tara, forcing a grin on her face. "*See?*"

But Emily was on a roll.

"You really do need to get out more," she said. "And no, your Aunt Bessie's 60th at the old fogies' club last night does not count. It will do you the world of good to go to the staff party tonight. And you never know, you might even meet the man of your dreams. There will be other departments there. The whole shopping complex is going!"

"I already have met the man of my dreams. And I let him go."

Tara took a last spoonful of cold vegetable broth and pushed her bowl to the side. Emily worried about her, she knew that and she was right – she did need to get out more but a posh do at the King's Head with her colleagues and greasy Michael from Menswear was not where she wanted to be heading to that evening.

"It will probably be cancelled because of the weather," she muttered, aiming to convince her own self more than her co-worker. "I'll just play it by ear. If it's still snowing by eight I'm sure I won't be the only one who has cold feet."

"They probably wouldn't even notice if you didn't show up anyhow," said Emily.

"Exactly," Tara replied. "They'll be too busy bitching about who got the biggest bonus and who couldn't handle their mulled wine."

"And don't tell me – that ladder in your tights that you told me about means you couldn't possibly go anywhere because, after all, there's nowhere near *here* you could buy another pair. And the food will be rotten and the free drink will be too expensive and it's at the King's Head and there's no way you would ever go there again and –"

"Okay, okay, you've made your point. I am full of excuses," said Tara. "I just don't think there is any need for all that false mingling and air-kissing under the mistletoe with people you would rather stab than socialise with."

"Oh bah humbug!" said Emily and she lifted their dishes and took them to the sink, her high heels clicking on the porcelain floor. "Well, I am off to the front line again to sell more smelly stuff. I love Christmas and I love any excuse to party. Are you sure you're only thirty-three? It's time you started acting it!"

There was no doubt about it, despite being the same age Tara and Emily were like chalk and cheese, even though they managed to be best friends in the workplace. Emily was tall and leggy with wavy dark hair and a magical personality. Tara was petite and blonde and after working hours she was a secret wallflower whose idea of a good night was one glass of wine in front of a roaring fire with a chart-topping bestseller.

She used to be more sociable. She *tried* to be more sociable nowadays, but the more she tried the more she failed and now, at the ripe old age of thirty-three, she'd had one cringe-worthy experience too many of busting her gut to let her hair down. She looked great on the outside, but inside she felt like she had passed her sell-by date.

The festive do tonight was marked in her mind as a personal challenge to learn to live again, to do that thing that sounded so easy but felt so impossible – to 'move on'. She had been through the wars and she deserved a night out. She worked hard in Harvey's department store all year round and she took great pride in her job as head of Beauty and Make-up. She knew her Elizabeth Arden from her Clarins inside out and was an expert in all things Gaultier. She was popular and pretty and had a team of staff who admired her sharp business savvy and slick knowledge of how to make every customer leave the store feeling that extra bit more beautiful than when they came in.

The office party tonight was her big chance to get on with her life. A chance to prove to herself that she was bigger and better than any heartache and that she could move on after their relationship hit the rocks involuntarily when Adam had gone to Canada for a job offer he just couldn't refuse.

He had begged her to come with him, pleaded with her even, but as much as she longed to pack up and go she had a young child to think of and uprooting him from his friends and taking him away from his father who loved him just wasn't an option.

"Whatever happens, I want you to be happy," he had told her on their last long-distance call.

She had cried like she had never cried before. Like a grief worse than death, she had bid him a final farewell and tried her best to look to the future, but a whole year later she had only taken one step forward and two steps back.

She accepted with devastation that he would have met someone else by now. They had tried to keep in touch at the start but the pain of the distance, the time difference and the long lonely nights tossing and turning and missing his arms around her made her finally call quits to their late-night phone calls and daily Skype conversations.

With Emily gone now to see to the customers, she allowed herself just five more minutes of wallowing in self-pity and wondering what could have been.

She began by drifting back to their first meeting. Their first *actual* meeting which was a long time after the first time they had emailed and weeks after they had spoken on the phone.

He was a Sales Manager, far away in County Cork, for a well-known brand of cosmetics and without having a face to put to his name, they had exchanged email conversations that started off punchy, to the point and businesslike but soon turned to friendly banter and then undeniable flirtation.

"I would love to hear your voice," he had told her one day in an email and just as she read it her phone had rung and she knew it was him. Hearing him was like a bridge over the 300-mile gap that sat between him and was better than any written correspondence they had exchanged in the few weeks before.

"You sound different than I expected," she had told him, giggling like a schoolgirl down the phone as Emily almost did cartwheels in excitement. Like the other girls in the sales team at Harvey's, Emily was as intrigued and excited at the growing romance as Tara was herself.

"You sound beautiful," he had told her. "I want to meet you, so badly."

"I want to meet you too," she'd told him with longing.

Tara remembered every word of that first phone conversation like it was yesterday. They'd exchanged mobile numbers and for three whole weeks afterwards they had talked at any given moment – on her lunch break, on her way home, when her four-year-old son was tucked up in bed, as she drifted off to sleep. When they weren't talking they were texting. When they weren't texting they were thinking about the next time they would talk. From a very long distance and in a very short space of time, Adam had become the love of her life and she hadn't even met him yet.

He arrived in Belfast on a bitter cold December evening two years ago and she had arranged to meet him at a posh hotel, The King's Head, for dinner in town. They had planned in advance every moment of that first encounter. What to wear, what they might say when they came face to face. Would they kiss straight away or would nerves get in the way? Yes, he could have turned up to work in an official capacity with a range of fragrances to tempt her into buying, but that would have felt wrong and unsatisfactory. They wanted to do it properly, like a real date of a young couple who had longed to be together for what seemed like an eternity.

Emily came to baby-sit Callum. Promising him a movie treat and a bedtime story, she had waved Tara off as she left for The King's Head in a taxi with her heart leaping in anticipation and her stomach feeling like it was jumping up and down. Her head told her to expect disappointment – they had discussed that too. What if their meeting was a let-down? What if, in real life, they didn't click as much as they were both hoping for?

The moment itself, when it finally came around, was more mind-blowing than either of them could ever have imagined.

"I'm about five minutes away," she told him on the phone as the taxi weaved its way through city-centre traffic. "Can you please come outside and meet me? I'm so, so nervous!"

The taxi drew nearer to the hotel and she could feel her hands shake as much as her voice as she spoke to him.

"This is weird," he kept saying. "I can't believe we're going to meet up at last."

"Just keep talking to me," she said. "It's like I'm talking to my best friend on the phone but going to meet a complete stranger in real life."

"I will never be a stranger to you," he had reassured her.

She saw the sign for The King's Head and her heart was thumping by now.

"Are you outside?" she asked him.

"Yes, I'm here. Oh my God . . . oh my God I can see you! Tara, I can see you!"

The taxi pulled up and she saw him, holding the phone, still talking to her as if she was miles away. His smile . . . she would never forget how he smiled right then.

He opened the car door and she climbed out as gracefully as her legs could carry her. He was taller than she had imagined, much more handsome than any photos they had exchanged. His hair was darker too and his eyes . . . oh, she could have died happily one day in the faraway future while staring into those eyes.

They both hung up their phones as the moment they had looked forward to unfolded into reality.

"You're real," he said, gently taking her hand and touching her face as if she was a dream come true. "Oh my God, this is real. This is happening."

Then he leaned in and kissed her, softly at first – and then passion and weeks and weeks of longing took over and they embraced like the long-lost lovers they really were.

They never did have dinner that night. There wasn't time to eat.

And so their love had continued . . .

Winter turned to spring and spring to summer and their love blossomed as they met up at every given opportunity that their busy lives and the distance between them allowed. They both knew they would each have major changes to make if they were to be together full-time. He would have to make a move up North, she would have to introduce a new man into her son's life and they had pledged to do it, but then the offer to go to Canada with a huge promotion and the promise of a life he could only have dreamed of came along and turned all their plans upside down.

At first it looked like it could be a new life for both of them, the chance of a new beginning and a future that she longed to spend with him and she thought she would be able to pack up and go. He had booked their tickets, arranged for her and

Callum to follow him out once he had everything set up. Then just before she drove him to the airport she got cold feet, knowing that her reasons for moving to a new country were unfair to her son and his father who loved him with all his heart.

"When will this pain ever go away?" she would ask anyone who would listen as days without him turned into weeks. "Surely someone, somewhere, has some secret to fast-forwarding to a cure for this nightmare I'm going through?"

"You've done the right thing," some would tell her. "Callum needs his dad."

"You should have gone!" others would say. "You were mad to let him go there alone!"

"If he really loved you he wouldn't have left you behind."

Those were the comments that stung the most. *If he really loved you . . .*

But no matter what people said, no matter what anyone did, no one could give her what she wanted.

She wanted *him*. She pined for him, she longed for him and no matter how many times she was told that time would heal, the aching just wouldn't go away.

She had never been close enough to a man to even smell his aftershave since, apart from a drunken snog with greasy Michael from Menswear last year under the mistletoe when she had more brandy in her than a Christmas pudding. She had left that night with a goody bag, a bruised ego, a stagger due to too much alcohol and a family of blisters that had taken up home on her poor feet. Michael would be there again tonight and she knew she would have to swallow her shame of that horrible incident with a polite nod and a wish for a happy and peaceful Christmas even though she would rather stuff her own head up a turkey's ass than offer him season's greetings under the mistletoe again, however much his leery smile told her he was expecting it.

There was no way she was going to the party tonight. She would grab a bottle of wine on the way home, cancel the arrangements with Callum's dad who had agreed wholeheartedly to have him for the night, and listen to sad songs just as she always did when the overwhelming loneliness took over her very insides just as it was doing now.

"Sorry? What? I was miles away."

Tara looked at the clock as Emily's voice brought her back to reality. Shit! It was well after lunchtime. Her little trip down memory lane had taken longer than she intended.

"A childminder who has everything?" said Emily. "A retired lady allergic to alcohol in perfume? A neighbour who is spending Christmas in hospital? Come on, lady, I need some help out here!"

Tara followed Emily out onto the shop floor and wiped a tear from under her eye before painting on her best front-of-house smile. She loved serving customers and Emily's chit-chat always helped to distract her mind from the admin side of her job that haunted her with memories of Adam. His emails, the phone she first spoke to him on, the cards he used to send her, still all lay in a drawer in her desk. She couldn't bear to get rid of them. Not just yet.

"Would you like this wrapped, sir?" she asked a rather dapper elderly gentleman who knew exactly what he wanted.

"Yes, please," he said. "It's for someone very special."

Tara withdrew to the wrapping-table which was equipped with gold and silver paper, gift-tags, cards and sticky tape.

"Wife, for definite," muttered Emily as Tara wrapped the gift. "You see, why can't all men be like him? No beating around the bush. He knows what she likes and he gets it. No bullshit, no hanging around, no –"

"I don't think it's for his wife," murmured Tara. "It's a fragrance for a younger woman."

"Maybe he has a young wife? Maybe he's a sugar daddy. I bet he's minted. He looks rich, doesn't he? Doesn't he, Tara?"

"He does," she said. "Yeah, he does. But no matter what he is, or who he is, he has very good taste. That perfume has been my favourite since it first came in . . . it was the first range I bought from –"

Emily glared at her and strode back to the counter. "Would you like to attach a greeting, sir?" she asked the man.

"Yes, indeed. Can you write 'To My Fiancée', please?"

"Certainly, sir."

Fiancée? The girls exchanged a glance as Emily went back to the table.

Tara wrote the greeting on a little gilt-edged gift-tag, attached it and then handed the gift over to the customer.

"What the –" said Emily after he had left. "We were miles off there."

"Lucky girl," said Tara. "That's my favourite. As I was saying –"

"Oh, here we flippin' well go again!" said Emily. "Honestly, you're starting to wear me out as much as yourself! If I said Kylie Minogue was just in, you would find some way of relating it back to you know who! Why don't you just put yourself and the rest of us out of your misery and go find him?! Go to Canada, Tara! Go there for once and for all!"

Emily left a customer open-mouthed as she stormed away from the counter.

"Maybe I will!" called Tara after her, hot tears stinging her eyes. "Maybe I bloody well will! And where are you going? There are customers!"

"To the loo, is that okay?" said Emily. "Oh, don't tell me, that probably reminds you of him too!"

Tara thought about it. She probably could relate it to him if she tried!

"Sorry, what can I get you?" she asked the startled customer who stood before her.

The man ordered his fragrance in haste. Mistress for definite, she thought. All men are tramps.

"Happy Christmas, sir. Have a nice day."

Tara knew she had to make the effort to show up at the party after Emily's outburst. In a way, it was the tough love she had needed to hear. She couldn't help it and she knew it wasn't healthy to keep relating everything she did in life, every single thing she did or said back to Adam.

Callum was with his dad for the evening so she had no excuses left not to go. Her taxi was waiting outside, she had bought new tights so the ladder-reasoning was gone and a run through with her straighteners had left her hair as glossy as any stylist could make it.

She took a sip from her glass of wine, reapplied her lipstick and told herself that she would and could be the life and soul of the party that evening.

"The King's Head," she said to the driver when she got into the taxi.

She would not let the fact that the party was on at the very venue where she first met Adam get in her way. She would have to face up to the ghosts of her Christmas past once and for all. She had to do it for everyone's sake, but most of all for her own. It would be closure. She hated it, but it would be closure.

As the car pulled up under The King's Head's infamous sign and she paid the fare, the flurry of snow grew heavier outside. Then her mobile rang and she reached into her handbag to answer it. No doubt it was Emily, calling to make sure she hadn't chickened out.

It wasn't Emily.

It was Adam.

"Tara, I can see you," said his beautiful familiar voice and when she looked out of the window, she saw him standing there.

"Oh my God! Adam! What the –?"

He opened the door and she stepped outside, feeling like she was living some sort of cruel dream, just like those that had haunted her for months and months. She hung up her phone and he did the same.

"Adam?" she said again, her heart and mind scrambling to make sense of what was happening.

"You're real," he said, taking her hand, the other touching her face.

It was like she had stepped back in time, but it was real and it was now and he looked just like he had on that first night.

He reached into his jacket pocket and took out a gift-wrapped perfume. She read the tag that she had written herself only hours earlier.

To My Fiancée, it read.

"I sent someone for this earlier," he said. "I knew it was your favourite."

"It is," she whispered. She could barely breathe.

"I will never, ever leave you again, Tara," he said. "Will you marry me? Please?"

She looked up into his dark eyes and knew that she would happily die looking into them one day, way, way into the future.

"I will," she said.

"I hoped you might say that!" he replied. "Now, let's go inside. I think I owe you dinner in here?"

"I think you do," she said.

"Happy Christmas, Tara."

"Happy Christmas, Adam."

Fiancée, she thought, looking at the man of her dreams and her heart swelled with joy.

Fiancée, for definite.

Emma Heatherington is from Donaghmore, County Tyrone, where she lives with her three children Jordyn, Jade and Adam. She is the author of seven novels, two of which were written under the pseudonym Emma Louise Jordan for Poolbeg's Crimson range. By day, Emma works full time as a PR Manager in Belfast and, by night, she writes scripts for theatre and short film for audiences of all ages. She loves live music, celebrity-stalking, red wine and has a lifelong, very public, love for Marti Pellow (she will grow out of it one day . . . !) Emma's next novel, *One Night Only*, is due for release in Spring 2013.

Underneath the Mistletoe

Michelle Jackson

This wasn't how Anna thought she would feel on her thirty-fourth Christmas. At sixteen, she had thought that by now she would be living in a big house with her adorable husband and their beautiful children, waking from slumber to see what Santa had brought. But that was the foolish happy-ending dream of a teenager. She'd had her white wedding seven years before – it was the perfect day. All of her family and friends were there, looking fine, and Simon's family agreed that they were a perfect match – everyone had said so. For seven years she had hosted Christmas dinner for Simon's family and hers but the clink of the Waterford crystal glasses couldn't drown the heaviness pounding in her heart. She knew things were wrong, she had known for the last three Christmas dinners just how wrong. But still she had gone along with the charade of basting the turkey and icing the Christmas cake. At least she wouldn't have to do it this year. Her parents were hosting Christmas and had promised that they would serve her steak and not a single wrapped present would be opened in her presence.

Her brother, Donal, was only too delighted at the prospect of gulping down a steak before making his way to his girlfriend's in

Wexford – he would probably stay there for the New Year. Her mother had got used to the idea and was prepared for the imminent loss of her son. But it was the way that her daughter's marriage had ended so abruptly that had caused such shock and consternation.

For Anna it wasn't a surprise – she was glad that it had come to this. She'd always known that it would some day but now that the day was here it didn't hurt any the less. She had friends – good friends that would take her out and support her. It was not as if all of her friends were married yet – ironic how she was the first to be married and now she would be the first to be separated.

It had been going this way since she told Simon that she didn't want children. She spoke the truth. She had never known that longing but thought that her antipathy was like an itch that would just go away and someday she would wake up longing to be pregnant. But as the days and weeks of her marriage to Simon passed she wanted children less and less. She often felt really bad about it and bad for him.

She was too young for all that, wasn't she? But suddenly, at thirty-four and separated, she felt very old. Her pain felt like a boil that needed to be lanced – her seven-year marriage, her nine-year relationship could be summed up simply as a boil. She felt her heart ache, for although she didn't want him back – that was not an option, he was firmly in love with someone else – he had been hers once and they had uttered the words 'I do for as long as we both shall live.' Had she crossed her fingers at the top of the aisle – had he? She couldn't remember and now she didn't care. But why did it all have to happen at Christmas time? For some reason every emotion was amplified at Christmas.

As she drove the short distance to her parents' house she wondered how Simon would be spending this Christmas – their first apart. Simon had met his new girlfriend at work. It was a well-known fact that certain nurses saw their employment as an opportunity to land themselves a doctor. It just so happened that Simon's nurse wanted him. Anna didn't blame *her* – she was just a party to the entire sad event that had become her marriage break-up.

Anna's father opened the door to his daughter. He didn't ask if she had been to Mass – it would have been important to him at one time but in the midst of his daughter's pain he felt that it was insignificant. She followed him into the house where her mother had been careful not to place one Christmas decoration. Only the crib, nestled in the corner of the living room, was a reminder that it was a festive time of year.

They went into the kitchen where her mother was cooking the steaks.

As Anna hugged her, Donal pounded down the stairs and shook his bed-head on entering the kitchen. He walked over to his mother and nodded a greeting at his sister. "Smells good, Mum! I much prefer steak to turkey – we should have this every year."

Anna's mother tapped her son playfully on the wrist. "Have some respect for your sister – she's had a terrible few months."

"Ah, she knows she's been saved from a fate worse than death – Simon was always a prig – you'd only end up being one of them yummy mummies, Anna!"

Anna's mother coughed awkwardly as she had a habit of doing during these conversations. She realised that her chances of grandchildren were now in the hands of her wayward son. She had been very pleased that he had not impregnated any girls in his teens but now longed for a grandchild under any circumstances.

"Anyway, Christmas is all about kids – you always said that, Mum, and we don't have any in this family so it doesn't matter!" Donal said, taking a slice of garlic bread from the grill. "I love this food – top marks."

Anna's mother held her daughter's hand in a gesture of support as her son left the kitchen. "He doesn't understand, pet."

Anna looked into her mother's eyes – she seemed to understand how Anna felt better than she did herself.

Once the steaks were eaten they moved to the living room

where coffee and Pavlova were served. Anna shuffled restlessly in her seat. She wanted to be in her own home. Simon had said that he would be back in three days so at least she would have the house to herself for now – until the separation details had been legalised.

"Turn that Daniel O'Donnell off – he's singing Christmas songs," Anna's mother said.

"What do you expect him to be singing?" her husband huffed.

His wife cast him a killer glance and he changed station but only festive movies were showing on the other channels.

"Is it okay if I go now?" Donal asked, looking at his watch. He wanted to get going while there was still some light left in the sky.

"Of course, son – have a nice time." His mother kissed him resolutely and watched her daughter stand up to put on her coat also. "Going so soon, Anna?"

"I want to get home and call a few of my friends."

"Are you sure you won't stay? You can call them from here!"

Anna shook her head. Spending the night in her old bedroom would be one step too far – it would be admitting defeat. She would not return to her parents' care. She was a grown woman who would have to deal with her situation herself.

"Thanks for the offer but I really would rather be in my own house."

Her mother understood but it was such a solemn way to end the day – and so early too. Anna had tried her best to be in good spirits but it hadn't compensated for the lively banter that they had all come to expect at Christmas time – in a way it was like a bereavement. She wondered if her daughter would have been better off if she'd had a child – but she dismissed the thought when she pictured Simon. He was one person that she wanted to 'handbag' – an emotion that she had never felt before. Anna was saddened by this desire of her mother's and made her promise never to even speak with her wayward son-in-law. Reluctantly her mother agreed for her daughter's sake but secretly she hoped that the day would come as she passed him by on the corridor

of some hospital and she could just lash out and tell him how hateful he had been to her daughter.

of some hospital and she could just lash out and tell him how hateful he had been to her daughter.

Anna's father kissed her on the forehead as she left. She drove to her empty house. She never wanted to remember the rest of that Christmas Day but it involved copious boxes of tissues and a bottle of red wine which she drained from the comfort of her bed.

The next morning was bright and cold but her head throbbed and, although Christmas was technically over, there was something about St Stephen's Day that warned her she wasn't over the hump yet. The races were on later at Leopardstown and she and Simon had loved going there. She couldn't understand why constant reminders of him continued to crop up and the more she tried to forget, the more thoughts of him flooded her head. She was relieved when the telephone rang and she answered to the cheery familiarity of her friend Rachel's voice.

"Are you in form for Kate's party later?" Rachel asked.

Anna wasn't in form for any party. She couldn't face meeting anyone today – she just wanted to curl over in bed and sleep the rest of the year off. Annus horribilis it truly was.

The silence at the other end of the line didn't deter Rachel. "You have to come for my sake," she pleaded. "It's going to be filled with couples and I was at the Ghost of Christmas Past party last night playing whist with my aunts – it's not natural – I think I'm going to scream."

Anna felt bad for Rachel – singledom was getting to her friend. But Rachel was more fortunate than her because she wasn't already a failure in marriage which was how Anna felt. "Okay, I'll go," Anna said, regretting it the moment the words came out of her mouth.

"Thanks so much, Anna . . . oh, and Paul will only be there for a few minutes – Kate assured me of that."

The mention of Anna's old boyfriend made her wince. But it didn't stop Rachel in her tracks – she felt compelled to dish out the details.

"He's going out with a nurse from Galway now and will be dashing off to pick her up from the hospital as soon as she finishes her shift."

Was that meant to make her feel better, Anna wondered? Maybe she should have studied nursing instead of finance – losing her job six months before had been difficult to stomach but it was losing her husband shortly after that really added insult to injury.

Kate had done well for herself. She had purchased a penthouse apartment as property prices plummeted, bagging a real bargain. And now she was all loved up with her boyfriend Niall and Anna was happy for her. She had waited until she was thirty before committing herself to living with a guy and it seemed like common sense now.

The smell of mulled wine wafted through the front door as Niall answered and welcomed Anna and Rachel to his new home. Candlelight reflected off the cream-painted walls and the lights of the city below twinkled in through the tall windows. The towers at Poolbeg and the lights of Howth sparkled in a way that made Anna's heart sink. It was such a perfect party – such a wonderful evening. So different to the day before which she had spent denying her parents of their festive cheer.

She was in the middle of Christmas here. Fairy lights and mistletoe! Kate had hung a veritable bush over the doorway into the lounge. It was difficult not to hit your head against it on the way in. Why did people who were blissfully in love want everyone else to feel the same way as they did? Could they not allow those going through a difficult time to wallow in their misery? That was all that Anna wanted and she didn't feel like she was asking for too much. Kate had been miserable at Anna's wedding and Anna hadn't tried to impose her happiness on her – or had she? Anna had to think about that! Truth was she wasn't blissfully happy on her wedding day – more like deathly nervous and anxious about spending the rest of her life with Simon. She remembered feeling scared of the responsibility of being a grown-up and or a parent. But she didn't have to worry about things like that now.

She eyed a bottle of Chianti on the marble island in the middle of the kitchen and made a beeline for it. She would pour herself a large glass and find a corner in which to sit and sulk. She might even watch as the lovers lost themselves in the romance of Christmas. This was one party that she would be happy just to sit out. *But* Paul was making his way over to the bottle of Chianti at the very same moment – she had hoped that she wouldn't bump into him so soon.

He stood there looking far more handsome than she remembered when they were dating. Mind you, they were both plagued with spots and greasy hair in those days – unfortunate conditions of youth.

"Anna, great to see you!" Paul smiled as he leaned forward to plant a polite kiss on her cheek. "You look great."

Anna wanted the ground to open up and swallow her. He was so gracious, so lovely – he'd always been – she'd just never appreciated him. So this was her karma. Because she had truly never adored any man enough to want to have his children, this was her punishment – she could slink into singledom and look on as all the happy caring couples procreated and spent the rest of their lives in wedded bliss.

"You look good, Paul – and happy."

"I am," he nodded. There was nothing showy or hurtful in his comment. "I'm moving to Galway – I always loved the west."

Anna smiled. It was fate. It was nice to see things working out for him. It was good to see those around her in high spirits. But she wouldn't have been human if she didn't feel more than a little jealous. She was heading into court in the New Year to sort out the finances and put in place the legal side of her separation.

"I'm delighted for you," she said.

He beamed. "Thanks, Anna – it's kind of you to say so."

He didn't mention her predicament and she appreciated that. What was the point? It was enough to wish him well and share a glass of Chianti from the same bottle.

Rachel rescued her from Paul and dragged her over to the makeshift dance-floor in the corner of the living room.

"Come on, you love this one – it's Jennifer Lopez – 'On the Floor'."

Anna didn't like this song. It was Simon who had loved it and blasted it from their iPod whenever they had people around – although their socialising had been sporadic for the previous twelve months, what with all the hours that he had been working and overtime spent nursing his nurse!

The party was filling up and more familiar faces joined the group in the living room – even more were calling to the door and piling into the kitchen.

Anna needed to go to the bathroom and she left Rachel dancing rhythmically with a tall friend of Niall's who had told them already that he would be spending the night in the spare room.

A scented candle burned on the ledge in the bathroom and Anna looked over at the neatly placed razor and comb placed beside her friend's toothbrush. It was lovely for Kate to have found her man at last. Everyone deserved to be loved – everyone deserved to find their mate. Anna rested her head in her hands, elbows on her knees. Someone knocked on the door but she didn't want to move. She wanted to stay in the bathroom all night. There was obviously something wrong with her. She had messed up one marriage – she couldn't face the throngs of beautiful people outside all making love and merriment in this happy place. She decided that she would get her coat and slip out silently before Rachel noticed. She washed her hands with the heavily scented liquid soap and dried them in the fluffy towels. Had she ever gone to so much care and trouble to make her bathroom so luxuriant in her home with Simon? Even after the honeymoon? She doubted it. She took a quick glance in the mirror to check that her straight blonde hair was in place.

As Anna returned to the party she noticed that Rachel was getting closer to her new friend, her arms firmly wrapped around his neck, his hands on her waist. At least Rachel is sorted, she thought. Now was a good time to slip away. She went to the small cloakroom with coats bulging and falling from the hangers. At the back she found hers. She slipped it on quickly and pondered whether she should say anything to her hosts. A part of her prompted that it would be rude not to.

She ventured back down the corridor in the direction of the living room. She was almost under the doorframe when she felt two strong arms wrap around her waist from behind. They spun her around.

Anna was startled. A handsome face framed with a mop of curly black hair was only centimetres away from hers. She protested at first but the stranger's hazel eyes had a mesmerising effect on her. He smelt sexy too – he had obviously been dancing but his scent was divine. He didn't speak, he simply looked through her – she felt naked, as if he could see right inside her.

She lifted her arms in a gesture of resignation and glanced above their heads. They were directly underneath the mistletoe.

"You can't go without giving me a Christmas kiss," he said smoothly.

His tone made Anna think of chocolate but she didn't know why.

He slowly leaned forward and his lips looked warm and inviting. He paused for a second as she yearned to feel them on hers.

Anna started to tingle inside. It was the most gentle and sensual kiss. She couldn't remember the last time she felt this way. Was it the suddenness of the situation or the fact that it was so pleasant? She wasn't sure but she didn't try to fight it either.

The stranger cast his head back to survey his prize in greater detail.

Anna was melting – she wanted more. She looked up and into his eyes until she saw something that made her blink. The shape reflected in his eyes resembled that of a little child. She blinked again but still the image wouldn't go away. Was she imagining it – was she just emotional? She had to pinch herself.

"Are you okay? You look like you've seen a ghost?" he grinned. "Don't say my kisses are that bad!"

"N-n-no, no not at all – it was very nice!" she stuttered.

"Phew!" the stranger smiled and gently released his grip on Anna's waist. "You are free to go now . . . if you must!"

Anna would normally have felt defensive at such a remark but she was so transfixed by the aura and smell of this attractive man that she wanted to know more – she couldn't go home now. "I don't have to!" she blurted.

He beamed. "Oh good!" He started to peel her coat from her shoulders. "Come into the kitchen, let's get a drink."

And that was how it started. Anna took the stranger home that night. He was a work colleague of Kate's so she didn't have to worry about him being some sort of weirdo.

As she opened the door to her house, he stopped her.

"You haven't told me your name yet?" he said.

Anna smiled. She didn't know his either. And strangely she wasn't curious to know. It was only a little thing – it didn't matter what he was called. She felt as if she knew him already – she knew him better and in a more intimate way than she had ever known Simon.

"I'm Ryan!" he said.

She put a finger up to his lips and held it there. "It's okay. We don't need to say any more."

11 months later

Anna stood up on her tiptoes as she balanced precariously on the footstool. She hooked the branch around a nail sticking out on the doorframe. The mistletoe was firmly in place where it should be. What a difference a year had made! It was less than 360 days ago that she had walked under this very doorframe, insistent that not a single decoration should grace the walls of her home. And it *was* her home now – the settlement with Simon had been swift – he was keen to buy a place with his nurse and didn't want any baggage left over from his marriage. She felt a shiver. The snowflakes were falling hard outside. So much concern over the weather – but the logs crackled on her cosy fire now and she had stocked up well on provisions just in case the weather got worse. She threw her eyes around the room, checking that the holly on the picture frames was sitting just right – her Christmas tree was the most beautiful she had ever brought into the house. For a moment she closed her eyes and cast her mind back – that horrible feeling returned, reminding her of Christmas Day exactly one year ago.

But suddenly the door opened and she smiled, knowing that it was him. Anna had so much to be thankful for and she still thrilled at the sound of Ryan coming through the door.

He walked over to help her down from the stool.

"You shouldn't be doing anything strenuous – not in your condition!" he urged.

She giggled. "I'm pregnant – not ill. Anyway, I want to make this the best Christmas ever."

He spotted the mistletoe above their heads and dragged her closer to him.

"It's going to be the first of many and you are giving me the best present that anyone could hope for," he grinned.

And as he placed his lips on hers – underneath the mistletoe – she knew that it was going to be her best Christmas ever.

Michelle Jackson is the bestselling Irish author of five novels. *5 Peppermint Grove* is her latest, published by Poolbeg Press in 2012. Her other novels *One Kiss in Havana*, *Two Days in Biarritz*, *Three Nights in New York* and *4am in Las Vegas* have been translated into foreign languages including Dutch, German, Portuguese and Norwegian. In October 2010 her first nonfiction title *What Women Know*, which she co-wrote with Dr Juliet Bressan, was published. She also contributed to the Irish Epilepsy Society's collection *The Thorn and the Rose* published in 2011. She is a native of Howth, County Dublin, where she lives with her husband and two children. For further details her website is www.michellejackson.ie

The Christmas Pact

Linda Kavanagh

It was Christmas Eve, and as she pushed her way through the throngs of happy shoppers, Helen cursed under her breath. What on earth was the matter with these people? Why were they all grinning inanely, wishing each other Happy Christmas, as though there was something to be cheerful about? It was just a commercial festival nowadays – the best time of the year for retail stores. It was only one day, and then the madness and the orgy of self-indulgence would be over. In January, they'd all be paying off the moneylenders, and regretting their reckless seasonal spending.

Helen grimaced. Besides, she had no one to shop for anyway, and no one would be bringing her gifts either. It was at times like these, when everyone else seemed so happy, that she felt most alone. And knowing it was all her own fault made her feel even worse.

Helen had decided not to celebrate Christmas at all. There was little point in sitting all alone trying to pull both ends of a cracker by herself. But she did have a plan, and it gave her a morbid sense of relief. This would be the last time she'd ever have to feel so alone and unwanted.

Back home, she prepared Sailor's lunch. The tabby cat was hungry, and Helen felt a momentary pang as she reviewed her plan for Christmas. She would have to make sure that Sailor was looked after when she wasn't around any more. She'd leave a note outlining her instructions – maybe the new neighbours next door would adopt him – he spent much of his time in their home already.

Looking out the window, Helen watched the new next-door neighbours unloading their freshly cut pine Christmas tree from the roof of their car and carrying it inside, the children laughing and their dog excitedly jumping up and down as he tried to share in the spirit of things. Other people's happiness made Helen feel even sadder, and it made her review the life she might have had if only she'd behaved differently.

As it grew dark, a scattering of snowflakes began to fall and, watching from her kitchen window, Helen felt even more lonely. She recalled other Christmases, happy Christmases, a long time ago . . .

Dishing out an extra-large portion of cat food, Helen felt sad because old Sailor didn't realise this was the last time he'd ever see her. She had a tear in her eye as she took a final look around the house before stepping outside and closing the front door.

Creeping up the new neighbours' driveway, she stuck a note in the flap of their letterbox that asked them to feed Sailor, and maybe even adopt him. If not, could they find him a good home? He was neutered and vaccinated, and was no trouble at all.

Helen closed the neighbours' gate and began walking purposefully down the road. The snow was falling heavier now, and the local bus was disgorging the last of the Christmas shoppers, who were about to make their way home, laden down with last-minute purchases. Even though they looked weary from shopping, people were smiling and children were sliding along the fine layer of snow that now covered the ground. The arrival of snow seemed to have created a sense of magic, and a feeling that a white Christmas was going to make this year extra-special. Strangers smiled and wished Helen a Happy Christmas as they passed her, and she inclined her head in acknowledgement. For a moment, she almost felt a surge of Christmas spirit herself, but then she scolded herself for indulging in such frivolity. This kind of bonhomie was all very well for people who were loved, but she had no one who cared for her.

Helen made her way along the road, then up the hill and out of the village. The snow was now falling heavily all around her, and she had to brace herself against its onslaught. At least she could be certain that no one else would be up on the cliff in such weather. She'd be able to end her life in peace and solitude.

When she got to the highest point of the cliff, Helen was surprised and annoyed to find a young boy of about fifteen leaning against the wall that served as a parapet, and staring down into the waters below. She certainly hadn't expected to find another human in this deserted spot on Christmas Eve. Couldn't she even end her life in peace? Briefly she wondered if he could be a hoodlum about to attack her. Then she smiled grimly to herself – since she was going to commit suicide, what difference did this potential threat make?

There was a dejected look about the boy, and he didn't seem bothered by the snow that was already building up on his clothing. Helen wished he'd just go on home. The sea below looked dark, cold and bleak, and she didn't want to have to hang about for ages while this child amused himself. She wanted to jump in and get it over with as quickly as possible.

"What are you doing here?" she asked the boy pointedly. "Surely, on Christmas Eve, you have better things to do?"

The boy shook his head. He looked so dejected that Helen felt a sudden surge of pity for him. He looked as though he had no one in the world to care about him. Which was exactly how she felt herself.

Despite his loose snow-covered hoodie, Helen could see that his frame was thin, and he looked as though the wind might blow him over. Clearly the boy was experiencing a growth spurt – she remembered that Tom, her son, had also been a skinny lad in his teens.

When the boy didn't go, Helen's annoyance turned to anger. "Look, why don't you just go home?" she said sharply.

"I don't want to," he said sullenly. "Why don't *you* go?"

They glared at each other. Then the boy jumped up onto the parapet from which people from miles around traditionally leaped when they wanted to end their lives.

"I hope you're not planning to do anything stupid," Helen said anxiously.

"It's none of your business," the boy retorted. "If I want to jump, I will. Anyway, what are *you* doing here on Christmas Eve? Unless you're planning to jump too."

Helen acknowledged his words with a nod. "Well, yes, I have good reason for ending my life – I've made a complete mess of it," she told him.

As the boy teetered uncertainly on the edge of the precipice, Helen longed to reach out and grab him, but instinctively she knew that it would only make the situation worse.

For a moment, Helen hesitated, uncertain what to do. Then she decided that her own sad and pathetic story might be just what the boy needed to hear.

"I have no family or friends left because of my behaviour, and I've only myself to blame," she said, looking at the boy sharply.

The boy looked surprised, but he stepped back from the edge of the wall, sat down on it and turned to face her.

"What did you do that was so awful?" he demanded.

Helen grimaced, hardly believing that she was about to share the most intimate details of her life with an unknown teenage boy, but she felt that despite the difference in their ages, there was now some kind of bond between them, forged from their shared desperation.

"I stole my best friend's husband," she said at last. "How despicable is that? Annie and I had been friends since kindergarten, yet I put my own desires before hers and wrecked her life. She ended in psychiatric care afterwards, and she never married again. Needless to say, I lost the best friend I ever had."

The boy suddenly seemed interested. "Did you marry the guy?"

Helen nodded.

"Did you have any children?"

Helen nodded, stamping her feet to shake off the snow that was now sticking to her boots. "Yes, we had a son together." Her lip quivered. "But our relationship was doomed right from the start – no marriage can work when it's based on someone else's misery. And the spectre of Annie's pain was always there between us. We began to fight, and I quickly discovered that he wasn't the dashing hero I'd believed him to be. You see, back then I had no idea what love was really about – I didn't realise that you have to work at it, and that no one is perfect – least of all, me."

"So – what happened?"

"I told him to go – and he did." Helen's eyes filled with tears. "He was found hanged in his bedsit a few weeks later."

The boy bit his lip. "So you blame yourself."

Helen nodded, wiping away a tear. "I destroyed his life as well as Annie's. And Tom, my son, has always blamed me for what happened. He idolised his father, and I could never make it up to him for sending his father away. He grew to hate me and, as soon as he finished school, he moved away. At first, there was the occasional letter or phone call, but even they eventually tapered off, and I haven't seen him for years now."

The boy looked down into the water below. "That's really sad," he said softly. "I can see that you really care about your son. I wish *my* mum cared as much."

"Don't be ridiculous!" Helen said angrily. "Of course your mother cares for you. She gave birth to you, and has looked after you ever since. Even though you probably drive her mad at times, she'd do anything in the world to protect you. What do you think it will do to her if you throw yourself off here? Do you hate her so much that you'd want her to spend the rest of her life wondering how she failed you?"

The boy shook his head, and Helen thought she saw the glint of a tear in his eye.

"Do you have any brothers and sisters?" she asked gently.

"A younger brother."

"And a father?"

The boy shook his head vigorously. "Dad died of cancer last year."

"Well then, it looks as though you're the man of the house," Helen said firmly. "Don't you think your brother needs your help to grow up to be a man? Now that your dad's not around, you're his role model!"

"I'm no role model for anyone," the boy said gruffly.

"I'll bet you're his hero," Helen said softly. "And if you go ahead and jump, you'll make Christmas Eve the worst day of your mum and brother's lives. And forever more they'll hate Christmas, because that'll be the time they lost you."

The boy burst into tears. "But I can't live just for them – everything in my life sucks! I don't want to go back to school, but Mum keeps insisting I go – all she thinks about is education, education – but I can't cope with the bullying any more!"

"Have you talked to your mother about the bullying?" Helen asked, deeply affected by this unhappy boy.

The boy shook his head.

"Or your teachers?"

Another shake of the head.

"Then how can anyone help you, if they don't know what's going on?"

The boy turned to her, anguish etched into his face. "You don't understand – if Mum or the teachers got involved, I'll be bullied even more for telling on them!"

A sob rose in the boy's throat. He jumped up onto the wall again, and looked down into the black waters below. "I can't even stand up for myself!" he whispered, turning his tear-filled eyes towards her. "I always wanted to be in a band – Mum paid for music lessons and I've been saving up for a proper, professional guitar – but I'd never be able to get up on stage and play before loads of people, since I can't even deal with a few bullies!"

"There's no shame in being bullied – it's the bullies who should be ashamed," Helen said stoutly. "Anyway, people don't

165

bully unless they're hurting, themselves. These kids probably feel inferior, so terrifying others helps them to feel better about themselves."

"B-but how can I stop them?"

"I'm no expert, but it stands to reason that bullies can only succeed if you let them get to you. If they see you're not reacting, they'll get fed up," Helen said firmly. "Anyway, are you letting a bunch of silly, immature kids cheat you out of a great life? You're a bright young man – I can see that – so you've probably got a great future in the music business. Even a mediocre life is better than none!"

The boy looked at her angrily. "Well, yours didn't work out very well, did it? Otherwise, you wouldn't be here!"

Helen nodded. "You're right – I'm hardly the one to be telling you what to do. But if you jump, you're going to waste sixty or seventy more years when you could have been doing wonderful things – having a career you enjoy, getting married to someone you love, and having kids – it's all ahead of you."

"But *your* marriage didn't work out."

Helen sighed. "You're right – there are no guarantees in life. But why not hang in there, and see what happens? Of course there'll be disappointments, and sometimes heartbreak. But each time something good or bad happens, you'll learn something new about yourself."

"Then why didn't you take your own advice?" the boy said sarcastically. "Anyway, I've been through enough bad stuff already – after Dad died, my girlfriend left me, and now she hangs out with the meanest of the bullies. And she laughs whenever he calls me disgusting names."

Helen had to hide a smile. A girlfriend at fifteen? Wasn't he a bit on the young side?

She looked at him wryly. "If that girl could switch sides so easily, she doesn't deserve you, and you're better off without her. I dare say your mother's told you this already but, of course, the young think that older folk know nothing about anything – am I right?"

Helen saw the hint of a smile on the boy's face, and she was glad that he still retained some sense of humour.

For a few minutes, they stood together in silence, watching the snow as it now fell thick and fast before disappearing into the waters below, muffling all sound and creating a carpet of white all around them.

Then the boy turned to face her again. "You know, I can understand how your son feels – even if he wanted to see you, it'd be difficult for him to take the first step now, because he's left it so long. I'm sure he'd like to, but he just doesn't know how."

Helen nodded humbly. The young man was making a lot of sense. Why had she always felt angry and rejected when her son was around? Had her own behaviour driven Tom away?

As if he read her mind, the boy looked at her angrily. "You've a nerve telling me not to jump, yet you think *you* have the right to do it! What about your son? Don't you care how he'd feel? You say you've ruined two people's lives – do you want to ruin a third?"

Helen bowed her head. It felt strange to be spoken to in that tone of voice by a teenage boy, but she acknowledged the truth of what he was saying. She was a hypocrite to think that there was one rule for him and another for herself.

The boy looked searchingly at Helen. "Do you know where your son lives? Did you send him Christmas card?"

Helen shook her head. "I think he lives up North, but I don't know his actual address."

"Well, can you use a computer? If not, I could try to find his contact details through Google –"

The boy suddenly realised what he'd said, and he and Helen exchanged a smile.

"See? For a moment, you were actually looking to the future," Helen said gently. "You're on the threshold of something wonderful, and you want to throw it all away? I'd give anything to be your age again."

The boy's eyes filled with tears again. "But what if I made mistakes, like you did? And what if – like you – I was too stubborn to do anything about them?"

Helen was momentarily shocked. *Was* she stubborn? Was there something she should have done? Was there something she could still do?

For a moment she said nothing, mulling over his words in her mind.

"Anyway, you can't end your life until you've made things right," the boy added determinedly.

Helen gave a hearty laugh, startling the boy and surprising herself by its genuine, joyful sound. "Isn't it funny that we're both great at offering advice to each other?" She held out her hand. "Why don't we make a Christmas pact with each other, to forget about ending it all?"

The boy blinked, then nodded slowly. "Okay. As long as you promise me you'll try to contact your son – and write to your friend?"

Helen nodded back. It seemed strange to have a young boy making demands of an elderly woman, but then the whole situation was strange.

"Just tell your friend you're sorry," the boy added. "She may never reply, but even so you'll feel better for doing it. And if she does reply – you'll be glad, won't you?"

Helen nodded. "Okay, I'll do as you ask – as long as *you* agree to be the man in your family, and look after your mum and brother?" She smiled. "And promise me you'll ignore the bullies, and get that band of yours up and running?"

The boy agreed, and Helen noticed the slight upturn of his lips as the two solemnly shook hands. Helen was relieved that the boy no longer intended to jump, and she was even more astonished to discover that she didn't want to do it either. She'd just realised that while she could still help someone, life was worth living.

"Go on home –" Helen said, smiling in the dark, "– your mum's probably worried about you."

"I'm not going until you leave here, too," the boy said firmly. "We made a promise, right?"

"Well then, let's walk back to the road together."

Walking through the snow in companionable silence, they eventually reached the road, and Helen suddenly leaned up and planted a kiss on the boy's cheek. "Happy Christmas," she said.

Although he was surprised and embarrassed, Helen could see that the boy was pleased, too.

Bending down, he put his thin arms awkwardly around her, and she could feel how bony he was as they hugged. "Happy Christmas to you, too," he said, not bothering to wipe away the tears running down his cheeks.

At the bottom of the hill, they parted company, and Helen waved to the boy as he disappeared into the snowy night.

Standing outside her front door, Helen felt weird. She'd left an hour ago, never intending to be back again. She could hear Sailor meowing inside, and when she opened the front door he lunged at her affectionately, following her into the kitchen and wrapping himself around her legs, demanding her full attention. With a start, Helen realised that the cat needed her, and not just as a source of food. He actually liked being with her. As she held him tenderly in her arms, he purred happily.

With a start, Helen remembered the note she'd stuck in the neighbours' letterbox. Hopefully she could retrieve it before anyone found it . . .

Creeping up her new neighbours' driveway, Helen had just reached the door when it was flung open.

"Oh, it's you, Helen – come on in and have a Christmas drink with Des and me," said Sarah cheerfully as she stood by the door. "We've just got the kids off to sleep," she added, smiling. "They're so excited about Santa coming!"

"Thanks, Sarah – that's very kind of you," Helen said, suddenly feeling mean since she hadn't even thought of getting the new neighbours a gift. In fact, she'd nothing in the house at all, except stale crackers and cat food. Well, you don't go shopping when you're expecting to end it all, do you?

"I popped in earlier to invite you, but you were obviously out," Sarah added, as she ushered Helen into the warm kitchen, where her husband Des was just taking a batch of newly baked mince pies out of the oven. Suddenly, Helen's stomach rumbled, and she realised how hungry she was. Food had been the last thing on her mind an hour earlier, but now she was positively starving.

As if she'd read her mind, Sarah placed the fresh mince pies in front of her. "Help yourself, Helen," she said, "and let me get you a cup of tea to go with them."

A little while later, as Sarah was showing Helen to the door, Helen spotted her letter still sticking through the letterbox. Luckily, at that very moment, Sarah was momentarily distracted by one of the children calling from upstairs, and Helen grabbed the letter and surreptitiously slipped it into her pocket. There was no need for it any longer.

As she opened the door to usher Helen out, Sarah reached forward and gave her a hug. "Des and I were wondering if you'd like to join us for Christmas lunch tomorrow, Helen – unless you've other plans?"

Helen faltered. Previously, the old Helen would have said no. But the new Helen returned Sarah's smile.

"Thank you, Sarah, I'd love to join you all," she said sincerely.

"That's great! We'll see you tomorrow then – around one?"

"Yes, thanks, Sarah – I'm looking forward to it."

Leaving her neighbours' house, Helen didn't go straight home. Instead, she hurried through the swirling snow to the corner store. She had no presents for the children, but she had cash that she could put into Christmas cards for each of them, assuming she managed to get to the store to buy the cards before it closed. She'd also get a few bottles of wine to take to the Christmas lunch, some sweets for the children, and maybe a box of chocolates for Sarah.

Back home with her purchases, Helen wrapped the gifts for her neighbours while she listened to Christmas carols on the radio. She was beginning to realise that buying Christmas gifts wasn't really a chore – it said that you cared about the people to whom you were giving them.

Helen was humming along to her favourite Christmas carol when the telephone rang. Startled, Helen looked at it fearfully. No one ever rang, so she wouldn't bother answering it. Undoubtedly it was a wrong number. Then she remembered the promise she'd made to the boy to make changes in her life, so she reached out and gingerly picked it up.

"Hello, Mum? It's Tom here – I'm just ringing to wish you a Merry Christmas!"

Helen was speechless. Then she realised that in her astonishment, she hadn't answered him.

"Hello, son," she said warmly, "It's great to hear from you."

Thanks to the young boy, Helen realised the effort it had taken for Tom to lift the phone, so she responded affectionately to his call. The old Helen would probably have snapped at him, querulously asking why he hadn't been in touch for ages, and they'd have parted on bad terms yet again.

She could now hear the hesitation in her son's voice. "How are you, Mum? I'm sorry for not being in touch –"

"Well, what better time than Christmas to say hello?" Helen replied cheerfully. She would not let censure creep into her voice – these moments of conversation with her beloved son were precious.

"Where are you living now?" she asked.

Tom gave her his address and phone number, and Helen eagerly wrote it down.

Her son hesitated again. "Maybe I'll come to see you soon, Mum – would that be okay?"

"Of course, love –that would be wonderful!" Helen said warmly. "Your old room is always there for you." There were many things she longed to ask him, but for now they could wait.

With promises to talk again soon, they ended their call.

Feeling very emotional, Helen went to the drawer and took out a pen and paper. Then she sat down and wrote a letter to Annie. Pouring her heart out, she apologised for all the hurt she'd caused and asked for her friend's forgiveness. As she closed the envelope, she felt an amazing sense of peace. Even if she never got a reply, Helen felt cleansed by her actions.

It was going to be a great Christmas after all, and she'd have missed it if she hadn't met the boy at the cliff. Helen hoped that he, too, would have a great Christmas and that in some small way she'd helped him to realise that problems were usually temporary. She'd needed reminding of that fact herself.

Although she didn't even know the boy's name, she'd never forget him, and she'd start watching out for aspiring new bands. Maybe she'd even go to one of his concerts some day? She felt certain that the boy would achieve his dreams, and when he did, she'd like to think that she herself had played some small part in it.

"Oh, there you are, love – thank goodness you're back – I was beginning to worry about you."

The boy's mother hugged him, smiling. "You're freezing!" she said, tenderly. "Where on earth have you been? Come and sit by the fire – your brother's already tucked up in bed, eagerly waiting for Santa! It's the first time he's ever climbed those stairs so willingly!"

His mother looked earnestly into his eyes.

"Are you okay, love? I've been worried about you lately – you've seemed so distant. I know you miss your dad – we all do."

"I'm fine, Mum," the boy assured her, hugging her tightly. "I've just been sorting a few things out. I've decided to get a Saturday job at the supermarket so that I can save up for the guitar I told you about. I know now that I really want to be in a band –"

His mother looked pleased. "That's great news, love, because I've got a special surprise for you!" With a flourish, she produced a large gift-wrapped parcel. "Since you're too old for a visit from Santa, I got you this myself."

The boy's eyes opened wide as he studied its shape. It couldn't be – could it? Eagerly he ripped off the gift-wrapping, his face now wreathed in smiles. It was the actual guitar he'd intended saving for! Then an anxious look crossed his face. "But Mum –

this cost a fortune! And I know we don't have that kind of money . . ."

His mother smiled. "I wanted you to have a special treat, love. You've been so down lately that I wanted to put a smile back on your face."

"Thanks, Mum," he whispered, hugging her tightly, and burying his face in her sweater so that she wouldn't see that he was crying. How could he ever have contemplated hurting his mother and brother by jumping off the cliff? He owed that old lady big time. He'd take her advice and ignore the bullies. And even if it didn't work, he'd just concentrate on his music. They'd all want to know him when he was a famous rock star. Then, when the bullies queued up for autographs, he'd get his revenge by pretending he didn't even remember them.

Smiling, he took the new guitar out of its case, tuned it and began to play.

Linda Kavanagh is a Number 1 bestselling author. A former journalist, she has published six novels with Poolbeg. She likes to combines suspense with social issues, and her novels have tackled violence against women, bullying, the power of industry versus the individual and the past inhumane treatment meted out to women who became pregnant outside marriage. She hopes that her novels make readers think as well as entertaining them. She believes that animals are far more moral and decent than humans, since they don't deceive, cheat, steal and kill on the scale that humans do. But, of course, she'd have nothing to write about if people didn't behave so badly!

Since she is not a fan of Christmas, her story begins rather gloomily. But as the Christmas spirit exerts its influence, even she couldn't resist a happy ending . . .

Diva-licious Christmas

Pauline Lawless

Samantha flashed a smile at the doorman of the Four Seasons Hotel as she handed him the keys of her BMW convertible to be valet-parked.

"Good morning, Mrs Fleming," he greeted her, smiling as he tipped his top hat to her. She was a familiar face and a favoured client of the hotel.

"Good morning, Joe, and thank you," she replied, as she strode in through the marble doorway, confidence oozing from every pore. Slim, blonde and beautiful, she still retained the looks that had catapulted her to the top of the modelling industry fifteen years previously. Along the way she had also garnered a millionaire husband and lived a life of luxury in the gracious mansion she shared with him on Dublin's leafy Ailesbury Road.

She made her way to the room that she had reserved for her DWD committee, of which she was the chairperson. Samantha was a major player on the Irish charity circuit and today she had plans to shake things up a bit. The media were forever referring to them as Ladies Who Lunch, so the idea of calling themselves Divas Who Dine caused them all much amusement. Lisa, who of course could always be counted on to lower the tone, said it stood for Divas Who Drink! She was the first to arrive for the meeting.

"Jeez, the feckin' traffic!" she moaned, plumping herself down on one of the sofas, her skirt, as always too short, riding high up her thighs.

Samantha wrinkled her nose in distaste. "Good morning, Lisa," she greeted the other blonde coolly.

"Bloody hell! It's alright for you," Lisa replied. "You only live around the corner. I'm going to ask Jeremy if we can move to Ballsbridge too. I see the house across from you is for sale."

Samantha tried to hide her alarm at the thought of having Lisa for a neighbour. It was one thing having her on her charity committee but quite another to have her living just across the road. Lisa's husband, Jeremy, was one of the best divorce lawyers in Dublin and extremely wealthy. He was also a dear friend and was a stalwart of Dublin society, which was why Samantha had no choice but to include Lisa on her DWD committee.

Imogen arrived next followed by Alison and Beth. After much air-kissing and exclamations of envy at Alison's new studded Louboutins and Beth's Prada suit, they settled down to business.

"I think it's time we did something new," Samantha announced. "We've really got stuck in a rut with the same old charity lunches and balls every year. Our supporters are jaded and I think we should do something to shake them up."

"As long as it involves some gorgeous men, you can count me in," Alison drawled. Samantha looked at her coldly. Alison was rumoured to have bedded half of Dublin and was seemingly on a mission to bed the other half. In fairness, her wealthy husband was pushing ninety but Samantha thought a little discretion wouldn't go astray.

"A new charity has come to my attention," she informed the group. "It's called Charity Begins At Home, or CBAH for short, and in the light of the recessionary times we're in I think it would be a very admirable charity for us to get involved in." She looked at the others to gauge their reaction.

"Very good idea," Imogen agreed in her clipped English accent. Her husband was a diplomat and she was very top-drawer.

"Yeah, we should forget about Africa for a while and bleedin' look after our own," Lisa piped up.

"I don't think we should put it quite like that," Samantha reprimanded her, "but there is no doubt people in Ireland are suffering hardship too."

"Isn't Marcus O'Neill involved in that charity?" Beth asked.

"Yes. Actually, it was he who brought it to my attention. We were at the same dinner party last week." She found herself blushing as she spoke of him, remembering how attractive she'd found him.

Alison sat bolt upright in her chair. "You met him?" she asked Samantha, her eyes alight. "Is he as gorgeous as they say? Can you get me an intro?"

"Well, actually, you'll meet him pretty soon. I've asked him to come in and talk to us this morning and explain what his charity is all about."

"Well, well, things are looking up," Alison exclaimed, patting her hair and adding some more lip gloss to her plumped-up lips.

Just then a waiter came in with refreshments and they chatted together as they sipped their black coffees. The plate of biscuits was left untouched. All of these women were serial dieters. They were interrupted by a discreet knock on the door.

A dark curly head appeared around it and the women fell silent. Before them was possibly the best-looking man any of them had ever seen. Tall and well built he advanced into the room as Samantha got up to greet him.

"Marcus! How good of you to come!"

"My pleasure, Samantha." He shook her hand and looked at her, his dark eyes serious. She noticed again the pronounced dimple in his chin that was so attractive.

"Girls, let me introduce Marcus O'Neill."

In a flash the others jumped up to greet him, smiling flirtatiously as they shook his hand. Even Imogen acted out of character, fluttering her eyelashes at him. Alison held his hand as if she'd never let go.

"Thank you, ladies." He gave them a fleeting smile as he looked from one to the other. Samantha had the distinct feeling that he was sizing them up as he sat down on the sofa beside her.

"Would you care for a coffee, Marcus?"

"No, thanks. I'd like to get down to business straight away, if that's okay."

She nodded, smiling. He was obviously not one to waste time.

He gave them a brief history of how CBAH had come into being and of the others involved in it with him. He, it appeared, was the mover and shaker behind it. He was a dynamic speaker and they hung on his every word.

"I'm grateful to Samantha for giving me the opportunity to talk with you as I know of your Trojan work with charities."

They smiled at his words, each of them taking the compliment personally.

"But, as I explained to Samantha, it's time we started helping our own people, some of whom are in dire straights at the moment wondering how to keep their homes and put food on the table." His eyes were serious and he spoke with a passion which captivated them.

"Absolutely!" Alison agreed, her blonde extensions bouncing as she nodded her head in assent.

"Damn right!" Lisa said with conviction.

Imogen and Beth were both nodding vigorously. Samantha was pleased with their positive reaction.

"Added to these worries, parents are now worried about Christmas coming up. They naturally don't want to dash their children's hopes and dreams of Santa, and that's where you ladies come in." He looked at each of them intently.

"Jeez, don't tell us you want us to play Santa!" Lisa cried.

He looked directly at her and gave a little laugh. "Well, yes, in a way, but not physically."

"I'd play Santa physically with him anytime," Alison whispered behind her hand to Beth. Samantha didn't hear what she'd said but nevertheless frowned at her.

"What do you suggest?" Imogen was curious.

"Well, I don't think dinners or balls for the wealthy privileged few is appropriate, given the financial climate at the moment." His voice held a note of disdain and Samantha wondered if he was mocking them. "I was thinking of a more hands-on approach. There are five of you here and I'm sure if you put your heads together, you'll come up with something original." Seeing their blank looks he raised one eyebrow. "It shouldn't be all that difficult."

They looked at each other, baffled.

It was Lisa who broke the silence. "Well, we'll give it a bloody good shot."

The others murmured their agreement.

"Great! Samantha, as your chairperson, will coordinate things and liaise with me." He stood up to go. "I have every confidence in you, ladies."

The women were obviously disappointed that he was leaving them so soon.

"Can't you stay and have lunch with us?" Alison asked him, in the little-girl voice that she reserved for good-looking men.

"I'm afraid not." He raised one eyebrow again, which gave him a cynical look and made Samantha uneasy. "I have to get back to work and besides I don't *do* lunch."

Alison sighed dramatically. "What a pity! You would have livened it up considerably."

Samantha shook her head. Alison really was outrageous. No man was safe in her presence.

Marcus bade them goodbye and gave a tight smile as he exited.

"Wow, what a hunk!" Alison cried when he'd left.

"He's a bit of alright," Lisa grinned. "I wouldn't charge him a penny."

"Charge him? I'd pay him!" Alison exclaimed, earning another disgusted look from Samantha.

"Well, ladies? Shall we go in to lunch and discuss what we can do for CBAH?" she suggested, gathering up her things.

They adjourned to the dining room, chattering like a flock of birds. Marcus was naturally the main topic of conservation.

Over lunch they discussed ways they could help. They were all agreed he was right that balls and lunches were definitely old-hat and not appropriate. No, something extra special was needed. It was Lisa who came up with the idea.

"I saw something in Florida when I was there last Christmas," she told them, "and I thought it was a feckin' great idea."

Samantha saw Imogen squirm at Lisa's language.

"There was a Christmas tree in every store and mall decorated with little cards," Lisa continued. "Disadvantaged kids had written the thing they'd like from Santa on them and well-off people took a card and bought that present for the child. I thought it was bloody brilliant."

"What a great idea!" Samantha said enthusiastically.

"How did they distribute them?" Beth asked.

"The presents were delivered by the stores to a big warehouse, with the kids' cards attached, and volunteers then distributed them."

"How do you know all this?" Alison wanted to know.

"Well, I took a few cards and bought presents for some of the kids," Lisa admitted, embarrassed.

Samantha had heard Jeremy say that Lisa had a big heart. She was beginning to see that now. "That sounds like a very novel idea. What do you all think?"

"I think it's spiffing!" Imogen said excitedly.

"Yes, we could hire a warehouse as a distribution centre and take turns manning it," Samantha suggested.

"Hire, my arse!" said Lisa. "No feckin' way! We get someone to donate a warehouse. I'm sure our hubbies could afford to do that. They can always claim it back off tax."

"Great idea!" Samantha was so excited now that she even ignored Lisa's language. "Beth, your Robert has a fleet of vans, doesn't he? Maybe he'll give us a van at a discount to deliver the toys. What do you think?"

"He'll donate a van or as many as we need, or he'll have me to contend with."

They all laughed, never doubting it for one moment. Robert was the most hen-pecked man in Ireland.

"I don't know, it doesn't sound very glamorous to me. Has no one any better idea?" Alison said, looking at her long gel nails which were never intended for working in a warehouse.

The others shut her up with withering glances.

They decided to call the project 'Santa Trees'.

"I'll float the idea to Marcus tonight and see what he says," Samantha said, sure that he would love the idea.

Marcus more than loved the idea. "You're a genius," he said, making her blush.

She thanked God he was on the other end of the line and not beside her, to see it.

"Well, actually, it was Lisa's idea," she admitted.

"She's something else, isn't she?" he said and she could tell he was smiling as he said it.

"That's exactly what I was hoping for, something original, not just a fancy dinner for pampered rich people. Sorry, no offence intended," he added.

That was the second time he'd passed a snide remark about wealthy people. Was that the way he saw her? A pampered rich bitch? That's not how she was at all. She didn't need all those fancy dinners where one met the same circle of people over and over again. If the truth be told, she was fed up of the narrow Dublin social scene where everyone tried to outdo each other. Well, she'd show him. She could knuckle down and get her hands dirty with the best of them.

"Are you sure the other women are on for this?" he asked. "It won't be easy, you know. I got the impression from Alison that getting down and dirty was not on her agenda. What about Imogen?"

Samantha was amazed that he'd remembered their names and from the sound of it had sized them up pretty quickly.

"Oh, Imogen will be fine. She's spent her life around horses so she's used to mucking out, or in, as the case may be."

He laughed, a wonderful throaty laugh.

"Alison might be a problem but I'm sure we can find something nice for her to do. Maybe she could contact the managers of the stores or something, and publicity. She's good at that."

"I'll bet," he said. "If they're male, that is."

He seemed to have an uncanny insight into people. She wondered what he really thought of her. They arranged to meet up on Friday to discuss the plan. He seemed very pleased with what they'd decided.

Samantha's husband, Andrew, was a corporate raider and was hardly ever at home, his work taking him all over the world. It wasn't until she had seen the movie *Pretty Woman* where Richard Gere's character had also been a corporate raider that she began to understand just how her husband made his money. These ruthless men ruined lives and businesses in the name of acquisition. She'd been horrified by it and by his reaction when she'd tackled him about it. Her already ailing marriage deteriorated quickly after that, eventually becoming an empty shell. She accompanied him to the many dinners and functions that were required of her but their marriage was a sham.

When Andrew rang her that night, she mentioned Santa Trees to him. He was less than enthusiastic.

"I don't really think it's a suitable thing for you to be involved in," was his response.

"Why not?"

"Because, firstly, I'll need you to be available for a lot of functions in December and, secondly, I think it's beneath you."

They argued about it and she hung up, more determined than ever to go ahead with it. She guessed he wouldn't be donating to the warehouse after all.

The calls flew furiously between the DWD members over the next few days and within a week they had made terrific strides. Samantha had to admit that Alison had outdone herself. She'd targeted all the main supermarkets, department stores and shopping malls and somehow had managed to wangle a positive response from each and every one of them. Alison was in her element. She had plans for a big publicity campaign and had persuaded her husband, William, to finance it. She was energised as Samantha had never seen her before. What a surprise!

Lisa had secured a warehouse which Jeremy was willing to finance. He thought the Santa Trees project was brilliant and made a very substantial donation to help with the costs. Beth's husband had agreed to give them as many vans as they needed to deliver the goods. Imogen's husband had been persuaded to donate the trees. Samantha's job was to organise the cards to be hung on the trees and to choose the children who would benefit.

Samantha met up with Marcus the following Friday morning and felt a warm glow at his praise for their endeavours.

"Well, I take my hat off to you." He gave her a devastating smile. "I honestly had my doubts you ladies would follow this through."

"We're not just pampered trophy wives, you know. We genuinely want to make a difference."

"I see that now. Forgive me. I'm just an old cynic."

He smiled again and she felt herself soften. It was impossible to resist his charm.

"Now how do we choose the children to whom we give these cards? I'm in charge of that task."

"Well, that's where I can help. As you know I'm a social worker so I have lots of contacts with the various agencies. I'll contact them and explain about Santa Trees and then we'll take it from there. I'll be in touch as soon as I've done that.

Andrew arrived home that evening and was furious when she told him that she was going ahead with what he referred to as 'this ludicrous scheme'.

"I thought I told you I didn't want you doing this charity gig," he said firmly as he poured himself a whisky before dinner.

"I want to do it. It's important to me," she replied, equally firm.

"Oh, no doubt you'll have tired of it before Christmas comes around," he said smugly as he started reading *The Times*.

She was infuriated at his assertion and the way he'd dismissed her. It made her more determined than ever to see it through.

Things were moving at breakneck speed and every moment of Samantha's day was taken up with Santa Trees. The following week Marcus and the DWDs met in the warehouse that Lisa had procured. They all agreed it was perfect. Lisa beamed happily as Marcus congratulated her. Samantha showed them the three thousand cards she'd had printed in a Santa shape and with a photo of a Santa.

"Do you think that will be enough?" Alison asked.

"I'd imagine so," Marcus replied. "As it's only a new concept, it will take time for people to hear about it.

"I'm not so sure. The publicity campaign should make a big difference next week." She smiled at Marcus flirtatiously but he didn't react.

Samantha had brought two bottles of champagne in a cooler and glasses and they toasted Santa Trees in the empty warehouse, wondering what it would look like in the run-up to Christmas.

"Hectic, I hope," Samantha said as they clinked glasses. Marcus joined in, thanking them for their ingenuity and commitment. He was smiling much more than the first day he'd met them.

He had contacted the orphanages in Dublin who had emailed lists of the children's names, ages and wishes to Samantha. It was her responsibility to have these transferred to the cards. Marcus's social welfare colleagues had also forwarded the names and wishes of the needy children under their care. It was all coming together beautifully.

Marcus asked her if she'd like to join him the following day when he would be visiting women's shelters. They would meet some of the children to be included on the Santa Trees. She accepted, happy that he seemed to be seeing her not as 'a pampered bitch' any more.

Nothing prepared Samantha for what she saw that day. It was horrendous. It was like living a nightmare. In the first women's shelter they visited she saw women with children, all crowded into one small room where they slept on mattresses. Marcus explained that they had fled there to escape violence and abuse at home. These women were living in fear and it touched Samantha's heart. She was trembling from head to toe when they left.

"Are you okay?" Marcus asked.

"I never imagined anything like this existed in Dublin," she said, before bursting into tears.

Marcus put his arms around her. "I'm sorry. Maybe I shouldn't have brought you here. Come, let me take you for a drink."

He led her to a nearby bar where he ordered a brandy for her. She sipped it slowly and eventually stopped shaking.

"I'm sorry," he said. "I'm so used to seeing things like this that I forget how shocking it can be to experience it for the first time. Maybe it was a bad idea."

"No, no, it was a good idea," she said hesitantly. "I never knew places like this existed. I guess I'm out of touch with the real world."

"Well, it is pretty far removed from the life you lead." His voice was gentle.

"It's terrible. This shouldn't be allowed to happen. I wish I could do something to help them."

"Well, what you're doing will help them."

"It's not enough!"

She insisted on joining him for the rest of the day. They visited other homeless shelters and she knew that her life would never be the same again.

The Santa Trees project rolled smoothly on. The five women gave it their all. Alison had done a great job with publicity and advertising and even secured a spot on the morning TV show for Samantha to talk about it. They were inundated with support after that and even received many donations from people outside Dublin. They decided to use this money to buy food vouchers for those needy families who otherwise would not have had a Christmas dinner.

The trees had been delivered to the stores and all that was left to do now was transfer the names and wishes from the lists onto the cards. This was the most time-consuming job so Samantha called all hands on deck and the five of them worked solidly for three days and nights, in Samantha's house, to be ready for the launch the following Saturday. Marcus joined them every night and lent a hand. Bikes were the most requested items followed by Baby Annabelles and Barbies, Leapfrog Leap Pads and Transformers.

"I'm surprised they don't want video games," Ruth remarked.

"These kids don't have PlayStations," Marcus said simply.

On Saturday they all converged on the Stephen's Green Centre where the first Santa Tree was to be unveiled. They arrived early to hang the wishes on the tree. They all stood back to admire it. It was a sight to behold. There were crowds of people there and also media photographers and two TV crews. Alison's publicity campaign had certainly done its job. Two presenters interviewed Samantha and Marcus and the cameras also filmed people coming in and taking wishes off the tree. It was incredible and Samantha felt a glow of pride.

They all then scattered in different directions, to hang the wishes on the other trees all over Dublin. They met up that evening, happy and exhausted, to celebrate with a dinner. Their husbands joined them except for Andrew, who declined the invitation. Marcus was also partner-free, so Samantha didn't feel too bad.

The real work would start on Monday when the toys would begin arriving in the warehouse. Samantha had organised a roster so that there would always be two of them manning the warehouse at any one time. There were so many deliveries that Samantha and Lisa found themselves there every day. Lisa had turned into a real brick and the two girls were becoming firm friends. Lisa's language had even improved under Samantha's influence. As fast as the deliveries came in, they sorted and grouped them for redelivery. Samantha ordered another thousand cards and Marcus had no problem coming up with another thousand children's names from his social-work colleagues.

Samantha was glad to be busy as her relationship with Andrew had sunk to a new low. It all came to a head the Friday before Christmas week. Things had been maniacally hectic in the warehouse all week and she was feeling exhausted when she got in that night. She tried to ignore Andrew's snide remarks about her 'latest plaything', which is what he had started calling the Santa Trees. He had obviously had a few drinks and was cock-a-hoop about a huge take-over that he'd pulled off. It disgusted her. Some poor sod had lost his company and people had lost their jobs, no doubt, and he was rejoicing. When he insisted that she accompany him to dinner to celebrate, she flipped. The upshot of it was that she had packed a case and walked out.

She had no family in Dublin and didn't want to involve her old friends, so she rang Lisa and asked if she could stay the night with her. Lisa was very understanding and said she could stay as long as she liked. There was too much to be done in the warehouse to even think of looking for an apartment so she gladly accepted.

Christmas Eve, and all was finally done. All the presents and food parcels had been delivered and it was with great satisfaction that the group surveyed the empty warehouse. They were exhausted but elated. Marcus had worked with them for the past three days and nights and made a little speech as he poured the champagne he'd so kindly brought.

"I can't thank you enough, ladies. The first day I met you all I could never have imagined for a minute that you'd have been able to pull this off. Now, thanks to you, there will be four thousand happy children opening Santa presents tomorrow morning and many families sitting down to a wonderful Christmas dinner. I salute every one of you. To the WCWs!"

"WCWs?" they chorused together.

"Yes. I've renamed you the Wonderful Caring Women."

They all blushed with pleasure, Samantha most of all.

Lisa had to rush off as she and Jeremy were meeting up with friends. She had invited Samantha along but she declined. They had insisted that she stay with them over Christmas until she found a place of her own.

"See you later at home. We shouldn't be too late," Lisa said as she kissed her goodbye.

Marcus raised his eyebrow.

The others left shortly after, laughing as they called out "Happy Christmas!"

"Are you staying with Lisa over Christmas?" Marcus asked as they were locking up.

"Yes. I left my husband last week and have been too busy to look for a new place."

"Oh, dear! I'm sorry. Do you want to talk about it?"

"How many hours do you have?" she asked jokingly.

186

"As many as it takes. Come on, let's go for a Christmas drink. You've earned it."

Over a bottle of wine, she found herself telling Marcus about her marriage. He listened quietly without interrupting.

"So, you see, I just can't live that vacuous life any more. I want to do something more with my life. This project has shown me another way."

He was silent for a while and she wondered what he was thinking.

"You know, when I first met you," he said, "I honestly thought you were a pampered Barbie."

Samantha blushed with embarrassment.

"But I realised very quickly that I was wrong. There's much more to you than that. You're a fantastic organiser and worker. I could really do with you in CBAH. I can't run it by myself any more. It's too much. Would you be interested?" He looked at her hopefully. "The pay won't be huge. It certainly won't keep you in the designer gear you're used to."

She laughed. "Are you serious? I'd love that. I'd even do it for nothing. Besides, I have enough designer gear to last me the rest of my life."

"You're on! To the new director of CBAH!" He raised his glass to her. "To one very special lovely lady!"

She was blushing with pleasure when an obviously drunk guy came by their table, holding a sprig of mistletoe over their heads.

"Mistletoe!" he cried. 'You have to kiss the lady!"

"With pleasure," Marcus replied, grinning. He leaned over the table and kissed her slowly and fully on the lips. "Happy Christmas," he said huskily before he reached over and kissed her again.

It was the best Christmas present she'd ever had.

Pauline Lawless is the author of four bestselling books, *Because We're Worth It, If The Shoes Fit, A Year Like No Other* and *Behind Every Cloud,* all published by

Poolbeg. She is from Dublin and only started writing after she retired. She now lives in Belgium and spends winters in Florida. It was there she saw the Santa Trees in shopping malls which touched her greatly. She thought it was a wonderful idea and it was the inspiration for this story.

Crossed Lines

Kate McCabe

Lisa Kenny was in a bad space. It was three months since she had broken up with Jack Dunbar, her boyfriend of two years, and the intervening period had been the hardest she had ever faced. Now she was all alone in the world with just an empty flat and a little ginger kitten for company. And Christmas was only a week away. How was she going to get through it?

Her best friend, Sarah O'Leary, had suggested she take a holiday in some nice, warm place where the sun shone all day long.

"What you need is a change of scenery, Lisa. No wonder you're down in the dumps. You need a break, something to distract you."

It sounded like a good idea so Lisa got on the internet. She found there were lots of Christmas holiday offers. But the one that caught her eye was a week in Tenerife. It was called The Singles Special. As she read what was on offer, she found herself getting excited.

The Singles Special seemed to be designed for someone just like her. *Meet New Friends – Let Romance Blossom in the Sun*, the slogans proclaimed. The package consisted of six nights in a five-star hotel, including meals and discos and sightseeing trips which were tailored specifically for single men and women like her. The highlight was a Christmas Eve candle-lit party in the hotel. The total cost including flights came to €1200.

Lisa closed her eyes and let her imagination roam. She thought of the sun-drenched days and starlit nights, the scent of jasmine on the air and music drifting out onto the terrace. And always the possibility of romance, of meeting some good-looking man who would sweep her off her feet. If anything was designed to lift her spirits and get her out of herself, it was this.

She took out her credit card and was all set to book when she began to have second thoughts. If she went on this holiday, she wouldn't know a sinner. Of course that was the whole purpose. It was to meet new people. But would she be able to handle it? And what if she didn't meet anyone she liked? Would she feel lonely? And didn't someone say that the loneliest place in the world was in a crowd?

She put her credit card away until she had thought some more about it.

The truth was, she missed Jack Dunbar desperately despite everything that had happened. She knew she had no choice but to drop him. It had been coming for a long time. Her friends had told her he was bad news. They could see the way he treated her. But Lisa was blinded by love. She kept forgiving him and allowing him one more chance until the night he hit her with his fist and knocked out her front tooth. That's when she finally saw sense.

She called the police and they came and took him away. She packed as many of his clothes as would fit in two suitcases and left them in the hall outside her apartment. Finally she got a locksmith to come and change the locks. The next day, he rang and pleaded with her not to press charges. He said he would lose his job. He told her how sorry he was, how it would never happen again.

He sounded close to tears. He said it was just a moment of

madness that made him snap and lose his temper. He pleaded so hard that she finally relented. She told the police that she didn't want him prosecuted. But she drew the line when he asked her to take him back.

The sad thing was: Jack could be a lovely guy when he wasn't drinking. He was so kind and considerate. He paid her the nicest compliments, bought her lovely presents. These were the things that had won her heart when they first met. And of course he was stunningly handsome. He was the sort of man who could walk into a room and everybody would stop talking so they could stare at him.

Lisa still had fond memories of those early days of their romance. They had met in a bar off Dublin's Grafton Street where she was seeing some friends after work. Jack had walked in and sat down beside her and asked if he could buy her a drink. He had a cheeky confidence that made her sit up and take notice. And she only had to look into those smouldering brown eyes to feel her knees turn to jelly.

So, they had a few drinks and fell to talking. He told her he worked as a bond-trader with an international investment bank and entertained her with stories of some of the interesting people he had met. He kept up a stream of witty conversation that had her laughing. He told her she was the most attractive woman in the bar and when she finally stood up and said she had to go, he asked if he could see her again. She gave him her phone number.

A few days later, they met for their first date. He took her to the O2 to hear Leonard Cohen sing and afterwards they had supper in a romantic restaurant in Dame Street. He dropped her home in his nifty little sports car and kissed her goodnight. Lisa went to sleep with the thrill of that kiss still on her lips.

Before long, they were meeting almost every day. Jack wore tailored suits and custom-made shirts and hand-crafted Italian leather shoes. He had a generous expense account and took her to films and concerts and the swankiest bars and restaurants. He showered her with gifts of jewellery and perfume and sent her flowers at work so that her colleagues were green with envy.

Of course Lisa was completely blown away by all this attention. What girl wouldn't be? She went around with her head in a daze. She was seeing one of the best-looking men in Dublin. Because of his job, Jack was always getting invitations to glittering parties and social events. He took her to race-meetings and opening nights at the theatre. It wasn't long before the paparazzi were snapping them coming out of discos and their photographs were appearing in the papers. Sometimes she had to pinch herself to make sure it was really happening to her.

Six weeks after they met, he told her he was in love with her. They were in a chic little restaurant in Howth. Outside the window, they could see the yachts bobbing on the tide. The candles cast shadows on her face. Soft romantic music spilled from the CD player. His hand reached out and touched hers and she felt an electric charge run along her spine.

"You're so beautiful it takes my breath away just to look at you."

"Thank you," she whispered.

"I think about you all day long. I can't get you out of my mind. I want to be with you all the time. Why don't we move in together?"

Lisa had never lived with a man before. She knew it was a big step. It would be a public statement of their commitment to each other. It was almost like getting married. But it was so exciting that she only paused for a second before giving her consent.

"Alright, if that's what you want."

Lisa was twenty-eight and Jack was thirty-one. She was five-feet-five and he was six-feet-two. She was blonde, blue-eyed, slim, nice figure, good legs. He was built like an athlete with broad shoulders and dark Mediterranean good looks. She'd had only two serious boyfriends before she met him. Jack never talked about his old flames but Lisa got the impression that he had never been short of company.

Now that they had agreed to live together, the next decision was where it should be. Lisa owned a modern apartment in a renovated building on Baggot Street. It had one large bedroom with en-suite bathroom, a state-of-the-art kitchen-cum-dining-room and a cosy living-room. It was bright and airy, easy to heat and it had the great advantage of being close to her workplace – a solicitor's practice on Stephen's Green where she worked as a legal secretary.

Jack lived in a dazzling penthouse in Malahide with views over the marina. It was three times the size of Lisa's flat and had been tastefully decorated by a big-name interior designer. But if they lived there, it would take Lisa an hour to get into work each morning and another hour in the evening to get home. When she pointed this out, Jack didn't hesitate.

"You're right. There's no contest. We'll move into your place."

"Won't you find it cramped after living in the penthouse?"

He laughed. "I'd be happy to live in a shoebox so long as I had you."

"So what will you do with the penthouse?"

He shrugged. "I'll place it with an agent. There'll be no problem letting it. I'd say I'll get two grand a month, no sweat."

Once the decision was made, it was only a matter of arranging the transfer. Jack hired a van and moved his stuff across town and into Lisa's apartment.

"This is an important day in our lives," he announced once he had finished unpacking. "I think it calls for a celebration." He produced a bottle of champagne and two glasses from a bag and they drank to the success of the venture. Then Jack took her in his arms and smothered her in kisses. She offered no resistance when he gathered her up and carried her into the bedroom. Within minutes, they were naked and making wild love on Lisa's bed. It was the best sex she had ever experienced and when it was over, she was exhausted.

They lay in the crumpled sheets and she traced her finger across his cheek.

"Do you really love me?" she asked.

"Have you never heard the expression actions speak louder than words? Why else would I leave my penthouse and move in with you unless I loved you?"

"Have you ever lived with someone before?"

"Never. And the reason is simple. I haven't found anyone I wanted to live with till I met you."

They lay in each others arms till Lisa felt him stirring again. She felt her body jolt when he entered her. This time, the lovemaking was slow and tender and it built in intensity till Lisa felt herself swept away on a wave of pleasure.

Afterwards, they showered and got dressed and went off to a restaurant for dinner. The following morning when she woke, his head was beside her on the pillow. She closed her eyes and thought: I must be the luckiest woman in Dublin to have found a man like this.

All her friends were envious. They told her he was a godsend, easily the hunkiest man they had ever seen. Some of them advised her to get a ring on her finger as fast as possible.

"If I was involved with Jack Dunbar, I wouldn't let him out of my sight," Jenny Taylor said. "I'd keep him under lock and key. This town is full of rapacious females who wouldn't think twice about running away with him."

"He has to go to work every day," Lisa replied with a laugh. "What am I supposed to do?"

"Well, maybe you could hire a private detective to keep an eye on him."

She knew there was some truth in what they said. There were women out there who wouldn't hesitate to steal him from her, given half a chance. But the thing was: it didn't worry her. She trusted Jack completely. He was in love with her. She had heard it from his own mouth. And she loved him back. And Love could never thrive where there was suspicion.

But it wasn't long before some of her friends began to change their minds. The reason was Jack's drinking. Lisa had noticed it from quite early on, the way he always wanted to meet in pubs and have lots of wine with meals and then liqueurs afterwards. There were occasions when he would turn up to meet her on a date and she knew immediately he was drunk. And then there were the times when she was with her friends and he would begin slurring his words and she would see them exchanging glances.

He was drunk the first time he struck her. It was six months after they had moved in together. It was only a glancing blow, more a slap really and it didn't hurt her. The way it happened was stupid – they both agreed about that afterwards when he had apologised profusely and promised it would never happen again.

He had come home around eight o'clock, tired after working a twelve-hour shift in the bank. She smelt the alcohol on his breath straight away. He went into the living-room and flopped down in front of the television.

"I'm starving," he said. "Any chance you could rustle up some grub?"

She wasn't expecting to cook and had nothing prepared but she went off to the kitchen and scrambled a pasta dish together from some tins she had stored in the cupboard. But after a few spoonfuls, he pushed the plate away in disgust.

"What kind of crap is this? Even your cat wouldn't eat it."

"I'm sorry," she said. "You caught me unprepared. Would you like me to order something in?"

She went to smooth his forehead but he raised his hand and slapped her across the mouth with the back of his hand. Her face went scarlet with shame. Then the tears gathered in her eyes and tumbled down her cheeks. She ran to the bedroom and closed the door.

Poor Lisa was devastated. No man had ever hit her before. But immediately he followed her into the bedroom, got down on his knees and begged her forgiveness.

"I'm really sorry. I don't know what came over me. Please say you forgive me."

By now he was weeping too and Lisa felt sorry for him. He was working so hard. He was under enormous stress at that bank, his bosses always pushing him to get results. He took her in his arms and she felt all her hurt melt away. He covered her mouth and neck in burning kisses. He slowly unbuttoned her blouse and bent his lips to her breasts. In a few minutes, they were making love.

But he didn't keep his promise, although it was several months before he struck her again. This time he left a bruise on her cheek which she did her best to cover with make-up. Although she could tell from their reaction that people noticed. After that, the violence became more regular.

It was always a spur-of-the-moment thing and Lisa never knew when it was coming. Immediately he regretted it and was begging her forgiveness. Lisa learned to tip-toe round him when he had been drinking. The slightest thing could spark him off.

Then one day, her friend Sarah O'Leary called her and asked to meet for coffee.

"You can tell me to mind my own business but you're my best friend and I feel I have to say something. I know he's beating you."

Lisa was about to deny it but the look in Sarah's eye told her she would be wasting her time.

"He doesn't mean to. It's just that he gets stressed from his job and sometimes he loses his temper. But he always regrets it afterwards. He's a good man, Sarah."

"Not if he's abusing you, he isn't."

"All couples fight, you know that."

"They might have arguments. This is different."

"And sometimes I provoke him."

"Stop making excuses for him," Sarah said. "He's an abuser. And he drinks too much. And as long as you stay with him, the abuse will continue. You have to get rid of him, Lisa."

But the thought of leaving Jack was too much for her to contemplate. She told herself she could change him. Maybe he could get a different job where there wasn't so much stress. Perhaps she could persuade him to go to Alcoholics Anonymous and get help with his drinking. Maybe he could attend Anger Management classes. She knew that deep down Jack was the kindest, most loving man she had ever met.

But no amount of talking made any difference. Jack made plenty of promises but he never kept them. Then came the incident when he punched her full in the face and broke her tooth and Lisa knew she had reached the end of the line. She had no option but to put him out.

For weeks afterward, he rang her every day, sent her flowers and messages and told her his heart was broken and he couldn't live without her. He said he would do anything if she would only take him back. But she was resolute. All her friends told her the same thing. She was a very attractive woman. She would soon find a nice man who would treat her properly. She was better off without him.

Lisa took to the social scene again. She went to parties and discos with her friends. The weeks slipped away but no Prince Charming crossed her path. It seemed that all the suitable men in Dublin had been snapped up. Then one day her boss asked her to represent the firm at a legal conference.

It was held in a large city-centre hotel. Lisa got dressed in a smart business suit, white blouse and heels and set off with her slim black briefcase. The conference was full of people who seemed to know each other already and she felt a little isolated. When it came time for lunch, she went to the dining room and sat down on her own at a table in the corner. All around her, people were laughing and smiling and introducing each other.

She looked up when she heard a voice ask: "Is this table free?"

A young, fair-haired man was smiling at her.

"Yes," she said.

"Do you mind if I join you?"

"No, of course not, please do."

He sat down and stretched out his hand and she grasped it.

"Peter Brennan."

"Lisa Kenny."

"Here on your own, Lisa?"

"Yes, and you?"

"I don't know a soul."

He nodded towards the other tables where people were busy shaking hands and networking.

"They're not a very friendly bunch, are they?"

"That's putting it mildly. You're the first person who has spoken to me."

"Are you learning anything from the conference?"

"Not really. My boss asked me to come, just to fly the flag. I'd rather be at work to tell the truth."

He laughed. "You're very honest, Lisa. That's refreshing."

"I speak my mind, if that's what you mean."

The waiter came with the first course and as they started to eat Lisa managed to sneak a good look at Peter. He was about thirty, neatly dressed with twinkling blue eyes and a warm smile.

When lunch was over, he asked if he could sit with her. He said they could keep each other company.

"Be my guest."

So they found two vacant seats at the back of the room. Lisa felt better now that she had someone to talk to. When the conference ended about six o'clock he suggested they have a drink and they went to a wine bar. He told her he was single, from Belfast, and had been working in a Dublin law firm for eighteen months. As they were leaving, he said: "Perhaps we could have dinner some evening?"

Why not, Lisa thought. It's not as if my appointments diary is exactly overflowing with invitations. And besides, he's good company and not bad looking. I think I might enjoy dinner with him.

"That would be nice," she said.

"Give me your card. I'll call you in a few days."

She opened her bag and took out a business card. He slipped it into his pocket.

"It's been lovely meeting you, Lisa," he said as they left. "I'm really looking forward to seeing you again."

Lisa went home to her apartment with a light heart. For the first time since she had ditched Jack Dunbar, she actually felt good. She had met a pleasant man who was going to take her to dinner. It restored her confidence. She felt that she had turned a corner and things would only get better.

That night before she went to sleep, she thought about him

again. He was quite good looking although not as handsome as Jack. And he had a lovely smile. Perhaps this is the one, she thought. Perhaps this is the man I've been looking for.

But the days drifted by and he never called till she was forced to accept that he wasn't going to call. It was just another opportunity that hadn't borne fruit.

December approached and she began to think about Christmas. She dreaded it. The festive spirit would be abroad. Everybody would be out enjoying themselves and she would be alone. Her widowed mother was spending Christmas with her aunt in Limerick. She could go and stay with them but they were so old-fashioned and set in their ways. She knew it would be a trial. She'd be better on her own.

One evening as she was leaving work, she heard someone call her name. A figure stepped out from the shadows and she saw it was Jack.

"We've got to talk," he said, taking her by the arm. "This is crazy. We're just making each other unhappy."

"I'm not taking you back, Jack. You broke every promise you ever made."

"I've changed. I've stopped drinking. It'll never happen again."

"Oh, Jack, if only you meant it!"

"I *do* mean it."

"You mean it now but as soon as I take you back, you'll just slip into your old ways again."

"No, I won't. I've learned my lesson. I was thinking we might go off together to a hotel for Christmas. We could talk this business through. You could see the way I've changed. Please, Lisa. Just give me one last chance?"

"No," she said and walked off into the night.

But now that she had seen him again, she couldn't get Jack out of her mind. What would be so terrible about spending Christmas with him in some nice hotel? And he was right. It would give her a chance to see if he had truly reformed.

She knew what Sarah and Jenny Taylor would say. They would tell her she was crazy and deserved everything she got. But they weren't living her life. They didn't know how lonely she felt. They didn't feel the terrible sense of loss she had to carry around with her every day.

She could feel her resolve begin to weaken. She sat down again at her computer and called up the information on the Singles Special in Tenerife. *Meet New Friends. Let Romance Blossom in the Sun.* It sounded very attractive. Should she go to Tenerife or should she take one last gamble and go off with Jack to this hotel?

Just then her phone rang. She answered it and heard a strange voice.

"Lisa Kenny?"

"Who is this?"

"Peter Brennan. Remember we met at the legal conference?"

Of course she remembered. He was supposed to take her to dinner and didn't ring.

"Oh, hello, Peter. What can I do for you?"

"I'm calling to apologise for not getting in touch with you. You won't believe what happened. I lost your card. And this morning I found it in the lining of my suit. So here I am again. I'm dying to see you, Lisa."

She felt a wave of relief wash over her. Suddenly she had an inspiration.

"What are you doing for Christmas?"

"Christmas? I've nothing planned."

"Ever been to Tenerife?"

"Er . . . no."

"How would you like to spend a week there?"

"With you?"

"Who else?"

"I'd like it very much."

"Well then, start packing your suitcase."

❖❖

200

Kate McCabe is a former journalist whose duties took her to many exotic destinations in the United States, South America and Eastern Europe. Kate recently left work to devote her time to writing. She lives in Howth, Co Dublin, and is married with two children. Her hobbies include travel, cooking, reading and of course writing. Kate spends half the year at her second home in Andalucia in southern Spain – an area which features in many of her novels. Her greatest joy is walking the Andalucian countryside while she conjures up plots for her stories.

Princess Grace of Holly Lane

Siobhán McKenna

My name is Grace Gavin. I'm six-and-a-half (nearly) and I
live with my mum in Number 3 Holly Lane. It's just me
and Mum because my dad was taken away by hedgehogs.

My mum's name is Audrey. She was called after an olden day
movie star. I'm called Grace after an old movie star too, but mine
turned into a princess. There are black-and-white photos of
them in Nana's house. They were very pretty but I wish I'd been
called after someone in colour.

Nana Gavin buys me dresses and shiny shoes. Mum giggles and
says poor Nana wishes we'd behave more like princesses but me and
Mum, we wear jeans and boots that we can jump into puddles with.

Even so, Nana Gavin calls me her Princess Grace but I'm not
really a princess. I put a pea under my mattress once, just to be sure,
and I slept just fine. I've thought about kissing a frog but that's
gross and there's no frogs in Holly Lane anyway, just hedgehogs
and look what they did to my dad. I think my dad could have been
a prince and that's why he went away with the hedgehogs. I can't
find any books about a prince and the hedgehogs though. If there
was, my friends would understand why my dad had to go away.

Holly Lane has five houses on it but there's no holly bushes, except for a little one planted at the stone sign in the grass that says HOLLY LANE. Someone put it there to make it look like our lane was full of holly. What is it with grown-ups, always pretending things are something they're not? Mum says I shouldn't worry about such things and that I should just enjoy being six – she never says six-and-a-half (nearly).

Grown-ups think they know everything too but there's some things us kids are just better at. Like how to make a wish properly. You've got to really believe it can come true, or it won't. Sometimes though, grown-ups need children to show them the way . . .

It was five days before Christmas. Audrey drove slowly up the hill in Holly Lane towards her home. It was after dark, and ice was making driving difficult.

"Audrey, look out!" said her mother, Irene, gripping the handle of the passenger door.

A large dog ran in front of them. Audrey hit the brakes, causing the car to skid. It came to a halt and she glanced behind to check if Grace was okay in the back.

A man came into view, slip-sliding down the road and holding a dog lead.

"Bobby!" he called out before he whistled. The dog bounded back to him. Rubbing the dog, he clipped the lead on before approaching the car.

"I'm so sorry, are you okay?" he said as Audrey rolled down the window.

Irene leant across, ready to give him a piece of her mind.

"Yes, we're fine. No harm done," said Audrey quickly.

"You're the new people, aren't you?" he said, smiling broadly. His dog stuck his head in the window to investigate what was going on.

Irene bobbed from side to side trying to get a look at the man with the wayward dog. "Are you a neighbour?"

He leant down further. "Yes – David Kelly. I'm very pleased

to meet you." He gave a little wave. His face was somewhat shadowed by the single overhead streetlamp. But there was a spark of friendliness in his eyes that didn't require light to see. His hair was dark and his smile warm, if a little cheeky.

Irene's frigid stance relaxed as she thrust her hand forward, causing Audrey to press back against the car seat. David shook the hand.

"I'm Irene Gavin. This is my daughter, Audrey Gavin. She lives with her daughter Grace Gavin. I'm just visiting. Say hello to the nice man, Grace."

Discreetly, Audrey gritted her teeth. Grace waved from her car seat in the back.

"Hi, Grace."

Maybe it was the because of the dog, but Grace beamed back at David Kelly.

The dog started to tug on the lead. "I'd better be going."

Irene craned over even further until she was practically on Audrey's lap. "Why don't you call in for a Christmas drink later, David? It's just us girls."

Audrey shot her mother a look, not that Irene could see it.

David thumbed the rope of the leash. "Tonight's not great, I'm afraid."

A woman turned the corner, watching her step as she came down the hill. "There you are," she said to David. "Bobby run off again?"

"Yep. Karen, meet our new neighbour Audrey Gavin – and that's Grace in the back. And this is Audrey's mother Irene who is visiting."

"Oh hi! I've been meaning to pop in to say hello. Karen Kelly." She beamed.

Irene thrust out her hand again and shook Karen's before sitting back despondently.

Karen slipped her arm through David's. "Welcome to the lane, Audrey! We must get together. Tell you what, call in over Christmas for a drink. We'd love that, wouldn't we, David?"

"Thank you, that's very kind but we'll be visiting relatives," said Audrey, eager to get going.

"I thought Santa had come early there for a moment," said Irene, once Grace had gone up to her room.

Audrey looked confused.

"David Kelly, he's a handsome man, and gentle too."

"How can you possibly know that?"

"It's all in the eyes."

Audrey rolled her eyes. "His wife seems perfectly lovely too."

"All the good ones are either married or gay, is that what you're going to say next, Audrey?" Irene said, turning on the oven.

"No, I was going to say he's not my type."

"Of course." She threw her hands up in the air. "Why would you like the tall, dark, handsome and seemingly normal type!"

"I don't have time for a man, Mum."

Irene shook her head and exhaled loudly as she unhooked an apron from the back of the utility door. Grace appeared in her reindeer fleece pyjamas, halting the conversation.

"Mum, can I play with your phone?"

Audrey handed Grace her phone.

"Never mind phones!" said Irene. "There's work to be done. Gingerbread houses to make, and jelly tots to stick on. Meringue snowmen that need baking." She clapped her hands. Grace looked up and Irene peered at the screen of the phone. "What kind of phone has cartoons of Father Christmas throwing snow balls at elves?"

"A smartphone."

"It should be called a daft phone if you ask me," Irene tutted.

Audrey smiled and went over to give her a hug.

Irene was more tense than usual, upset she wouldn't be home for Christmas this year as her husband had booked a Christmas get-away to celebrate his retirement and their thirty-year wedding anniversary. Tonight, while her husband had his last ever office party, Irene Gavin was staying over with her daughter and granddaughter to ensure some traditions were upheld. Namely,

Christmas baking and the winter solstice trip to the Hill of Tara, where in the morning they'd set their intentions for the coming year and make wishes at the fairy tree.

"I do wish you and Grace were coming on holiday with us," said Irene.

"And give up being wined and dined by my big brother? Not a chance. Besides, it's your second honeymoon, remember?" Audrey pressed play on the Christmas CD. It wasn't long before they were singing, as scents of cinnamon and spice wafted in the warmth of the kitchen.

Later, as Audrey was putting Grace to bed, the child grinned at her from under the duvet. "Can I make two wishes at the fairy tree tomorrow?"

"Okay . . . Do you want to tell me what they are?"

"I want a dog, like Bobby." Grace's face lit up, but then she hesitated as she chewed the inside of her cheek. "And a special friend for you, like Nana says. So you won't be lonely any more. We could lock the gate so hedgehogs can't come in and take him."

Audrey brushed a wavy strand of blond hair back from Grace's face. "You talk in riddles sometimes, little lady." She laughed gently. "We'll see."

"That's what you say when you mean no," said Grace, her brow furrowed.

Audrey kissed her forehead and her face soon softened again.

As Grace settled down to sleep, a playful grin crossed her lips and Audrey wondered what plan her daughter was cooking up.

December 21st, and the air was crisp as the Gavin women stood on the Hill of Tara. There was great excitement as the people who'd gathered on the hill watched the sun, a giant orange ball, rise above the horizon.

"Can we see the fairy tree now?" Grace pulled at Audrey's jacket sleeve. The tip of her nose was red as her new coat.

Dark clouds had started to gather above them. Audrey shivered. "Yes, but we'd better hurry."

They walked over the frozen mounds to the fairy tree, a tree with twisty branches to which people tied ribbons, bows of sheep's wool and little parcels containing handwritten notes, crystals or coins. Audrey had brought a few lengths of red ribbon and a little sachet of oat flakes. Handing Grace a ribbon, Audrey lifted her up so that she could reach a branch.

"Make a wish as you tie the bow, Grace," said Irene as she tied her own ribbon and made a wish.

Grace stuck her tongue out in concentration as she tied the bow. Afterwards, they scattered the oats at the base of the tree trunk to feed the fairies.

As they walked back towards the car Grace asked. "Fairies look a bit like angels only smaller, don't they, Nana?"

"I suppose they do, Princess Grace," said Irene as she grasped her hand. She flinched suddenly as something plopped on her nose. Looking up, she saw the first of a flurry of snowflakes. "If you wished for a White Christmas, Grace, it looks as though your wish is already coming true."

At first, the snow brought great excitement. Then, as it continued to fall Audrey's anxiety grew. At least her parents had managed to get off before the airport shut down.

By Christmas Eve the steep hill to Holly Lane was almost impassable. The surface of the road was like an ice rink as layers of snow compacted. Audrey and Grace stood outside their house as Audrey tried to assess if she'd be able to drive to her brother's house tomorrow. Karen Kelly and an older gentleman, Mr Banbury, looked as though they were doing the same. Audrey and Grace joined them.

"I think it'll be fine as long as the snow stays off tonight," said Audrey, brightly. "We'll be able to drive tomorrow."

"You're joking, right?" Karen looked worried. "It's impossible to stop going down the hill – you'll veer straight out on to the main road. I think we're stuck."

"Santa will still get here, won't he, Mum?" Grace's face looked grave.

"Of course, Grace," said Audrey.

"Absolutely," said Karen.

Mr Banbury coughed, looking a little uncomfortable.

The cookies were eaten, the Diet Coke can was empty and all that was left of the carrot was the green leafy top. Santa had made it through the snow.

"Did you get everything you wanted?" Audrey asked.

Grace was eating a bar of chocolate from her selection box as she sat playing in the cardboard box her toy kitchen had come in.

"Yes, and I still have my fairy-tree wishes to come."

Audrey smiled, but didn't ask further questions in case Grace was still hoping for a dog. Besides, her pressing concern now was the amount of snow that had fallen overnight. With it, her heart had fallen too. They were snowbound.

"It looks like it'll be just the two of us this year, Grace."

"I'll have no one to play with – all day?"

"The snow is just too heavy, Grace. We can't drive to your cousins, but I'll play with you!"

Grace nodded sagely.

"Fancy pancakes and maple syrup?" Audrey said. "After, we can go outside and make snow angels and a snowman."

Grace grinned. Cocking her head, she asked, "Can I have a scoop of vanilla ice-cream too?"

"Go on then."

They decided to make the biggest snowman in the history of Holly Lane. They were compacting snow for the body when they heard a bark.

"Bobby!" Grace ran towards the dog.

David and Karen Kelly weren't far behind.

"Merry Christmas!" David called out. "Need some help?"

"Happy Christmas, David, Karen!" Audrey replied. "We're not going anywhere so we've all day to make Frosty here, but feel free to join in!"

"You're staying put then?" asked Karen.

Audrey sighed. "Yep, decided you were right – it's too dangerous to travel. We were to spend a couple of days with my brother and his family but . . ." She swept her hand at the blocked road.

"Our parents were to visit," said Karen. "They were bringing the pudding."

"And the wine," David piped up.

"They can't get here, so it's just the two of us now with enough food to feed an army . . ." Karen frowned. "Why don't you join us? If you were to be away you probably don't have any food in?"

Audrey winced. "No, we don't. A box of Tayto and some cakes we made. I do have wine though."

"Audrey Gavin, I knew I liked you!" Karen smiled. "We should knock on the doors of the other houses, see if anyone else is stuck and wants to join us."

One neighbour only lived on the lane for part of the year, during the summer months. That left just two houses – those belonging to Mr Banbury and the Old Witch, as Grace's new school friends had so eagerly informed her. Audrey enquired about the woman from the other mothers and had been told her name was Mrs Moerk – a name she tried to get Grace to use. Audrey had to admit though, the few times she'd seen the woman, her grey hair had been tied back in a tight bun and her long nose nearly appeared to meet her chin. The term *Old Witch* stuck

Mr Banbury said he'd be delighted to join them. "I had planned to stay put. Eat my nut roast and enjoy a glass of vintage port but now you're here why the heck not? I'll be a long time dead!"

"You're a vegetarian?" Audrey asked.

"How else do you think I'm such a fine specimen of a man, at my age?" He held his chin up as he pulled his stomach in. "I've even managed to hang on to my great sense of humour too." He laughed.

"Okay, that just leaves Mrs Moerk," said Audrey.

They looked at each other, wordlessly. David shifted from foot to foot, looking antsy. Karen averted her gaze.

"She'll say no anyway," Mr Banbury sighed. "It's not just her Nordic homeland that blows an Arctic wind."

Karen grimaced. "I don't think she likes me very much, I'm afraid."

They turned to David, who held his hands up. "Don't look at me! The last time I offered to cut her grass, she practically set the dogs on me."

"She doesn't have any dogs," Karen tutted but David didn't budge.

"Grace?" Audrey turned from left to right but Grace was nowhere to be seen. "Grace!" she called out again. "She was here just a second ago . . ."

"Bobby, Bobby boy, where are you?" David joined in.

Mr Banbury nodded for Audrey to take a look. She turned around to see Grace trying to ring Mrs Moerk's doorbell, Bobby by her side.

Unable to reach it, she started knocking – loudly.

The hall door half-opened slowly. A stern-looking Mrs Moerk peered down at Grace.

"Happy Christmas, Mrs Moerk." Grace beamed up at her.

Mrs Moerk's lips set into a thin line before she mumbled, "Many happy returns."

"Will you come to the Kellys' house for Christmas dinner? They've enough food for an army, they said, and Mr Banbury has nuts and my mum has tons of wine that even she can't drink all of."

Mrs Moerk raised her eyebrows but her eyes narrowed when she saw Audrey ploughing her way up the driveway. Karen was close behind her.

"Thank you, but no." She went to close the door.

"Why not?" Grace asked.

The woman stopped for a moment and looked at Grace, a flash of emotion crossing her eyes, before she gently closed the door.

"Come on, Grace. We've a snowman to build, remember?" said Audrey.

As they walked away, Grace looked back. She could see the shadow of Mrs Moerk watching them from her window.

Christmas in the Kellys' was a hands-on affair. Everyone pitched in with the preparations and cooking, even Bobby who licked up spilt gravy and stray bits of food as they fell to the floor. Mr Banbury asked that they call him John from now on. Despite the festive atmosphere, Audrey noticed that Karen kept twisting her wedding ring, and she and David didn't appear to be connecting as a loving couple do. David spent much of his time playing with Grace and Bobby, and his eyes kept wandering over to Audrey. She began to feel uncomfortable, worried that the addition of a single mother and her daughter was causing tension in the Kelly home.

"It's really kind of you and David to have us here. We're probably the last thing a young couple want on Christmas Day," Audrey said casually as she helped Karen set the table.

"David and I aren't a couple!" Karen laughed. "I'm his sister." She banged her forehead lightly with the heel of her hand. "Sorry, Audrey. I've a head like a sieve at times, I guess I assumed David mentioned it. Be a pet and pass me those forks."

"No, no, he didn't," Audrey said smiling, as she handed Karen the cutlery.

"I live in the UK. I split from my husband a while back. I came to stay with David until I find my feet again, which is taking longer than I thought."

Without meaning to, Audrey's eyes rested on Karen's wedding ring.

"I know, I still wear my ring. I never did change my surname but taking off the ring seems so final."

"You might reconcile then?"

Karen sighed. "He called, saying he'd made a mistake, and that it was over between him and the other woman."

Audrey blushed.

"I know, very convenient, hey? He's suddenly single and decides he wants his wife back. What about Grace's father, is he still on the scene?"

Audrey looked away.

"Forgive me, it's none of my business. It's just something Grace said earlier."

"What did she say?"

"Her daddy loved her, but the hedgehogs took him."

Audrey smiled and shook her head. "Grace's father and I were childhood sweethearts." She placed a linen napkin on the table. "When I got pregnant we were young but so, so happy." She smiled to herself. "Until the cancer, that is. He died shortly after Grace was born." She looked away. "It was Hodgkin's."

"The hedgehogs," said Karen softly.

Audrey nodded. "She'd have heard me say that we lost him to Hodgkin's," she smiled. "She never mentioned the hedgehogs to me though, until the other night. Knowing Grace, she was probably trying to make sure I didn't feel sad."

They were interrupted by the doorbell and then voices at the door as David opened it.

Curious, Karen had a look, then beckoned to Audrey to join her.

A nervous Mrs Moerk stood at the door holding a marzipan-covered cake and a bottle of brandy, her body rigid.

"I will not stay," she said, abruptly. "But I thought you might make use of these." She held the gifts out.

"Come in, Mrs Moerk," said David. "Please, do stay."

Stepping in, her eyes darted around nervously. Audrey and Karen greeted her warmly. Bobby wagged his tail.

Then Grace appeared, beaming.

"Perhaps I'll stay for a while," Mrs Moerk said, "just to be neighbourly."

Mrs Moerk did stay for dinner and after the dishes were cleared they sat around the table drinking coffee laced with brandy, and sharing stories. Mrs Moerk – Ursula – was Danish. She'd moved to Ireland with her husband in the seventies. Her husband was dead and her only son now lived in Ohio. His work kept him busy. She found the journey to the US too difficult. She hadn't seen her son in three years. They also discovered that she had been a professional ballerina, with the Russian State Ballet.

"That was in my youth," she brushed it off, though her cheeks flushed at the happy memories.

John Banbury was a widower. He had no children. The cars that they saw coming and going from his house were his nieces and nephews. He was lucky: spending Christmas alone had been his choice – not his only option. He was retired from the army and had seen many of the world's notorious battlefields. A native of England, his wife was Irish and they'd opted to retire here. Most of his extended family lived in Ireland anyway. It was where his heart and his wife lay.

Audrey watched her neighbours, who until today had been little more than strangers that happened to live on the same street. If the snow hadn't come, the chances were that they would have remained that way. No matter how much they protested that they were content to be alone today, their eyes told a different tale. But Audrey's eyes rested on one face more than the others.

Grace and Bobby were curled up together asleep in front of the TV. David gently lifted her.

"I'll walk you home," he said to Audrey.

Having said goodnight to everyone, she set out with David on the short walk, two doors down the road. She held on to his arm – because of the slippery snow, she said.

"Was it me or was there a spark between John and Ursula?" David asked, smiling.

"Definitely. Whatever they want to call it, that was a date they were setting up. Neighbourly indeed!"

"Rambo and a Prima Ballerina, living in our midst! Who'd have guessed? There might even be wedding bells on Holly Lane before long."

They got to Audrey's door.

"I'll take her from here," she said. She moved closer to David to tuck her arms under Grace. She could feel the warmth of his breath on her face.

Grace shifted, and flung her arms around David's neck.

"Why don't I lay her down on her bed? She's more likely to stay asleep that way."

"Good thinking," Audrey nodded, briefly wondering if she'd left her underwear to dry on the hall radiator.

Once Grace was tucked up in bed, Audrey offered David a nightcap.

Somewhere between talking, laughing and wishing the night would never end, he kissed her. There was no mistletoe, no roaring log fire, but there was a Christmas tree, with its twinkling lights, and a white angel that looked down upon them.

If Audrey Gavin had made just one wish, that kiss was surely it.

That was last Christmas. This year, there's no snow, but that's okay because we've got something better. In a few days, my mum and David are getting married.

Karen is home too with her new boyfriend. She giggles a lot when he's around and she's always kissing me, which I'm getting a bit big for, but I say nothing because she seems so happy. She doesn't twist her wedding ring any more. Maybe because she doesn't wear it any more. Like I said, grown-ups are very confusing.

And the best bit? David said that Bobby is my dog now too. I did get all my wishes, just not in the way I thought I would. The fairy tree's way is much better.

Nana Gavin will be really happy to see me in a dress for the wedding and I won't be able to make faces because it's Mum's big day.

"You'll look like a princess, Grace!" Nana keeps saying in a high voice as she's running about bossing everyone. She's very happy me and Mum didn't go on holiday with her and Granddad and that we got stuck in the snow instead.

I wonder has she thought about how my name is going to change now too. I'll be Grace Kelly, just like the real princess. Maybe that's what Nana wished for that day in Tara, and her wish has come true, like she wanted, only different. I'm guessing that the fairy tree had something to do with that too.

Siobhán McKenna's literary career was lauched in 2011 when she won the Poolbeg/TV3 Write a Bestseller competition with her debut novel *The Lingerie Designer*. The win was further endorsed when she was shortlisted by the Irish Book Awards as Best Newcomer. Her writing is influenced by her experience of the business world, wanderlust for off-road travel and the dynamics of modern Irish families. In addition to being an author and mother of two, she is a representative of Deepak Chopra, MD, in Ireland.

The Spirit of Christmas

Marisa Mackle

"Ladies and Gentlemen, welcome to Dublin. On behalf of the Captain and all the crew on your flight this afternoon, I'd like to wish you and your loved ones a very Happy Christmas. Please have a safe onward journey and we hope to see you again on board very soon."

Heather put away the PA, applied another coat of red lipstick and stuck on the Santa hat that all the airline cabin crews had been given to wear Christmas week. She was tired. It had been a very busy week with the flights full to capacity with people coming home for Christmas from every corner of the world. There was a great buzz about working as an air stewardess at this time of year. Passengers were in terrific form, armed with mountains of presents and as much good will. You could visibly see the excitement in their eyes as they disembarked from the aircraft, eager to meet their friends and families in the Arrivals area where Christmas carol singers were stationed and a jolly fat Santa was walking around, posing for photos with delighted kids.

After she had said goodbye to the last of the passengers from the Paris flight, Heather thanked the other cabin crew members and wished them a Happy Christmas. Alison, who was ten years younger than her, was so full of excitement about Christmas that you would almost think she still believed in Santa and Mrs Claus. She had told Heather that she couldn't wait to go to her local pub tonight and see all her friends from school and college, many of whom had emigrated to places like England, the USA and Canada over the last couple of years as work in Ireland had become increasingly hard to come by. Alison's eyes shone as she told Heather that they would all meet in the local pub for drinks and then go back to her house for a bite to eat. They would hook up again the following morning out at the Forty Foot in Sandycove to jump into the freezing cold sea, and then treat themselves to a hot whiskey when they emerged minutes later, their limbs red with the cold. Heather found herself involuntarily shivering as Alison talked about the Forty Foot. It was a very popular swimming spot all year round with hardy Dubliners, but Heather couldn't think of anything worse than donning a bathing suit on the twenty-fifth of December and plunging into deep, dark, bitterly cold water in the name of fun. Mind you, she would have liked to be going to a local pub somewhere to meet all her friends. It would be nice to meet up in a warm cosy establishment with people that you hadn't seen in ages, to swap memories and catch up on all the news. That wouldn't be happening for Heather this year though. The pub nearest to her small inner-city apartment was not the most inviting of places. In fact, the only time she had been in there was once when she had popped in to get some change. It was a place with iron bars on all the windows and doors. She wasn't quite sure whether the bars were designed to keep the punters in or out.

Eager to get a foot on the first rung of the property ladder, she had bought her apartment in Dublin city at the height of the property boom. She had been convinced that property was rising and rising and that prices were showing no signs of slowing down. Every day when she had come into work, one of the pilots or flight attendants seemed to be talking about how much the value of their properties had soared in recent years. And after waiting and waiting to see if property prices would ever eventually go down, Heather had decided that they more than likely wouldn't, and had secured a ninety per cent mortgage from a building society for a city-centre shoebox with the wrong sort of postal code. Then, almost immediately after she had signed on the dotted line, property had begun to tumble spectacularly. Now her little shoebox, which was so badly soundproofed that she could hear her neighbours flush the loo, was already worth less than fifty per cent of what she had initially paid for it. She was almost sick thinking about it. And what made things worse was the fact that her own mother kept saying to her, "I told you not to buy in that area. All those apartment blocks will become slums in the next ten years. You'll never be able to sell." Jesus, she should have listened to her for once in her life! Why had mothers such an irritating way of always being right?

Heather took the two bags of mince pies from the cart under the trolley. They had been left over from the passengers. She would keep one bag and offer the other to the captain.

She knocked on the cockpit door and then opened it slightly. Captain James Kirby had his head bent in paperwork. "Sorry, Jim. I was just wondering if you'd like these to take home to your family. They haven't been heated so they're perfect."

He looked up with a fairly surprised look on his handsome, sallow-skinned face. "Thanks, Heather. But are you sure you wouldn't like them for your own family?"

She found herself blushing. "Oh, no. I mean, I have a bag for myself. There were lots left over."

"Well, thanks very much. I will take a bag then. They'll come in handy over the Christmas. You know the way people are always calling."

Heather looked away. Nobody would be calling into her tiny one-bedroom apartment in a dodgy area of the city. It wasn't a place where the neighbours dropped in to each other. She had only met her next-door neighbours once when she'd knocked on their door in her dressing gown at around one in the morning to ask them to turn the TV down.

Heather handed the mince pies to the captain and he took them gratefully. He had a kind face and when he smiled his eyes creased in the corners. She didn't know how old Jim was but she would say he was in his late forties. He had a kind face and he was always very nice to the cabin crew, unlike some of the other pilots who would act like mini-gods and press the call bell all the time looking for fresh cups of tea even if you were run off your feet in the cabin.

She left him to his paperwork, shut the cockpit door and buttoned her coat. There was a strong icy breeze coming from outside that would slice through you. Heather shivered. She wondered whether there would be snow this Christmas. There had been snow in Ireland last Christmas for the first time in years. Her mother hadn't stopped complaining about it. Heather's mother detested snow with a passion. She said she was afraid of falling and breaking her hip and wouldn't leave her house except to go to Mass.

Heather pulled the hood of her uniform coat over her head to keep her ears warm. There was no point catching a cold now. Christmas this year was going to be lonely enough without being sick too. She was halfway down the steps of the aircraft when she heard her name being called. She turned around to see Jim at the open door in his short-sleeved white shirt. "Heather!" he called, not seeming to notice the bitter weather. "Come back here a minute."

She left her bag on the steps and moved towards him. Was everything okay? To her surprise he handed her a bottle of red wine. "This one's a good year," he said.

"Oh, I couldn't –" she began.

"Honestly, take it. I bought a crate at the airport. I don't need them all."

She was touched by his kindness. She remembered himself and the co-pilot going into Charles de Gaulle airport at the turnaround. One of the cabin crew had also gone in with them. Heather had just thought they were going in for a cigarette break. She hadn't realised they had been stocking up on booze.

But why wouldn't they? It's what people did at Christmas time. It was important to have something to offer people when they called.

"Thanks," she said. "I really appreciate that."

"Don't drink it all at once," he laughed. "Merry Christmas!"

He gave her a swift peck on the cheek and she found herself blushing. The touch of his lips was warm against her cold cheek. She walked purposefully across the ramp towards the airport terminal. The airport was busy with parked planes getting ready to transport people home across the world, and inside, people in the terminal were hugging each other, revelling in the warmth of Christmas.

To her horror, Heather felt her eyes well up. She took a tissue from her coat pocket and dabbed them. She shouldn't start crying. That would be only ridiculous.

Carol singers were singing at the tops of their voices, and cameras were flashing as families and friends took homecoming pictures of one another. Heather walked swiftly through the crowds with her small black wheelie case. It wouldn't take long until she was home. Well, if you could call her tiny lodgings a home.

She was soon at the staff car park, putting her case in the boot of her Ford Ka. She longed for a cigarette now but she had been off them six months and didn't want to go back there. She took a deep breath. This will pass, she told herself – in two minutes I won't even want one.

She started the car and headed for her apartment. The sound of 'Jingle Bells' was still ringing in her ears. The happy scenes that she had just witnessed at Dublin airport had made her feel sad. She felt no part of it. She was skipping Christmas this year. Last year it had been so, so different.

Last Christmas she had spent in New York. With her fiancé, Simon. She had flown there with work and the airline had put the crews' families up in a fabulous hotel for three nights and had put on a spectacular lunch on Christmas Day complete with wine and champagne. Herself and Simon had gone Christmas-shopping soon after arriving in New York. She'd been dying to visit Sak's but there was only one place that Simon had on his mind: Tiffany's. They had picked out the ring together an hour after he had got down on one knee at the ice rink in the Rockefeller Centre. It had been the happiest day of her life. What a pity that he had since changed his mind and that last Valentine's Day he had decided that marriage, perhaps, wasn't for him after all.

When Heather arrived home at her shoebox apartment the first thing she noticed was that the Christmas wreath that she had hung up on her little balcony was missing. She leaned out to see if it had fallen onto the street below but there was no sign of it. It had completely disappeared. With a heavy heart Heather acknowledged that it had been stolen. She was disgusted. What kind of mean-spirited person would make off with somebody else's wreath? Some little brat must have scaled the wall, maybe as a dare. Maybe he did it to make his mates laugh. Disenchanted, Heather turned on the small electric heater with a sigh. She shouldn't be that surprised really. A lady who lived in the same block had gone to the shop a few months ago and came back to find her mobile phone and her laptop stolen. Somebody had climbed the wall and got into her apartment through an open window even though she'd only been gone ten minutes.

It just didn't even feel like Christmas. She wished she was going somewhere or doing something. She envied Alison, the younger stewardess, whose eyes had shone when chatting about her plans for tonight. No doubt right now she would be putting on the false eyelashes and the skyscraper heels. Heather wished she could meet somebody even for a quick drink. But there was no chance of that happening. It would feel very sad to be phoning people at this late notice. She would just have to stay in. Then she remembered the bottle of wine that the captain had given her. It was probably a very good wine. She would have that, watch a DVD and eat a couple of mince pies. Maybe *A Christmas Carol* would be on TV. They normally showed it on Christmas Eve, didn't they?

She took off her uniform, hung it up in her wardrobe, put on a pair of slippers and settled down for the evening. What was all the fuss about Christmas anyway? The festival had become so commercial in recent years. After all, they had even started running the Christmas ads on TV before Halloween this year. It was madness.

Heather screwed the cap off the bottle of red wine. She sniffed it and approved. It smelled very nice and rich. She would leave it open a while and let it breathe. She turned on the TV and started flicking through the channels. She wasn't going to let herself get downbeat about Christmas. This time tomorrow it would all be over and then on Stephen's Day everything would be all back to normal again.

The phone rang making her jump.

"Hello?"

"Heather, can you hear me?"

"Yes, I can, Mum. How are you?"

"Fine. I am at Puerto del Carmen now. Kitty collected me from the airport and I had to stretch my legs a bit. I didn't like being cooped up in that seat for four hours. The man in front's head was so big he was blocking my view of the screen so it was hard to see the film."

"What's the weather like there, Mum?"

"Well, it's dark now but it's clear. I can see the stars in the sky. Kitty got the forecast and said that the next few days are going to be sunny, thank God. You know how I hate the cold, love."

"I know – well, it's got pretty cold here now. It's about two degrees."

Heather knew that telling her mother how cold it was now in Ireland would make her very happy. Like most Irish people, she would enjoy the sun a lot more knowing that people back home were cold and shivering.

"Kitty wishes you a Happy Christmas."

"Well, tell her I said the same thing," Heather said.

"It sounds like you are in the room next door and not thousands of miles away."

"It does, doesn't it?"

"I'd better not stay on the line. I don't want to be running up Kitty's phone bill ringing from so far away."

"Okay. Happy Christmas, Mum."

"Happy Christmas, darling. You won't forget to go to Mass tomorrow and light a candle for your poor deceased father? I always think of him at this time of year."

"Me too, Mum. Have a lovely night tonight and enjoy your week. You'll have a ball. Love you."

"I love you too, darling."

Heather put the phone down. Her mother certainly seemed happy to be staying with her sister in a sunny climate this Christmas. No fuss. No bother. No fretting about family members coming to dinner or the hassle of washing up. Mind you, who could blame her? Her mother's widow's pension didn't stretch so far in these tough economic times. Herself and Auntie Kitty would enjoy the time together. Kitty didn't have any children and had moved to the Canaries years ago. She seemed to have a good social life over there mingling with other ex-pats. Heather had been out to visit Auntie Kitty herself before. Although she had really enjoyed the holiday and swimming in the sea in December, she didn't really see the attraction of living there all year round. The sun was lovely but even endless sunshine got a bit boring after a while. There was something quite nice about wrapping up against the elements in the winter with a warm woolly coat, hat and scarf. Or relaxing in front of a roaring log fire with a terrific book. For the first time in her life Heather wasn't spending Christmas with a loved one. She had always spent Christmas with her parents and since her father had passed away, having bravely lost a tough battle against cancer, she had spent Christmas with her mother. And last year with her fiancé, well, ex-fiancé now.

It still pained her to think that he was gone.

To her horror, Heather noticed a lone hot tear escaping down her cheek. It was the second one today. This was ridiculous. She brushed it away quickly. She didn't want to be miserable this

Christmas. She was a grown woman and Christmas magic was for kids. She thought of the children who had been on the flight earlier on, looking out the plane window to see if they could spot Santa on his sleigh while they were up in the air. It was so heartening to watch them. It was at times like that when Heather wished she were a mum. How exciting it must be to live in a house full of enthusiastic kids on Christmas Eve! She herself had loved Christmas as a child: hanging up her sock over the mantelpiece, waiting for Santa to arrive down the chimney to enjoy a glass of whiskey and a large slice of Christmas cake. Her father had loved Christmas too. Heather's family had always been the first family on the road to put the tree up in the window. Her dad had always bought her an Advent calendar too, and they had taken turns in opening the windows every day right up to the 24th where there would always be a Nativity scene with Mary, Joseph, Baby Jesus, and the shepherds. Then on Christmas Day they'd all go and see the big crib in the church after Christmas Mass, and light candles before coming home to tuck into a delicious turkey dinner, followed by trifle, pudding, and Christmas cake washed down with copious amounts of Coca Cola before retiring into the sitting room with a family tin of Quality Street. Oh, the memories . . .

The phone rang again making Heather jump. Who could it be? Surely her mother couldn't be calling yet again.

"Hello?"

"Heather?"

She frowned. Who was this?

"It's me, Eileen. I'm just phoning to wish you and your mum a happy Christmas."

Heather broke into a smile. It was so nice to hear from Eileen who had been her best friend from college. She hadn't seen her for the last few years as Eileen lived in England now.

"Hey, Eileen, it's so good to hear from you. Happy Christmas to you too. How is the weather where you are?"

"Same as the weather where you are. I'm in Ireland!"

"Really? In Galway with your family?"

"No, I'm in Wicklow."

"What are doing there? You never told me you were going to be in Ireland this Christmas."

"I didn't know I was going to be."

"Is Niall with you?"

"No."

"Where is he?"

"I don't know."

Heather was confused. Eileen and Niall were inseparable. Although they had never married, they were closer than nearly every married couple she knew.

"What do you mean?"

"I mean just that I have no idea where he is. I haven't seen him for quite some time.

"You mean he's missing? Have you called the police?"

Eileen gave a hollow laugh. "No need for the police. I don't know where he is but I do know who he's probably with. A French girl called Dionne. We had planned to travel to France next year, so Niall thought he'd get a few lessons first . . ."

"Oh God! So what are you doing in Wicklow?'

Heather couldn't remember her friend having friends or family in Wicklow. Eileen was from Galway.

"I'm here because I had to get away from England. I wanted to come home to Ireland, but not home to my family and their endless questions and their prying, and my mother telling me that it was always suspicious that Niall had never put a ring on my finger, and my brothers saying that I should have seen it coming."

"But Wickow?"

"Yes, I'm in a small guesthouse here in the middle of the woods. It's perfect. There's a log fire burning in the sitting room, and a huge Christmas tree in the window, all covered in fairy lights and paper lanterns. The landlady, Maura, is lovely and so thoughtful. When I checked in earlier, she had left a Christmas card on my pillow along with a mince pie and a Christmas cracker. The only problem is that I've nobody to pull it with."

"I know the feeling," mumbled Heather.

"What?"

"It sounds lovely," she said in a louder voice. "I wish I'd thought to do something like that. Escape to a little guesthouse in the woods. It wouldn't have occurred to me to book in somewhere on Christmas Eve."

"But aren't you spending Christmas with your mum?"

"No. She's in the Canaries with her sister."

"So you're on your own?"

"I am."

"Well, come down here. I'm in a twin room. There's lots of room for you."

"Ah no, I couldn't intrude on you like that."

"Intrude? Don't be ridiculous. I'd be delighted to have the company. The room is paid for so don't worry about money."

Heather was slightly horrified that her friend thought she might be worried about the cost. "Eileen, it's not the money, it's just that it's far away and –"

"Nonsense. You could be here in an hour. The skies are clear and there's no ice on the roads. Please come."

"I'm not prepared or anything."

"Okay, well, I understand. I'm putting you under pressure and I didn't mean to. How about we meet up on Boxing Day instead?"

"I'm working unfortunately. We have a choice between working Christmas or New Year. I chose to have the New Year off this year. Bummer."

"Okay, well, I'd better go and get ready."

"Ready?" Heather sounded surprised. "Are you going out?"

"Oh, no, nothing like that. The landlady, Maura, has invited everyone downstairs to join her for some mulled wine and nibbles at nine. At first I told her that I didn't really want to. You see, the reason I'm here is because I don't really feel like socialising this year. I told her I'd rather stay in my room."

"I suppose a glass or two wouldn't hurt . . ."

"Funny. That's what she said. Maura's an older single mother and . . . I don't know . . . I felt kind of sorry for her so I said I might join her for a glass but that I wouldn't like to put my name down for definite."

"Of course, that's understandable."

"So look, I'll give you a shout again soon, Heather. And look after yourself, won't you?"

"I will, Eileen. Merry Christmas, and a Happy New Year too."

Heather put down the phone. It didn't sound too bad, did it? Mulled wine and nibbles, instead of sitting in a little shoebox in the middle of a city by oneself? She eyed up the red wine the captain had given her. There was nothing stopping her screwing the top back on, quickly packing a bag, and heading for Wicklow. In an hour's time she could be in a lovely warm guesthouse, sipping mulled wine, and chatting to her old school friend beside a lovely Christmas tree.

She reached for the phone. It rang and rang and rang. Then it rang out. Sugar! Eileen must have gone to have a shower. Heather left a message. Could Eileen phone back immediately? She did ten minutes later.

"Have you changed your mind?" Eileen sounded pleased and excited.

"I have. I'll see you in an hour. Just give me directions.'

Eileen explained how to get to the guesthouse. "I'll save the cracker until you get here."

"Thanks," Heather said. "I didn't think I would mind spending Christmas alone, but then . . ."

"Maura said that lots of people think they want to spend Christmas alone but then they change their mind. Her guesthouse is always full on Christmas Eve. Last-minute bookings."

"How many rooms are there?"

"Just three but they're full."

"I see. Okay, I'm on my way. And Eileen?"

"Yeah."

"Thanks for thinking of me."

Fifteen minutes later, she was on the road. The streets were quiet now with very little traffic. It seemed that everyone belonged somewhere this Christmas. Even Heather. And it was a good feeling. It was nice to belong.

❖❖

Marisa Mackle is the *Irish Times* bestselling author of *Along Came a Stork*. Her first novel, *Mr Right for the Night* was a No. 1 bestseller in Ireland and she has published over twenty books including the children's book, *Girl in the Yellow Dress*, which was illustrated by the former Miss World, Rosanna Davison. Marisa's books have been translated into a dozen languages and her romantic comedies are popular with women the world over. Marisa keeps herself busy by writing a weekly column in the *Evening Herald* and dividing her time between her homes in Dublin and Spain. She has one child and the two obligatory cats that every writer should have. Her latest book is called the *Secret Nanny Club*. Marisa would like to wish all her readers a very happy Christmas. She can be contacted through her website www.marisamackle.ie

Blood Ties

Rosemary McLoughlin

The most popular afternoon programme on national television was to be axed, and the most popular person on it, Joe Durkin, was to be let go because he had no skills that could be used anywhere else.

The show was called *It's All Relative* and it had run successfully for twelve years, reuniting blood relations who had never met or who hadn't seen each other for decades. It was still holding on to its first place in the daytime ratings but the economic downturn had claimed it as a victim. The cost of flying a presenter and a camera crew to Canada or Australia, solely to capture the sight of people bursting into tears after being told an unknown relative was searching for them, could no longer be justified in these austere times. Most of the exclusively local stories based in Ireland and UK had been used up years previously, so there was no hope of drawing on them to fill up the hour and cut down on expenses.

The members of the crew were disbelieving when they heard the news. They had thought the stories would never stop coming. Divorce had proven to be as fertile a source in the present day as adoption had been in the past for producing the initial separations.

The stories were still there but the money from advertising had dried up.

All except Joe were to keep their original jobs for the new programme which would cost little to produce. It was to be called *The Smell of an Oil Rag*. Ordinary people would appear on it to share their austerity tips and demonstrate their money-saving stratagems. The old folks who had lived through the Emergency would have a chance to shine at last. Gardeners, handymen, seamstresses, whole-food cooks, decorators and inventors would be the stars of the show. Various advertisers had already shown an interest. Joe's gift of excessive empathy that produced tears every week, turning him into a minor celebrity along the way, would be of no value in the new chirpy, upbeat show.

The crew knew there was no use speaking to the bosses on Joe's behalf. Hundreds of lay-offs were expected in the following months. The bosses knew as well as they did that Joe had no qualifications and no drive so there was no way they would make an exception for him. He had secured the job in television in the first place through pull – his mother had known someone with influence – and it was never expected he would be promoted beyond his lowly position of gopher. The fact that he was likable wasn't a strong enough reason to keep him on.

But there was one thing they could do for him to send him off in a blaze of goodwill, and they sat around plotting the best way to go about it.

Poor Joe would have to give up his rented apartment and go back home to live with his mother, they sympathised, in between plotting.

"At least he doesn't have a family to support," said the floor manager. "That's some consolation."

"I think it would be more of a consolation if he had one. He'd make a terrific husband if only some woman could get near enough to attach a set of jump-leads to him," said the director.

"He doesn't need jump-leads," said Fiona, a researcher. "He's fine as he is except for that damned shyness that holds him back."

"A curse, that. Let's hope some perceptive woman will spot his good qualities one day and have the patience to draw him out," said the cameraman.

"I'd make a play for him myself if I wasn't old enough to be his mother," Fiona went on to say. "I'm going to miss his big warm presence around the place. He's one of nature's gentlemen."

"He is that. Poor Joe. Life just isn't fair. He's not likely to get any sort of job in Ireland in this economic climate. Especially with his lack of initiative."

"He'll probably have to emigrate."

"Can't see that ever happening. If he's shy with us, imagine how he'd feel facing a whole continent of strangers. Besides, he's too attached to his mother to go anywhere."

"His adoptive mother, you mean," smiled the director in a significant way. The rest of the crew smiled back as they began to pack up.

"I knew I'd be the first one shoved out," Joe had told his mother after he had first heard the news. "It's not as if I have any real input. Anyone off the street could do my job."

"I don't think that's true, dear," Anna had said. "You are special and the viewing public are mad about you. I'm sure the powers that be are aware of your value and will find another position for you before too long."

She was trying not to think about the prospect of having an unemployed, unqualified son of thirty-five having to give up his apartment and move back in with her just at a time when she was at a low ebb herself, mourning her own mother, only three months dead, and dreading the thought of Christmas without her. Though God knows why, thought Joe. It was such a relief to be rid of the nasty old bag. If his mother knew what had gone on at home while she was at work she mightn't have been so grief-stricken. His grandmother had been the bane of his life, hissing at him that he had bad blood inherited from his wicked birth mother and would end up just like her, bringing nothing but shame on his new family. The devil couldn't wait to punish him and had a scorching trident ready to push him into everlasting flames where he could be reunited with his evil mother at last, and serve them right, the pair of them with big, black stains on their souls.

Anna didn't have the money to send him to college. His grandmother did, but told him privately it would make her sick to her stomach to invest in someone with tainted blood. Joe left home soon after his excellent Leaving Certificate results were published and took a job driving a forklift in a warehouse. Worried about his increasingly solitary ways, Anna called in a favour from a friend who worked in the national television station who secured him a position of gopher on *It's All Relative* where he would be part of a team and have to socialise. The subject matter of the programme caused Anna to hesitate, but not for long. Joe's lack of social skills needed to be addressed before he became too set in his ways.

"You have a great gift with people," said Anna, who had judged the move to be a success. "Everyone you meet likes you and opens up to you. You're a good listener."

"No one cares about that. Crying's all they're interested in and that's not something to be proud of."

"I can't agree with you there. A soft heart can only be a good thing."

Tonight Joe noticed how his mother wasn't meeting his eye as she was talking, and she looked nervous as she sat down opposite him at the table.

She dropped her fork on the floor and he jumped up to fetch another one for her.

I bet she's wondering how her widow's pension is going to stretch to feed both of us when I'm no longer bringing in a salary, he thought, tasting the first mouthful of her perfectly prepared meal. She's not the only one who's worried. I bet she wishes she'd picked a different baby when she came to the agency and chose me. Someone who by now would have a career, a house, a wife and some children. Someone she could be proud of. Not a dud like me who hasn't managed to acquire even one of those.

Joe was positive the crew had been talking about him when he arrived for work at the beginning of the final week of the show. There had been a babble of voices, and then as he approached, silence, and then an over-enthusiastic welcome for him. Their greetings all sounded a bit false.

What's going on here? he asked himself. First my mother acts all peculiar, and now my friends are talking about me behind my back.

"For Part One we have a full brother and sister, Bluey and Kiera, who have never met, even though they're both living in Australia – Bluey all his life on the west coast and Kiera for the last ten years on the east," said the researcher, handing everyone a set of photographs.

Joe looked at the photo of the girl for a long time and felt himself gliding into the euphoria of impossibly perfect love.

"Come on, Joe. Hand it over," said the floor manager. "Wow! I can see why you were hanging on to it. She's a real stunner, and she has such a sweet expression. Is this an old photo?"

"No, it was taken recently. She's just broken off a long-term relationship and has decided to come back home to live, much to the relief of her family and handy for us. Arrived yesterday. She's just turned thirty, and her brother is thirty-two. She's all right, but he's not. There's a lot of bitterness on his part. Understandably. It took a lot of persuading to get him to go on the show at all. I'm only hoping that he's not going to create a scene live on air."

"What's the Australian footage of him like?"

"Great stuff. Heartbreaking in a good way. He didn't know anything about his biological parents and hadn't tried to find them. He was adopted at birth and taken to Australia straight afterwards. The adoption was not a success. He left home at fifteen and went bush, as they say there, and hasn't contacted either parent since. When we told him that after his adoption in

Dublin his mother and father subsequently married each other and had three more children, all girls, he was full of rage, and who could blame him? He'll be flying in on Tuesday with a big chip sitting on his shoulder, and you'll be doing the minding, Joe, as usual. From what I've heard you'll be put to the pin of your collar making sure he co-operates."

"Oh, no fears there. Joe will manage, won't you, Joe? We have the utmost faith in Joe, don't we, gang?" asked the director, looking around at everyone with a mischievous look in his eye.

The 'gang' chorused agreement.

Joe reddened. Was he actually being made fun of? A couple of the young ones giggled and whispered to each other behind their hands.

"What do we have after that?"

"A mother wanting to be reunited with her son."

"The usual. Here in Ireland?"

"Yes. That saved us a few euro."

"Thought we'd run out of home-grown ones ages ago."

"There's still a few keep popping up here and there."

"Any photos?"

"No. Neither party wanted to be taken so I didn't push it. You'll be seeing them soon enough. That's it, folks. Hard to believe we have only six more days in existence. Make the most of it."

"Come on, Joe," said Fiona, the researcher. "Let's go over to the cafeteria for a coffee – just the two of us – and have a nice, long chat in peace."

"Do you think he suspects anything?" the director asked when the two were out of earshot.

"Nah. He's not the suspicious type."

"All the machinery is in place. Only a couple more pieces of the jigsaw to be found and we'll be away on a hack."

"Leave it to Fiona. If anyone can winkle out secrets, Fiona can."

Fiona had recently heard Anna's story after waiting impatiently

234

for years. Anna had told her way back then that she couldn't say a word while her mother was still alive. She couldn't take the chance of a loose remark in front of her mother. Just the thought of it filled her with fear. But now the mother was dead and Anna had agreed at last to tell her story about Joe's adoption, especially as it would boost his profile among the viewing public, and who knows what offers might come in after the show?

All that was left for Fiona to do was to winkle out of Joe his side of the story to add extra pathos.

She did have worries about the surprise element of this production. Usually all parties signed permission slips before they took part in the show. The producer said he would take full responsibility. He didn't expect any problems since Joe was such a trooper it wouldn't cross his mind to let his mates down.

"We're going to miss you, Joe," Fiona said, as the two picked up their coffees and Danish pastries before settling opposite one another at a table for four.

Joe slumped forwards. "Would you ever put your scarf on that seat? Can't bear the thought of anyone joining us to offer their sympathies." He had already put his coat on the third seat after noting a few faces across the room turning towards him with interest.

"I know the crew are being a bit odd," said Fiona, doing as he asked, "but they're all jumpy at the moment, thinking the axe might fall on them as well before they get to take up their new positions. And they're all really genuinely sorry to see you go."

Joe didn't trust himself to comment on that remark. They have a funny way of showing it, was what he would have said if he'd spoken.

"Remember the early days, Joe? Remember the first time Andy turned the camera on you? Here, have half this Danish. I'm on a new diet." She put the half on his plate before he had time to answer. "Will you ever forget the reaction?"

How could he forget? It was so mortifying at the time. The viewers were expected to cry three times for each reunion during the one-hour show, but the members of the crew were meant to stay professionally detached. He had been crying quietly along with the audience for months whenever two people who hadn't seen each other for years were reunited. He couldn't help himself. He was deeply moved each time, and wondered if that had anything to do with the fact that he had never tried to find his own birth mother who was out there somewhere. His adoptive mother, Anna – a pearl beyond price – had been so good to him he didn't want to appear disloyal by searching for her rival, who was a bad egg, anyway, from what he had heard.

The day Andy the cameraman noticed Joe standing in the background crying quietly and had swung the camera around and caught him, exposing him to the public for the first time, was the day Joe had become a minor celebrity. The papers and magazines were full of the story of the man who hadn't become cynical and jaded through constant manipulation of other people's misfortunes for use as entertainment, but was in fact genuinely affected by each individual story.

There had been an unseemly argument after that. The ratings had soared. The fact that he was handsome and that his face didn't contort as he wept – the tears rolled unhindered down his face – had endeared him to the viewers. Joe had said he didn't want to become an exhibit detracting from the serious nature of the programme. The truth was that the prospect of people looking at him caused him to suffer agony. Why not just ignore him, he pleaded. "Ignore you?" squawked the producer. "Are you cracked? We stumble across a unique crowd-puller and you expect us to ignore it?" The producer offered to raise Joe's wages in line with the increased advertising revenue his fame had brought to the station. Joe didn't want to profit from other people's miseries and declined any extra payment. All he ever wanted was to quietly do his job out of the camera's view, but that option was denied him from that time on.

So he continued to cry, the cameraman continued to focus his camera on him at the crucial moments and *It's All Relative* continued to do well in the ratings.

"It just doesn't seem fair," he heard Fiona saying as he

brought his mind back to the present moment. "The show would have been considered pretty ordinary without you."

"I don't agree with that. Haven't I said all along that the stories were strong enough without any tricks?"

"You're being too modest as usual. Do you know something? I believe there's no limit to how far you could go if you only asserted yourself a little."

"You should know by now that's not in my nature," he said.

That was the opening Fiona needed to find out what his nature was, where it had come from and what had shaped it.

Joe let himself be drawn in by her sympathetic, warm regard. He was very fond of her and felt relaxed in her presence.

It was only afterwards he felt she had taken advantage of his vulnerable state, softening him up with a motherly tone, a black coffee and one-and-a-half Danish pastries to find out what he had kept secret until then. But at the time he had felt only relief at talking truthfully to her.

"I don't mind who knows, now that my grandmother is dead, God rest her shrivelled soul," he said before telling her the story she wanted to hear. His so-called father had put his eye on Anna, his adoptive mother, and practically laid siege to her to get her to marry him so they could adopt his sister's son – that was Joe. "He didn't want me to go to strangers, so he said, and he wanted to be able to see me grow up. Anna was a motherly type even then, and my father had complete trust in her. Then as soon as the whole thing was legalised he scarpered with his sister, who turned out not to be his sister at all. Left my mother high and dry, literally holding the baby of two con artists. She returned home to Dublin eventually so she could go back to work to support us while my grandmother looked after me and she never saw her husband or my mother again."

Joe was glad to see Fiona was finding the story as extraordinary as he did whenever he thought of it, which was often because of the weekly showing of *It's All Relative*.

She continued to ask him questions and he continued to answer them for a further ten minutes before she made a move to leave. "You're a lovely man." She smiled across at him.

"You'll be a great catch for some lucky woman. I was only saying to the crew the other day that I'd make a play for you myself if I wasn't such an old one."

Joe thanked her for the compliment that said more about her good nature than his appeal. He stayed behind and ordered another coffee. His forbidding expression deterred anyone who might have entertained thoughts of joining him at the table from making a move.

He wanted to make sense of it all – his mother acting all nervy and distant, his friends making fun of him behind his back, Fiona showing an interest in him and paying him compliments.

The only conclusion he could come to was they all thought he was a loser and, now that he was soon to become unemployed, felt free to show their lack of respect for him along with a curiosity about what made him tick.

He was quietly angry by the time he had processed his thoughts and left the cafeteria without finishing his coffee. People at other tables stared after him, puzzled.

It was the day of the final show of *It's All Relative*.

Joe was feeling strung out with nerves and Bluey, the prickly import from Australia, wasn't helping Joe's state of mind by pacing up and down, opening the door of the soundproof room and wanting to go out to catch sight of his sister before their public reunion in front of the cameras. In the end Joe threatened to call security if Bluey didn't sit down and keep the door closed.

Joe studied him while they were waiting. He didn't look anything like his dazzling sister. One would never pick them for siblings. Not that that was anything new – he had often noticed how there was sometimes no family resemblance between a reunited pair, and wondered if either the researchers had made a mistake or one parent's genes had dominated so markedly that they had only allowed the other's recessive ones to line up. Or, as he sometimes suspected, the mother had told a lie about the paternity of the child in the first place and there wasn't any genetic link at all between the child and his supposed father.

What if those displays of intense joy that such occasions elicited were directed at the wrong person? A person with no genetic connection whatsoever? Was it all in the mind? Did it matter?

Joe didn't want Bluey's resentment towards his birth parents, who unknown to him were seated in the audience and were already crying, to be directed towards the adorable Kiera and he determined that if he upset her in any way he'd knock his bloody teeth in.

He had worked himself up to a pitch. He was a man in love.

Kiera came on first and took her seat on the couch. The presenter guided her through her story of how for ten years she had been on the same continent as her brother, whose existence she wasn't aware of, and how thrilled she was that she would be meeting him in a few minutes' time. Joe thought he had never seen anyone look so sublime, or behave so endearingly.

The floor manager signalled to Joe to bring on Bluey. Kiera, radiant with anticipation, was looking towards the door. Joe wondered what would happen if Bluey and the floor-sweeper walked out at the same time. Would Kiera instinctively know which one was her brother or would she have to be told? Joe, in a voice of authority he didn't know he possessed, instructed the security guard to keep Bluey in the soundproof room for a little longer, before putting his earphones, identity card, clipboard and microphone down on to a chair, and walking out of the shadows on to the set and sweeping up the joyful, weeping Kiera into his arms.

One of the thoughts that crossed his mind as he hugged his 'sister' was that at least they couldn't fire him for doing such an outrageous thing, seeing he was already redundant, and even if they could, it would have been worth it to feel those divine arms around his neck for those few seconds.

There was consternation on the floor, babbling in the audience. Joe was forcibly pulled out of Kiera's arms by the security man who was supposed to be watching Bluey, who had escaped from the soundproof room in time to give Joe a punch in the face before they were all bundled out of shot and the engineer switched quickly to commercials, much to the disappointment of the viewers at home. A tabloid journalist who had been sitting beside the parents bolted towards the exit, shouting into his mobile phone as he ran.

The security guard came in to find Joe to tell him the director wanted him back, bleeding face and all, standing in his usual place on the floor, even though in this half of the show he wasn't in charge of any of the participants.

The audience seemed unusually skittish. They must have been told something during the commercial break that Joe hadn't heard. What he had heard was that there was a twist to the usual format to celebrate the last ever programme. Instead of the birth mother coming to find her adopted child, it was the adoptive mother coming on to find the birth mother that her son refused to look for.

He should have guessed, and he might have if his mind hadn't been so full of Kiera.

His mother Anna was guided out and seated on the sofa. She looked over at him, as he stood out of view of the camera, and began by saying, "Joe, I have to tell you that I'm sorry. I've told you a whole pack of lies and now at last I can tell you the truth."

He looked behind him and saw all the crew grinning at him and giving the thumbs-up signal. Fiona was crying.

Anna had become pregnant in Dublin at the comparatively late age of twenty-three to a work colleague who was engaged to someone else, she explained. In fear of her mother's reaction, she went to England and stayed in a charity Mother and Baby Home until her baby was born. There was no husband, no sister with a baby son, no wedding, only an unmarried mother in a home. The idea at the Home was that babies born there would be adopted out to wealthy, childless couples who would give them every material and spiritual benefit they could possibly desire. Only selfish girls kept their babies, the unmarried mothers were told, condemning their children to lives of shame and deprivation. Despite that warning, Anna was determined to keep hers and was lucky to obtain work for four years as a live-in housekeeper to an old lady who allowed her to bring the baby with her as long as he didn't cry too much. He didn't – he was such a good-tempered, docile child. "And he still is," Anna added with a smile. When the old lady had to go into a home, Anna was forced to return to her mother's house with a story that was so unbelievable her mother believed it.

And so did I, thought Joe.

"I'm sorry, Joe," she said. "I couldn't risk telling you while my mother was still alive. You might have let it slip when you had drink taken and she would have thrown me out and publicly denounced me. I was afraid of her all my life."

Not half as afraid of her as I was, Joe thought sadly.

"So your adopted son Joe wasn't adopted after all," the presenter spelt out. "He was your natural son all along." He turned towards Joe at the same time as the camera caught the tears coursing down his face. "Joe, come out here and greet your birth mother whom you last saw five hours ago."

Joe left his post and enclosed Anna in his second joyful hug of the afternoon.

The members of the audience were on their feet, crying, cheering, laughing, clapping and stamping. The beaming, emotional crew were standing around in the background, trying to get a look without coming into shot.

Joe looked over Anna's damp shoulder at them. "You gangsters," he said affectionately. "You set me up."

Joe filled in and signed the form granting permission for his part of the show to be aired. The writing was a bit jerky as each member of the crew came up to give their good wishes and slap him on the back while he was trying to complete the details.

Joe felt such a surge of happiness he wondered how he could ever have entertained such negative thoughts as those of the last week and how he could ever have believed his grandmother's assertion that his blood was bad.

A year later Joe married Kiera on the set of the newly commissioned series *Who Dares Has a Pretty Good Chance*, which was soaring in the ratings. Bluey was the best man.

Press photographers jostled to get close-up shots of the man who had inspired the title and theme of the show and had been appointed as its producer. The public had clamoured to have him present it, as they wanted to see his face on screen, but he said he wasn't up to that yet.

"I'm still shy, you know. That hasn't changed."

A perplexed Kiera, her hand holding Joe's, looked over at Anna. "What's he talking about?" she asked.

--✦✦--

A member of a large family, **Rosemary McLoughlin** was reared as Rosie Fahey in a small village called Tyringham in NSW, Australia. She saved up enough money to travel to Europe for a two-year working holiday. It was in Powers Hotel, Kildare St, where she worked as a waitress and barmaid, that she met her future husband, Kevin. They have lived in Dublin for the last forty years. They have two adult children, Cian and Orla. In her fifties Rosemary began to paint. She will be exhibiting her first solo show in the Leinster Gallery in Spring of next year. In her sixties she began to write and found that the story she was telling began to take over her life, to the exclusion of her painting, until *Tyringham Park* was completed. Writing turned out to be so exciting and consuming that she wished she had taken it up thirty years earlier, and mourns the wasted hours. At the moment she is halfway through her second book, *Twelve Thousand Miles*.

The Gift of Love

Mary Malone

Carleen's face broke into a smile of relief as she read the text from Lucas. Jingle Bells, Jingle Bells . . . shouldn't be too long more . . . X She replied with a single X.

With Christmas exploding around her, every shop, pub and restaurant draped in tinsel and fairy lights, she was looking forward to this one more than any other. And, to her delight, temperamental Lucas seemed in a festive mood too.

Tossing her phone on the pine coffee table, she hummed softly and went to check on the mince pies baking in the oven, inhaling the delicious aroma lingering in her kitchen. With nothing to do but wait for her guest to arrive, she poured a generous measure of chardonnay, increased the volume of her music and danced around her living room. Wineglass held aloft, her hips swaying to the upbeat tempo booming from her iPod, she grinned impishly at her reflection in the over-mantel mirror, recognising a wild look in her expressive green eyes, her flame-coloured hair flying behind her as she twirled around and around, glossed lips waiting to be kissed. Anticipation filled every pore, her heart exploding at the promise the evening held.

Loving (and lusting after) Lucas was driving her wild with desire, their intense chemical connection unlike anything she'd ever experienced. It had been only six weeks since their eyes had met across the bank's boardroom table and in that short space of time he'd invaded her body, mind and soul. Thoughts of him rolled inside her head every moment of every day, seeping into her dreams at night, her hunger for him seldom far from her mind.

"Is it you who'll be renegotiating our quarterly terms and conditions?" Lucas had enquired after that initial credit meeting.

"Yes," she'd stammered, her stomach somersaulting as his caressing tone melted her inside.

"Could you spare another half hour of your time this morning? I'd like to brief you on company priorities, finer details that were excluded on today's agenda."

"The bank's cafeteria serves very good coffee. We could continue our discussion there," she suggested.

"I had something more culinary in mind," Lucas said. "There was a delicious smell of baking coming from a French café a short walk from here. I'd love to try some of their bread."

Carleen laughed. "I know the one you're talking about and you're right, it's irresistible. I often take the long way home to avoid indulging. Their bread and cheese selections are mouth-watering."

"What are we waiting for? Lead the way," Lucas instructed.

He turned up the collar of his navy wool jacket as they left the building and held an umbrella over Carleen as they hurried to the café.

Remembering it clearly, she was filled with warmth. Normally detesting the rain, she'd never been more grateful for an excuse to huddle close under a large golf umbrella!

Their 'terms and conditions' conversation quickly turned personal and realising their 'morning coffee' had almost extended to lunchtime, Carleen had jumped from the chair in shock. "I have to run, I've a conference call at twelve forty-five," she explained, zipping up her beige parka jacket and taking her wallet from her brown leather handbag.

"My treat," Lucas insisted with a smile, waving away her offer to pay.

"But it's a company expense," she teased, a playful glint in her eye, her bravado spiked by a mixture of strong coffee and attractive company.

"Carleen," he said, his tone turning serious, "I'd like to see you again. Will you come for dinner with me?"

Swallowing hard, she felt caught between avoiding any form of fraternisation with a client and following her heart and screaming 'Yes!' But her ringing phone cut through the moment, preventing her from having to make an instant decision.

"Saved by the bell," Lucas grinned.

"Sorry but I have to take this," she apologised, hurrying from the restaurant as her colleague transferred a disgruntled client through to her mobile.

But she needn't have worried about the untimeliness of her call denying her a chance of an evening with Lucas. Before she'd left the office that afternoon, he'd emailed her the minutes of their boardroom meeting, including his personal mobile number as a postscript and asking her to text him a response to his earlier invitation.

Feeling his lips on hers at the end of their first official date, Carleen had let go her inhibitions about mixing business and pleasure. At thirty-two years old, she'd had more than her share of one-night-stands as well as the experience of two serious relationships, enough involvement with the opposite sex to recognise powerful chemistry and feelings that up to now she'd believed had only existed in romantic novels. From that moment on, Carleen's heart was captivated by Lucas, her head debating furiously, urging her to take things slowly but losing every battle to the overwhelming passion she was experiencing with her new lover. Her imagination already on overdrive, thoughts of his sensual touch heightened her senses, raising them to a level she hadn't known existed *pre-Lucas*.

Since that first kiss, Carleen's life was dividing into two neat compartments, *pre* and *post-Lucas*. *Post-Lucas* mostly represented a heady, all-guns-blazing excitement. *Pre-Lucas*, dull by comparison, was fading into an imaginary cobweb in the recess of her mind.

Time dragged between opportunities to trail her fingers over his muscular body, their mutual obsession with each other often scuppered by altered arrangements – dates broken 'unavoidably' by Lucas on every occasion. Sensitive to the newness of their relationship, she'd restrained from harassing him for explanations, accepting his apologies and hiding her intense disappointment.

The track on her iPod changed, mournful lyrics filling the room and interrupting her reflections. What's taking him so long, she wondered? She glanced at the clock, biting her lower lip, insecurity nudging its way inside her. As though on cue, her phone beeped.

"Please don't be cancelling," she muttered, her heart thumping, creases lining her forehead as she read the text.

Sorry! There soon. Promise. xx

Two kisses this time, she thought, relief coursing through her again. At least he's not postponing our evening. Letting out the breath she'd been holding, she typed an immediate response, more than just a kiss this time.

So excited about getting into Xmas mode. Can't wait for you to get here. XX

She dropped the phone on the coffee table once more, spirits rising again as she listened for his ring on the doorbell, imagining running to greet him, visualising leaping into his arms, kissing his face, touching him, feeling his body mould around hers, inhaling his trademark musky scent.

Soon, she hoped.

But an hour and two more 'excuse' texts later, he still hadn't arrived, the clock chiming in hurtful reminder as another playlist came to an end, the mince pies cold and mournful on the kitchen counter, the aroma of Christmas baking faded.

He's not coming, Carleen's conscience screamed. *You're facing another disappointment, another night stuck in alone.*

246

Shut up, shut up, she thought, shaking her head, refusing to accept that this was true.

Picking up her phone in desperation, she began to type.

Lucas??? What's going on? Are you cancelling?

Reading the needy text repeatedly, she cleared the words from the screen without sending. A nagging text was liable to send him running in the opposite direction. She drained her wineglass, unsure about another refill. I'll wait until he gets here, she decided, moving to stand by the fireplace, careful not to disturb her artistic array of Christmas decorations on the mantelpiece. Taking great care arranging the red and gold trinkets across the wooden ledge, she'd sprayed the display with 'snow' and assessed her work, tweaking the arrangement critically before switching on the glistening fairy lights and bringing the room to life.

Three weeks after their first date, they'd shared a magical weekend break in London, the build-up to Christmas infectious, the magnificent array of decorations difficult to resist. Arguing playfully over the theme colour with Lucas had been fun, a taste of normality. Eventually agreeing on the rich ambiance of red and gold, they'd lugged the delicate items as hand-luggage on the plane home that Sunday night, huddling together in the darkened cabin, fingers entwined as the roar of the engines on the runway signalled the end of their fantastic weekend.

Her heart leapt with relief at the sound of her phone ringing. He's probably outside the door, she thought, grinning as she hurried to answer.

"Hi there," she chirped.

"Hello, Carleen. I've been waiting for you to phone."

Disappointment warred with guilt when she heard her mother's complaining tone.

"I should have called, Mum. I'm sorry." Contacting home had completely slipped her mind. Well, not entirely if she were honest. But she was stalling for time, didn't want to disappoint her mother by refusing her annual invite for the holidays. Damn, damn, damn!

With only one week to go, she needed to break the news now. "About Christmas, Mum," she began.

"Family should be together at Christmas," her mother interrupted. "I don't want to hear any lame excuses. What's going on lately? You seem distracted. There's something or somebody you're not telling me about."

Groaning inside, Carleen dragged her fingers through her hair. Trust Mum to see right through her. "I'm going to try something different this year, have Christmas in the city instead of travelling. The weather forecast's not great, a threat of snow and poor driving conditions," she improvised. *Why can't I tell my mother there's a man in my life?*

Because you're afraid he'll disappear.

"Christmas alone, afraid of a bit of snow? You want to be alone on Christmas Day when you could be with your brother and sisters and parents?"

"Of course I want to be with you all," she said in exasperation, her plans to spend the holidays with Lucas foremost in her mind. Regardless of how selfish she felt, she didn't want to change those plans, knew she couldn't even if she'd wanted to. Her heart wouldn't let her. "I'll come for New Year instead," she offered as a compromise.

"But New Year's Eve isn't the same. Your brothers are both on duty and your sister has some gala dinner that night. Please, Carleen, come home for Christmas! You've already missed stirring the cake and pudding. You never said why you didn't make it home that weekend?"

A guilty blush spread over Carleen's face. Answering the door to a delivery guy and receiving an enormous bouquet of fresh flowers from Lucas that Friday had spurred her to call home and forgo the eighth of December tradition where every family member took part in the Christmas baking regime. CU@7.X had been printed on the accompanying card.

"Carleen, are you still there?"

"Sorry, Mum." Taking a deep breath, she answered her mother's previous question, the truth behind the memory piercing. "It was a work thing that weekend. I wish now I hadn't bothered. Turned out to be a big build-up to nothing."

Crying bitter tears when seven o'clock had come on Friday, Saturday and Sunday without a visit from Lucas, her phone the bearer of a series of excuses by text. He hadn't even had the manners to call and still she'd waited. And amidst her sorrow, she'd craved the smell and warmth of her mother's kitchen, regretting her decision to miss the fun and laughter with her family, stubborn pride preventing her from changing her mind and turning up unannounced.

Her mother's sigh came down the phone. "Well my dear girl, life's like that sometimes, little more than bitter disappointment. But your home and your family are always here for you. Make sure you remember that, if you change your mind. No invitations required, the door is always on the latch."

"Thanks, Mum," Carleen said, the lump in her throat making her voice catch. "I'll call you Christmas Eve."

Sitting staring into space with her mother's words rolling in her head, her music continued to play, romantic lyrics stinging Carleen's heart. She fought against threatening tears, the sentiment of the songs growing ever more poignant with her increasing despondency. Would their Friday night remain another unfulfilled dream? What was her position on his priority list? Was he making a fool of her? Had he somebody else? The suspicion raged inside her head but, still too much under the influence of their intense passion, she refused to confront the possibility.

"Lucas," she pleaded aloud in the empty room, "you promised nothing would get in the way of tonight!"

Hating how she'd allowed their relationship to obliterate the life she'd had *pre-Lucas*, she suddenly longed for the Friday night ritual of joining her friends in the lively bar opposite the bank. By now they'd be discussing the week's highlights, sharing baskets of hot food and trying to be heard over the din of the background music, their spirits and laughter soaring as they celebrated the beginning of a weekend of socialising.

Post-Lucas, however, these gatherings were something she'd attended less and less, uttering feeble excuses to her colleagues and rushing straight home instead, sacrificing more and more with every passing day, instinct forbidding her from publicising her relationship with a client.

Her inner voice snarled, *You sit at home waiting and Lucas arrives when it suits. Why can't you see what's staring you in the face? He's hiding something, all is not as it seems.*

Carleen's heart took another nosedive, truth a difficult pill to swallow. Spurts of pleasure with Lucas carried an expensive price-tag, glorious, short-lived highs followed by excruciating lows when he became vague and distant, a see-saw of emotions from one day to the next and a difficult balance for Carleen to control.

Another song coming to an end, she scrutinised her reflection closely, stunned by the level of desperation staring back at her. Momentary silence forced her to accept reality. He wasn't coming. Again on cue, her phone beeped. She swallowed the lump in her throat, blinking furiously to stop her tears falling. She clenched her fists, manicured nails digging into her palms. Another beep. Heart pounding, she opened the text.

Unavoidable diversion but hope to still make it. L

No kiss this time was her first observation. God damn it, she thought. How pathetic am I? Interpreting his level of interest by the content of a text message? He hasn't shown up! Isn't that a much clearer message to read? Damn you, Lucas! She set the font to capital letters, typing quickly, for once ignoring her heart and allowing the voice inside her head full control.

IF IT'S TOO MUCH TROUBLE, MAN UP AND SAY SO! STOP DANGLING ME ON A STRING!

"Why did I expect tonight to be any different?" she wondered, remembering the solemn promise he'd made earlier as they'd parted company outside of the Georgia hotel where they'd attended the bank's Christmas clients' lunch. Waiting until the officials had left, he'd pulled her against him, his smouldering eyes boring into hers for the briefest moment before their lips met. His touch had its usual magnetic effect, leaving her shaken, dazed and completely under his spell.

Refilling her wineglass, she switched to a new playlist, harsh, loud music in keeping with her increasing fury. Spotting the untouched pile of decorations in the corner, she was tempted to kick them over and stamp on them – in the same way he had trampled on her excitement.

Decorating the tree – an essential part of the build-up to their first Christmas together – would have been fun. She dropped to her knees and opened the boxes of lights, plugging them in and watching as they twinkled and flickered, the diverse array intended to intensify the atmosphere and accentuate their lovemaking. Untangling the long lengths of cable, she imagined the powerful explosion they'd have shared at first, closely followed by gentle and slow teasing, no doubt reaching repeated crashing climaxes throughout the evening and into the early hours. Classic perfection . . . if he'd arrived.

Reaching for the remote control, she silenced the music, knowing any hopes she'd had of partying were over. Turning on the television instead, she flicked mindlessly through the channels, Christmas cheer in mocking abundance, the final insult being another beep from her phone.

She didn't need to pick it up and read it. The routine was all too familiar. He wasn't coming. Pressing the power button on the TV remote, she watched the picture fade from the screen before unplugging the Christmas lights and allowing darkness fill the room.

Saturday dragged for Carleen, her attempt to cancel a pre-arranged get-together with friends falling on deaf ears.

"But you can't cancel our Christmas night out," her friend Sophie insisted. "You've barely answered our texts in weeks! We miss you, Carleen. Anyway, the others are already on their way!"

Sophie's guilt trip had the desired effect. Carleen knew it was too late to back out now. It would be a waste of time mentioning exhaustion after a restless night's sleep, tossing and turning and watching time crawl by. "Okay, okay. Keep your hair on, Soph! I'll be there as arranged but I might have to leave early."

"Whatever's eating you, Carleen, you can tell us."

"It's nothing, Soph." Nothing I can divulge anyway, she thought, biting her lip.

"We'll see you at seven at the restaurant. Don't you dare let us down!"

Carleen couldn't help smiling. She'd forgotten Sophie's dogged determination and sharp intuitiveness. Opening her wardrobe before she could change her mind again, she took out the midnight-blue dress she'd bought for the occasion, a short sassy number she'd fallen in love with as soon as she'd spotted it in the window of her favourite boutique.

Laying her outfit and accessories on the bed, she went to the adjoining bathroom and stepped into the shower. Squirting liberally from the plastic bottle of luxurious gel she'd intended to massage on Lucas's skin, she inhaled its sensual perfume, closed her eyes and stood under the flow of warm water. "Damn you, Lucas," she muttered, remembering the unopened text messages on her phone, self-protection preventing her from reading his excuses. "I'm not sparing it for you when you couldn't even bother turning up!"

The dress hung loosely on her, emphasising her recent weight loss. Taking a narrow silver belt from her wardrobe, she pulled it tight around her waist, the accessory shaping her enviable figure and instantly improving her look. Perfecting her make-up and hair, she gave a last glance in the mirror and smiled at her reflection, grateful Sophie had convinced her to go.

Her attention on the contents of her silver clutch bag, she stood outside her house checking she had her keys and wallet, failing to notice an unexpected guest walking up the footpath until he was at her side.

"*Wow!*"

"Lucas!" Carleen jerked her head up, paling under the carefully applied foundation and bronzing powder designed to camouflage exhaustion, her mouth drying as she came face to face with her lover.

"Why haven't you answered my texts?"

"Lucas, now isn't a good time."

"You look stunning! That outfit's irresistible and I can't wait to get you out of it! But first we need to talk. I owe you an explanation."

She gaped at him, unsure how to answer his unabashed expectancy, his proximity unnerving. Her heart betrayed her, soaking up his compliments, making her glad she'd worn her short faux-fur jacket over the dress instead of her ankle-length wool coat. She bit her lip, tasting her strawberry gloss. What should she do? She fumbled with her purse, checking for her keys once more, concentration wavering as she struggled to maintain a distance between them. A few minutes wouldn't make much difference to her evening. He wants to talk.

Are you out of your tiny mind? What about the avalanche of tears you shed last night? Carleen's subconscious was having none of her melting, traitor heart.

Before Carleen could respond to Lucas, another unannounced visitor arrived.

"Great, you're still here. I'm glad I caught you in time." Sophie appeared behind Lucas, dark curls bouncing on her shoulders as she hurried past him. "Aren't you going to introduce us, Carleen?"

"Weren't we meeting at the restaurant?" Carleen's tone was sharper than intended.

"I asked the taxi driver to swing by, thought we'd travel together," Sophie pulled her friend into a bear-hug, whispering in her ear, "and just in the nick of time it seems too! I can see why you've been ignoring us for this specimen of good looks!"

"Lucas, this is Sophie," Carleen said, looking from one to the other without enlightening either of them any further.

"We met in primary school," her friend volunteered, eyeing the tall, athletic type with appreciation.

"Friends for quite a while then," Lucas commented, a grin crossing his face. "Nice to meet you."

Having him and Sophie in such close proximity shocked Carleen into merging life *pre-Lucas* with *post-Lucas*. What had possessed her to neglect family and true friends for someone who constantly disappointed, people who'd shown her nothing but kindness? And now, despite her shabby treatment, they continued including her in their Christmas celebrations. They loved her and she'd given nothing in return.

"Where are you from, Lucas?" Sophie filled the silence.

Deep in thought and self-deprecation, Carleen tuned out of their conversation.

Lucas's jovial attitude, his dismissal of the disappointment he'd caused her and his expectation that she'd fall at his feet without question filled her with a mixture of fury and shame – fury with the man who proclaimed she excited and fulfilled him and shame with herself for acting so foolishly. She stared at him now, recognising the boyish excitement in his eyes. He's twenty-four hours late and expects a welcome like nothing has happened. Instead of apologising, he's behaving like an errant schoolboy who has missed dinner.

Why so surprised, her inner voice sneered. *Isn't that the behaviour you've encouraged? Don't you jump around like an excited puppy when he makes an appearance? If Sophie hadn't arrived wouldn't you be in his arms now?*

Six weeks ago, Carleen thought, I was a woman with a brain, an opinion and self-respect. And now my life's revolving around Lucas. It's unhealthy, unreasonable and totally unacceptable. At what point did I let go my hold on dignity?

The morning you huddled under his umbrella, her subconscious snorted.

I'm responsible, not him, she realised. I chose to wait around and make myself fully available. I could have continued with my existing social life and expected him to fit around it but I didn't.

"Sophie, we should get going. The girls will be waiting." Carleen's voice trembled, her discomfort evident. She didn't want to lose him but she needed to get their relationship on a more normal footing. "They won't hold our table, not this close to Christmas."

Lucas's face fell. "Can you spare me a few minutes before you go? There's something I should explain."

"Want to share our cab? Then you can talk to Carleen on the way," Sophie invited.

"I wouldn't want to intrude." He looked expectantly at Carleen, holding her gaze. "I've got the car. Perhaps I could drop you?"

The waiting taxi driver revved his engine. "I'm losing fares sitting here, girls," he called through the open window.

"It's a girls' night out, Lucas, been arranged for ages – call me tomorrow," Carleen managed after a few stammered attempts, grabbing Sophie's arm and hurrying to the car before changing her mind. More than anything she'd wanted to accept his offer. But tonight was for her friends and, if she meant anything to him, he'd call her tomorrow.

"Why haven't you told me about him?" Sophie squealed as soon as taxi driver pulled away from the kerb. "He's gorgeous!"

Attempting a smile, she looked at her friend. "I've been asking myself that question too," she sighed. "But, Sophie, I owe you and the others a huge apology. I've been so self-obsessed. I've a lot of making-up to do." Her head pounded, the sound of Bing Crosby's 'White Christmas' reverberating around the car, increasing the pressure in her pounding temples.

"Carleen, don't be silly! We'll always be here for you. We love you!"

"And I lost sight of that. I don't deserve friends like you, Soph," she insisted, clutching her hand and squeezing it tightly before glancing surreptitiously around, just in time to see Lucas's car take off in the opposite direction.

"Are you crying?" Sophie lowered her voice.

Carleen sniffed and nodded, blinking furiously to try and prevent any more tears from falling. "Sorry, Sophie. I'm shattered, didn't sleep a wink last night."

"Lucas?" her friend enquired.

Nodding, Carleen shrugged her shoulders. "He's amazing but totally unreliable."

"And you've fallen for him?"

"Big time, but at a price I'm ashamed to say. I've been foolish.

I'm thirty-two, acting like a fifteen-year-old, prepared to overlook anything rather than lose him!"

"The face on him when you told him you were on a girls' night out! That will make him try harder for your affections," Sophie giggled. "Christmas brings the best and worst out in us all."

Carleen squeezed Sophie's hand in hers, already fretting about not giving him those few minutes he'd requested, fearful she'd pushed him away. "He stands me up more often than not."

"I'm here if you want to talk," Sophie replied as the taxi pulled up outside the restaurant. "Try and put him out of your mind for a few hours. It'll help you rationalise the situation."

With her friends' help, Carleen managed to get into the spirit of their reunion, their relaxed company a poignant contrast to the stress she'd been under recently.

"I can't believe the night's over already," a semi-drunk Sophie said wistfully as they waited for taxis outside the busy restaurant. "Won't any of you go on to a night club? Going home now makes me feel old!"

The others laughed with her but were resolute in their decision.

"Taxi!" Carleen hailed the first cab, hugging her friends one last time before jumping into the back of the car, surprised when Sophie got in beside her.

"Thought you'd slope home alone and cry yourself to sleep? We're having a sleepover and that's final."

"Sounds perfect." Taking her mobile phone from her bag for the first time since she'd left Lucas earlier, she noticed fifteen missed calls. Guessing they were all from him, she resisted temptation and turned off her phone. Tonight was about reuniting with the friends she'd taken for granted. Tomorrow she'd hear what Lucas had to say and maybe they could start afresh.

"I've got you a really cute gift, but it's not wrapped," Sophie mumbled before resting her head on Carleen's shoulder and drifting to sleep.

"Tonight you've shown me the importance of the best gift in the world, one that doesn't require wrapping," Carleen whispered to her friend. "The gift of love and friendship."

First thing in the morning, she decided, regardless of what happens with Lucas, I'll call Mum and let her know I'll be home for Christmas after all. Everything else could wait one more day.

❖

Mary Malone lives in Templemartin, Bandon, Co Cork, with her husband Pat and sons David and Mark. Working full time in the Central Statistics Office as well as being a published author, life can be hectic for Mary at times, and she often writes late into the night to meet deadlines. But seeing her books sitting prominently on the shelves in bookshops and receiving complimentary correspondence from readers makes the hard work and persistence very worthwhile. Mary has had four published novels, with her fourth title, *Love Is The Reason*, becoming a bestseller. Her fifth book, *Where There's A Will*, delves into the thorny subject of inheritance and family secrets and will be published by Poolbeg in Autumn 2012. Mary is currently working on her sixth novel. For more information, visit her website, www.marymalone.ie.

Evening News

Miranda Manning

Sarah found a seat on the Luas and had just sat down when it lurched into motion. She was glad of the twenty-minute journey ahead. She needed time to sort out her thoughts. She watched as the Christmas lights lit up the puddles on the pavement outside, glinting almost as brightly in the shimmering water as they did overhead. Her fellow passengers were typical of commuters everywhere – careful not to make eye contact, hoping not to be forced to sit close to someone who was wetter than them. No conversation – some had iPods while others clearly were listening to the radio on their phones. The people standing were swaying in motion with the Luas. They were probably just anxious to get home.

It was Friday. It should have been a good day. She always looked forward to the weekend. Despite their difficulties, she and Brendan and the kids always made a point of doing something interesting together rather than just letting the couple of days slip by. It might only be a walk in the Dublin Mountains but since the children were getting older a trip to their favourite shopping centre was more the norm. But they did it as a family – it was part of their routine.

But this evening Sarah had a problem – made more complicated by the fact that it was good news really. Having worked on a temporary basis as a copywriter at the advertising agency for almost twelve months, she had been told today that the woman she was replacing had decided not to return to work after her maternity leave.

"The job is yours if you want it, Sarah," Phil, her boss, had said. "Your work is always highly imaginative. I was regretting that I would have to let you go but now I don't so all is well. It's a win-win situation. It will mean a raise as well. You are now a member of the permanent staff. Congratulations!"

The other copywriters took her out to lunch to celebrate. She should have been delighted. Heaven knows she needed the job and the raise would come in handy as well. It had been her salary that had paid the mortgage for most of that year. Brendan had been made redundant more than fifteen months earlier and they were trying not to touch his not very large lump sum until they had to. It was their rainy-day fund and so far they had been able to manage without it except when the car needed new tyres. Brendan had quite enjoyed the role reversal involved in being a house husband at first. The children were all at school now and initially he had enjoyed tackling all the little jobs in the house which he hadn't had the time for when he was working. He had even taken up woodwork at the local tech and they were both very proud of the bookcase he had made for the sitting room. They were even considering if he could replace the shabby carpet in the sitting room with a wood floor but decided against it until he was a bit more experienced.

But as time went on there seemed less and less for him to do. The housework almost did itself and the children were good at doing their share. The interviews were getting scarcer and Sarah could see that Brendan was beginning to lose heart. He was beginning to feel redundant in life as well as in work. She knew that it was a feeling that many housewives had when the children started school and there didn't seem to be much to do. She remembered the feeling well even though it had been easier for her. She had other housewives, who were in the same boat, to moan to. For Brendan there was no one. House husbands were fairly thin on the ground in their estate.

259

They tried to continue living their lives normally when Brendan was made redundant. They budgeted carefully and were still able to go out occasionally in the evenings with friends, though after a few months they decided it was cheaper to invite people to their home and that worked well too. But it was hard on Brendan when all the men seemed to talk about was work. He stopped playing golf when one day after a game the others in the foursome wouldn't let him buy a round of drinks in the bar afterwards. They said they had enough, but he knew they only wanted to save him the expense and they all went home early.

Yes, it was surprising how insensitive well-meaning people could be. Today at lunch they had all been enjoying themselves until the junior in marketing said, "Brendan need never go back to work now. He'll be delighted when he hears the news – he can be a gentleman of leisure for the rest of his life!" Sarah could have cried, but just then Phil popped a bottle of champagne and called for a toast and the moment passed. They were a great crowd really and Sarah loved working with them. Apart from the salary which had become essential to her and Brendan, she would have missed her job and the cheerful company if she had been let go.

The Luas glided to a stop and an old man got on and sat beside her.

"It's a terrible day," he said glumly, as the rain trickled from his raincoat to form tiny meandering rivulets on the floor.

"Terrible," agreed Sarah, hoping that this wasn't going to be the start of a long discourse on the weather, but she needn't have worried.

The old man took out a soggy evening paper and began to study the sports results.

Men are all the same, she thought to herself. That's what Brendan would have looked at first too.

She sighed when she thought of Brendan. He was probably putting the finishing touches to dinner. She knew he would be pleased for her when he heard her news but he wouldn't be human if he didn't feel at least a small pang of regret that he hadn't been the one with the promotion. She hadn't rung him from the office. She wanted to be there when she told him.

Nearing her stop, Sarah turned up the collar of her coat in readiness for the cold and the rain. She had never felt less Christmassy in her life even though she and Brendan had budgeted carefully for it. They had bought carefully and they were sure that they could give the children the Christmas they deserved.

"Excuse me," she said to the old man as she stood up.

He got up reluctantly and stepped back to let her out. There were quite a number of people getting off the Luas. It was close to the end of the line so no one got on. Before long she was on the street heading with no great enthusiasm for home. She wondered vaguely why Brendan hadn't come to collect her from the Luas, as he usually did when it was raining.

"Sarah!" she heard her next-door neighbour calling. "Sarah, I was wondering if you would be interested in going to a fashion show on Tuesday? It's at the school and all funds go to the new gym."

"I'm not sure, Jane. I'll give you a ring. Is that alright?" Sarah didn't want to be a cheapskate but the money spent on the fashion show would be money she wouldn't have for something that might be essential. And it didn't stop at the entry fee – there'd be the raffles and you couldn't go to something like that without having a glass of wine or two. She would definitely have to think about it.

"Fine," Jane's reply seemed a bit curt. "Oh, by the way I met Brendan in the supermarket today. He seemed to be buying up the store – smoked salmon, olives and I thought I saw a bottle of champers peeping out of the trolley. Did you two win the lotto or something?"

"Not that I know of but I hope so," Sarah replied. She never did think much of Jane's sense of humour. Still, there must be something afoot if Brendan was buying posh nosh and it was with a degree of curiosity that Sarah turned her key in the front door.

"Hi, Mum!" she was greeted by Aoife, her twelve-year-old daughter. "Wait until you see the dining room!"

Sarah went into the dining room to find it decorated for

Christmas – a little earlier than they would normally do it. It wasn't yet the 8th December. There were lighted candles on the table and it was laid with their best cutlery, their dark-green Christmas table-cloth and red-and-green napkins. There was a blazing fire in the hearth and Brendan was laboriously trying to open a bottle of champagne. She didn't know what to think as she looked at the smiling faces of her husband and her children.

"We're celebrating," John, their son, said. "But Dad wouldn't tell us what we are celebrating until you came home."

"And I'm not going to tell anyone until your mother has dressed for dinner in a manner worthy of the scrumptious meal which is about to be served."

"You clown!" Sarah laughed as she rushed up the stairs. Whatever had happened, her own news would have to wait. She had the quickest shower in history before slipping into the red dress she had bought in the January sales a few years earlier. She knew she looked good in it and that Brendan loved it on her.

"Do I pass?" she grinned as she opened the dining-room door, doing a little pirouette as she did so.

"Wow! Just wow!" Brendan grinned while John made an unsuccessful attempt at a wolf whistle. Brendan poured the champagne and he had even got sparkling non-alcoholic wine for the children so that they wouldn't feel left out.

"Now, I want to propose a toast to Mum, who today landed herself a permanent job, because she is the best copywriter they have!"

"How did you know that?" Sarah grinned

"I rang the office, but you were at a meeting. The person who answered the phone told me. But please keep quiet, everyone. I haven't finished."

They all looked at him expectantly.

"To Dad, who today received a very satisfactory job offer which I shall be very happy to accept!"

The place was in uproar. Sarah couldn't believe it.

"What job? When did you hear? Where? When do you start?" The questions came tumbling out.

"Calm down, love. We can't have you overexcited or you won't have an appetite for the meal which I cooked with considerable care." Brendan grinned. "Remember the interview for the job in Executive Clothing a few weeks ago?"

"I thought you heard that job was gone."

"Well, that can't be true, because I start on the 1st of next month. What a start to the New Year!"

It was obvious he could hardly believe his luck.

"Does this mean I can have acting lessons?" Aoife was always one to get her priorities straight.

"Yes, but only if you promise to become the next Saoirse Ronan!" Brendan laughed. "Now isn't it time we all had something to eat?"

They served the meal together and it was just perfect.

"I'd say this is going to be a great Christmas," Brendan beamed.

"But Dad," Aoife said, "we always have a great Christmas!"

❖

Miranda Manning took up writing as a hobby when she was a stay-at-home mum and her moods swung dramatically from 'all sweetness and light' to 'demented mother of three'. She had a number of short stories and articles, on subjects ranging from breastfeeding to left-handed women, published in women's magazines and local newspapers – not to mention the *Cork Hollybough*. She particularly likes the short story as a genre because she can complete them quickly and move on to something new. She has been a runner-up in more short story competitions than she cares to remember but never the outright winner. Always the bridesmaid! However, that pattern changed recently and her novel *Who is Alice?* will be published by Poolbeg in 2013. She currently works as an office manager and is a bit less demented. She has three adult children and lives in Galway.

Gin and Holly

Helen Moorhouse

"Oh, Elsie, you gave me such a scare!" Peggy Crisp woke with a start and a sharp intake of breath as she saw a face peering at her, looming over her favourite armchair.

Her friend, Elsie Dawson, formed an apologetic 'o' with her mouth. "I'm ever so sorry, love. I didn't mean to frighten you," she said softly, standing up straight as Peggy regained consciousness

Peggy, the older of the two women, wiggled her ample frame slightly in her chair to push herself upright and blinked at her surroundings, as though she had never seen them before.

"That's alright, dearie," she replied. "Ever so good of you to come, of course."

"I hope you don't mind that I let myself in?" asked Elsie politely. "Only I wanted to get here before they arrived."

Peggy blinked, thought for a moment, and then nodded her head. "That's today, of course," she mused, almost to herself. "I'd almost forgotten . . ." She suddenly realised that her friend was still standing before her, hands clasped demurely at her waist. "Oh, where are my manners? Do take a seat, Elsie."

"Don't mind if I do, Peg," Elsie replied, and lowered herself gracefully into the armchair opposite, tucking her skirt neatly underneath herself to avoid creases and crossing her ankles. She pointed politely at Peggy. "I can see you're all ready for the off anyway."

Peggy looked down at her appearance. She ran a red-painted fingernail along the lapel of the rich brown fur, savouring its feel. Of course it was frowned upon nowadays to wear something like this, especially when it was the real thing. But she had never been able to deny herself the pleasure of the full-length coat. And its warmth.

"Truth be told, Elsie," she said, as if revealing a confidence, "I sometimes wear this old thing round the flat when it's parky outside. And inside, of course." She nodded toward the sash window behind Elsie which framed a vista of the snow-covered roof opposite, barely distinguishable against the pressing white of the sky as yet another snow shower prepared to burst through and make a listless, silent descent on the city below.

Elsie responded by giving a "*Tsk!*" and rolling her eyes. "I know," she replied. "How long has it been snowing now?"

"Five days, give or take," replied Peggy. "And it's frozen solid out there. I can't even get out my own front door with it. Packed ice it is. Treacherous. I'd break every bone in my weary old body like china if I so much as put a toe outside."

Elsie nodded in agreement.

"The cupboards are bare and all. Not a drop of milk or a teabag left in. I'm so sorry I can't offer you a cuppa, Elsie."

Elsie dismissed the thought with a grimace. "Not at all, my dear," she sniffed. "No need to trouble yourself. Anyway, you know me. I'd take a glass of gin over a cup of rosie any day."

Her grin was contagious and Peggy returned it for a moment before frowning in disapproval. "Now, now, Elsie Dawson!" she chided. "Mother's ruin. You, of all people, should know that."

"A small one couldn't hurt!" protested Elsie, smiling. "It *is* Christmas after all!"

Peggy gasped. "Christmas Eve, Elsie, of course. Of all the days to have a bare larder!"

"Well," replied her friend, "you won't have to worry your

head about shopping for yourself for much longer, now, will you? What time are they due?"

Peggy glanced at the delicate silver wristwatch – a gift from long ago. She shrugged. "Any time soon, I should think. My neighbour, Sandra – lovely girl, even though her hair's a funny shade of pink – well, she's been dealing with it all. Made all the arrangements, bless her. I should really give her a little something to say thank you."

Elsie's voice was calming as she said, "I'm sure she won't mind, Peggy, love. You've got enough on your plate with the move, especially at Christmas time. Will your Nigel come to see you, do you think?"

The name made Peggy harrumph. She gave a dismissive flick of her once razor-sharp chin and looked again out of the window. "I expect so," she grunted. "He generally throws his head in on special occasions."

Elsie grinned. "Sons, eh?" She followed Peggy's eyes as they travelled from the window to the small table at her left hand, beside the armchair. To the delicate pewter picture frame guarding a treasured snap. She recognised the young Peggy, her hair dark and her eyes bright, posing on a settee beside a Christmas tree, the baby asleep in her arms, the small boy clutching a wooden train and staring straight at the camera, his expression sulky.

"Never changed, did he, your Nigel?" offered Elsie softly.

Peggy surprised her with a smile. "He was six years old in that picture," she said. "Christmas 1960 and Nigel in a huff because he got a train when he wanted a car." She took a deep breath. "You're right, of course. Hasn't changed a bit, the ungrateful little –"

Elsie cut in suddenly. "I don't suppose you *have* any gin, do you, Peggy?" She glanced around the flat, taking it all in. She had always supposed that someone younger would think the flat old-fashioned. A two-bar fire rested in the grate of an actual empty fireplace. Their chairs were angled slightly toward it to create an impression of convivial companionship, resting on a brown-and-green rug which covered most of the centre of the room, leaving bare boards only at the edges which couldn't be seen, for the most part, with the clutter of sideboards and shelves and china cabinets that Peggy had brought to the flat with her. There was a lot there for such a small room but you couldn't fault Peg's housekeeping. She had always kept the place like a new pin.

Elsie looked back at her friend to find that her look of disapproval had returned.

"I don't keep it in the house, Elsie Dawson," she said coldly. "I had a friend once, you know, who got on the back of a fella's motorbike after he'd had a skinful of Gin and Sins. Her and all. And I don't need to tell you what happened."

Elsie suddenly clapped her hands together with delight. "Gin and Sins, Peggy! I can't remember the last time I had one of those. What was in them again? Gin – of course – and lemon juice – and *orange* juice – why, they were practically good for you! – and there was one more thing . . . What was it? Dubonnet, wasn't it?"

Peggy rolled her eyes. Preaching abstinence to Elsie was like talking to the kettle. "Grenadine, I think you'll find," she replied drily, as if against her will.

Elsie thought for a moment, looked puzzled, and then shook her head. "I don't think so, Peg. I'm sure it was Dubonnet. I remember asking for Dubonnet from that waiter in the Crystal Club who didn't know how to make 'em."

Peggy tutted. "It was *Grenadine*," she growled. "*I* used to drink the occasional Dubonnet and Gin – the Queen Consort's drink of choice. It had a bit of class about it."

Elsie leaped in again, her glee girlish.

"Ooh, you're right as always Peggy Crisp!" she exclaimed and smacked her lips. "What I wouldn't give to taste one of those!"

Peggy said nothing this time, just gave a grunt and a sigh, shaking her head slightly. Thus it had always been.

"That was some Christmas, though, wasn't it, Peg?" asked Elsie suddenly, her voice rich with playful memory. "1950. Panto. The Lyceum. Do you remember?"

It was Peggy's turn to smile wistfully. "How could I forget?"

she sighed. "Both of us in the chorus line and before I knew it you were principal boy . . ."

"Aladdin," interjected Elsie, lost in memory. "I never for one minute thought that I'd be on that stage so young . . . all me dreams coming true. All the sequins and the smell of that panstick. And who'd have thought that I'd end up falling in love with the Widow Twankey? What a pair we were! Didn't know if we was coming or going, me and Clive . . ."

In an instant she snapped out of her reverie and glanced nervously at Peggy who had pursed her lips at the name.

"Oh come on, Peg – you liked him too!" protested Elsie. "All those good times we had down the Rose and Crown after we'd come off stage!"

"In *Sheffield*, Elsie!" exclaimed Peggy. "Freezing cold, it was, in that lodging house run by Mrs Whats-er-name . . ."

"Leech."

"Leech, yes. And a right bloodsucker she was and all. Couldn't have been more aptly named. No hot water, as I recall, and I'd swear she never changed the sheets – just turned them over when she could get away with it! And as for the smell of cabbage, my word! Cabbage for every meal, cabbage sandwiches, fried cabbage . . . she'd have given us cabbage for *breakfast* if she could have got away with it!"

Elsie laughed out loud. "Oh, good times, Peg!" she giggled. "But remember Christmas Day? Stuck up there in the frozen north, and all of us homesick and miserable and no performance to look forward to till the Boxing Day matinee –"

"And she cooked a goose," interrupted Peggy, her own mind finding itself reliving the sounds and scents of the lodgings. "And some more cabbage, of course . . ."

"And she had holly everywhere. Only decoration she'd put up 'cos she got it for free from the bush in the front garden, the mean old thing. But she let us use her gramophone, do you remember?"

Peggy nodded, a smile playing on her lips. Elsie fell silent as Peggy stared into space and began to sing in a reedy voice, an echo of what it once had been when they shared a stage . . .

"*If you were the only girl in the world . . .*" she sang.

"*. . . and I were the only boy . . .*" finished Elsie, her own voice cracked and shaky. The years had not been kind to their talents, but the women sang on, together, for a moment, lost in their own memories of that December. A hush fell on the room as they reached the end of the chorus, broken only when Peggy looked out the window and gave a little gasp at the thick white flakes which fell straight down, silent, like feathers from the sky.

"There's the snow again," she said softly, shaking her head.

Elsie turned in her seat to look at the scene behind her.

"That'll delay my lift I should think," said Peggy gravely. "The gritters can't keep up with it all, so Sandra says. I wonder if she might like something from here? After all, I can't take much of it with me." Her eyes scanned the room rapidly, taking in all of her life's belongings.

"I suspect you have everything you need," offered Elsie, consolingly. "And I'm ever so sure that your Nigel will look after the rest for you."

"I'm sure he will!" Peggy scoffed, shifting in her chair. "Especially when it all turns up on *Cash in the Attic* or one of those dreadful programmes. Just so long as that David Dickinson doesn't get his hands on my silver teapot! What time is it?"

Peggy glanced again at her wrist, stared for a moment at the face of her watch, tutted and tapped it vigorously with the forefinger of her right hand. "Bloomin' thing," she said under her breath. "Only gone and stopped . . ." She glanced upward at the mantel where a small, plain alarm-clock sat. She gave an exasperated sigh. "There's no way it's that time . . ." She looked back at her arm and struggled with the catch on the watch, removing it abruptly and tossing it on the side table. "Perhaps Sandra could have that," she sniffed. "If she can get it fixed – because Lord above knows I can't be bothered again."

Elsie looked alarmed. "Why, Peggy!" she exclaimed. "You can't leave your watch! That was your engagement present from Ron!"

Peggy looked her friend square in the face. "And what a happy union *that* turned out to be!" she snarled sarcastically.

Elsie sat back in her chair and squirmed, uncomfortable. She'd forgotten that Peggy could be like that sometimes.

Peggy's face was filled with righteous indignation as she continued.

"He started the way he meant to carry on, Elsie, I tell you. Didn't even have enough to get me a proper ring. *'I'll save up and get you a ring that sparkles like the sea!'* he promised me a thousand times. Even when Nigel came along there was nothing on my hand but the plain gold band they'd prised from his nan's dead fingers. Gave me the creeps, that thing."

Peggy paused for a moment, the fury rising inside her at the memories.

"Scrimped and saved I did. Every penny I had to hide from him. I was never so glad as when he did a bunk and that's a fact. No, Sandra can't have that watch, as it happens. I wouldn't give it to her. Bad luck it's brought me, I'm sure of it. Now *that* . . ."

Elsie followed the finger that pointed to a china cabinet under the window.

"That is what I'd take with me if I was taking anything at all," Peggy said. "My sauceboat. The china sauceboat with the hand-painted ivy."

Elsie frowned as she looked back at her friend. "Whatever for, Peg?" she asked, bemused. "I don't see as how you'll be making much gravy where you're going."

Peggy's expression softened as she gazed to where she knew the precious jug was. She couldn't see it in the dark of the winter's evening, but she'd stared at it often enough to know its exact location. "Not gravy, Elsie," she said quietly. "Parsley sauce. Denis's favourite was parsley sauce with a bit of gammon, mash and peas. He'd have eaten it every day of the year if I hadn't put me foot down for the odd lamb chop."

Elsie couldn't see her companion's face any longer in the dark of the room, but she knew that a smile was dancing on her lips.

"I always think of him when I look at it. More than anything else. More than his old slippers and I slept with them under the bed for long enough, lord knows. More than his tatty old cardigan that he used to wear pottering round his allotment. That sauceboat – that stood for every meal, our whole life together, me and Denis. What we had, what we built. What he gave me . . ."

The smile had gone, Elsie could tell. A silence followed for a moment.

"How old would she have been now, Peg?" Elsie asked quietly.

Silence again.

"Forty," came the response. "Forty-one on December twenty-fifth. Christmas Day. Tomorrow."

"Do you miss her Peg?" asked Elsie.

There was silence again, followed by a long sigh.

"It's a funny old thing to say, Els," came the hushed response, the words slow and measured, "but I don't miss having a grown-up daughter – grandkids, even – on account of how I wouldn't know what that felt like. But if you think that an hour of a day passes that I don't feel the weight of her in my arms, that I can't call to mind the smell of her little warm head, the sweet scent from her breath after a feed . . . my little Penny Toffee I used to call her . . ."

Silence again.

"I'm sorry Peg," whispered Elsie. It seemed irreverent to speak aloud.

A sniff. "That's alright, Els," came the response. "It's all a whole lifetime ago, eh? Time to move on now."

Elsie paused before she answered. "That's right, Peg," she said softly. "Us dancing girls. Let's go on with the show and all that."

Elsie heard Peggy shift in her seat again.

"Looks like an explosion in a down-factory out there," Peggy said, clearing her throat and looking out of the window again.

Elsie turned. The orange street lights had been lit while they spoke, one of them directly outside Peggy's window. In its glow, the thick white flakes pelted down, one after the other in quick succession. The two women watched in silence for a moment until Peggy broke it again with song.

"I'm . . . dreaming . . . of a . . . white . . . Christmas," she sang softly, joined after a line or two by Elsie, falling into a familiar pattern.

It was the clatter of footsteps and voices in the hallway that disturbed them.

"Ooh," said Elsie. "This'll be them now."

There were two men's voices, from what they could make out, making chitchat with a woman who must be Sandra.

"This is it," they heard her say as the footsteps drew to a halt outside the front door. "This is Peggy's flat. Peggy Crisp. She's lived here years, since her husband died . . ."

Peggy drew a sharp breath through her teeth as she heard a loud bang on her front door, followed by another. "Steady on," she muttered as she heard a third and finally the door opened.

"I think her living room's through there . . ." they heard Sandra begin, only to be interrupted by one of the male voices.

"Don't worry, love, we'll take it from here," he said. "When are you due by the way?"

They heard Sandra give a giggle, a short, hopeful laugh full of excitement and promise. "Tomorrow, actually," she said lightly. "Christmas Day, of all days!"

"Whoo!" they heard the second man's voice exclaim. "You sure you don't want to come back with us, just in case?"

"Oh God, no thanks!" they heard Sandra exclaim, all the happiness gone from her voice.

"Stan's only kidding, love," the first man said apologetically. "Not a funny joke. Now you go and put your feet up – Sandra, isn't it? We'll take it from here . . ."

"If you're sure," said Sandra. "Merry Christmas, then."

"Many happy returns," said Stan. "Dev, can you find the light-switch, please?"

With that, Peggy and Elsie listened to Sandra's footsteps tread back along the hallway, one heavier than the other. "Sciatica," explained Peggy, moving across the room to be beside Elsie. "Poor love is crippled. Like I was with Nigel."

They watched as the two men in their uniforms came through

the living-room door and flicked the light-switch just inside, then stood taking in the scene before them. One was tall, dark-skinned, fit and handsome while his colleague was considerably shorter and tubbier.

Elsie spluttered. "Ooh, I bags the Eastern Promise!" she stage-whispered from the side of her mouth to Peggy who smacked her arm instinctively.

"Elsie Dawson," she hissed in return. "You can't say stuff like that nowadays – people take offence!"

"Get you!" replied Elsie. "Just 'cos I don't like the look of yours much!"

She cackled a little too loudly, causing the shorter, fatter man – Stan – to look around the room nervously and shudder. "Don't think there's much room for surprises here, Dev," he said abruptly. "Let's get this done as fast as we can and get out, eh?"

His colleague didn't reply. He was too busy checking Peggy's pulse, gently laying her arm back on to her lap when he didn't find one. "Poor old thing," he said softly and respectfully. "It's freezing in here. No wonder she didn't make it, even with that coat on her."

"And at Christmas too," observed Stan. "Christmas Eve. In the snow. It should be all ice-skating and last-minute presents, shouldn't it, Dev? Carols and midnight Mass and hot whiskeys and that."

Dev sighed briefly as he looked around the flat. "I wouldn't know, Stan. For the twentieth time, I'm a practising Muslim. Now did you bring the bag up or do I have to go down and get it?"

Peggy felt Elsie's warm fingers clasp her arm and she turned to look at her friend, surprised by how young she looked up close, her hair neatly permed and dark, her lipstick red as berries, like it always had been.

"I think it's time for us to head on, then, Peg," she said softly but with an urgency to her voice. "You alright with that?"

Peggy glanced around the room. "Ever so glad it's you here to give me a hand with this, Els," she gulped. "I wouldn't have had the faintest what to do otherwise."

Elsie smiled softly at her dearest, oldest friend. "Least I could do," she replied warmly. "Having gone off on you so young and all."

Peggy smiled back. "Wish you hadn't, Elsie," she managed. "Bloody Clive and his Gin and Sins. And bloody you for getting on the back of his bike!"

Elsie made her apologetic pout once more. "Like I said, sorry, Peg. Still, I'm here now though, aren't I? Now we have to make tracks, have you got everything?"

"I think so, Els. Just one last thing though . . ."

Elsie watched as Peggy crossed the room to gaze at the photograph of herself taken that Christmas, all those years ago, a baby daughter in her arms, a surly son by her side.

Stan shivered as he felt something walk over his grave.

"He'll be alright, Els, won't he? My Nigel?" said Peggy.

It was the first time that Elsie had ever heard Peggy so hesitant, so unsure.

"He'll be fine, Peg," she replied. "He's a big boy now."

Peggy paused for a moment, staring at the scene. "Suppose he will," she said. "He'll have me boxed and delivered in no time at all, I expect."

She looked straight at Elsie, delivering the line with a broad grin. Elsie cackled loudly and Peggy joined her.

Stan shuddered again, looking around him nervously.

"We nearly done, mate?" he asked Dev. "Only this place don't half give me the willies."

"Nearly done, Stan," sighed Dev.

"We ready for the off then, Peg Leg?" asked Elsie at the same time, holding out her elbow so that Peggy could link her.

"Rightyo then," said Peggy, a tremor to her voice.

Elsie smiled warmly. "First night nerves, my love," she said reassuringly, watching as her friend strode across the room, a long-absent spring returning to her step. "But nothing to worry about. Let's be having you, then. Let's not keep your Penny waiting any longer than we have to, eh?"

Helen Moorhouse is the author of *The Dead Summer* and *The Dark Water*. Originally from Mountmellick, Co Laois, she lives in Drumcondra, Dublin, and is a wife, mum, daughter, sister, aunt and great-aunt. After many years spent behind-the-scenes in radio, Helen now works as a freelance writer of articles, speeches, scripts, shopping lists and occasional birthday cards. Her interests include TV, movies, eating, sleeping and things that go bump in the night. Pre-toddlers, she dabbled in acting and wallowed in reading and hopes one day that she might again finish reading something that isn't geared solely toward Age 1 and up. For more of her scribblings, see www.helenmoorhouse.weebly.com

The Photograph

A. O'Connor

It was tradition for as long as anyone could remember for all the family to go and stay at Great-aunt Rachel's house, Woodstown, the day after Christmas. It was a wonderful opportunity for the extended family to meet up, catch up, swap news and stories. As Rachel had never married or had children of her own, it was as if she belonged to the whole family and at seventy-five remained a vivacious and warm hostess. This tradition was being interrupted this year as the forecast had predicted heavy snow and recommended no travel after Christmas Eve. So it was decided that anyone who could would travel to Woodstown on Christmas Eve and spend the entire festive period there with Rachel.

Craig kept the car at a steady pace on the country roads as the forecast was being proven right and the falling snow was already making driving conditions difficult.

"Is Rachel's house much further?" he asked his fiancée Sophie who was peering out, trying to spot any landmarks. Sophie was Rachel's great-niece, and her favourite.

"It's impossible to say in this weather – I said we should have left earlier," she said irritably. This was the first Christmas Craig was due to spend with her family, and they were due to announce their engagement that night, which meant her nerves were on edge.

As a large stone gateway came into view, Sophie said, "Thank goodness! There it is. I had visions of us spending the night in the car on the side of the road!"

Craig drove through the impressive stone pillars and made the journey up the long winding driveway. At the top of the drive was a large two-storey granite period house, with tall Georgian windows which were all illuminated with welcoming glows of light. As they parked alongside the several other cars in front of the house, Craig and Sophie grabbed their cases, dashed through the pelting snow to the front door and rang the bell loudly.

A minute later Rachel's housekeeper Fiona opened the door.

"Hello, Fiona – what a night!" said Sophie as they moved quickly into the hallway, shaking the snow off themselves.

"And it's due to get worse. Freezing temperatures later, they say," said Fiona, giving them a welcoming smile. "They're all in the drawing room."

She took their coats from them and went off to hang them in the cloakroom.

"We'll pop in to say hi, before we go upstairs to change," said Sophie as she took Craig's hand and led him across the hall.

As Craig looked around the beautiful antique-furnished house, he inhaled the rich aromas of cinnamon, sage and onion, and the turf fires that filled the house. Sophie said Aunt Rachel always made a fuss at Christmas and that was why everyone enjoyed going there so much. And as they passed the gigantic tree in the hall, sprinkled with twinkling lights, and the abundant holly, ivy and mistletoe everywhere, he could see this was no lie.

On entering the drawing room they found about twenty people already there, all of whom were Sophie's relatives including her mother, father and sister.

"Looks like we're the last to arrive – as usual!" said Sophie loudly.

There was a chorus of "Sophie!" and everyone greeted Sophie and Craig warmly with hugs and kisses.

Craig knew them all well at this stage. The only person he had never met was Great-aunt Rachel herself and he had heard so much about this kind and generous woman, he was looking forward to it.

An elegantly dressed woman in her seventies approached them and gave Sophie a hug. "Welcome, my dear. Delighted you could make it."

"We nearly didn't, Aunt Rachel. Craig is a veritable Scrooge – wouldn't leave the office early, even on Christmas Eve!" She took Craig's arm and drew him forward. "Craig, this is Aunt Rachel."

Rachel stepped forward and kissed him on the cheek. "Regardless of what Sophie says, everyone else here has been singing your praises. Seemingly you can do no wrong!"

"Well, that's good to hear. Thanks for having me."
"Why don't you let Fiona show you kids to your room, and then you can come and join the party," advised Rachel.

"See you in a short while," said Sophie, and she and Craig went to join Fiona.

Upstairs, there was a blazing fire in the bedroom's fireplace and Craig warmed himself near it as Rachel changed into her cocktail dress.

"How long has Rachel lived here at Woodstown?" asked Craig, admiring the four-poster bed.

"All her life. It was her and my grandmother's family home. Rachel stayed on here and kept the house and the riding school going when her own parents died and my grandmother moved away and got married."

"Bit of a lonely life."

"Rachel – lonely?" Sophie burst in to laughter. "Rachel's never been lonely a day in her life. The house is always filled with friends and relatives."

"But she never got married, or came close to it?"

"There was somebody once, a brief engagement. She never talks about it, or nobody else does either, for that matter,"

Sophie said, checking her appearance in the mirror before turning and smiling at him. "Come on, let's join the others."

The party down in the lounge continued through the evening amidst a continual procession of brandy, hot whiskies and ports, finger foods, mince pies, cake and chocolates.

"Don't forget to leave some room for the dinner tomorrow!" warned Rachel over the laughter and talk.

She then joined Craig who was stood beside the fire. As he chatted to Rachel he found her engaging and good company, genuinely interested in hearing all about him.

"I do hope now you've found us in Woodstown, you'll be a regular visitor," said Rachel.

"I'd like that," smiled Craig. He looked over at Sophie who was standing by the Christmas tree and making a face at him while she tapped her watch. Seeing it was nearly ten o'clock, she was anxious to make their engagement announcement. He nodded at her, made his excuses to Rachel and went and joined Sophie.

"*Ahem!*" said Sophie loudly as she tapped a spoon against her crystal glass.

Abruptly the room became quiet.

"Sorry for this interruption, everyone – but – I have an announcement to make. Myself and Craig are getting married . . . we're engaged!" She stretched out her hand, proudly displaying the diamond ring.

There was a cheer as everyone rushed to them to offer their congratulations.

"We're thinking June or July," said Sophie. "And either Italy or the South of France for the honeymoon."

As Sophie chatted away happily about the wedding arrangements she surveyed the room looking for Rachel, but couldn't see her. She went up to Craig who was chatting to her father.

"Did you see Aunt Rachel anywhere?" she asked.

"No, not since earlier," said Craig.

"It's very strange – she didn't come up and congratulate me. Did she to you?"

"No, she didn't," said Craig.

"Let's go find her, see if she's alright," said Sophie.

Craig put down his glass of port and they went out into the hallway and checked the other rooms downstairs. When they opened the door to the study they were surprised to see Rachel sitting on a couch crying softly to herself, clutching what looked like a large photo frame to her.

"Rachel? What's wrong?" asked Craig as he closed the door behind them.

They quickly went and sat beside her.

"Nothing! Nothing at all! You go back to the party and don't mind me, I'm fine."

"You're obviously not, or you wouldn't be crying like this," said Sophie, full of concern.

"I'm just being silly," said Rachel, as she quickly tried to wipe away her tears.

"Aunt Rachel, what's the matter?" asked Sophie softly as she placed her arm around her and held her tight.

"It's just – it's just when you announced your engagement, all the memories came flooding back."

"What memories?" asked Craig.

"Of my own engagement . . . You know I was engaged briefly once?"

"I had heard. I never brought it up, because people said you didn't want to discuss it," said Sophie.

"You see, Edgar and I – that was his name – we had our engagement party on Christmas Eve as well, when we announced it to everyone here at a party in the house. Fifty-five years ago this very night."

"Oh, Aunt Rachel – I'm so sorry, how insensitive of us!" Sophie was mortified.

Rachel managed to smile and patted Sophie's knee "How were you supposed to know?"

"But I should have checked it with you beforehand to make sure it was alright."

"It *is* alright! I don't want you to fret over it. As I said, I'm

just being silly . . . But it did bring back all the memories."
"What actually happened – with the engagement, with Edgar?"
asked Craig.

"Craig! That's none of our business," snapped Sophie.

Rachel managed to smile. "It's alright. You're entitled to ask,
after finding me in floods of tears on your engagement night."
She sighed loudly "Edgar deserted me. He ran out on me just
after our engagement party."

"Rachel – that's appalling!" said Sophie.

"He never even said goodbye. He just disappeared and I never
saw him again."

"No explanation? No conversation?" Craig's face creased in
concern.

"No, nothing at all. He just left. He wasn't from around here.
I presume he went back to Dublin where he came from."
"Did you not try and track him down? Try to find out why he
ran?" Craig was amazed.

"No . . . I let him go. He obviously didn't want to be with me
any more – so what was the point of trying to find out where he
had gone to?"

Craig looked at the photo she was holding close to her chest
and asked, "What's that?"

She let the photo down on her lap. It was a large black-and-
white photo of a group of people dressed glamorously in
cocktail dresses and tuxedos, gathered around a Christmas tree.

"This was taken that Christmas Eve here in the house fifty-
five years ago tonight, just after our engagement was
announced," explained Rachel.

Sophie studied the photo. "That's you, Aunt Rachel!"

"Yes, standing beside my fiancé, Edgar, blissfully happy . . .
that's my sister – your grandmother, Sophie . . . my parents . . .
the rest were all friends of ours."

"Who's that?" asked Craig, pointing to a stunning woman
dressed in a long black gown.

"That was my cousin, Vivienne."

"She was very beautiful," said Sophie.

Craig noticed Rachel bristle as she said, "She seemed to think so. Anyway – everyone is going to wonder what's become of us. We better go back and join the party."

"Are you sure you're alright?" asked Sophie.

"Yes, I'm fine now. In a funny way, I'm glad I've spoken about it, after all these years." Rachel stood up and put the photo on the desk in the study. "I've always kept this photo hidden in this desk – but I've hidden the past long enough. Maybe it's time to air it."

"I'm sorry, Aunt Rachel," Sophie said sympathetically as she put an arm around her and they returned to the party.

"Come on, everybody, let's open the champagne! We've an engagement to celebrate," said Rachel as she grabbed a bottle of champagne and began to open it. "I only ever drink this brand – it gives you quite a hit!"

Craig was waiting for an opportunity to sneak out and have a cigarette. He waited until the excitement of the engagement announcement had calmed down and everyone was playing charades before he slipped out to the hall and into the cloakroom, put on his coat and stepped out the front door. The blizzard had stopped falling and now everywhere was covered with a thick layer of snow. As he lit up his cigarette and began to walk down the drive, the full moon was causing the snow crystals to glisten and sparkle. True for the forecast, it was now freezing and the snow was icing over. He followed a path from the drive that led down to a walled garden, the snow scrunching under his feet as he went. He sat down on the wall and thought of Aunt Rachel and the broken heart she had nursed for fifty-five years. All the unanswered questions she must have been left with when Edgar ran out on her. All the conversations she must have had with herself, trying to fathom why he did what he did. Never really understanding why, or getting closure. He sighed and flung the cigarette into a bush, before standing up. He started heading up the pathway back to the house but suddenly slipped on some frozen ice. He felt himself tripping through the air and coming down to land on the pavement, hitting his head first.

Craig blinked a few times, and slowly sat up. He felt disorientated. Standing up, he shook the snow from his coat. He wondered if he had blacked out when he had fallen. Hearing music coming from the house now, he realised the game of charades must be over. He carefully walked up the path to the driveway and continued up to the house. Through the windows of the house he could see people dancing.

He climbed the steps to the house and, opening the door, let himself in. He took off his coat and to his astonishment saw he was wearing a tuxedo. He shook his head in confusion as he had been wearing smart-casual clothes for the party. Amazed, Craig inspected the tuxedo.

He suddenly heard a voice.

"There you are! I've been looking all over for you – where have you been?" said a woman coming out of the drawing room who walked towards him, grabbing his hand. Craig didn't recognise her from Sophie's relatives who were staying at Woodstown, and he wondered if she was a neighbour. She did look somewhat familiar. But why was this woman looking for him? He allowed himself to be led into the drawing room by her, where couples were dancing to Frank Sinatra's 'Strangers In The Night', which was booming from an old-fashioned record player.

"It's our song," whispered the woman as she held him close and started to dance with him.

He anxiously looked around the room for Sophie as he tried to draw back from this woman. He then noticed he didn't recognise any of the people in the house, and the men were all dressed in tuxedos and the women were in 1950s style gowns and cocktail dresses.

"I'm sorry – I think I've come back to the wrong house," he muttered, but as he looked around the drawing room, he realised it was definitely Rachel's house, Woodstown. Everything apart from the people was the exact same.

"Wrong house? What are you talking about? Oh, you are silly, Edgar," said the woman as she laughed.

"*Edgar!*" shouted Craig. And as he looked down at the woman, he realised why she looked familiar. She was Aunt Rachel, but she was a young Aunt Rachel, the one from the photograph.

"Edgar?" asked the young Rachel curiously as she continually walked towards him as he tried to back away from her.

As he reached the fireplace, Craig turned to look into the mirror over it. But it wasn't his face looking back, it was a different face. It was Edgar from the photograph.

The music was suddenly stopped abruptly.

"Can I have everybody's attention, please?" said a distinguished-looking man standing by the Christmas tree.

"Rachel and Edgar, could you come over and join me," said the man.

Rachel excitedly grabbed Craig's arm and pulled him over to the tree.

"Friends and neighbours, you're all very welcome to the traditional Christmas Eve party here at Woodstown. And this Christmas Eve, I've some very good news – the engagement of my eldest daughter Rachel to Edgar Jones!"

Craig looked at Rachel in horror as the crowd clapped loudly and cheered.

"Everyone together now for a photograph," said Rachel, and everyone lined up in two rows in front of the Christmas tree. Craig found himself standing beside Rachel and, as he looked down the line at everyone, he realised he was posing for the photograph Rachel had shown them in the study earlier.

"Smile everybody!" said the photographer as he clicked his camera.

Sinatra's 'Strangers In The Night' began to play again. Rachel was being surrounded by everyone offering congratulations. Craig backed into a corner beside the Christmas tree as he stared at the scene in front of him.

"You make a lovely couple," said a voice that was smooth as velvet beside him. He turned to see the speaker was a beautiful young woman dressed in a long black gown. He remembered her from the photograph in the study and Aunt Rachel had said she was her cousin, Vivienne.

Vivienne stared at him and said, "What's wrong, Edgar? You look like you've seen a ghost."

"It's very warm in here," he said, untying his bow tie.

"Maybe you need some air." She looked at him intently, before bending forward and whispering, "Give me a couple of minutes, then follow me . . . I think there's some explanation needed, don't you?"

She drew back from him, smiled, and walked through the crowd and out to the hallway. He saw her put on a long coat over her gown, grab an open bottle of champagne from a sideboard and leave through the front door.

Craig looked around the festivities of the room and then hurried out to the hall. He grabbed his coat and slipped out the front door. He looked at all the cars parked outside, and realised they were all 1950s vintage.

"Hello!" he called.

"Down here!" came Vivienne's response and he spotted her down by the walled garden.

He ran down the drive through the snow and down to the garden where he found her sitting on a wall, drinking from the bottle of champagne.

He was so confused, but Vivienne had said she could explain everything.

"Please tell me – what's going on?" he demanded.

"Why don't you tell me, darling!" she said back. "You were supposed to dump her today, and instead you announce your engagement!"

"I don't understand . . . "

"Don't you? Well, I understand everything now. You've been playing me for a fool, Edgar. Seeing me behind Rachel's back. Telling me she meant nothing to you. Telling me I was the one you really loved. Telling me you were going to leave her and come to me. And it was all lies!"

"Vivienne!"

"She just had too much on offer in the end, was that it, darling? Woodstown, the house and all the land. She's going to inherit it all, and you just couldn't bear to part with all that, could you? Because, let's face it – you can't love her. Not dreary boring little Rachel – when you could have me!"

They could hear the front door of the house slam and they both looked up to see Rachel standing there on the steps.

"Edgar? Edgar!" Rachel called into the night.

"Well?" asked Vivienne. "Final chance – who's it going to be – me or her?"

Craig stared at her in bewilderment.

"I see," said Vivienne, nodding and taking a drink from the champagne bottle before placing it down on the wall, and saying bitterly, "I hope the two of you will be very happy."

Vivienne marched up through the gardens towards the house. She stopped as she passed Rachel.

"Oh Vivienne, have you seen Edgar anywhere?" asked Rachel.

Vivienne looked Rachel up and down and sneered. "Oh yes, I've seen him alright. I've just left him down by the walled garden . . . You're welcome to him, darling . . . I've finished with him anyway." She continued up the steps and back into the party.

Rachel walked slowly in confusion down to the walled garden to find Craig standing there.

"Edgar, what were you doing down here with Vivienne? What's been going on?" Rachel's face was alarmed and anguished.

"Believe me, I have no idea what's going on!"

Rachel studied him intently. "Well, I'm getting a good idea what's been happening . . . between you and Vivienne." She put her hand to her face and shook her head "Please tell me you haven't, Edgar. Not with *her*. Not with Vivienne!"

"Rachel –"

"How could you?" Her voice rose as she walked towards him. "Did I mean nothing to you? Are my parents right? Are you marrying me for the money? For Woodstown? After I defended you to them. After I defended you to them all. And now they'll all be laughing at me. Everyone will know. Vivienne will make sure they know. *She'll be laughing at me – how could you do this to me?"* Suddenly Rachel's hand grasped the champagne bottle Vivienne had left on the wall. In a swift movement she raised the bottle into the air and brought it down on Craig's head.

Craig slumped to the ground. He slipped in and out of consciousness, but could make out Rachel dragging him further into the walled garden towards the wood.

Craig woke up with a start and felt the cut to his forehead where he had fallen. His head was throbbing. He managed to sit up and looked around him. He was on the pathway where he had slipped and banged his head earlier. He managed to stagger to his feet and slowly made his way up the drive to the house. The house was in quietness as he let himself in through the front door. The party was over and everyone gone to bed.

"Craig, is that you?" came the panicked voice of Sophie from the drawing room. She came rushing out and gasped when she saw the cut on his forehead.

"What happened to you?" she asked as she led him into the drawing room.

"I went out for a cigarette and slipped and hit my head. I must have passed out," he explained as he collapsed on the couch.

"Those bloody cigarettes! I told you they would be the death of you, in one way or another!"

"Oh don't go on, Sophie, please!" he begged.

"That's right, Sophie, he's had quite enough drama for one night," said Aunt Rachel as she stepped out from the shadows into the firelight.

He got a start at seeing Rachel and tried to sit up.

"Now, now, you just try and relax," she said, putting a hand on his shoulder.

He recoiled.

"You've had a nasty shock. You must have been out there for ages. You're lucky if you're not suffering from hypothermia."

"And yet you don't even feel cold," said Sophie as she felt his forehead and cheeks.

"Probably got a temperature," said Rachel. "I'll get the doctor to take a look at you in the morning. We don't want to take any chances."

"There's no need," objected Craig.

"There's every need," said Rachel. "In the meantime, I'll get you a stiff drink."

"I do wonder about you, Craig, I really do!" Sophie was close to tears. "I was worried sick."

He looked up at the mantelpiece where the 1950s photograph was now positioned.

"Who put that up there?" he demanded.

"I did," said Rachel. "You know, talking about it earlier made me feel so much better. It was like I released all the ghosts. So I thought I'd put the photo up here, in the room where it was taken."

Craig stared at the photo, vividly remembering posing for it.

And yet how could it be? He remembered Edgar's surname being Jones during the engagement toast, but Rachel hadn't mentioned his surname earlier in the study when she talked to him and Sophie about her fiancé.

"Rachel, your fiancée, Edgar –what was his surname?" asked Craig.

"His surname?" Rachel looked confused. "His surname was Jones."

"Why on earth do you want to know that?" questioned Sophie.

"Just wondered," said Craig.

"Well, let me get that drink for you," said Rachel, walking across the spacious drawing room to the drinks cabinet.

Craig whispered to Sophie. "We'll have to cut our visit here short. I have to go now."

"Has that knock to your head stopped you from thinking straight? There's a severe weather warning," snapped Sophie.

"We have to leave – something urgent has come up in work."

Sophie adopted a non-compromising look and muttered, "Stuff work, Craig! We can't leave Woodstown after dear old

Aunt Rachel has gone to such effort for us. We'll be spending the full Christmas period here."

Rachel turned around from the drinks cabinet and said, "Now, I'm afraid all the port and whiskey is drunk so it will have to be champagne for you, Craig."

She cradled the bottle of champagne as she walked towards Craig and smiled. "I do like this particular brand of champagne. I always think it gives you such a – hit."

A. O'Connor is the bestselling author of seven novels including *Talk Show, Property* and *Full Circle*. A graduate of NUI Maynooth and Trinity College, A. O'Connor's latest book *The House* will be published this Christmas. *The House* is a novel set around one house at three different pivotal periods of Ireland's history. Part historical fiction, part contemporary, the novel follows the fortunes and misfortunes of the Armstrong family in the 1840s, 1910s and the present day. *The House* is a sweeping read set against the Great Famine, the First World War, Ireland's independence and the present. A tale of betrayal, deceit, revenge and obsession – about one house, one family and three generations.

Christmas with Elvis and Roy

Geraldine O'Neill

Iknew I should have switched the bloody phone off when I arrived at the airport.

Sorcha's voice is crackling in my ear as I walk across the blowy, wet tarmac.

"Marianne – I can't believe you're going away!" she says. "Leaving him alone at Christmas is the worst thing you could have done."

"He's not alone. Daniel is *never* alone!"

"That's a bit of an overstatement . . . and what about our New Year party? I was depending on you."

Sorcha lives in the same road as us. At times it's a bit too close.

"I'm sorry, but I need to get away." I don't know why she was depending on me, as I'm not in the least bit talented at making the fiddly canapés Sorcha's parties are famous for. "You'll find someone else . . ."

"*Who?*" she asks.

"One of your friends whose life isn't falling apart!"

I notice some of the other passengers looking at me as they pass by and I suddenly realise I'm shouting. The glass of wine I downed in several quick gulps when my flight was called has just hit me. I took my time over the first two glasses and, if I'd thought about it, I would have left half of the third one because it's a half too much.

Sorcha is yapping as I walk along and my hair is flying all over the place. An unruly bob an inch too short to tie back in the usual handy ponytail. The hairdresser was so preoccupied chatting about her new sparkly top that she just kept chopping. I tuck a wing behind my ear and thank God no one will know me where I'm going.

"The weather might not be that great in Spain," Sorcha says. "It could be the same as Dublin. I know you think it perks you up – but you're not guaranteed sunshine at this time of the year."

Why the hell did I ever tell her that I thought I might have SAD syndrome after reading a magazine article about it? She's like a bloody elephant, and it's always the uncomfortable things she remembers.

"The weather is the last thing on my mind . . ."

"Listen, Marianne, have you told him how you feel? I'm worried that this is all a spur of the moment thing that you'll regret."

"I've had enough – I'm not waiting in for him any more. I'm not wasting my time cooking meals that he doesn't come home for. You wouldn't take it from Andy."

Sorcha rolls her eyes. "He's the opposite. Likes his meals on the table at six o'clock every night. Boring to the last." She pauses. "You can't compare them. With Daniel, I think it's just work."

"Well, you can only bump into so many old friends and colleagues that drag you off for a drink. He must think I'm stupid."

"What do you mean?"

"It's obviously a cover-up for something else."

"Another woman?" There's a silence. "Have you any evidence?"

"Do you mean have I checked his phone?"

"Oh, no . . . don't lower yourself to that," she says. "That's only for desperate women. Marianne, please don't go! What about your new Christmas tree and wreath?"

"I don't care."

The queue is slowly moving up the aircraft steps.

"How long are you going for?"

"I've time owing at work. I can have a couple of weeks off — more if I feel like it."

"Come home for New Year. Going away will give him the wake-up call he needs, and he'll be all over you at the party."

My finger locates the 'Off' button on the phone. "I'm boarding now."

"I'll ring and keep you up to date on things back here . . ."

I'm relieved to get a seat in the middle of the plane, just in front of the emergency seats. I hate flying, and I read somewhere that the middle of the plane is the most stable in turbulence. There's a thin, older man sitting by the window. He doesn't make any eye contact as I sit in the aisle seat leaving a spare seat between us. I flick through the magazine I bought at the airport, and realise that the wine has helped as I feel my eyelids fluttering just before take-off.

It's a calm, easy flight and I sleep through most of it. I waken a couple of times – first, when the drinks trolley passes, and again when the man beside me needs to use the lavatory. Afterwards, I doze off again.

I waken with a shock as we hit the ground at Malaga airport and then go into automatic pilot sorting my hand luggage and passport. As I make my way into the terminal, I wish Sorcha was here to see the Spanish sunshine and feel the warm air. I could phone her, but my mobile is staying switched off. I don't want to hear Daniel's excuses, and I don't want to have to report it verbatim back to her.

I collect my case – a mix of summer and winter clothes – everything thrown in un-ironed without my usual carefully ticked-off list. I've only brought my small make-up bag, hoping Mum will have everything else I need. Who will notice if I haven't my special body-building shampoo or my straightening serum?

My mother is waiting for me.

It takes me a few moments to recognise her. Her hair is longer, and her mousey colour is a vivid shade of plum. She looks younger than her fifty-odd years. Compared to her, I am suddenly the mouse. I worried about her moving to Spain after Dad died two years ago, and thought that my life would change dramatically, but we quickly got into a routine with me visiting her often at the apartment five minutes' walk from Malaga city centre.

She has kept our family home back in Dublin and she comes back and forward every few months, and we phone and Skype regularly. In a funny way we are closer now than we were when she was in Ireland all the time. I suppose it was my fault – at the beginning of our romance, I had no time for anyone but Daniel.

Mum wraps her arms around me. "I'm so glad you came."

I fall into the warmth of her neck and the comforting smell of the *CoCo* perfume that she's worn forever. "So am I."

There is a chicken Caesar salad, garlic bread and a cold bottle of my favourite Chablis waiting at the bright airy apartment which is perfect with only six of everything – knives, plates, chairs and wine glasses. My mother calls it her 'doll's house' and keeps it uncluttered of all the stuff she has collected over a lifetime back in Ballsbridge.

After the meal we open another bottle. Normally my mother would be careful with drink – but things aren't normal.

She starts hesitantly. "I'm delighted you came . . ."

I take a big gulp of wine. "I'm going to have to start being single all over again and I couldn't face doing it at Christmas in Dublin. I would have had to hide away."

"You know Oliver and Orla are always there for you."

"I know." My younger twin brother and sister who are both happily married with kids. Oliver in Donegal and Orla in Cellbridge. "But I didn't want to be a wet blanket over their Christmas – be a spectre at the feast."

"They love having you."

"The kids would want to know where Daniel is – and I would have to explain it to all their friends . . ."

Mum's hand covers mine. "Are you regretting walking out?"

"I'm regretting I didn't go sooner. I'm regretting that I've wasted another two years on him."

We drink more of the wine, talk and hug each other a lot, then we go to bed. I fall asleep as soon as my head hits the pillow.

It is late next morning when the deep blue sky creeps through the slits in the shutters that it all comes back to me. I lie there filled with dread in case I have overreacted. I run it over in my mind and let out a low sigh when I arrive at the same conclusion. I was right to cut my losses. Daniel has once again proved that he is incapable of changing. He might say he loves me and he might even believe it, but he can't change.

He cannot say 'No'. He cannot refuse a final drink. He cannot come home when he says he will. I cannot depend on him. There will always be something or someone to steal his attention. I will never be enough.

And that decision to walk away leaves me technically homeless and boyfriend-less again at thirty-six years old. I have our old family house to go back to but it's not the same. Mum said she still has the fifty-thousand deposit for a place of my own that she has kept safe for me – money that the three children got when my father died. It will get me a decent mortgage and buy more than it would have done pre-recession.

The thought of house-hunting gives me a tight feeling in my chest.

I look at my phone on the bedside cabinet and wonder if Daniel or Sorcha have been trying to contact me. I don't switch it on to check. I have nothing to say.

I shift off the bed and walk across the cold marble floor to press the switch which lifts the metal shutters on the French windows. They rattle into life and as they move upwards sunlight floods the room. When I slide the window open to step out onto the decking area, I can feel a definite warmth. I reckon the temperature must be in the late teens.

Mum must have heard the shutters going up because she calls out from the kitchen to see if I'd like coffee and croissants.

I haven't given food much thought for the last few days. "Great," I call back.

"And how do you feel after sleeping?"

"Better – glad I've come."

We sit in our pyjamas talking as we have breakfast, and then Mum tells me that she's met a new friend.

I immediately know what the plum hairdo is about. "A man?"

"Yes," she says, flushing. "Although he's not actually new . . . we met a long time ago back in Dublin. He's been living over here about five years."

"How did you meet up?"

"We bumped into each other in the local hotel."

I can't imagine her with a man. I thought she'd had enough with dad. Maybe she's lonely out here. "Do you see as much of Patricia and Margaret?" These are two Dublin friends who have been living in Spain longer than Mum and who encouraged her to move to an apartment near them.

"Oh, yes," Mum says. "We meet up every other morning and I go swimming and to Zumba classes with them."

She doesn't sound desperate for company. There's a look in her eyes that makes me wonder. "Do you like him a lot?"

"Yes," she says. "I do . . . I've always liked him, but we were both married back then."

"Is he like dad?"

She shakes her red hair. "Not at all. He's very easy-going."

Dad – a retired policeman — was the opposite of easy-going. His pleasant personality changed after he fell off a ladder and banged his head. How Mum put up with him all those years I'll never know. When we complained, she told us that he was a good provider and he loved us all. He just didn't know how to show it.

"What's his name?"

"Frank."

"And am I going to meet him?"

She nods, her face scarlet now. "There's a show on down in

one of the local hotels tonight. I thought we might go and catch up with him later."

"What kind of show?"

She laughs. "A tribute show – Elvis and Roy Orbison." She's always loved Elvis.

"I don't know if I can bear it!"

"You enjoyed the Robbie Williams tribute last time you were here."

"That's different, years of difference."

"We don't have to go."

I can tell she is disappointed. "Going out will take my mind off things back in Dublin."

As we carry the things back into the kitchen, I ask about the weather forecast and what I should wear.

My mother shrugs. "It won't be cold, but it won't be boiling either and it should be dry so we won't need umbrellas."

After my shower I throw on a blue chambray shirt, cream jeans and navy deck shoes, and I roll a cardigan up and put it into my shoulder bag. Mum's shampoo and the Spanish water has made my hair too fluffy and flyaway, so I stick on a black hair-band until I buy my usual products.

Mum wears a black sweater and denims with a bohemian-style scarf. I'm still amazed at how well she looks.

We walk into Malaga city centre and look around the shops. There are Christmas decorations and Christmas music everywhere. The phone remains switched off. We stop for a cappuccino and a pastry at my favourite café.

"Shall we have them inside?" my mother checks. "There's a bit of a nip in the air."

I look at the blue sky and think of the Irish weather I will be facing when I eventually return. There are a few other people outside, admittedly mainly smokers. "Shall we chance outside?"

Mum smiles and nods. A bit of me feels she would agree to anything to see me happy. We take our trays outside. We chat for a while then we fall into a comfortable silence as we eat and drink. Every time my thoughts drift back to Daniel, I force them back to the sunshine and the elegantly dressed Spanish women passing up and down. They are dressed for winter in their coats and boots and scarves, dictated by the calendar. The ex-pats like Mum and holiday-makers like me are conspicuous by their dedication to summer wear whatever time of year the sun shines.

When we arrive back home I spend an hour ironing all my crumpled clothes. A little knot in my stomach keeps reminding me of Daniel. I force him out of my mind by concentrating on smoothing and straightening the fabrics. I know I've made the right choice.

I hang all my perfect clothes in the wardrobe, then Mum and I take magazines outside with glasses of cranberry juice. My mother's phone rings and I guess it is Frank when she goes to the upstairs balcony to talk in private.

"We'll meet him after the show," she tells me later. "I thought you and I would go into town earlier and have tapas beforehand with Patricia and Margaret."

She is trying to fill every moment for me, so I haven't time to think. But I can't stop it. If I'm not fighting thoughts of home I'm dreading the awful show tonight and meeting Frank. I can tell it's important to Mum. So important I don't chat about it or make jokes as I usually would.

The tapas bar is down a small side street beside Malaga Cathedral. It is decked out in Christmas paraphernalia. We sit inside as it is chilly out. Margaret and Patricia look fantastic, they are cheery and chatty and after a brief mention of my runaway situation, they tell me about all the people they know who have made new lives in Spain. I wonder if Mum has asked them to suggest I move out here. I make it clear that it's only Daniel I've left behind, and that I intend to return to my life in Dublin.

"You'll be grand," Patricia says. "Look at your mother, starting all over again, who would have believed how she met her old boyfriend again . . ."

My mother's head jerks up and the topic of Frank is dropped.

We drink two bottles of wine between us and as we walk along to the hotel where the Elvis and Roy show is on, I feel like a mousy loser again compared to the three vivacious retirees.

The opening bars of 'Pretty Woman' blare and then Roy appears on stage to loud applause. The jet-black nylon wig and dark glasses are hilarious, and I cringe when he starts singing as he looks too intense and his first notes are dodgy. I glance at the three women to see if they noticed, but they are clapping and singing along. Roy's voice warms up and he becomes bearable.

When he finishes, Margaret turns to me. "Isn't he fantastic?"

It's politic to agree. "He's very good."

When he starts singing 'It's Over', their faces look mesmerised.

At the break in the Ladies', Patricia asks me how I feel about meeting Frank and I shrug.

"He's lovely, when you get to know him. He's not a bit like your father – he's a bit of a one-off."

I don't know what Mum has said about my father, so I just nod.

"At our age," Patricia says, "you have to grab life while you can. I lost my oldest friend last year in a car accident and another friend is dying of cancer."

That really cheers me up.

Elvis has the same initial effect on me as the Roy performer when he starts. I cringe again as he struggles for the first note of 'In The Ghetto', and then suddenly he's coasting along. He's wearing a white rhinestone cat-suit which is a couple of sizes too big – one The King would have worn in his later, fatter years. And I'm certain he has borrowed Roy Orbison's nylon wig. I find myself singing along, and later agree with the others that he's exactly like the real Elvis.

When he sings 'Always On My Mind', Daniel comes floating back into mine. I wonder what he's doing and how he has reacted to my disappearance. The phone is still off. Elvis rounds off with his festive hits, 'Blue Christmas' and 'White Christmas' leaving the fans misty-eyed as we move out into the bar for a drink. I notice my mother's gaze flitting to the door every so often and her hand is slightly shaky when she lifts her gin and tonic.

Patricia turns around and says, "Look who's here!"

A nice-looking man of average height with grey hair, jeans and a well-ironed striped shirt comes towards the table. He leans down and kisses my mother on the forehead. My heart shifts a little as she is glowing in a way she never glowed with my father.

She gestures towards me. "Marianne, this is Frank . . ."

He comes around to shake my hand. His eyes are warm and friendly.

"Lovely to meet you. Did you enjoy the show?"

"Yes," I nod. He is well spoken. "It was very entertaining."

Margaret touches my arm. "Does Frank remind you of anyone you've met recently?"

I stare at him. There's something vaguely familiar, but I'm not sure. I look back at her and shake my head.

Frank grins and sinks into the chair beside me. "You're a bit younger than the usual audience. I suppose you'd prefer Robbie Williams or Amy Winehouse?"

"The performances were good, but I couldn't believe the dodgy wig they were sharing and Elvis's rhinestone boiler-suit . . ."

"I believe it's the same guy doing both acts."

"My God, I would never have guessed," I smile. "Although he could do with investing in two wigs."

There is a deafening silence, then my mother says, "Marianne . . . are you sure you don't recognise Frank? We didn't say because we thought it would be a surprise."

My heart quickens. I've obviously said something wrong.

He starts to laugh. "I'm flattered she doesn't know!"

"Frank," Mum says in a strangled voice, "is Elvis and Roy."

The world suddenly stops. My mother is in love with an Elvis impersonator. Can my life get any more tragic?

After the taxi drops Mum and me back at the apartment, I turn on her. "I can't believe you're seeing a man who does such a ridiculous job for a living."

"I'm proud of him." Her voice is trembling. "He's a talented performer and musician, and he brings a lot of enjoyment to people."

"It's ludicrous. He's a cheap ten-a-penny club act. All your friends back in Dublin will laugh when they hear."

"I don't care. My real friends who know Frank all like him, and they think he's good for me."

"What will Oliver and Orla say?"

"I was hoping that you would explain it to them when you got back."

"Explain that you've lost your mind? Explain that you're behaving like a love-struck adolescent? He's not Elvis Presley, Mum. He's not real."

"Frank is very real. Our feelings are very real." Her face is white, her voice determined. "It's probably the worst time for you to meet – but it would be unfair to hide him away over Christmas. And I couldn't dis-invite him because things didn't work out with you and Daniel."

"So Elvis and Roy will be here for Christmas Day?"

"Yes," Mum says, tilting her chin. "Frank will be here."

"I wish I'd never come."

"Marianne, please let me explain about Frank . . ."

I shrug her off. "I'm too tired to listen."

I hardly sleep. At seven o'clock in the morning I feel so bad that I might as well check my phone. I have twenty-three missed calls. Most are from Daniel, Sorcha and an unknown number.

I go to voicemail. The latest message is from the number I don't recognise. It's from Sorcha's husband, Andy. Surely he's not phoning me on her behalf about the bloody New Year party? The time on the voicemail is eleven last night. I listen. He's asking me to call him back.

I stare at the ceiling until I hear Mum rattling around, and then I wonder what I am going to say to her. There's a knock on my door and she comes in carrying two cups of coffee. She sits on the end of my bed.

"Frank and I met at a teachers' in-service training day over twenty years ago. He is a highly qualified music teacher."

She is telling me this because of the club-act comment.

"I could talk to Frank in a way I never could with your father, especially after his accident. We used to meet up for a coffee now

300

and again, but after a while our feelings were getting stronger and we both decided that it had to stop."

I look down at the floor.

"It wasn't an affair," she stresses. "We never allowed ourselves . . . but I was upset . . ." She tilts her chin. "In all the years since, he was the first thing I thought of when I woke every morning."

"What about Dad?"

"He never noticed anything. He never spoke about anything personal. You know that was always his way."

There is no point saying anything more about Dad. We all knew what she had put up with. "Was Frank married?"

"Yes, but no children. His wife died over ten years ago. She was a bad diabetic. Everyone at school knew them so it was all the talk."

"Why didn't you go to him then?"

"Because I had a husband and I had three children I loved."

"Did you speak to him after his wife's funeral?"

"No. I had no contact details for him, and I still didn't think it was right. I never saw him again until Margaret and Patricia brought me to the hotel two years after your father died." She lowers her eyes. "They knew I had always loved Elvis Presley."

I think of my mother waking up thinking of this man every morning. "And did they know you had always loved Frank?"

She shook her head. "I told no one. I wouldn't have done that to our family. The girls think we were just teaching colleagues who met up again. Are you angry at me for finding another man, or angry that it's Frank?"

I shrug. "I don't know . . . I just find his job an embarrassment."

"It's only a hobby . . . he has his own lovely place out here and a very good pension. He loves the music . . . and I love it too."

I look towards the window. The sky is cloudier today. But then tomorrow is Christmas Eve.

She stands up. "I just wanted you to know. I'll go and put some croissants in the oven."

My phone rings. I click 'answer' to hear Sorcha crying.

"The message that Andy left you is all lies!" she says. "It was completely innocent and he's blown it into something huge. He's ruined Christmas for us all! I invited Daniel in for a drink because I felt sorry for him. Andy went to bed and we stayed up talking, then Daniel started looking up flights on my computer to follow you out to Spain."

My stomach lurches.

Sorcha goes on. "We both drank a bit too much and fell asleep on the sofa. It was completely innocent, we were just lying together – but Andy came down and went berserk and then ran out. Daniel left of course, mortified. When Andy came back he told me he had left a message on your voicemail saying we'd been having an affair, but it's all lies! We're just good friends and I'm a married woman."

"Stop right there, Sorcha!" I suddenly say. "Don't tell me he's on his way?"

"No," she said, "by the time he checked again this morning, the last available seat had gone."

I am overcome with relief.

"I'm sure Daniel's hoping you'll patch things up and thank God Andy has calmed down now. I didn't know he had it in him to be so jealous."

Something in her tone tells me she is enjoying the drama.

"Goodbye, Sorcha," I tell her. "Happy Christmas and don't ever call me again."

I lie in silence for a while, then I get up and go into the kitchen. I go towards my mother and put my arms around her. "I'm sorry. Frank's a lovely man and I hope you'll be happy together."

She looks at me in amazement. "Why the big change?"

"Because I don't want you to spend another twenty years waking up thinking of a lost love. And what you said made *me* realise that I don't want to wake up in twenty years' time wishing I wasn't with Daniel."

I go back into the bedroom and pick up the phone. I smile and think of Roy's song. "It's over," I text. "Put the apartment on the market."

⚜

Geraldine O'Neill grew up in a small mining village, in Lanarkshire, Scotland. The second of six children, she contracted polio as a baby during the last 50s epidemic. She moved to Newcastle-upon-Tyne to train as a teacher, and there she met her future husband, Mike Brosnahan, whom she married in 1977 and had two children. The family relocated to Ireland in 1991. Around 2000 Geraldine's old polio condition came back to haunt her and a range of symptoms led to her being diagnosed with Post-Polio Syndrome. She controls the condition through lifestyle management and 'listening to her body'. She is an active member of the Irish Post-Polio Support Group. Geraldine has been writing since the early 90s and had gained a number of awards for her short stories before embarking on her first novel. She has also had a number of poems published. She has been involved in various community writing projects and workshops, has given readings at literary festivals and talks on her writing career. Geraldine has had nine novels published in Ireland and abroad, and her tenth book will be published in spring 2013. Her books are also available in e-book versions, large print, audio and various foreign translations.

The Reluctant Snowman

Jacqueline Strawbridge

Orla had been receiving brusque letters announcing residents' association meetings all year. Back in January, the meeting theme had been speeding. In February, it was cracked pavements. There had been litter meetings, tidy-garden meetings and, once, a 'pick up dog-poo' meeting, whose letter she had thrown straight into the bin.

Now it was December and though she'd known about the meetings for nearly a year (she couldn't understand how they had dropped under her radar before that), she'd been to exactly none.

Yet lately she'd had this vague notion that it would be a good idea to 'get involved' in something. At thirty-nine, she lived alone. Since she had broken up with her boyfriend (she hated using that word at her age), she was at a loss. All she did was work and sleep. At work, she didn't have any friends. She didn't know why. She felt lonely. And that is why she decided to go along to the last meeting of the year.

Yes, Orla thought, as she marched with purpose into Number 64 a fashionable half-an-hour late, she would make more of an effort. She imagined herself, apron on, spooning out jam (her concept of neighbourliness was a mystifying patchwork of an *Ireland's Own* article she'd read and a childhood memory of eating jam from the spoon at a neighbour's house) to an eager crowd, then modestly grinning while the chairman of the association made an impromptu speech about how unbelievably improved life had been since she moved there.

Orla, a prim woman with a precisely cut dark-brown bob and intelligent (her own compliment) brown eyes, was still in this cinematic reverie when she realised she was the focus of attention.

There in a dark and densely tinselled living room, the only light a miniature fire that looked like it had been built by fairies, sat eight or so people, all blinking at her. She felt faint. At work she often led meetings in the boardroom where, she thought with a pinprick of shame now, she had held no pity for the interns who shuffled in late looking mortified. Which is what she felt now.

Suddenly irritated, she strode forward to the nearest person, a stout, red-faced woman, and stuck out her hand. The woman inexplicably gripped Orla's left hand and used it to lever herself up. As Orla tried to introduce herself, the woman used a stick to deftly push her down into the seat.

"Ssssh," she said, pointing reverently at a disgruntled-looking man across the room. "Sean was just telling us –"

"Ladies, when you're finished," Sean said sternly.

Jesus, thought Orla, looking around. The room had lost interest in her and were staring intently at Sean, a tall, well-built man in his sixties who had a small dash of the Sean Connery about him.

Orla surveyed the room. Aside from the stout woman (who she learned was called Peggy), there was a dishevelled man of around fifty, two women in their forties (one with an apron on, Orla was pleased to note), an extremely young couple with their hands intertwined, a man in a smart suit (handsome, thought Orla, imagining the story she'd tell her grandchildren about how she met her husband), two very old men (one of them looked about a hundred), and – Orla had to stop herself gasping – Joan Collins.

Orla couldn't believe it. Perching languidly on a pine stool was an older woman wearing an elegantly cut scarlet suit. She had fabulously long legs, which wound around each other endlessly and eventually crossed at her ankles, daintily situated above a pair of gold-studded Louboutins. She wore a pussy-bow chiffon blouse and through it you could see she had on a spectacularly fancy bra. A bra like only Joan Collins would have, Orla thought in awe. The woman's hair was dyed a glossy black and was swept up off her distinguished face. And what a face! There were wrinkles, but it was as if they had been painted on to flatter her luminescent green eyes, three faint strokes on each side of her face. She wore deep red lipstick and her nails were painted a pristinely fashionable shade of nude.

Who was this woman? Orla couldn't take her eyes off her, studying her as she listened to Sean speak. The woman had her eyes half-closed, as if she were applying all her powers of concentration to Sean's rousing words.

"It takes all shapes and sizes," said Sean. "Nobody should be ashamed!"

There was silence, and the young couple coughed in tandem. The stout woman tapped her foot, as if she was getting ready to break out into a jig. Perhaps she was, Orla thought idly. She had no idea about what really went on at these meetings. The presence of Joan Collins had thrown her. She felt that anything could happen.

Dragging her attention away from Joan, Orla looked at the man in the smart suit, who was preparing to speak, signalled by a theatrical clearing of his throat and a loosening of his rather, Orla noticed only now, flamboyant tie.

"Look, guys," he began, before briefly flicking his attention to Orla, "I'm Russell by the way – you?" As Orla mumbled her name, he continued, "Guys, doing it together – it'll be fun!" He stood up.

Jesus, thought Orla again. Was he going to do some kind of performance piece? He certainly seemed to be gearing up for it. She looked down at his feet, and noted he was wearing salmon-coloured brogues. She sighed. She wouldn't be marrying him after all, she told her future grandchildren, whose lineage she couldn't yet know.

Russell raised his right hand inspirationally. "It's Christmas! Let's do it. I've always wanted to . . ."

He flipped his fancy tie over his shoulder as he sat down with a flourish, clearly annoyed at the interruption. One of the ancient-looking men had outshone him by standing halfway up before changing his mind and sitting down again, looking over at Orla, curtly nodding and saying, "Larry. Number 57. Lived there sixty years," and then turning to Sean with a smart salute and saying "I'm in."

The young couple looked over at Orla. "The O'Briens." They pointed at each other, the girl chirping, "He's Jim," the boy – he couldn't have been more than nineteen – saying, "And she's Jen." Then, as if they had rehearsed it, simultaneously, "Just married, Number 15." They both laughed, looked at each other conspiratorially and chorused, "Okay!"

Orla was feeling ashamed now, because she had been so taken with the neighbourhood Joan Collins that she didn't have a clue what everyone was agreeing to. She couldn't even guess. Why was salmon-shoes so enthusiastic? And the young couple looked trendy and normal. What were they looking so pleased about? Larry was 'in' too. In what? she wondered, gazing over at Joan again, who was sitting in the same sensual half-eyes-shut position. Perhaps she was meditating, thought Orla. That would explain her beautiful skin. Meditating gave you lovely pinky skin, she'd read somewhere. All that oxygen, it must be.

". . . and I'm going to do it too, honestly. I'm up for anything now!"

Orla jerked back to reality. The dishevelled man was speaking. For a moment, she felt she was in the middle of an AA meeting. The man, who when Orla glanced up said, "My name is Joe," looked as if it had been a huge effort to speak at all, and was now glowing in relief that he'd said his piece.

"Well done, Joe!" said one of the women in her forties soothingly, leaning over to touch his arm affectionately.

"Maeve," she said to Orla, then looked at Sean and said, "Of course I'll do it."

"Ah, good woman yourself!" Russell leapt up again, sitting down swiftly under the weight of a filthy look from Sean.

"Peggy?" Sean said.

Peggy tapped her foot again, and placed her hand on Orla's shoulder, as if they were both now posing for one of those grim nineteenth-century portraits.

"Don't be ridiculous," she said, standing up straighter as she dug her hand into Orla's shoulder.

"I'll take that as a yes," Sean continued, flashing Peggy a smile, which elevated his features so handsomely that Orla decided, yes, he was the absolute spit of an elderly James Bond.

She looked at Sean with new interest, glancing from him to Peggy and back again. Definitely something going on there. She bet these meetings were a hotbed of affairs. She looked over at Larry's friend, who was idly pulling at his nose hair. Perhaps not. Sean and Peggy though. Wouldn't you have thought it would have been Joan Collins? Well, it just goes to show you, thought Orla triumphantly. There's Peggy, plain and puffy-faced and carrying some sort of walking stick, and glamour-puss over there couldn't even get a look in with Sean Connery!

The woman with the apron on, which, Orla noted with disappointment, was a dress and not an apron at all, stood up to leave. She grinned wearily over at Orla, saying, "Leanne, next door!", then said to the room "I'm not going to tell the kids about it – it will just confuse them – but yeah, it's a great idea. It's Christmas, it would almost be a sin not to."

"Bye, Lee," said Larry, standing halfway up before sitting down again.

His friend, John, stopped fiddling with his nose hair, and shouted out as Leanne was leaving, "I'll be round at six!" before turning to the room and saying, "Well, if my daughter says she'll do it, I'll do it too." He picked wax out of his ears and wiped it on his trousers. "Though I don't want to see any melons," he cackled.

Orla looked at him with disgust, and he hung his head, muttering, "John. Number 18."

The room fell silent. It would be Joan Collins's turn next, thought Orla with excitement. She was still in the same pose, signs of life traceable only by a change of the position of her hand, which had now moved from her lap to underneath her chin. Not a waddle of flesh in sight! Plastic surgery, Orla told herself snarkily. It had to be.

Orla realised she was staring, snapping back to reality as Peggy nipped her shoulder, saying, "Orla. Orla, Number 49."

That's me! Orla thought with a start. "Er . . . Orla, Number 49."

Everyone, apart from Joan Collins, said, "Hello, Orla Number 49!" which made her giggle nervously. She quickly flicked through escape strategies in her head. How on earth could she hide the fact that she had been sitting there for so long without knowing what they were talking about? She would look like a fool! Should she just say yes? To what though? It could be anything. But it must be something to do with Christmas, she reasoned. What had the letter said? What had John just said? She couldn't remember. Her mind had gone blank. She wished she was more like Joan. Did Joan take fish oil?

"Orla's lived here for three years," said Russell, quite accusingly she thought. But when she caught his eye, the expression was merry.

"I only just . . ." began Orla apologetically.

Larry nodded encouragingly. Then Joe wiped his hands on his trousers, and stood up, taking the attention away from Orla.

"Mine . . . er . . ." Joe paused, cleared his throat and then squeaked, "Well, it's more like a cucumber." He stopped and surveyed the room bashfully. "Because it's very big. That's what the woman said anyway," he said, looking around for support.

The young woman interrupted enthusiastically. "His is enormous. I can't wait for you all to see it! " she said.

Joe sat down again abruptly. Orla was sure he had more to say, but had given up. He was blushing furiously. Maeve tugged at his arm again, smiling up at him. Another affair, thought Orla. And he looked like he needed a good –

"Go on, Orla," said Peggy, who had adopted her, in what capacity Orla didn't know, but she suspected it would be a lot to do with aiding her restricted mobility. Panicked, Orla flicked through Christmas-themed things in her head. Mince pies, Santa, the baby Jesus, presents, pine trees . . . Look, she told herself sternly, you'll just have to ask them what's going on.

She stood up. It seemed appropriate.

"The thing is, I don't even . . ." She trailed off because, without warning, Joan Collins had stood up, eclipsing the rest of the room.

"Joan," she said, stretching out her hand.

Confused and wondering briefly if she should kiss it, Orla sat down instead, nearly missing her chair in shock. So it *was* Joan, she thought, astounded. You knew these celebrities existed under the radar, but wow, Joan Collins. She hadn't even known that Joan had Irish connections.

"Joan O'Leary. The top terrace."

Orla stared, still dumbstruck.

Joan moved forward, ballerina-like, slipping sensuously through the narrow gap between Larry and John's chairs. Peggy pursed her lips. Jealous, Orla thought. The atmosphere in the room was electric, the only sounds the howl of sudden hail outside and the faint crackling of the minuscule fire.

With Joan standing there, the room took on a new glamour, as if it had just been promoted from living room to ballroom. Even Joe, his desultory demeanour taking on a certain shabby charisma, seemed to shine. Peggy let her walking stick fall deferentially to the ground. Larry stood halfway up, and remained there, his legs shaking with the effort. Jen and Jim dropped each other's hands and sat up straight, while Sean bowed his head, as if the Pope himself were about to speak.

Would Joan agree to do it too? It seemed important that she did, that was certain.

"You all know what I did for a living. I've done this countless times."

John let out a strange, high-pitched schoolboy laugh, very odd coming from a ninety-odd-year-old.

Joan glanced over at him and he hung his head again.

"It's alright John," she said. "I know what you're thinking." She paused. "And yes, I enjoyed it. I wouldn't change it for the world."

Now it was John who was blushing, making his leathery skin appear even more burnt.

The silver tinsel sparkled, as if in applause. Orla shifted in her chair, agog. Joan was looking around the room, her green eyes scooping up the admiring glances like an opera diva after her final performance.

Those shoes really were gorgeous, thought Orla, trying to get a closer look at Joan's legs to see if there were any veins popping out on them. There were none.

"I'd do it again in a heartbeat." She paused again.

Orla looked around the room for the cameras, or at the very least, Blake Carrington.

"I'll be Miss July. And no jokes about how juicy I am. I've heard it all."

With that, she swept out of the room. Everybody stood up en masse and Orla thought they were all going to start clapping. Instead, the room broke out into noisy chatter.

"Alright, everyone, settle down," said Sean, although he looked as excited as everybody else. He shook his head, as if in disbelief. "This calendar is going to be . . ."

"Better than *Playboy*!" laughed Peggy, tapping him playfully with her stick.

So that was it! They were making a calendar, Orla thought in relief.

"We'll need somewhere private to take the photographs," said Jen.

Sean averted his eyes, and replied, "Yes, yes, sure we're all in it together. It's a first for me, a first for all of us – except Joan of course!"

Calendar. Private. Photographs. The truth was finally dawning on Orla. Melons. Miss July – oh my God! *It's more like a cucumber because it's so big.* Well! She'd felt sorry for Joe, but not any more. They were making a naked calendar!

Just as she was imagining with horror what Larry would look like with no clothes on, Peggy nipped her on the shoulder and said, "Orla, you'll do it? It's for the local children's hospital."

They all turned to stare at her and Orla found herself saying "Yes . . ." before everyone in the room whooped and cheered.

The gathering dispersed and, as Orla walked back to her house, hopping delicately between the slushy puddles, she couldn't quite believe what she had agreed to.

A nude calendar with Peggy and Larry and shambolic Joe — and Orla herself! Who would want to see that? Orla shivered in the cold and shook her head. She'd have to find a way to wriggle out of it, that was all.

As she turned her key in her door, Leanne popped her head out of her front window and said, "Peggy just called. Delighted you've agreed! Hopefully we'll all get to know each other better."

They certainly would, thought Orla grimly, but before she could say anything, Leanne disappeared again.

Then Orla felt something stir deep inside her. She'd been so lonely all year, and now here was her neighbour popping out her head to chat to her as if she were an old friend. She stepped into her freezing hallway and shook the slush from her shoes. She'd do it! If Joan Collins could do it at nearly eighty, then she could do it too.

Upstairs, she undressed and studied herself in the mirror. Her waistline was still intact, her breasts were – well, they were there. They weren't saggy or anything. Orla Cassidy, she smiled to herself, I can't believe you're going to strip off for a calendar. She climbed into bed, still naked, and drifted off, though it took longer than usual as she started to worry about what she would tell her boss when she handed in her notice because of the film and book deal that would inevitably come. She dreamt of Peggy running nymph-like through the street, chased by a naked Sean, who held her stick aloft as if it were a prize.

She woke up the next morning to a loud buzzing noise. It took her a while to work out that it was her front door, which nobody had ever rung before.

No sooner had she opened the door than Peggy, breathless, leaned forward and rested her hand on Orla's shoulder.

"It's happening sooner than we thought," said Peggy. "Tonight!"

"What? Why?" said Orla.

She was wide awake now. She wasn't ready. She had been planning to not eat for at least three days and get her hair dyed darker, and maybe even Botox her lips so she could out-Joan Joan.

"No!" she almost shouted, and Peggy teetered back.

"No? Why ever not, dear?"

"I'm not ready," stuttered Orla, "I don't even know if I should have agreed to this in the first place!"

But by now Peggy had turned away, shouting over her shoulder from the gate, "It'll be fine. See you at the top terrace at seven. Just bring yourself – you don't need any clothes."

For God's sake! Was she even to *walk* there naked? What was wrong with these people? And the top terrace! That was Joan's house.

She closed the door, and sat down on the stairs. It was only then that she realised she still had no clothes on. Peggy must have got an eyeful. Mind you, she hadn't said anything. Perhaps they all stripped off all the time. Perhaps they were swingers.

She looked at her watch. It was seven o'clock. She had twelve hours. That wasn't necessarily a lot of time, she reflected, especially since she had to squeeze a day's work in between.

That day, Orla got the following done: a Brazilian wax, attachment of false eyelashes, an eyebrow tint, an all-over body scrub, a semi-permanent hair dye (on her head – she wasn't Jean Harlow) and a pedicure. It had been a Herculean feat, of which she couldn't deny she was proud. Maybe she'd tell Leanne about it later.

As evening fell once more, Orla undressed in her bedroom and looked at herself again. It was a mammoth improvement on this morning.

So why did she feel so full of dread? She felt no giddy, *Calendar Girls*-style excitement. Stripping off was just so very un-Orla. She was much more likely to apply layers on than strip them off. What if Larry or John or Joe, or for that matter, Peggy, were perverts?

She felt defiant now. For one thing, she wouldn't be walking over there naked! She put on her dressing gown. She had stolen it from a hotel. It was absurdly fluffy. It was also bright white and so when she put it on, she looked like a snowman. A very reluctant snowman, she thought darkly, as she pulled on her black wellies, an old flat cap and shuffled out of the house.

Outside, it was snowing heavily and she could barely see in front of her. Good lord, she shivered, how had Larry or John survived this naked walk?

And how was she going to survive seeing them with no clothes on? What if she did something stupid when she saw them – oh!

She stopped dead in her tracks, her arms hanging down by her sides, pulled in close to her body to keep out the cold. What if she *enjoyed* seeing them naked? Oh my God. It was *she* who was the pervert! Snow stuck thick and fast to her dressing gown, and she stood there for a moment, frozen with panic.

Inside the house above her, a little boy looked out with wonder at the snowman who had appeared so suddenly in the night. It was magic, he thought solemnly, for he knew it hadn't been there just minutes before. He lay back down on his pillow, hugging himself. How he loved Christmas!

Outside, Orla began to walk again. This was all Joan Collins O'Leary's fault, she thought, on the verge of tears as she rang the doorbell of the top terrace. Who else would have suggested such a thing? All she had wanted was to become involved in a Christmas cake sale or a mince-pie bake-off and now it had come to this! Yes, she thought bitterly, it was last chance saloon for Joan. A last flashing of the flesh, a last hurrah, a —

The door swung open and for a second Orla couldn't see anything. She felt a warm blast in her face, and could hear joyous bursts of laughter in the background. She heard a cork pop open and the clink of glasses. Well! They were really going to town.

Then her eyes began to focus. Standing before her was a six-foot tall broad bean.

"The name's broad bean. Sean Broadbean!" the broad bean joked and Orla saw that it was Sean – she could just make out his features as his face was painted green. Sean threw back his arm, pointing to the living-room. "You're wearing a dressing gown! Is that the new thing? He leaned forward to pull her in. 'Come in out of that cold and join the party. My wife's the sweetcorn!"

Orla entered the room and saw lots of huge fruits and vegetables milling around. There was Peggy, wearing a yellow body stocking with green sleeves. "Grab a drink," she yelled over. "The pictures are being taken in Joan's kitchen, the light is perfect."

Orla stood still.

There was Larry, dressed as some sort of turnip. "I'm December," he said proudly.

And Jen and Jim, both with purple tights on and padded-out, purple leotards. "Passion fruit and blackberry!" said Jen as Jim self-consciously checked to see if there was a gigantic green stalk still attached to his head. They wandered off, hands still held.

There was Maeve and Joe deep in conversation, Brussels sprout and carrot respectively (it was a particularly large carrot, very like a cucumber – Orla saw that now), and Russell, dressed as a broad bean too. He looked a bit huffy, Orla noted.

"Before you say 'broad bean'," he said, "I'm Mr May. Asparagus. Thought it would have been pretty obvious actually." He flounced off to pour himself another drink.

John was dressed in pale grey and looked like a jellyfish. "I'm a mushroom," he said, standing up to offer Orla his chair.

"Er . . . no, thanks," she said.

Leanne, dressed as a lettuce, sidled up next to her and squeezed her arm, laughing. "I like your style. Sometimes I wish I had the balls to go out in my nightgown!" Orla smiled weakly. "I guess everyone will be getting a fruit and vegetable calendar from Santa this year! Wait until you see Joan," she giggled. "Honestly. I don't know why she's not still on TV."

Joan was holding court in her kitchen, dressed as a strawberry. She had a chic little green beret on, and a bright red, billowing mini-dress, the endless legs sheathed in red fishnets and red stilettos.

Joan saw Orla and beckoned her in. "Hello darling!" she said, kissing her on each cheek. "Oh well done, dear, you wore a robe! I used to wear one myself on the way to the studio, back in the day. What's the point in getting dressed only to get changed again? Of course, my robe was terribly glamorous."

Joan shoved a red costume into one of Orla's hands and a glass of champagne into the other. "I thought you'd get a kick out of being a ravishing radish. You remind me of myself when I was your age – which was only recently, of course. Happy Christmas!" Joan floated off again.

Clutching her costume, Orla looked up and saw Leanne smiling at her. She had a feeling she wouldn't be lonely any more.

Jacqueline Strawbridge is currently an assistant features editor at the *Irish Daily Mail*, a job where she gets to read and write all day and therefore loves. Originally from Derry, she lived in Greystones, Belfast and Dumfries in Scotland, before returning to Dublin in 1999 to do the MPhil in Creative Writing at Trinity. She moved to La Maddalena, an island off Sardinia, in 2000, where she taught English (and had fun on a Vespa) for three years, before returning to Dublin to lead a more responsible life. She worked as a stage manager, an English teacher and director of a children's summer language school before discovering, at twenty-eight, that working in newspapers suited her perfectly. Since then, she worked in *The Star, The Evening Herald* and *The Irish Independent* before her current position in the *Mail*. During a brief stint of freelancing she had her short play *Eggshell* produced by Fishamble, and trained a guide dog called Edgar for the IGDB – she is very proud of both.

Going Up in Flames

Áine Toner

"I swapped the Baby Jesus' head with yours."
And so he had. Chief Designer Andrew had done a feat of cutting out to superimpose my bonce onto a small Holy Child's, which, along with the rest of his tiny baby body, was wrapped in swaddling clothes and lying in a manger. Which would have been bearable had my picture not been one of me, magazine editor Orla Bracken, doing my infamous 'drunk reindeer' impression at last year's staff knees-up.

The rest of my team, the talented bunch who comprised *Wahey!* magazine, also featured in the bizarre nativity re-enactment. Nuala (Deputy Editor, poker-straight hair, envy of all the magazine team, male and female) was Mary but then she always had a fondness for blue. Sub-editor Sarah was a Wise Man swathed in exotic fabrics, as though straight from the Bethlehem version of Net-a-Porter. Even intern Connie was present: we imagine no shepherd ever wore fluorescent-pink nail polish but we were clearly going for a post-modern, proto-feminist interpretation.

What do you mean you've never heard of *Wahey*!? We're positively brimming, nay, *saturated* with helpful hints and tips to make your life that bit easier.

You probably wouldn't admit to buying it – we dub ourselves our readers' guilty pleasure – but the dedicated team (read: will do anything for a byline) have produced some of the most outrageous journalism Ireland has seen in years. Purely by accident, with ill-advised headlines that cause us to burst our giggly bags in the office and cause threatening solicitor letters to be sent to our Managing Editor (more on him in a minute).

Examples? The interiors shoot, in a well-known city-centre department store, entitled *Know Your Knockers and Knobs* placed beside an advert for health self-examinations. Or the sex feature illustrated with Lego men and women, their little yellow bodies entwined in eye-watering positions. Seen and replicated by a Lego-loving child on Christmas morning much to his mammy's outrage. Or the line *Tits Up*, supposed to be detailing the rise in our winged feathered friends but illustrated with birds of an entirely different nature.

So our non-threatening, non-aggressive Christmas scene was supposed to *Wahey's* gift to its readers. I wanted to go down the traditional route of fifty cent off your next issue and a coupon for a free mince pie in your local supermarket. I was overruled.

As you'd expect, being the star attraction in the greatest story ever told was not top of my 'must get this finished so we can shut up shop for Chrimbo and eat rings around ourselves' list. The seventy-five complaint letters and phone calls we'd received *this morning* about a seemingly harmless cookery feature were.

Chesney 'Cheesy' O'Rourke was Ireland's best-known vegetarian chef. Probably Ireland's only vegetarian chef – despite a 1840s plague almost wiping out our national foodstuff (potatoes), we still hadn't really embraced the idea that meat could sometimes be off the menu.

Chesney was always harping on about preserving animals, keeping them on the fields and off our plates. It had taken months of planning to snare him from rival publication *Yoohoo!*, a wooing that included the ingestion of more than one questionable Fakin' Bacon Roll (made in Chesney's manky kitchen – clearly the man believed in letting everything, mould included, roam free).

Eventually we convinced him of his rightful place on *Wahey's!* contributors panel – the remainder of whom would not be getting the annual gift of liqueur chocolates and a sparkly card because he was costing a knee-knocking really-have-you-lived-in-a-bubble-for-the-last-three-years-there's-a-recession-on fortune.

Back to our festive food photoshoot and it had all gone well. To a point. We'd been so careful. Ish. The problem was, Chesney had all the popularity of his 1980s namesake but none of the talent (hold your tongue, 'I Am the One and Only' is a modern classic). His recipes merely amalgamated loads of ingredients. Which, I realise, is what *all* recipes are but at least most have the rationale that ingredient *x* may just complement ingredient *y*.

Chesney had 'created' an exclusive Christmas dinner for the *Wahey!* populace, all you need to feel smug about not eating the cute and cuddly turkey that was now frolicking through bitterly cold fields, tired, upset and lonely because all his mates were indoors and sporting a tan.

Having not been present at the time of going to print four days ago – I had, ahem, an important meeting vital to the magazine's expansion – the *Wahey!* team had chosen an appropriate heading to fully showcase Chesney's delectable dinners. Appropriate if you worked on lads' magazine *Geezer*, that is, or enjoyed opening seventy-five almost identical letters of complaint.

'Ches's Nuts Roasting on an Open Fire' assaulted your eyes as soon as you opened the spread. Andrew and his partner-in-crime, senior designer Matt, had even replaced the o's with little flames of fire. The recipes required you to have an iron stomach as it was – sprout soufflé and flame-cooked imposter sausages anyone? – but the obscenely large fluorescent-orange font, coupled with one particular image, made it belly-churning.

The photograph was of Chesney standing in front of a barbecue – why let this family pastime be summer's exclusive bedfellow, he argued – wearing a pale-coloured tight-fitting top. So pale and so tight-fitting that it blended into the background colour, making him look like he was . . . yep, topless. And given that you couldn't see the bottom half of Chesney O'Rourke, you could think that he was standing in front of a barbecue, warming more than just his meat-free sausage.

It would be a picture that would haunt me for the rest of my days.

"Did we really suggest he's cooking his dangly bits?" I asked weakly, having just read another 'you should be ashamed of yourself' letter complete with a religious tract that urged us to pray for our souls. In fairness, I was more worried about my career at present.

"'Fraid so. We thought it was fun. But we thought you'd change it," said Nuala, reaching for her fourth luxury deep-filled mince pie in thirty minutes.

It's a little-known fact that magazine employees turn to food in desperate times. Other industries chain-smoked. We chain-ate. If magazine companies tell you that they don't buy into all those sugary snacks and treats, they're lying.

Matt, a notorious gym bunny who hadn't been in the same room as a carbohydrate in five years, was currently inhaling a family-sized bag of cheese and onion behind the office Christmas tree. I doubt the crisps even touched the sides of his mouth.

Staff Editor Bea had her back turned to the food-frenzied team while she snaffled as many chocolate teacakes as possible from the 'Only Break This In Times of Emergency' cupboard. Sales Manager Susanne, not usually seen on our floor, too busy was she selling advertisement after advertisement, was pacing up and down clutching four chunky Kit Kats.

Wanting to impress, Connie was attempting to break the Guinness record for the amount of snowmen-shaped Christmas-tree-chocolate decorations she could fit into her mouth at the same time. She wasn't quite up to our standard, bless her, but she was trying.

"Where were you at print time?" asked Nuala, suddenly suspicious of my absence, through a mouthful of mincemeat and pastry. "I had to send the magazine myself."

"Out," I said, stating the obvious. If I had been here, Ches's nuts would have stayed either in a baking tray or fully clothed.

"Christmas shopping? Did you buy us our presents?" yelled Art Director Andrew hopefully from across the room.

Despite the *Wahey!* team having the combined age of 328, it got really excited about presents. Anything. A jar of sweet and sour sauce was received with much the same reverence as a trip to a luxury spa. New stationery, albeit emblazoned with obscure company logos from businesses we'd never heard of, was as prized as getting that must-have mascara that can't be bought until November 2016. We just loved free stuff.

Christmas presents for the team delivered by the editor were sacrosanct and meant me spending every lunchtime in the three weeks leading up to the holidays scouring the shops for something suitably thoughtful. Little tokens of appreciation that bring holiday cheer to our group and make people less likely to say rude things about your leadership behind your back. Until now.

"No, and you're not bloody getting any after this," I said.

Cue silence as furiously active jaws slowed then stopped while the Waheyers mulled this over. Nuala eyeballed Andrew warily. No gifts? Not even six of the same gift wrapped in different paper? Not even a Lindt chocolate Santa? She must really be angry.

Seizing the moment before they returned to their emergency intake of any foodstuff, I said: "Has Chesney telephoned? His PR? We were only on shelf yesterday. Connie, take petty cash and buy as many of the fecking magazines as we can. Let's erase naked Chesney from the public's memory as quickly as possible."

Connie skedaddled out the door as quickly as our readership surely would once they spotted our interpretation on a naked chef.

"His PR rang – said Chesney hasn't seen the article yet and he's doing all he can to prevent him from picking up a copy," shouted Bea in a fake-happy voice.

"Let's hope he can bewitch him with a battered carrot – or a honeyed parsnip, whatever these vegetarians eat," I said, dismissing the whole race of non-meat eaters. Now was not the time to be politically correct.

I'd like to think of myself as the hero of the hour, swooping in to resolve our tiny technical issue but I was trying to cover my very scared behind from being fired two days before the arrival of Santa. Hiding all available copies would give me enough time to make up a semi-convincing lie to cover us with our *very* gorgeous Managing Editor Leo Glass.

Even his very name made me quiver and my heart flutter. Yes, I know it's a cliché to find a co-worker handsome but it's slim pickings in Magazine Land. And really, Leo was hot. He was like a Disney leading lady's really attractive father. Habitual bachelor of course, living in a manly apartment in the city centre, drinking old-fashioneds and moisturising his lusciously toned body and running a rugged hand through his salt and pepper hair. Yum.

By cover 'us', I mean really mean cover me. All's fair in love and career ladders. If we were going to be hauled over the barbecue coals, at least I had enough wit to attend a pre-Christmas job interview.

So sue me. No, don't. I imagine Chesney's solicitors are working on that. A lady's allowed to broaden her employment horizon, no? To seize the chance to improve her skills? Well yes, that's lovely and everything, but after a slight misunderstanding at the *Wahey!* Christmas party – I might have misunderstood that I was a sexy magazine editor when in fact I was a drunken scut energetically gyrating against aforementioned Managing Editor. Let me tell you: there are some songs you should *never* dance to provocatively – and '*Away In A Manger*' is one of them.

After suggesting that Leo and me 'call in sick together' the next day, nudge, nudge, wink, wink, and being politely rebuffed (imagine), I should have gone home, garlic and cheese chip in my handbag. I did not. Instead I made the lovely sexy man who pays my wages listen to what I'd exactly do to all of One Direction if I got the chance. With vigorous hand and hip gestures. Morto.

Waking up the next afternoon, congealing mayonnaise

slathered across my face, I realised I needed to leave *Wahey!* ASAP. Cue days of manic CV-updating-and-discreet-emailing until I received news of a position as deputy editor in *Yoohoo!* magazine. Our direct rival that we never bothered worrying about as its content was about as interesting as an out-of-date selection box in July. It was significantly less money than what I was on, and a lower position, but rumour had it the *Yoohoo!* team had unlimited access to buns and cakes from its neighbouring delicatessen. Not to be flippant, but I loved cake, especially free cake. I could be swayed by cake.

It wasn't that I necessarily wanted to leave *Wahey!* but I had to. My team, rather than pretending my outré actions never happened, spent a great deal of team reminiscing. And there was a whole lot more One Direction being played than was needed, with my crew pretending to be the famous five and Simon Cowell. Actually, they were quite funny – not that I would ever tell them so.

So four days ago I donned my best dress and highest heels to visit FLIP (Food, Lifestyle and Interiors Publications) Media to interview for *Yoohoo!* I should have been in the office sending our beloved if provocative magazine to print; instead I was putting forward my six-point plan for achieving magazine nirvana in our rival company.

"Why leave *Wahey!*?" asked Timothy Scanlon, Managing Editor of FLIP Media and definitely not a person against whom I'd want to bump and grind. He smiled. He shouldn't, his teeth were manky.

"I've learned a lot with *Wahey!* and I will always treasure my time there but I'm ready to employ my talents elsewhere," I say.

Clearly the right response. Manky Teeth Scanlon sat back and smiled broadly. Time to avert my eyes.

"We're an energetic team in *Yoohoo!*," he explained, "Full of get up and go! Usually get beaten by the *Wahey!* team but if you come on board, well, that won't happen, will it?"

I looked around the *Yoohoo!* office. 'Energetic' was stretching it, the employees looked to have as much joie de vivre as a one-legged snowman in a bum-kicking competition. They looked . . . bored. The editor, Michelle Huntman, was dressed in a Kim Kardashian getup that she was filling out in all the wrong places. I don't quite know how completing a Sudoku grid was advancing *Yoohoo!* but maybe she did things differently. One man was reading *Wallpaper* magazine and looking like he'd rather be anywhere than this office.

Plus, there was no dancing, no frivolity, hell, there wasn't even an advent calendar to fight over like in chez *Wahey!* Get up and go? I think it got up and went.

But beggars and choosers . . . I turned around to Timothy and smiled. "Not at all, I'm very competent at leading a team."

"Excellent, excellent. Well, don't think it's all work and no play, Orla, the *Yoohoo!* team enjoy regular shindigs in Starz bar – we're all great, great pals."

Any establishment that had to add a 'z' to its name to jazz it up was no friend of mine. But again, I needed employment urgently so I smiled beatifically and repeated my mantra that had got me through the darkest of publishing days: *There is a happy land far, far away, where you get beans and chips three times a day.*

"But let's remember, Orla, you wouldn't be leading the team, you'd be second-in-command," said Timothy.

Was that a smirk on his manky toothy face? Idiot.

It has been a long time since I had been second-in-command. I liked being in charge – you got away with a lot of angry/ withering/frustrated looks for no reason. And you're officially allowed to raise your eyes and sigh dramatically like you're an extra in *Casualty*. And people made you endless cups of tea in your favourite *Go Away I'm Editing* china mug.

I wasn't sure I could be the Dancer or Prancer to Michelle's Rudolph but I would try. At least she'd be the one copping the flack if we screwed something up. And, truth be told, she did have a rather prominent red hooter, so it sort of fitted. We clearly wouldn't have the same craic as in *Wahey!* but maybe that was a good thing? Maybe I should start the new year in a new office, far away from unclothed cooks and blasphemous pictures. I nodded at Timothy.

He outlined the working conditions and I began to relax when the words "clothing allowance" were uttered. I could do this. It was Christmas, the time of goodwill to all those working in publishing, I could say goodbye to dodgy headlines and hello to regular hours and someone else being in charge. Result.

"Any questions?" he asked, sucking his teeth. He wasn't showing himself in the best light but I had to overlook his idiosyncrasies for up to 25 per cent off Cos clothing.

"Where do you keep all the food?" I asked. "The *Wahey!* team has a hamper full of goodies for afternoon snacks. I didn't spot yours."

Timothy looked at me like I'd suggested we do a lingerie photoshoot with Santa and Mrs Claus. He shook his head.

"Oh no, Orla, there's no food hamper here," he said. "We don't approve of eating between meals. All food is consumed in the *Yoohoo!* kitchen and any 'goodies' as you call them are donated to our sister publication, *Cabinet*."

"*Cabinet*?"

"*Cabinet* – a guide to all your cupboard repository needs," beamed Timothy. "A massive seller in the wood industry. They rarely see the outside world so we like to give them our treats. It's a share-and-share-alike company."

What in God's name would *Cabinet* share with the *Yoohoo!* team? Would I be coming home of an evening laden with slabs of unpolished pine? All the hinges I could carry?

I looked up at Timothy to find him thrusting his hand in my direction. I shook it. Clammy. I hate a man with clammy hands.

"Welcome to *Yoohoo!* May I be the first to congratulate you," he said, moving a little too close for my liking. I looked up to spy a rather miserable sprig of mistletoe hanging from the ceiling.

Timothy caught me looking at the near-dead plant and licked his lips hungrily.

"For Christmas?" he said, moving ever closer.

"I'll see you in the new year," I said swiftly, dodging his sweaty palms and heading for the exit. I'd have rather snogged a slab of pine.

So you can appreciate my predicament. For four days I have had two jobs: one with a team who were only interested in my presents, the other with a man only interested in my presence.

But I still needed to address the Chesney debacle now. I wanted to sit down in a darkened room with my friends Mr Pinot and Mr Grigio. Where the hell was Connie and those mags?

As I went to my desk, ransacked by the emotional eating *Wahey!* team because I had hidden all the decent biscuits under a pile of *Marie Claires*, Nuala sidled over.

"Er, Orla," she began, looking a bit shifty.

"Yep," I said, flicking on my computer and opening my emails.

"Connie's just telephoned. She's standing in the supermarket and there aren't any copies of *Wahey!*"

Relief flooded my face. Maybe the printers had accidentally sent the magazines to Outer Mongolia instead of Ireland. It's a common mistake. Really, I wasn't sure if Outer Mongolia even existed which is why I'm editor of *Wahey!* and why *National Geographic* has never called.

"That's brilliant, Nuala. *Phew!*" I said, pretending to wipe my glistening brow.

Funny how Nuala wasn't looking too pleased.

"Er no, you see, she asked the manager and he said they've all sold out."

"What's sold out?"

"*Wahey!*."

"Nuala, do you mean '*Wahey!* the magazine I work on that prints indecent photographs of well-known cooks is sold out?'"

"I do."

A pause.

"Did they sell out because you already bought them and hid them from our readers?" I ask.

"No."

"Did they sell out because Cheesy O'Rourke wants to wallpaper his vegetarian boudoir with them?" I ask, suddenly repulsed by the very thought. Cheesy by nickname, cheesy by nature, he was always a bit whiffy. Any woman wanting a bit of jiggery-pokery with Ches would need to be devoid of a sense of smell.

"No."

"Then why the hell are they not there?"

"Because the *Wahey!* readers fancy a bit of redecorating . . . with Chesney's meat and two veg," commented a very sexy voice.

Aha, our Managing Editor arriveth.

God, he looked good. Even in a pair of reindeer ears and a fetching knitted jumper decorated with a skiing polar bear. The pattern had come free in our sister publication *Cuppa?* and its appearance had caused something of a national yarn-emergency. Hundreds of knitters circled craft stores around the country to get enough wool to create at least five jumpers each.

I was so distracted by Leo's company I wasn't really listening to him. Nuala had to dig me in the ribs, probably a lot more forcefully than necessary, to wake me.

"What? Yes? What?" I said while Nuala looked on with disgust. She couldn't really see the whole 'Leo is a sexgod' thing. More fool her.

Leo smiled and walked to my desk.

"It appears the *Wahey!* reader loves the idea of a naked Chesney," he placed an email from SuperNosh, a national supermarket chain, on my desk, "even if we don't."

I pretended to read the email but I really just picked out the main words: 'unprecedented demand', 'reorder immediately', 'possible advertising liaisons'.

"This is . . . a good thing?" I said uncertainly.

Leo's smile went to full beam. "Absolutely it is! Susanne is on the phone securing a year-long partnership with SuperNosh and we've asked the printers to roll out another 50,000 copies."

Lovely. It was quite appropriate that I left on our highest-selling issue.

"And you're not . . . mad about Chesney's bits, attached or otherwise?" I asked.

Leo's pretty face frowned.

"I wouldn't say I was happy with what was done," he said, glaring at Nuala who was shaking behind me, "particularly given the number of complaints we received already."

"That was my fault, Leo," I said. Since I was leaving, I could say what I wanted. "Nuala did her job as I wasn't here to do mine." That sounded quite professional – I surprised myself.

Leo looked at a now less shaky Nuala and back to me.

"Very well, Orla. I can hardly complain considering the financial boost Chesney's given us. Might even try some of those recipes, eh?" he said, adjusting his reindeer ears.

Nuala sniffed and rejoined the *Wahey!* team, now gorging on a box of mulled-wine-flavoured cupcakes. We also ate when we were happy.

I turned to Leo. Now I just needed to tell him . . .

"And er, Orla, just a thought. Remember the office party?" he said, turning a faint shade of pink.

"Indeed. I just wanted to apol–"

"Don't. It was all done in the heat of the night. Spirits were raised as high as employees' hemlines."

"Right. Great. Well, I have an announce–"

"Where do you want this, Orla?" shouted Matt, clutching a battered box full of mistletoe. We were meant to be distributing it to new subscribers. Another job to be sorted out by yours truly.

"Leave it there," said Leo, reaching over and plucking a delicate, healthy strand from the top.

Great, now he's away off to pucker up to his impossibly gorgeous girlfriend. Merry Fecking Christmas.

"Orla, would you . . . do you . . . would you like to . . ."

Oh God, he's going to let rip.

"Fancyadrinkovertheholidays?"

"Excuse me?"

Leo moved a little bit closer. Please note: I made no effort to let him not invade my personal space..

"Would. You. Fancy. A. Drink. Over. The. Holidays?" he enunciated, rolling the mistletoe in his hands.

"Yes, please," I blurted. "But there's one thing, I'm leaving–"

I looked around to see the *Wahey!* team beaming after finding their carefully hidden Christmas presents. Paper was flying everywhere. They weren't a bad bunch.

"Are you?" asked Leo with a smile.

Was I? Swop panic and mayhem for free buns and clothes? I thought it over.

"No," I said. "I think my place is exactly here."

And then I made use of the mistletoe. *Wahey!*

❖❖

Áine Toner has been editor of *Woman's Way* since September 2008, having been promoted from the role of deputy editor. As editor, she has responsibility for the co-ordination, production and content of the magazine, but is also author of the soaps pages, fashion articles, celebrity interviews and the books pages.

When she's not talking about the soaps on *Ireland AM* every Monday, she's reading everything she can get her hands on – but has a particular fondness for thrillers that scare the beejesus out of her. Books are her favourite thing and she feels delighted to be associated with the calibre of Irish writers in *All I Want For Christmas*.

Áine has significant TV and radio experience, regularly contributing as a panellist on topics such as health, fashion, beauty and the soaps. She can be found on Twitter at @aineltoner where she uploads musings on reality television and cake.